ENIGMA SERIES XI

CHINA DOLLS

TIERNEY JAMES

Publishing Coordinator – Sharon Kizziah-Holmes
Cover Design by Sweet 'N Spicy Designs

P R E S S

Owasso, OK

ISBN – 978-1-965460-42-9 (Paperback)
ISBN - 978-1-965460-43-6 (eBook)

DEDICATION

Katie Rose

In 2002 I traveled to China with a friend who was adopting a ten-month-old baby girl. I had no idea how she would affect my life that first day I held her in my arms. A feeling of unconditional love and joy filled my heart. The realization how blessed I was to witness her transition from an orphan to an American citizen, became the catalyst to the Enigma Series.

One afternoon while I watched her nap so her new mother could slip out and buy a few gifts to take home, a story began to form in my head about my future heroes Tessa Scott and Captain Chase Hunter. They travel to China and rescue a baby girl who would change the world. Of course, it took me a while to get to that story you are about to read because I had to create the Enigma Series from the beginning. Finally, I am back in China finding my baby girl who I love so very much to this day.

This book is dedicated to my beautiful Katie Rose who continues to surprise and make me proud. Like baby Lotus in this book, I know your very presence on whatever path you choose to follow, will change the world for the better in small and big ways. I know this because you have changed me. I love you.

ACKNOWLEDGMENTS

Paperback Press – A big shoutout for Sharon Kizziah-Holmes who formats and finishes up my books to publish. With attention to detail and being a terrific listener to what I envision for each new project, she never lets me down. Even as I begin each book, she is there to advise and encourage me to keep going when I lose focus. I call her my #1 hand holder when I get crazy.

Decadent Publishing Editors
Kate Richards – A huge thank you to the person who has made me a better writer. She continues to inspire, encourage and teach me on this journey called writing. I'm always amazed that she puts up with my constant questions, blunders and writing potholes. She addresses these with humor, facts and patience.
Nan Sipe – She is the rock star of line editing and proofreading. I'm so grateful she took the time to go through this book even though she was preparing for her upcoming wedding. The kindness and devotion she showers on each of my projects humbles me.

Sweet N Spicy Designs - Jaycee DeLorenzo once again created a beautiful cover for my latest in the Enigma Series. I'm not sure if I could ever use anyone else. Because she has created all my book covers, Jaycee knows how to read me and what I need for each project. It is one less thing I have to be concerned about in the publishing process.

Lipstick & Danger Street Team – These folks never let me down. They are always ready to get the word out about my book news, read ARCs, and whatever I need done to stay sane. Thank you so much!

It goes without saying – I am so proud of my family. They love asking about my projects, how I come up with such ideas, and support my traveling (especially my husband) when it is required. Some of my greatest joys are when my magnificent seven grands pile into my office, sprawl on the floor with art supplies, notebooks, novels and ideas for their own stories and junk journals. It sometimes turns into musicals where they sing and dance, making me laugh and happier than I ever thought possible. They are my reason for living a full and joyful life.

Writers of the Purple Page – These ladies are not only authors but good friends. Together we keep each other on track, both for our projects, life's ups and downs, and a chance to share a good belly laugh from time to time. Travel companions for conferences and book signing events, these ladies never miss a chance to eat, drink and be merry. You are loved.

PROLOGUE

L oud voices dragged the teenager from his sleep fog. The sound of a lamp crashing followed by tears caused the boy to sit up on his straw mat as he pushed the thin blanket off his body. He spotted his sister across the room, wrapped in a sheet who sat on the edge of her cot.

"Chase, what is it?" Her voice trembled.

The squeaky door pushed open, and their father, Dr. Hunter, thundered in and pulled the boy to his feet. "Get dressed. Both of you. Be quick about it," he ordered. "They're coming for us."

"The soldiers? But I…you said—" Chase reached for his shirt lying on the floor and shook it to make sure the bugs were gone.

"No time to explain. Just do it. Get your backpacks. Are they ready?"

"Yes, Daddy." The girl slipped off the cot then pulled her day clothes from the foot of the bed over the nightshirt. "I'm scared."

He hurried over and pulled her thin body into his arms and kissed her cheek. "We're in danger. The monks came to warn us. They're waiting to take us to a safe place. Hurry. There isn't much time."

Chase's father turned to him and placed a hand on his shoulder. His voice held concern. "This may be hard to hear, Son. But you need to take your sister and escape this place."

"What about you and Mom?" He grabbed their backpacks from a stool and knocked a curious mouse onto the floor.

"We'll be right behind you. We are going to make one last check on our patients, secure the clinic, and head out with some of the others. They are depending on us. It will also give you a better chance to avoid the soldiers."

"No," cried Christine as she ran into the next room.

"Come say goodbye to your mother, Chase. We'll be together soon enough. You have to be the man in charge. You're tough, hardheaded, and have the best instincts of anyone I've ever known. Take care of Christine until we join you. Don't take unnecessary chances and avoid the soldiers. They will lie and trick you. The Buddhists monks are our friends. Remember that."

"Yes, sir, I will."

"I'm proud of you, Son. I know you're almost seventeen, but you've been a man for a long time in this place. China will try and kill you, so I need you to go forward, no matter what. Get to the States if we can't catch up. The monks will get you over the mountains into Tibet. Your grandfather will have someone there for you. But be careful there as well. The Chinese do not like Americans meddling in the Free Tibet movement."

"How long will you be? Where should we wait?"

Even without him saying a word, Chase saw the truth in his father's eyes. This was goodbye. Forever.

"Son, may God protect you and your sister." The father pulled his son into his arms and held tight. "I love you. Always remember that—and don't look back. Promise me."

Chase stepped back. "Promise. But I will wait for you and Mom. I'm not leaving China without you."

His father's lips trembled. "Just don't look back. We'll be together again someday. It is what we believe."

~ ~ ~ ~

The darkness deepened in Captain Chase Hunter's eyes as his chin lowered in anticipation of the coming attack. With fists raised, he waited patiently, letting the opponent measure the threat. A slow melodic tune he remembered from his childhood in China, where he learned to fight from one of the Buddhist monks in the village, played in his head. The tune never varied, except it often came from a seven-stringed guzheng and other times, it was a flute. It never failed to keep him focused and keenly aware of his surroundings.

A sense of calm fell over him like a warm blanket, knowing his ability to overcome his opponent was imminent. The man's eyes narrowed and he continued standing in a fighting stance, some eight feet from him. He charged, emitting the yell of a gluttonous Taotie. Chase felt inclined to let a slow smile spread across his mouth, knowing it would unnerve his opponent.

At the last second, the opponent hesitated but managed to send a roundhouse kick to his head. The attack was met with a hammer-like punch that sent him off-balance. The opponent staggered backward while the battle-hardened soldier delivered shockingly brutal punches to his solar plexus. With one side kick to his thigh, the opponent yelped and held up his hand to stop.

"You do not play fair, Captain Hunter," the opponent declared as he bent over to catch his breath.

"Neither does the enemy, Dr. Wu." The soldier's voice grew flat and void of emotion.

"I am not your enemy."

Chase stopped unwrapping his hands to stare at the Enigma psychiatrist and switched to Chinese. "But I am yours." He walked toward the exit of the Enigma gym. "I'm starting to like these therapy sessions. Sign me up for next week," he called over his shoulder.

Grabbing his bag off the floor, he answered the vibration of his phone. Dr. Wu did the same. That couldn't be good.

The ID number caused both men to stare toward each other.

"A crisis is an opportunity riding a dangerous wind," Dr. Wu acknowledged as he joined Chase at the door. "I had hoped this would not involve you."

"I knew it to be only a matter of time."

"So be it. You are ready."

"I'm not sure one is ever ready to confront the past."

CHAPTER 1

The cries of seagulls mixed with the bark of seals basking on the nearby rocks surrounding the narrow island gave the three-year-old hours of delight. Chasing seagulls and counting seals resulted in long walks along the shore with his mother. This led to painting pictures, collecting pebbles, and reading stories about the land of his birth. Jun Hie enjoyed the distraction because it made the child laugh, which in turn resulted in his wife's tears subsiding. Tears that both annoyed and broke his heart, sidetracking him from the work he should be doing.

Even now, from inside their temporary home, Jun watched out the window at the child talking and running along the shore as his mother chased, then gathered him in her arms to offer tickles. The happy sound reminded him of the failure to protect his family from the Red Dragon, a beast of hidden agendas posing as a man. Why had he trusted him?

He should be grateful his son survived and lived long enough to reach the United States. But the regret weighed heavily on his ability to think. The bitterness choked him into not caring if he lived or died.

How could he have left her behind? At five months old, she was beginning to sit up, and become a little person who charmed even his stoic personality. No wonder his wife couldn't forgive him for forcing her to escape even though he promised he'd send for the child when he came to America. Yet his little girl remained in China.

He'd taken her to a place where she would be cared for better than in the typical Chinese orphanage. The little baby girl cooed at him as he placed her in a basket outside the gates then rang the bell. He didn't even wait to see if they came for her. The Red Dragon promised to stand guard until she was safe. Or did he actually give her up to the evil general who offered a ransom for such a prize?

He knew they would post about the little girl, as required, to see if someone stepped forward to claim her. If no one did, she would be put up for adoption. Lots of Americans wanted a baby, and China was more than willing to dispose of little girls. It remained a failed policy, creating a shortage of brides for a generation of young men.

The plan involved having his daughter adopted by an American couple, who, for a generous fee, would turn the child over to him once they arrived in the US. That never happened. Once the American couple landed in Beijing, they disappeared after going on a tour to the Great Wall. An investigation by the US government failed to materialize since no one knew the couple was there, and they had no family to speak on their behalf.

"What are you thinking?" His wife had come inside from the deck without him hearing her.

"That I am a failure as a father."

"You saved your son and me."

"But I left Lotus with a stranger on the advice of someone I hardly knew." He shook his head. "What if…" Why finish his thoughts out loud? He turned back to study his son enjoying the waves crashing on the shore. At the touch of his wife's hand on his shoulder, he faced her in hopes of forgiveness.

"Your friend comes today. Bargain with him to bring her to us. They cannot say no. Many will die if they refuse. This country should know what is at stake. And the Red Dragon must die if that is the only way to get her back. I never trusted him."

"You speak of dreams that cannot come true. But I will find Lotus, even if it means my life."

"That is all I can ask." A tear squeezed from her eye and trailed down her cheek as she turned away and exited to the deck where the boy jumped up and down, pointing at a whale in the distance.

This was a place of peace. Could they stay here forever, or would he be killed or sentenced to a life behind bars when the government knew what he'd done? Justice from the US would be less severe than China's. At least here, his wife and child would not pay for his sins.

~ ~ ~ ~

"It has been a long time, Jun." Dr. Wu gave a slight bow rather than extend his hand. He wasn't sure which would be more appropriate since the man had lived in China his whole life.

"Yes. Many years. And your parents? I saw them several times in Hong Kong, but you had already left for the States to finish medical school. They were proud of you. They tried to arrange a marriage, as I remember."

"They live in Chinatown in San Francisco. I suppose they are still trying to find a suitable match, but my work is demanding, and I'm not sure a wife would be understanding, especially an American wife."

Jun Hie nodded his understanding. "Not so different from a Chinese wife these days, I am told." His wife entered with a tray of hot tea and traditional Chinese snacks that included dim sum, steamed buns, dumplings, spring rolls, and various pastries. Wu reached for the sweet treat mooncake. It was something he enjoyed after immigrating to Hong Kong as a teen. There were also red bean buns and sesame Bs, another traditional small dish to serve with tea.

"You have gone to a lot of trouble. I thank you," he acknowledged Jun Hie's wife who offered a smile of gratitude then turned back to Jun Hie. "Do you want to discuss the weather?" Small talk before Chinese business was proper etiquette. Jumping directly into business matters was considered rude. The weather was a safe topic for small talk. He then suggested some travel options his family might enjoy.

"Who knows you are here?" Dr. Wu decided to move forward with business.

"Your government made it possible for us to leave after I approached your embassy in Beijing.

"Very unusual."

"I became involved in something I wanted to escape. I met a person who agreed to help me and put me in touch with someone at the embassy. I thought since he was a high-ranking officer in the military, he could help me. At first, the American embassy pretended to not want to help us. Then, out of nowhere, while I was on business in the Gansu Province, I was contacted. We had no time to pack. New papers had been prepared, and time was of the essence."

"Why have you reached out to me?" Wu inquired after taking a sip of tea. "I have no means to help you."

"I researched your career and wondered why there were no published papers, clinics you associated with, or even a private practice."

"There are many doctors in California who fill that void. It was not for me."

"You have chosen to work at a nondescript university that promotes engineering and science."

"Yes."

"Many of those students go on to work in government and"—he raised an eyebrow—"projects that some would consider dangerous."

"What do you want of me?"

The old friend began talking about his little baby girl who had been left behind when they escaped to the States. Taking two children would have alerted the authorities who searched for him.

"How can that be?" Wu asked. "The one-child policy has been relaxed the last few years. It is not breaking the law to have two children, and some even have three."

"True. But to embrace such a practice is expensive, and many have yet to be able to afford such a luxury. I have done well for myself and my family. Because of my special standing with the scientific community and the government, I was watched with much interest. When I began asking questions about the program several clinics instituted, I was warned to fall in line."

"What program are you talking about? We already know the coronavirus had its roots in Wuhan, maybe even starting in the open markets there. I know those places have been shut down, and the general thought is that it began in a lab."

"It is not the labs in Wuhan but several places in the Gansu Province to the north. There is a lab in Lanzhou and another in Wuwei where I worked." He narrowed his eyes. "It was once your home, was it not?"

"Yes. We fled because of a colonel who took great delight in routing out people he thought to be enemies of the Communist Party."

"Especially Buddhist monks and Christians?"

Wu remained silent as he lifted his cup to take another sip of tea. He locked eyes with the man and decided to wait him out.

"Is that how you knew the young Chase Hunter?"

"I know of no such person," Wu lied, keeping his pulse calm and his face void of expression. "Who is he?"

"Someone who needs to know the man who killed his parents is also the man who plans a most unusual attack on this country. He is a general and wields much power."

Wu set his cup down and stood. "Why have you not gone to the FBI?"

"I have. They were more concerned about what the Russians are doing in Ukraine or how to save Israel than listen to a Chinese scientist who holds life and death in his hand."

"You have told me nothing. I do not play guessing games, nor will I be tempted to fall for a trap without a clear picture of what you are talking about. If you have something to say to me, then you should speak plainly."

The wife entered with their little boy. Pain filled her eyes as she raised her chin at her husband. "Tell him," she begged. "Tell him the truth so we can get our little girl back. I am tired of waiting."

He stood and nodded to his wife. The tone of his voice became submissive, and his eyes pleaded for mercy.

"The Chinese hunt me. The FBI made sure I had a safe place for us. It was not easy. They are investigating the claims I shared with them but could not promise to rescue my child. They have been slow to investigate."

"Investigate what?"

"The children adopted from China in the last five years, around the world, are going to die."

Wu cut his eyes to the wife who had tears rolling down her cheeks. "How?" Wu asked cautiously.

"I will tell you when you convince Enigma to go get my child—now."

"I know nothing of this Enigma."

"Lies do not become you, Dr. Wu. Enigma is whispered among the powers that be, even in China. They are the henchmen of the president with permission to solve problems at any cost. This is one of those problems."

"How long do we have?" He spoke evenly so not to give away his rising concern.

"You may already be too late for some."

"Then why should I even help you?"

"Because I can save the rest."

"Then do it."

"I will. As soon as you bring my daughter back to us, I will break the code for all the China dolls that Americans so desperately wanted to adopt. If you don't, with so many children dying, chaos will begin, demands for answers, fear that all children can be affected—"

"Can all children be affected?" Wu thought of his friend Tessa and her children.

"I've said enough. Thank you for coming, Dr. Wu. It was my pleasure to see you again. I look forward to our next meeting."

"Your confidence that there will be another meeting is something I cannot promise."

He offered a bow. "Then it will be a sad day for this great country."

CHAPTER 2

"Mom, Chase, come quick. Something is wrong with Mrs. Ellis." Daniel ran into the kitchen where his parents were fixing dinner. "She's screaming for help."

"Stay here," Chase ordered Daniel. "Where are your brother and sister?"

"Heather is upstairs, and Sean is at the Ellis house. We were playing video games with Micky when something happened. Sean said to come get you."

Tessa wiped her hands on a dish towel and hurried out the front door, following Chase across the street. He was already on the phone dialing 911.

Chase burst through the door, where they found Mrs. Ellis on her knees next to her daughter who lay unconscious on the floor. "An ambulance is on the way. What happened?" He knelt by the child and took her pulse. His days as a Ranger medic still came in handy from time to time.

Tessa got down next to Mrs. Ellis and took her hand that stroked the three-year-old child they'd adopted from China as an eighteen-month-old. "Let Chase check her out, Gloria."

"She's not breathing." Chase started chest compressions, unsure of how hard to press on a child this age. Fortunately, the paramedics entered and took over as her eyes opened and she gasped for breath.

"My baby," the mother cried as Tessa and Chase helped her stand. "Chase, thank you," she sobbed. "I've got to get to the hospital."

The paramedic said she could ride in the front with the driver. Tessa volunteered to take Mickey home with them. Sean Patrick stood near his friend, looking helpless. No way he had ever been this close to death, and his wide eyes and twitching fingers indicated how frightened he was. Being a tough kid, Sean Patrick tried to be as macho as his new stepfather.

Chase walked over and put an arm around Mickey's shoulders. "Come on. There's nothing we can do here. I forgot to ask if your mom called your dad. Can I do that for you or go to his work?"

The kid nodded acceptance then looked up at Chase. "You saved my sister's life, Captain Hunter." It was not uncommon for Sean's friends to call him Captain, as if they were part of his personal fighting squad.

"I only revived her, son. Those guys will make sure she gets to the hospital safely then the medical staff will see what's going on. I know where your dad works, so I'm going to run on over there and get him to the hospital." He turned to Tessa. "You okay, babe?"

Tessa faked confidence as she connected gazes with Chase. "I'll be fine." She loved how no matter what the circumstance, he always cared about her welfare. "Boys, how about I make you some supper. There's sloppy joes on the stove."

"Is my sister going to be okay?" Mickey followed Tessa to the door.

"I think your sister will get the care she needs. Healing is their jam," she offered in a confident tone. "Okay?"

"Okay," he repeated.

"Sean Patrick, can you take Mickey over to the house and call your brother and sister to supper? Chase and I are going to close things up here and make sure everything is secure. We'll let the dog out one more time too, Mickey, so don't worry."

"Thanks, Tessa."

Where Chase was always called Captain Hunter, she was

always just Tessa.

As the boys walked across the street, several neighbors made their way to the house to find out more information, which they didn't have.

"Did she hit her head, Chase? Did you see anything suspicious?"

"No. Nothing. She's so little. I wanted to ask Mickey if she'd ever had seizures or some other problem since arriving from China. Those kids from the orphanages don't have a good start in life to begin with. Maybe something happened there before she left. Dropped. Got an untreated infection. The ER will know where to send her. I'd better get over to where Hank works." He leaned in and kissed her shortly. "Tell Heather…"

Tessa rubbed his forearm. "That you'll be back soon to give her a rundown."

Her youngest and Chase were nearly inseparable. Most of the time, Tessa wasn't sure who was actually in charge when they were together. The boys complained their sister could get by with murder with Chase in charge. However, when they needed to circumvent chores or wanted something, they weren't shy about using her as their advocate.

~ ~ ~ ~

Chase parked the car then ran toward the ER doors when he heard the rotor blades of a helicopter. Usually, such a sound gave him flashbacks of his time overseas in dangerous combat situations. He had a gut feeling this was worse. After being ushered to the area where they'd taken three-year-old Olivia, he spotted her father and mother. They stood with arms around each other. Three doctors took turns speaking while a flurry of activity around the child seemed to indicate something more serious had occurred.

"Hank?" Chase asked as the doctors began giving orders to the nurses and checking vitals.

"They're airlifting her to Sacramento Children's Hospital." Tears pooled in the corners of his eyes. "I need to go get my car to drive us there."

"No. Let me take you. I've got some connections that can provide an escort so we'll make good time."

Hank lifted his chin in acceptance as he walked to the side of the bed where Olivia lay, pale and taking shallow breaths.

How did a parent cope with such fear? His thoughts went to his three stepchildren. His love for them had exploded all reasoning inside him. If anything ever happened to them, would he survive? He'd fought Taliban, terrorists, evil scientists, a host of drug dealers, and corrupt politicians, but imagining one of his kids in a hospital bed wasn't anything he wanted to experience.

As promised, his friend Officer Michaels from the Grass Valley Police Department escorted them to the hospital in Sacramento. Chase focused on driving ninety miles an hour on the two-lane road. Once on the interstate, his body relaxed, but he needed to exercise an abundance of caution.

He'd let Tessa know about the new developments when he got to the hospital. When he let the Ellises off at the entrance, he parked the car and called her. There wasn't anything to tell yet, but he knew she'd be worried. He asked about Sean Patrick.

"He's very quiet. I think he got really scared. Mickey appears to be engrossed in the movie they chose. I'm baking some cookies. Daniel is telling some really corny jokes to make Mickey laugh."

"And Heather?"

"She's sticking to me like glue. Oh wait. She wants to talk to you."

The conversation was short, asking when he would be home. How was Olivia? Then ended with "I love you, Chasey," which was the best part.

"I told you not to call me that." It was a continued joke between them.

She merely giggled then called him Daddy Chase. She could have called him Frankenstein, and it would have been music to his ears.

"Help your mother, and save me some of those cookies. I know your brothers will pig out on them or bite a few to make sure they're done." She promised to hide some just for him. What more could a dad ask for?

"Geez, I'm getting soft," he mumbled to himself. He ran a hand over his face then grabbed a book out of the car console in case he had a long wait. Books had been his go-to distraction ever since he was a kid. It was a mystery by Lori Robinet he'd been meaning to read for some time. Maybe it would take his mind off whatever this was.

Once inside, he knew almost immediately things were not going well with little Olivia. The doctor stood outside the waiting room doors with a grave expression as he spoke in a quiet voice to her parents. He remembered not so long ago having to wait outside similar doors when Tessa had a miscarriage. *Why does love have to be so painful?*

The doctor returned to the ICU area, leaving the Ellises to stand staring at each other.

"Hank?" Chase asked then placed a hand on Gloria's back to offer comfort.

"She's really bad. They're running tests, but—they only give her a 50/50 chance of surviving. She's having multiple seizures and even coded on the way here. There's a chance she"—he choked—"may have brain damage."

Chase wanted to say he'd pray for her, but he couldn't. Most of his adult life had centered around the motto of *when your number is up, it's up.* Why bother God changing it? Had he prayed for Tessa? He thought maybe he had, but couldn't remember the words. Was it when she got into trouble from time to time?

No. He just fixed it himself. Self-reliance had proven to be a useful drug in his mental tool kit. Why put his faith in something that had pretty much ruined his life at an early age?

Tessa had come to him, full of faith, hope, love, and promise of a better life. She was both brave and compassionate to a fault. Agent Nicholas Zoric, an accomplished artist, often painted her as some kind of avenging angel who saved a warrior, who was him.

He used to hate those paintings and complained the Serbian needed a life and some art lessons if that's all he could paint. Yet, he'd often slipped off to the man's studio to admire the paintings before he and Tessa became involved. To say he was obsessed with the woman was an understatement, for most of the years he tried to deny his feelings.

"They said there's swelling on the brain. They want to do surgery to relieve the pressure."

"I should call Mickey," Gloria said, rubbing her hands together and walking over to her purse. "I didn't bring my phone," she mumbled.

Hank took his from his pants pocket. "You'll only upset him. Let's wait until we have good news."

She refused and clearly needed to talk to a healthy child. After speaking only a few minutes to him and saying they were waiting for good news, she asked to speak to Tessa. Chase knew the boy would most likely be spending the night, since both sets of grandparents lived in Reno. They'd promised to head out right away.

"Can I stay until your family gets here?" Chase asked. "You shouldn't be alone."

The only close family Chase had was Enigma. Other family members lived in North Carolina or Washington DC. If something like this happened to him, Enigma would step in like they had when Tessa miscarried.

The doctor returned several hours later and told the Ellises Olivia died on the operating table.

~ ~ ~ ~

Tessa's heart broke for the Ellises. She had just sent all the children to bed with an extra hug for Mickey. Sean Patrick insisted he take his bed and used an air mattress to sleep on the floor next to Daniel's. All three of the kids had gone above and beyond to make Mickey feel comfortable and distracted.

Then Chase called. He cleared his voice several times then coughed as if clearing his throat.

"She didn't make it, Tessa. They're in there with her." He paused for a long time. "I'll bring them home soon. Could you—I don't know."

"Yes. Be safe. We're waiting for you. Like always. I love you."

"Tessa?"

"Yes."

"I don't know what I'd do without you."

"Are you all right to drive? I can send one of the team to help."

"I'll be better when I get home."

CHAPTER 3

General Sun Li had no proof the American doctors were leading a few desperate villages to believe in a higher power that promised to take care of them. The fact was he knew about these religions after being in the States for his college education. That's where he learned that missionaries were sent to countries as healers, teachers, and project managers to show goodwill and influence.

To kill them often stopped most from being replaced. The people would revert to being suspicious and afraid to deviate from the path set for them by the government. It was frowned upon to become dependent on outside forces such as the United States.

Even the Shaolin monks befriended the two American doctors. They accepted their children and taught them their ways, shared food, medicine, and even traveled with the monks to visit the sick. It was messy. General Sun Li remembered how he hated the admiration the Americans gathered no matter where they went.

The monks helped them escape. The torture they endured did nothing to loosen their tongues as to where the children of the missionaries had gone. To this day, it was a loose end he longed to tie up. At the time, the thought occurred to him to hunt them down in the States and finish what he started. Since the family had connections in Washington, it was decided not to pursue it. Besides, missionaries were not allowed to even be in China. The reports at the time indicated the children had died crossing into Tibet.

"General Li, sir, there was a call from Colonel Zhou Xiang. Do you wish for me to send him a message?" His assistant stood at attention and avoided eye contact when he turned to face him. No one really enjoyed bringing him good or bad news. It was best they remained fearful.

"What did he want?"

"To let you know he will be in Lanzhou in a few days and would very much like to speak to you. Should I make room for him on your schedule?"

"Make it as inconvenient as possible. I have no time for inconsequential requests like he is prone to do."

"Yes, sir. Thank you. I will do so immediately."

General Li flicked his fingers out as if he were swatting a fly. The assistant pivoted and quickly strode off toward the office building. Turning back toward the mountains, his thoughts returned to that night so long ago. Colonel Zhou Xiang was only a major then and disobeyed a direct order. By the time he'd discovered the conspiracy, the incident had garnished an unfavorable light on himself. There was nothing to be done— except wait for the day when he could take his final revenge.

For the first time in many years, he replayed the memory of the unfortunate cleansing of the village. He closed his eyes and remembered as if it were yesterday.

Darkness had ebbed away. He was Colonel Sun Li then and wanted to finish this quickly. The orders were given to his men to leave the trucks and to search the village. It meant dragging women and children out into the chilly air and ramming rifles into the backs of the men. The sound of begging, crying children and angry peasants annoyed him. It was all a distraction to why he'd come.

The American doctors.

"They are gone, Colonel Li," a foot soldier announced as he saluted.

"Keep looking. Did you check their house, the clinic?"

"Yes, sir. The beds in their home were still warm. They

couldn't have gone far. The beds were empty in the clinic."

Why were the Americans even here? Spies? He'd been to the States. Doctors were rich and obsessed with their own importance. They lived like little emperors and were never short of supplies for the sick or broken people who came to see them. They were worshiped and lifted to great status.

He considered the Hunters, both doctors, living in this northern province where life was hard for the common man. They got permission to open a clinic with supplies coming to them from a place in North Carolina. The man was tall, big boned, and fair-skinned like a Viking. He stood out in this country of people who appeared short in his shadow. His wife, also a doctor, was dark skinned, an American Indian, he was told. Why would she not want to treat her own instead of these poor, miserable people? Both of the children were more Chinese than American now.

The questions he possessed never ended. Three weeks ago, the pieces began falling into place. They were Christian missionaries. There was no indication they were openly preaching their religion. After all, it was forbidden in China. Even the Buddhists had to tread lightly and, with time, their importance had diminished. The country must come first, not some magical spirit in the sky that promised a better, more perfect life without the powers in control of—well, everything.

The government knew what was best for them, not Western imperialism. That's why missionaries were expelled in 1949 by the Communist Party. Colonel Li never practiced any faith-based ideology. He aligned with Communism, believing religion could function as an alternative to the party, which could possibly undermine loyalty to the supreme government.

He had met the Hunters several times. Devoted to their work. If the patient couldn't pay, they let them do what they could. Their kindness garnished praise and devotion in this small community just outside the city of Wuwei. What was their gain?

Something caught his eye, causing him to turn toward where his second lieutenant slid out from behind the wheel of his vehicle. The soldier moved slowly, twisting his neck this way and that, looking—for what? The Hunters? If it weren't for him, he might never have known about the missionaries in the first place. The second lieutenant walked beside his superior officer, Major Zhou

Xiang.

"Major, do you know where they may have gone?"

"No, sir. This is wide-open country. Plenty of places to hide. The monks are their friends. Perhaps they went to the monastery. Should I send a few men there to look?"

He stood rigid, his focus narrowed as he stared into the eyes of the colonel.

"Yes. There will be someone there who knows. Be sure that you"—the colonel smiled and arched an eyebrow—"encourage them to be forthcoming if they plan on continuing whatever it is they do up there. It would be tragic to lose such a beautiful structure in this hideous outpost."

For a few seconds, Colonel Li felt suspicious of the man before him as he continued to glare menacingly at his superior officer. "You do not approve of my methods here, Major?"

"These doctors did nothing but honor our people, sir. I do not understand why they are being punished."

"They are missionaries," he growled.

"There is no indication they pushed their religion on these people. Not one has ever admitted to being a Christian, only that the doctors took care of them."

The colonel had turned back toward the darkness when he saw something move.

"Halt!" he yelled then pulled his rifle from his shoulder.

The major pulled his handgun and aimed toward the figures running toward the trees.

"Fire, Major. It's the Americans. They're splitting up. I'll take the man; you shoot the woman."

"Yes, sir." The sound of gunfire added to the chaos surrounding them. As the two Americans ran back to each other and grasped each other's hands, more shots rang out as they fell forward in the mud.

Both men lowered their weapons. They walked briskly to where the couple lay and used their boots to roll them over.

Colonel Li took a deep breath and eyed his major. "Finish them." When the junior officer didn't respond, the colonel glared at him until he responded.

"My pleasure, Colonel Li."

A smile toyed with one corner of the colonel's mouth. Walking away, he heard four more shots into the bodies of the Americans.

Even today, he felt no remorse.

~ ~ ~ ~

"The Ellises have more company," Daniel told his brother as he pulled back the sheers on the front window.

"Those guys are awfully dressed up for a Saturday." Sean Patrick nudged his brother over to get a better look. "I think Mr. Ellis is crying."

Tessa stood up from her reading chair and joined them. "Hmm. Interesting."

She noticed how Hank rubbed his face then pointed toward her house. A man and woman followed them inside. Seconds later, her phone rang.

"Tessa, this is Gloria." Her voice quivering, she paused then spoke in a more controlled tone. "Hank tried to call Chase, but it went straight to voice mail."

"He ran in to work for a bit. Are you all right? Is there anything I can do?"

"The FBI are here. I'm not sure we're up to talking to them or going over information about Olivia. Could you come over?" Her voice cracked. "I don't know if I'm coming or going. Mickey wants to visit with your boys."

"Say no more. They can play in the front yard. My bunch need to burn off some energy. I'll be over in a jiff." She clicked off and snapped her fingers at the boys. "Get your sister. She's upstairs. Mickey is coming over for a while, and you three need a good game of kickball."

"Everything okay?" Sean Patrick started toward the stairs.

"I think the Ellises are just having a hard time. I'm going over to meet these new friends."

Sean Patrick halted. "But they really aren't friends, are they?"

"Get your sister," she said, peeking out the window again as another black SUV pulled up in the drive across the street.

Mickey zipped past her and waved to her brood.

"There's a car coming," she warned.

He waited patiently for it to pass then joined the kids in the yard before she went inside.

There were four FBI agents in the living room speaking in low voices. One she recognized immediately. He locked gazes with her and nodded. The thought occurred to her his head might explode if he acted civil to her in front of others. That, she wanted to see. He took a step in her direction then pivoted away when Gloria came up and slipped an arm around her.

"Thank you, Tessa. We asked them to wait until you could come. I just felt we needed someone with a clearer head."

"What's going on?"

"Apparently our baby isn't the only one who died of this condition."

A chill ran up Tessa's spine, thinking about her own children. "Why is that of interest to the FBI?"

"Last night, two families contacted us who also went to China with us to adopt. Their children also died in the last six months."

"Were they from California?" she asked, turning her head toward Agent Martin who studied them intently.

"One was from Oregon and the other from Arizona. We've all tried to stay in touch. The other two families called us on the day of—the funeral, but I just couldn't talk about it yet. But I'm wondering if they even knew about our baby. Maybe something…"

"Why are the FBI here, Gloria?" Tessa already knew why. Their phones were bugged, and the FBI intercepted the phone calls. Whatever the problem, if Agent Martin was involved, it was a disaster waiting to happen.

"Who are you?" A well-groomed female agent extended her hand toward Tessa.

As she grasped the agent's hand, Agent Martin joined them to make introductions. "Agent Talbot, meet nosey neighbor Tessa Hunter." His expression reminded her of a sly fox planning his next mischievous incident.

The female agent's eyes widened. "My pleasure, Mrs. Hunter. Agent Martin has spoken often of you."

"I'll just bet he has," Tessa said in a low, stern voice. "Gloria, could you make these agents some coffee. I have a feeling things would go better if we all had something warm in our hands."

"Oh, yes. Sorry. The neighbors have brought so much food.

There's lots of pie."

Agent Talbot volunteered to help. As she stepped away, Tessa cut her off. "No questions or comments unless it's about the weather. If you can't wait until I'm present, then—"

Agent Martin pulled Tessa back as he addressed his agent. "Go on. No questions, Agent Talbot."

"Yes, sir."

Agent Martin waited until Mrs. Ellis entered the kitchen then shifted his attention back to Tessa. Their relationship was rocky, but the last couple of years they'd found common ground to trust each other.

"Why are you here?" Tessa diverted her attention to the other two agents sitting on the couch across from Hank. They appeared to be expressing condolences and doing a lot of head bobbing.

"You know I can't tell you that, Tessa." He pushed his coat back to place his hands on his hips.

"Well, I'm not going anywhere. And if you don't tell me, I'm making a call to Enigma."

"Ouch." He pooched out his lips in a flippant response. "I'm shaking in my boots. Go ahead. I guess that means God's-gift-to-saving-the-world Hunter isn't home."

"This family is grieving their dead child. Whatever you want to know can wait."

"Actually, it can't. But since you'll probably get involved in this mess anyway, I'll let you stay."

"What mess?"

"There are more dead kids with the same thing as little Olivia. There's concern that this is the beginning of another disease that affects children."

"You mean like polio?"

"Worse. Now, can you be a good little housewife and keep your mouth shut during the interview?" She opened her mouth to speak, but he raised his eyebrows. "Please tell me you can't. I would love to cuff you and haul your ass off to Sacramento for the night."

"I would love that too. I could use a night away. That way you can babysit my kids since they think of you as their grumpy but funny uncle."

"Are you threatening me, Tessa?"

"I am."

"You annoy me."

"You're a liar, Agent Martin. You think I'm adorable."

He narrowed his eyes and clamped his lips in a tight line. "I see all those Enigma misfits are still filling your head with a lot of nonsense. I'm not part of your fan club."

"I repeat. Liar."

This time, one corner of his mouth lifted just as Agent Talbot returned to invite the others to the kitchen where dessert and coffee were on the table.

CHAPTER 4

R ed Dragon. General Sun Li enjoyed the speculation that he was that man. There would always be people who believed in myths and legends, or, as he liked to say, lies and conspiracies. The fear in people he came in contact with brought him respect and the truth when needed. Why not use this story of a mythical man to heap chaos on those who opposed the Communist Party?

Standing with his hands fastened behind his back, General Sun Li surveyed the snowcapped mountains to the north. They were rugged and harsh, much like himself. No one dare tell him his demand for absolute loyalty could be construed as an obsessive-compulsive disorder.

China was destined to be the number one superpower of the world. He would help make that happen by sowing seeds of chaos among their enemies. China's intent remained to destroy democracy. Beijing promoted peace, of course, and refuted any idea they were an aggressor of an authoritarian dictatorship.

No matter they continued to take control of the Spatly Islands in the South China Sea. It remained a part of the plan. With the Americans heavily involved with the wars in Ukraine and Israel, the leadership turned to him to inject an unexpected problem, much like the one with COVID. No one expected it to have a domino effect and shut down the entire world for months as it had. With COVID, even China endured the repercussions of a sloppy accident, shutting down their economy and world influence.

The Americans were well aware of the rift between Japan, the Philippines, Taiwan, Vietnam, and Malaysia over who owned the rich fishing rights in and around the Spatly Islands. China's interests lay in the significant oil and natural gas reserves. Such an acquisition meant China would also be in control of major maritime trade routes. It wouldn't take much to transform them into strategic positions to monitor and demonstrate a powerful military force in the South China Sea.

A bird screeched overhead, drawing his attention momentarily as his thoughts turned to Taiwan. It remained to be a place of interest; a sore spot that wouldn't go away. However, it continued to be the world's undisputed leader of raw semiconductor manufacturing, a prize worth taking. No wonder the Americans sold them weapons, sent diplomatic groups from their aging congress, and strutted around like the biggest, bad boys on the planet.

One corner of his mouth lifted to form a smirk. Nothing gave him more pleasure than being given the responsibility to create a diversion from what his country planned to do. The United States continued to be a mighty military force with a short fuse and lots of money to spread around for support. Americans tired of hearing about war. Those wars were a gift to China. Along with Europe, they would have to deal with another problem that would hit closer to home: their children.

~ ~ ~ ~

The Enigma team sat at ease around the conference table. The director took inventory of the team as they settled in for the unexpected meeting.

Although Carter Johnson never saw a mirror he didn't like, the director couldn't help but admire him. The former astronaut propped his feet on the long table. He smacked his gum as Samantha Cordova approached seductively carrying two cups of coffee. With a wink in her direction, Carter's expression went from confident to confused when she set one of the cups of coffee in front of the resident artist and interrogator, Zoric.

The director often oscillated between trusting the Serbian and thinking he formed from someone's nightmare. Yet Captain Hunter had seen something worthwhile in him when he brought him into Enigma. Agent Samantha Cordova treated him with a lot more respect than the ex-astronaut.

"What the hell, Sam?" Carter reached for the cup on the table. Zoric wrapped his leathery hand around it then leveled one of his disgruntled frowns. Carter withdrew. "Just kiddin', buddy."

"I'm not your buddy," the Serbian grunted then took a sip. "Thank you, Sam."

"Is the other one for me?" Carter reached for the cup Sam held to her lips.

Setting it down on the table, she smacked his feet to the floor. "Keep your filthy cowboy boots off the table, you worthless Texas tumbleweed. I swear you were raised in a barn." She pulled out the rolling chair and sat down to drink her coffee.

Carter chuckled and leaned toward her. "You didn't mind that a couple of nights ago, Miss High and Mighty."

Laughter broke out among the others. Even Vernon, the tech genius, glanced over at Carter and chuckled. He too, had been invaluable to the team with his street smarts and ability to hack anything.

Ken Montgomery rubbed his chin and eyed Samantha, much like he often did Tessa. The director wasn't sure if he was interested or just admiring the scenery. The man had a soft spot for the Grass Valley housewife ever since she saved his life. However, there was no denying he was a soldier through and through. All the director had to say was, "I have a job for your unique skill set," and he was packed and ready to go.

Part of the team were on other assignments; no one asked where or why. If it didn't have anything to do with today, they weren't going to worry about it. The director knew how tired they were from the last eighteen months, having been from Syria to the mountains of Georgia. Both places created emotional roller coasters. The team suffered injuries that not only attacked the body but the brain.

"Thank you everyone for coming in on a Saturday." The director opened his notebook then folded his hands over the pages as he took a moment to make eye contact with each person. Somehow this always made them sit a little straighter in their chair and slip their phones out of sight.

"Where's Tessa and Chase?" Zoric grumbled as he checked the time. "He rips us about being late. This family thing is messing with my head."

"Well, you can leave anytime you feel you're not up to the job." Chase stood at the door, having failed to remove his sunglasses. He shoved them into his bomber jacket pocket and moved to the coffeepot.

"You look like hell, Chase," Carter voiced in his thick Texas accent.

The director took a deep breath and pointed to the chair nearest him.

After pouring himself a cup of coffee that resembled crude oil, Chase rolled the chair out. The tomfoolery ended among the team, taking their cue of decorum from the one they'd follow into the lion's den when called upon.

"Sorry I'm late. Tessa isn't coming. I'll catch her up to speed when I get home."

"Not coming?" Samantha snapped. "If I did that, you'd threaten me with a few months at that Space Force dump in northern Greenland."

"I might do that anyway, just for the hell of it." Chase spoke with a voice as warm as ice water as he cut his narrowed eyes over at his top agent. "You're beginning to annoy me."

Samantha stiffened. Chase often disciplined her but never showed her anything but respect. She'd always been the favorite until Tessa had entered the picture. The two women mildly tolerated each other, which was an improvement from wondering if there would be an unsolved murder that needed a creative cover-up.

"What's with you?" Carter leaned in and managed to draw his captain's angry expression to him. "Is Tessa okay, or are you two in a spat?"

"Whatever goes on between me and Tessa is none of your damn business. And she's fine."

Just as Carter formed an inappropriate retort on his lips, Director Clark held up his hand. "Enough." His attention went to the man who was like a son to him. "Chase." That was all he had to say to his best man at Enigma; the one he depended on to lead the others into danger with the threat of never coming back.

It had been a long time since he'd seen Chase this hostile. The director acknowledged how the man clamped his mouth to a hard line. Even though his jaw tightened and released, he complied by drinking his coffee. The director continued.

"This is a developing situation that feels time sensitive."

"Aren't they all?" moaned Zoric.

"You have a point, but this time the president is hoping we're ahead of the game instead of already a code red situation. Vernon, can you bring up the information on the screen, please?" The focus turned toward the rear of the room where the wall turned into a computer screen.

"Statistics tell us that more than 160,000 Chinese children, mostly girls, have been adopted into families all over the world since China opened its doors to international adoption in 1992. That was primarily due to the one-child policy they instituted to help with their bulging population problem."

"Why so many from China?" Samantha inquired. "There are plenty of countries who have adoption programs. How many of the Chinese children came to the US?"

"Roughly 82,000 of those were adopted to the United States alone. The number has steadily decreased over the last few years. The reason people go there is because of cost. They are the least expensive, where Bulgaria is the most expensive."

"How many recently?" Chase asked then drained his cup.

The director continued. "Recent records show that over an eight-year period, Americans adopted roughly 2,300 children. Most were between the ages of one and two years old. But they have instituted stricter guidelines for adoption, and the length of time couples have to wait is sometimes off-putting, not to mention the $40,000 price tag."

"Dr. Wu has some information the FBI didn't take seriously at first, and we're not exactly sure what we're dealing with. What we do know is that we are about to be hit with another dangerous disease that attacks children." The director sound grave.

"The person who removes a mountain, begins by carrying away small stones."

Dr. Wu entered the room and took a seat next to Chase. He did not often attend these meetings since his job was to stabilize the members after they were in a life-or-death situation. Sitting down next to the captain stunned them into silence, considering the two rarely agreed on anything.

CHAPTER 5

"The person who removes a mountain, begins by carrying away small stones." Dr. Wu's usual no-nonsense voice now carried a hard edge. There were a few eye rolls, which he expected. What he didn't expect was Captain Hunter's support.

"Hear him out," the captain snapped as he stood and poured himself more coffee. He also made Dr. Wu a cup of tea and set it down in front of his notepad. The expressions on their faces guaranteed a captive audience for once.

It was no secret the captain had given him a hard time for years, not allowing him to assess his team, calling him names like mindbender and Dr. Hocus Pocus and ignoring suggestions for a healthier team.

"It has come to our attention that many of the children adopted worldwide were implanted with a time-sensitive virus."

"Children?" Zoric said, lighting a cigarette. "Why do that to kids?"

"They were orphans. They were abandoned and most often girl babies, another strike against them. At first, it was only an experiment. We don't have statistics on this, but it has gone on for years, and we are unaware of how many infants died. Keep in mind, these orphanages are often overcrowded. Sometimes, there is one caretaker for twenty infants. Adoption solved a lot of problems in this regard. It was a blessing, as Tessa likes to say, that so many people began taking these children."

Carter shook his head. He was the one who loved kids and wanted a family. "So, they quit? Right?"

"Apparently not. This virus is a mix of polio and spinal meningitis. It causes inflammation in the brain and spinal cord membranes. There is some evidence it can spread through airborne respiratory droplets: a cough or sneeze."

"Here we go again," Carter groaned. "Another pandemic."

"Dr. Wu, could you just spell it out for us without giving all the drama and backstory?" Chase appeared to be chewing the inside of his jaw, and his eyes had that impatient gaze that meant he was tired of being Mr. Nice Guy.

"Of course. The children are dying at an alarming rate. Ten so far in the last month. No one paid much attention until the adoptive parents started contacting each other. One of those parents worked for the Center for Disease Control. The CDC took an immediate interest and contacted other parents along with the FBI. From there, an alert was sent to hospitals across the country with the express directive not to cause a panic."

Dr. Wu went on to relate his visit to the scientist hiding outside San Francisco.

"There's a vaccine, right?" Samantha asked.

"Sadly, no." Dr. Wu turned his attention to Chase and nodded to him. "Perhaps you should share the story you've lived through the last few days."

The team once more turned to their leader and demonstrated concern and interest. Chase told them about the Ellis family and their little girl from China, the emergency, her death and funeral, and ended with how his family had been affected.

"Along with the Ellises, we all had to be vaccinated both with a polio booster and meningitis shot. Everyone in our neighborhood was required to take it as a preventative. Tessa and I"—he paused and looked down at his hands then up at the ceiling—"are terrified for the kids. The boys were at the house when Olivia collapsed. I was on scene and resuscitated her. She coded again when the medical transport flew her to Sacramento. After she was stabilized"—Chase took a deep breath then let it out slowly—

"Olivia died on the operating table. She was three years old."

You could have heard a pin drop, and the team did not make eye contact with Chase. It was likely they'd never seen their leader this moved. The captain didn't get upset. He either got even or solved the problem with extreme prejudice. The outcome was always the same. Crushing a threat was what he did, what the team did. How do you crush a threat like this?

"Let's take a short break," the director suggested. "I have a call coming in from the FBI. My assistant is bringing in some food. I want you to know we'll fix this. I'm not sure how. But we will. We always do."

When the door shut behind the director, each team member tried to offer the captain condolences, but it was more awkward than comforting.

"Sorry. It's been a rough week and I apologize for biting your heads off. Holding an innocent child in your arms and knowing she is probably not going to make it, isn't something I'll ever forget."

"What about Tessa's kids? No signs of illness?" Ken Montgomery was the epitome of a career soldier, a man's man, and Chase's long-time friend.

"So far, so good."

"It appears that only the adopted children from China are at risk at this point. However, both of those diseases are contagious, so the FBI and the CDC are making recommendations for families to be confined if no signs of illness have occurred. We also know that over the period of experimentation, some children were given a placebo and show no signs of illness. Others, depending on the year they were born, may have been given various strains. Several children in Germany showed signs of the same illness but recovered."

"How many are we talking about?" Samantha asked.

"Out of the thousands that have come to America, we've only reached about one hundred as of this morning." Dr. Wu unwrapped a tea bag then placed it into the steaming cup of water he removed from the microwave. "It's a tedious process that requires a lot of manpower and support of what these families need, not to mention vaccinations even if they are showing no signs of the disease."

"Why? I don't get it? This is insane? What's to gain by it?" Vernon closed his computer and made eye contact with the captain. "Chase?"

"Hell, if I know, kid."

"Captain Hunter?" Dr. Wu had always been very formal with these people. It gave him a sense of superiority over them with a touch of respect. "Could I have a moment, please."

It was customary for the two men to also show a certain amount of hostility toward each other, but this time, Dr. Wu saw none as the captain followed him into the hall. "There is a lot going on down here, and you're involved. If you go to China—" Dr. Wu warned.

"I'm not."

"Okay. But I wanted you to know that the man they are looking at and may have started this program is General Sun Li. I believe you know him." Dr. Wu waited for a reaction then continued. "Is he not the man who killed your parents?"

"You already know the answers to these questions, Dr. Wu. Why drag me out in the hall and taunt me with the past?"

"There is yet another interesting fact you should know."

"You mean the fact that the Lieutenant Zhou Xiang who finished off my parents with a gunshot to the head was part of your inner circle? And that your father told him my parents were missionaries, which led to their deaths as well as the death of innocent men and women in the village? Are those the facts you're talking about?"

"There are three truths: my truth, your truth, and the truth."

"More Chinese gibberish. Spit it out, Wu."

Since the captain had grown angry and stopped calling him by his title of doctor, it was time to be honest.

"I was a boy like you. My family escaped because of the warning of Lieutenant Zhou that the soldiers were coming for you."

"Thanks for the heads-up, Wu. You still have your parents. My sister and I nearly starved to death running for our lives then spent our teenage years reliving that nightmare of seeing our parents killed."

"We were in Wuwei. My parents sent word; I promise you." Even though Chase's six-foot-one body stepped closer to Dr. Wu and towered over him in a threatening stance, he showed no fear.

"How about this Chinese proverb, Wu. To tell only half the

truth is to give life to a new lie."

"I have never lied to you."

"The only reason you're still working for Enigma is because you healed Tessa after her ordeal in Afghanistan. She has an affection for you I just don't understand. And I appreciate the fact that even though I've been somewhat of a jerk to you, you continue to help my team survive. I can't believe I'm saying this, but you brought me back from the brink of some pretty rough times too. But that does not mean I believe your father tried to warn us of the attack."

"Would you believe that the Red Dragon is alive and well and may have the answers you seek?"

Chase glowered at him and took a step back. "I'm listening."

~ ~ ~ ~

Chase passed Agent Martin's car parked out front when he pulled into the garage. Walking inside, he heard Tessa talking to someone in the kitchen.

"Agent Martin," he said, hanging his keys on the hook by the door.

"Daddy." Heather reached for him from atop the island. She was the only one of the kids who recognized him as their stepfather, dad, or paternal figure. He grabbed her into his arms and gave her a squeeze so she'd scream with delight, then kissed her. "Uncle Dennis is going to stay for supper. He's going to barbeque for us."

"No doubt the steaks in our freezer," he said with contempt.

"Oh no. He's going to make burgers from our freezer. Mommy said she'd make real French fries too. That way you guys could chat outside while he grills. Sound like a plan?"

"Yes, it does. And what are you going to be doing while we cook?"

"I'm going to set the table and make some lemonade. Uncle Dennis wanted beer, but Mommy said no way, Jose."

Tessa walked over and rubbed his back then landed a kiss on his cheek. "Uncle Dennis," Tessa teased, "has been in the neighborhood all day. He's been kind of a pest. There were other agents too."

"Uncle Dennis sent them away not long ago." Heather wrinkled her nose at the FBI agent. "Are you going to spend the night? My Barbies like it when you do."

"Absolutely not. Every time I sleep over, those ugly dolls end up in my bed and goose me."

The little girl covered her giggles with her hand then scooted off to watch a movie with her brothers.

"You know, Special Agent Martin, Tessa and I bought you one of those blow-up dolls to help you feel more comfortable with the Barbies but even she refused to have any part of you." Chase lifted his chin to stare down his nose at the agent.

"Very funny." He paused. "Sorry about this last week. Nobody should have to go through that. Let's go fire up the grill."

Chase nodded then kissed his wife on the mouth and offered an attempt at a grin. "Keep the kids in here."

"Will do. Are you okay?"

"Yeah. Dennis and I need to talk is all."

While the grill heated, both men munched on some chips and dip Tessa brought out with the burgers. The conversation eventually moved from baseball to current affairs. "I'm guessing Tessa doesn't know the president is involved and wants you to go to China to get that baby."

"No, she doesn't. I promised Tessa we were done with dangerous jobs, or at least she was. I could take care of the family, and she could teach or continue doing analytical evaluations for geopolitical conflicts. I don't want the kids to grow up without a mother and be stuck with that jerk who is their biological father."

"But you said yes."

"I said yes for both of us."

Agent Martin released a long breath. "I hope you know what you're doing."

"I hope so too."

~ ~ ~ ~

The nightmare returned, after he went to bed, of that murderous night that changed the trajectory of his life. All he could do was ride it out.

"We must hurry, Chase. The soldiers are nearby. Please. I

promise your father." The Buddhist monk tugged at his arm in spite of the teen's resistance.

"Chase, you heard Momma. She made me promise to see that you obeyed the Shaolin monks."

The monk straightened then pulled his shoulders back. "Do I need to force you? Because you know that I am more than able to do that."

"You are an old man," Chase growled as he turned toward the village where chaos had broken out with dogs barking and terrified voices overpowering the darkness.

The monk reached out and grabbed the boy between his shoulder blades and spun him around to apply pressure on his neck, drawing a grimace, but the young man complied. "That is better, young Master Hunter."

Gunshots rang out, followed by screams. A Shaolin monk raced up leading a family of three who Chase knew well. The boy was his own age, and his parents had often helped in the clinic his family operated. Like himself, the boy practiced the Shaolin way and learned kung fu along with his American friend.

"Where are my parents?" Chase demanded.

"We must go. They are searching for you," the new monk declared in a loud whisper as he hunkered down. He managed to push the second family behind some rocks, but Chase refused to avoid the horror, in spite of his promise.

The two monks led the five deeper into the night. With several houses on fire and military vehicles with searchlights swarming in, Chase suddenly spotted his parents running toward them. His father was pulling his mother, and he thought he heard her crying, a sound he'd never heard from her.

Even though the Shaolin never turned him loose, the teen walked backward, his heart in his throat when a soldier dismounted from the open-air military vehicle and stormed toward the American missionary doctors. The soldier never ordered them to stop as he removed his rifle from his shoulder and aimed. The younger Shaolin monk hurried his sister and the second family toward others who waited to protect them. But the older monk slowed, the young man using his strength to resist.

When the shots rang out and Chase's parents fell forward, a deep wounded cry tried to escape, but the monk covered his mouth to silence any hint of sound. The stubbornness collapsed, and he fell in step with his teacher. Tears gushed like rain as he ran to catch up with Christine and the others.

Their journey had just begun when he heard a voice.

"Chase!" came a distant voice.

He tried to stop for only a second and listened, all the while being shoved forward into the darkness by the Shaolin monk.

"Chase! It's me. Chase!" It was the voice of a woman.

"Don't look back," the Shaolin insisted.

"Chase!"

This time the voice was right behind him. He jerked free of the monk and turned.

"Tessa?" he whispered. "What are you doing here? It isn't safe."

"Chase! Wake up! You're having a nightmare."

Her hands touched his face as he gasped.

"Breathe, Chase. Breathe. Wake up."

Chase gulped in air until he came back to reality, his heart hammering against his chest. He was hot. Touching his face, he felt something wet. Sweat? Tears?

He reached to the spot next to him when Tessa left the bed and rushed into the bathroom. She returned in seconds with a cool wet washcloth and dabbed his cheeks until he took it away from her and covered his face completely. He swung his legs off the bed and bent his body forward.

"Another nightmare." Tessa spoke softly as she crawled behind him and massaged his shoulders. "Back in China again?"

He nodded then stood. "You were there this time."

"I was calling you back. I could tell you were having a nightmare."

"You had never been in my dream until tonight. You were wearing a Chinese military uniform." His voice could not express any kind of emotion while remembering how she appeared.

"It means nothing, Chase." She raised up on her knees and pulled him back into her arms and kissed him on his chin then cheek. "I love you and will never leave."

The touch of her body against his slowed his breathing and put his heart back in rhythm. She was his rock, his salvation, his world. How could he ask her to return to China with him? The land of his birth, his childhood, and his transition into manhood threatened to open wounds it took years to heal. The scars throbbed when he anticipated the worst when it came to his family.

A knock at the door then sniffles as it pushed open brought little Heather into the bedroom, rubbing her eyes.

"What's wrong, baby girl?" Tessa hurried to her and lifted her up into her arms.

"I'm scared. I heard yelling." She laid her head on Tessa's shoulder and hugged her neck.

Chase pulled on his T-shirt and pulled it down over the waistband of his pajama bottoms. He walked to Tessa's side and laid a hand on Heather's back, drawing her attention. She pushed away from her mother and into the arms of the soldier who walked to the rocking glider and sat down. They were inseparable most of the time.

"I guess we woke her up. Poor baby," Tessa whispered.

"My fault. I need to get a handle on this."

"Maybe Dr. Wu can—"

"No. I don't need his help. I have you and the children. That's all I want or need."

"Why won't you tell me why you distrust him? Babe, I will understand." Tessa reached down and ran her fingers through his thick black hair. "Please. I hate seeing you like this. We need you 100 percent. Whatever the director wants us to do in China isn't as important as your mental health. We can say no."

"I already said yes." He stared up at her, and her fingers withdrew. Although her face was cloaked in darkness, he'd broken a promise to never keep secrets or commitments from each other. It pained him to reveal he'd done both. "We'll talk in the morning."

She shuffled back to bed and lay in the middle. When Heather fell back asleep, he carried her to snuggle next to Tessa's side then climbed in on the other side. Draping his arm across both of his girls, he kissed Tessa on the shoulder and whispered, "I love you," and drifted back asleep.

CHAPTER 6

The Red Dragon observed the general from afar. The pompous man held little regard for the people he swore to protect. Power was his god, and those who stood in his way paid the price with destruction of one kind or another. All these years, he followed the man's rise in rank and evolved into a figure without a conscience.

The destruction of temples, Buddhist monks, those who dared speak up against tyranny, and children, left Red Dragon no alternative but to advance his work and presence. The smell of blood hung in the air, and he discovered he liked it.

Rumors of a conflict circulated in dissident groups that his country would be ill advised to do at this point. The Americans made weapons and ammunition like there was no tomorrow. Maybe in reality there wasn't. China would do nothing, while Eastern Europe and the Middle East demanded attention. In recent months, Americans, known for their short attention span to world events, had begun to tire of war. It was ill advised to make a move on any prize his country coveted, transitioning the focus to them rather than abroad. Perhaps he had time.

He tired of tracing the general's movements and lowered the

binoculars. The man embodied everything corrupting his country. Turning toward the fields where the poor toiled for a livelihood and slept in the caves along the ridge, he envied their satisfaction with their lives. For generations, they had been here and, with any luck, nothing would change.

He strode toward the cliff and stopped at a pond of water that had filled from the last rain. Peering over the edge, he examined his appearance. Once again, he surprised himself at the transformation; a strong muscled body clad in leather armor that gave him the appearance of an ancient warrior.

Squatting, he could see his face clearly; a thin mustache was barely visible and needed to be removed when he left this place. His hair had grown too long, giving his angled features a sharp dangerous outline. Although his eyes were large, and interesting, a darkness on the bottom rim made him appear threatening. The lips formed a slight frown and were thicker and wider than most men's.

It added to his no-nonsense ambiance, which he used to keep from too much interaction with normal, everyday people. They avoided him like the plague, even when he wasn't dressed like a warrior.

Red Dragon slipped into his home, a cave house in Northern China called a Yaodong, built into the side of a cliff along a gorge to avoid the wind and maximize the use of sunlight and water for farming. His cave featured a vaulted room with clay walls peppered with stones on the outside and arched openings to several other rooms. He kept the basics here but not much else. Neither dragons nor warriors needed the things that made them soft and unprepared.

It was his safe place. He let his attention take in every corner. Perhaps a dragon needed such a place to remain safe. How long could he keep hidden from the world and the truth of his identity? Treachery grew throughout the land, and he knew the importance of remaining undiscovered until the time he could make a difference.

The China dolls needed him more than ever, as did the old woman who took care of them. She had sacrificed much for the babies in her orphanage. With her help, they found a new life with American and European families who offered them a better future, including a promise to never let them forget China. These were children no one wanted. This he understood. So, he protected them from getting caught up in General Sun Li's latest scheme.

Tomorrow, he would return to walk among the powerful forces of China like the masses. It was his duty as well. He reached for a journal lying on the cot he used as a bed. Opening it, he thumbed through the pages, examining his transformation in sketches.

Somehow, he'd always known his destiny meant a kind of isolation in order to right the wrongs of powerful men. He thumbed through more sketches of those he had loved. Gently, he closed the book and held it to his chest, carrying it to hide it in a crevice in the wall.

One more night was all he required.

~ ~ ~ ~

"This will be great." Robert laughed as he slapped his hands together.

He was the kids' biological father, and Chase hated it with a passion. He felt jealousy, regret—that he hadn't killed him when he had a chance—and unease anytime the kids were in his care. Did he love them? No doubt. Did he appreciate the gift Tessa had given him with their birth? Probably clueless on that front. Part of the reason he wasn't in the picture anymore was due to his lack of participation in their lives.

Then, one day, Chase burst into Tessa's life, changing the way she perceived not only the world but her husband. He felt a little guilty about that at first, but the guy deserved what he got, which was booted to the curb. His lies and ignoring the angel called Tessa, caught up with him.

Robert extended a hand to Chase and, as usual, he paused then clamped it in a viselike grip. He never shied away from leveling a stoic glare to emphasize his disapproval when handing the children over to him for a visit.

"I've been really looking forward to this, guys," he chuckled, ignoring Chase's death grip. "We're going to have a great time."

"Where's your itinerary, Bobby? I mean Robert." He hated being called Bobby.

"I have it, Chase." Tessa tied off the ends of Heather's pigtails. "A resort in Palm Springs. That's pretty swanky, even for you,

Robert."

"I-I have a meeting there," he stuttered, avoiding eye contact.

"A meeting? What about the kids. Who is going to be watching them?" Tessa got in his face.

Chase wanted to stand back and enjoy the show as she whipped her ex into shape, but the kids were frozen in place as their parents got ready to duke it out.

"Kids, why don't we put your bags in the car while your mom talks to your—dad."

Sean Patrick picked up his duffle bag. He kept his eyes on his parents and backed toward the front door.

"Sean Patrick is capable of babysitting his brother and sister while I'm at work."

"Work? This is supposed to be a vacation for the four of you. You assured me they'd have 100 percent of your time. And Sean Patrick is not a babysitter."

Chase shooed Daniel and Heather outside, but Sean Patrick remained in the doorway.

"He's going to tell Mom I'd be a lot better behaved and more responsible if she hadn't babied me. I'm a pain in his neck." He glanced up at Chase and twisted his mouth. "I take better care of them than he does. I would bet money his girlfriend, Phoebe, will show up and take over babysitting us."

"Phoebe? Since when is there a Phoebe?" Chase relieved him of his duffle bag and tilted his head toward the steps that led down to the circle drive.

"Couple months, I guess. Not sure. We haven't met. But he talks about her a lot."

"Does your mom know?"

He shrugged. "Not sure. I never said anything. Phoebe isn't the first. There was a Paula for about two weeks then a Karla, I think, who might have been jailbait."

Chase chuckled. "Jailbait? How do you know what that is?" He tossed the bag in the trunk.

"I get around." The teen cocked his head and smirked at him.

"I can see that. You got your cell phone, right?"

"You'll be in China hobnobbing with the commies."

"We explained that, Sean. Mom and I are designated guardians to transport an adopted baby girl to a high-profile government official. Straight up not a problem. Are you worried you might need backup?"

"No. I'm worried you will." His smirk turned to a frown. "I heard you talking to Agent Martin about Olivia and the other dead kids. There's something else, isn't there?"

"Maybe. I'll take good care of your mom. And if you don't want to go with your dad, tell me, and I'll make other arrangements. It's fixable."

"Chase? What if—"

"No what-ifs. If you don't want to go, then don't. I'll deal with Robert. If you go and need a responsible adult, you have a phone. The Ervins are staying here in case you should call. They'll be able to reach us. Carter will come get you in his plane. You've got his number too. He's staying in-country."

Robert and Tessa came briskly down the front steps. Both wore plastic smiles and pretended to be cheerful.

"What's it gonna be, son? Say the word, and I'll make it so," Chase spoke through gritted teeth.

"Don't die, Captain." Sean Patick gave him a soft punch to the gut. "Think of me lying around at the pool staring at all the girls in string bikinis."

"You'd better keep an eye on your sister and Daniel. Promise."

"Promise. And you'll keep an eye on Mom?"

"Affirmative."

"If you're going into the unknown, I guess a few days at a resort is not the worst thing that can happen."

They gave each other a high five, which was a huge show of affection from Sean Patrick.

"Go kiss your mom. She's already getting weepy-eyed."

Chase followed Robert around to the driver's side after getting a hug from Daniel and Heather. Robert hurriedly slipped behind the wheel, but Chase stood so the door couldn't be shut. He leaned in and lowered his voice.

"Keep it in your pants, Bobby. If I hear Phoebe distracts you so that these kids get so much as a hangnail, I'm coming after you. Understand?" Chase resisted wrapping his hands around the man's neck, knowing how easy it would be to snap. "Remember that little surprise you got in that hotel room in San Francisco a few years ago?"

Robert jerked his chin up, and his eyes widened in surprise. "I was taken by some gangsters. The FBI had to get me out. How did you know about that?"

Chase patted him on the shoulder. "I was the guy who took you." He waited a moment for the realization to sink in. "I repeat. Do you understand you are to give these kids the best vacation ever and pretend to be the rock star they want you to be?"

He swallowed hard and nodded. "You don't scare me."

Chase chuckled. "I will. Trust me. So, if you screw up—better bring a pair of clean underwear. You'll need them."

He started the car as Chase closed the door. Sean Patrick checked his brother's and sister's seat belts much to their groans about him being too bossy as they pulled away. When they passed him, Sean raised his chin and gave him a thumbs-up. The kid was so much like he'd been. Wonder if there were any Shaolin monks that could give him some training? Dr. Wu was about the closest thing to it these days.

Tessa came to stand next to him and waved to the kids as they drove out of sight.

"What did you say to Robert? He was white as a ghost."

"Told him to have a good time," he shrugged.

"No. Seriously.

"To have a good time—or else. Well, that's the short version."

She sighed. "You always know the perfect thing to say."

This made him laugh. "You are so bad, Tessa Hunter."

CHAPTER 7

The flight felt endless. Tessa listened to an audiobook while Chase oscillated between checking out the passengers and reading a book he'd purchased in the gift shop at the airport. He rarely listened to books on tape like her; said he didn't want his ears clogged up with a voice that could drown out trouble. The man was always on his game.

"Aren't you the least bit excited about going back to China?" Tessa nudged him.

"Yes."

"Yes, what?"

"Yes. I'm excited." His eyes drooped toward sleep.

"I've already read several books about the places we'll be. I'm sure you have more insight. Talk to me."

Chase opened his eyes. "Stay close. Don't let anyone talk you into going to their school, community meeting, or—"

"Blah. Blah. Blah. I know that."

"Do you? Because every place we go, you attract trouble like a heat-seeking missile, not to mention questionable characters you tend to find some redeeming quality in. You can't be Miss Congeniality here. It will appear suspicious and most likely expose you to the darker side of life. With that blonde hair and those blue eyes, you'll stick out like a sore thumb. And not in a good way," he quipped. "Promise me you'll not be on some divine mission to save the world."

"Promise." Part of the reason she hadn't completely fit in with other Enigma agents was due to an overabundance of interest in a person's culture, background, and family, of course. Enigma saw everyone as the next bogeyman. She imagined people as a romantic adventure worth exploring. "People can be redeemed, Chase. You are a perfect example. I remember you as a scary guy when we first met."

"I'm still a scary guy. You're just numb to it." His lips tightened as if trying to hide his amusement when he reached for her hand. "Besides, I'm not a sociopath like you have a habit of attracting."

"That's not true," she protested.

"There's a long list. Want me to recite the names?"

"No thanks." The lights dimmed in the cabin; many of the passengers were already asleep. "Tell me the beautiful things about China. What you loved. Tell me about your family. I know so little of them." She laid her head on his shoulder. "Let me in. Just a little. Help me understand why you are the way you are. All of it."

He patted her cheek. "I don't want you to be afraid of me."

She took his hand and kissed it. "You are a dangerous man. I've never been surprised by that. Do you think I'd let you be with my children if I were concerned? A man who can put a tutu on and do the daddy-daughter dance at a Christmas recital to make a little girl happy is the man I love. The man who makes the world a safer place for me and the children is someone I never want to lose."

Chase leaned back in his seat and closed his eyes. "Okay. I didn't live the romantic version you have in your head."

"I know," she whispered, snuggling closer. "Tell me what you can."

~ ~ ~ ~

Robert studied his children enjoying the indoor waterpark at the resort he'd chosen for their vacation. They were growing like weeds. These getaways gave him moments of satisfaction and regret. How had he let this happen to his life? Had he really been so self-absorbed? Lying to Tessa about their marriage had been the final straw for her. Reminiscing at their life together, he realized how much she'd tolerated.

He had pursued her with every romantic trick in the book until she couldn't help but fall in love with him. Knowing he was her first experience with love and sex, he became complacent with their relationship; figuring she'd never want anyone else. Things began to unravel after their third child was born. Sometimes he imagined a checklist in his head of what he could have done differently.

Whatever the reason, she gravitated toward a new group of strange friends from the university where she worked. Her confidence level eroded his ability to control her. Trying that had been the wrong approach.

Enter a muscle-headed oaf into the picture; Captain Chase Hunter. He taught languages and French literature at the university. The surprise was that he had a doctorate in languages. Guess he wasn't as dumb as he looked. Apparently, his military training had left some very rough edges.

The idea the man threatened him with bodily harm sounded ridiculous. Maybe if he worked out and grunted answers like Captain America did and helped make dinner, he could win Tessa back. The kids would have to be a part of the plan, of course. Even they were a bit taken with the guy, Heather especially. Sean Patrick not so much. Daniel liked everyone, just like his mother.

"Penny for your thoughts," came a silky voice behind him. He turned to see Phoebe, a much younger woman than Tessa he'd invited to get acquainted with his family, or what was left of it. They had met at a dinner party several months earlier through the work he'd done for a client. They had recently bumped into each other at a conference in San Francisco. They hit it off and started making excuses to have dinner or visit a new art exhibit. When she said she'd be moving to Palm Springs for six months, he decided it would be a good place to take the kids on a trip.

"Phoebe." He kissed her shortly on the lips. "You look stunning as always."

Her slim figure was only about five foot one and had the poise of a princess. The shiny-black hair fastened in a bun with chopsticks begged to be touched. The burgundy suit hinted she'd just come from work. Robert let his eyes roam over her flawless, porcelain skin that gave her round eyes the appearance of a fawn. From the Carolyn Crocodile handbag to the Dior pumps, every inch of her reeked of money and good taste.

Like himself, she was an attorney, but her clients were celebrities and high-profile businessmen. He'd come to expect that she traveled a great deal. For whatever reason, Palm Springs would be her base for at least six months. The idea that she showed so much interest in his work and admired his choice of the kinds of cases he took gave him a much-needed boost to his ego.

It didn't hurt that she hung on his every word and asked the kind of questions about what he liked and disliked, that left no doubt in her fascination with him. She became a comfort to him, creating a safe place to talk about Tessa and the children. It didn't take long until the idea of winning his ex-wife back didn't feel like an important goal or even what to do about Mr. Muscle Head.

"You were deep in thought," she said, following his line of sight. "Are those your children?"

"Yes. They're very loud." He chuckled. "Sure you want to have dinner with us tonight?"

"I am. But I have a better idea. I know you wanted to have dinner here but I'm staying at my uncle's home since I won't move into my condo for another day or so. It's a beautiful place. I took the liberty of asking the chef if he would fix a special dinner for us tonight. There is a pool. The children could swim. The pool is heated and it is quite lovely. And we have horses. All kids love them. I could show them the barns and trails we use. I just need to let him know for sure. That way you can see where I live."

"Are you sure about this?" He leaned in and whispered, "They're pretty rambunctious. I don't want to scare you off."

She casually slipped her hand in his without taking her eyes off his kids. "Trust me. I love kids. And I know yours are going to be extra special to me, Robert."

"Okay. Can't say I didn't warn you." He released her hand and placed his on her back. "Want to meet them?"

She glanced at her watch. "I better get going, and I need to call the chef. I want to get out of these clothes and take a bath. Besides, they're having so much fun. I don't want to ruin that. This is your special time to be with them. You're such a terrific dad. I love that about you." She placed a cool hand on his cheek. "I'll text you the address." She kissed him lightly and backed away. "I'm so excited to have this evening, Robert. Thank you for sharing your family with me." She blew him another kiss.

Robert fixated on her as she walked away like a confident tigress. He checked to see if his feet were floating on air. "Man, Robert, you sure can pick 'em," he mumbled.

~ ~ ~ ~

Phoebe got in her Porsche and dialed a number. "How'd it go?" the male voice asked.

"How do you think? They're coming over tonight. He's so full of himself, this should be an easy one. From what he told me a few days ago, his ex and her husband are on their way to Beijing."

"Keep up the good work. Everything will be ready."

~ ~ ~ ~

"Tessa?" A rough hand rubbed hers. "Tessa?" The sound of someone far away called her back. Opening her eyes, she pushed herself upright in her seat. Sunlight came through the window, and the smell of coffee reminded her she needed caffeine. A yawn and a stretch followed as the flight attendant stopped next to them.

Chase ordered coffee for both of them and a bowl of something she didn't recognize. He lowered her table tray then placed the coffee in front of her. "It's congee. Chinese porridge. It's warm and will stick to your bones. I haven't had it in years."

She took a spoonful to taste. "What's it made of?"

"Rice. It's also known as zhou, jook, or chok. Lots of ways to serve it so you don't actually get tired of it. We had it every morning growing up. It was one thing we could afford." He took a big bite and smiled. "I had forgotten how much I loved it. Think the kids would like it?"

"Put enough sugar and fruit in it, and they'll eat it." She took several more bites then sipped her coffee. "Where are we?"

"About thirty minutes out. You going to finish that? I'm starved."

She passed her bowl to him, encouraged at his appetite, which had been lacking since Olivia died. They sat in silence until the flight attendant removed their breakfast dishes.

"I see land," she said with excitement. "So, you think we'll get to see the Terracotta soldiers?"

"No." He stretched his neck to peer out the window. "We won't be close to there. According to the itinerary, we'll have plenty to see along the way though." He chuckled. "You remind me of a kid getting ready to enter Disneyland for the first time."

"Last night—the stories you told me. You were happy."

"Until I wasn't, so let's just drop it."

The sound of the landing gear groaned into place. Tessa pressed her face against the window. "Oh my gosh! We're here." She leaned over and kissed him on the mouth. "You're home."

CHAPTER 8

Three couples waited inside the terminal, along with a man checking items off on a tablet. He smiled a great deal and occasionally pointed as if giving directions to the other three couples. Tessa and Chase joined them, having been given instructions before they left San Francisco. She had gone over everything a hundred times to make sure she was prepared.

"You're going to wear the ink off the paper," Chase mumbled after watching her several times.

"I want to be organized so they know I'm a good adoptive parent. This is so different from anything I've ever done."

"The instructions aren't going to change."

"You've barely glanced at them."

"I memorized it the first time. Put it away. We got this."

"Okay. Okay. Okay." But her anxiety was due more to getting a baby than the directions as to what to do. The shock of how much she wanted to hold a squirming baby in her arms again and be a new mom for the fourth time surprised and thrilled her. There remained a part of her that hadn't quite healed from having a miscarriage months ago. Even though she understood this new baby would be given back to her parents, for just a short time, she would belong to them.

Other than making sure she was healthy, both physically and mentally after the miscarriage, Chase had not mentioned losing the baby. At the time, he had been heartbroken and tried his best to be the strong one. But he wanted a child and chose not to put pressure on her about the idea. Could he have changed his mind, knowing how it might affect her health a second time?

"There." Chase nodded. "That's the guy, standing with those other people who resemble someone who has been dropped behind enemy lines." His chuckle bordered on sarcastic. "They're scared out of their minds."

"You'll have to admit, we're not in Kansas anymore."

"It doesn't seem to bother you."

"I've dreamed of coming here my whole life. I just didn't think it would be to get a baby."

"Ready?"

Tessa nodded.

"Aw, you must be Mr. and Mrs. Butler," the Chinese man said, extending his hand to Chase then giving a slight nod to Tessa. "My name is John, and I will be your guide while you are here. I trust your flight was uneventful." His English was perfect. "I'm going to step over here and make sure our transportation is ready. Please get acquainted. I won't be long. If you need to freshen up, the public toilet is down there." He smiled way too much.

Two couples were younger than Tessa and Chase. They were in their early thirties, she guessed, and their fancy luggage suggested they might have money. The Rickmans were from Springfield, Missouri, the Olsons from St. Paul, Minnesota. The third couple appeared to be older, maybe mid-forties, and were from Plano, Texas. They introduced themselves as the Williamses.

"You ladies want to go with me to the restroom?" Tessa pointed toward a sign.

The wives quickly followed her and started chatting right away, except for Mrs. Rickman who kept turning her head around her like a scared rabbit being stalked by a hungry falcon. Tessa walked alongside her and spoke softly as they entered the restroom. There was a long line of Westerners for one of the stalls. The other two stalls had no line.

"Come on, ladies. Let's try these." Tessa swung the stall door open to reveal a porcelain urinal embedded in the floor. Their faces twisted in horror, making her burst out laughing. "Called a squatty-potty. You can stand in line for the regular toilet or drop 'em like a native. Me? I gotta go." She stepped inside and closed the door.

Tessa wondered if they'd follow her lead. This experience wasn't new to her since she'd been in places where if you had to go, you went to the closest bush or rock. Hadn't they ever gone camping? At least it was a restroom. She waited outside and could tell by the scrunched expressions when they emerged what door they chose.

"Everything okay, ladies?" They either nodded or shrugged when Tessa chuckled. "You must be going to be new moms. Better get used to being peed and pooped on. After a while, it's no big deal."

"So, this isn't your first rodeo?" the Texas mom, Mrs. Williams asked.

"Nope. Got three at home and decided we needed an even number. We went to a seminar about foreign adoption, and here we are."

"Well, that is admirable dedication," Mrs. Williams admitted. "We always wanted children. Just never happened. Thought it was now or never. Hope I'm not too old to get the hang of it."

Tessa's heart warmed at her concern. She patted the woman's hand. "Don't you worry. I'll help while we're here. It's not easy with a little one, but you'll get so much joy from your sweet girl. Trust me. It was a good decision."

"I like you already." Mrs. Williams took a deep breath. "How about you ladies?"

The other two gave a quick summary of their desire to adopt for various reasons, and the four women instantly became friends.

"That took longer than I expected. Did you have to show them how to use the toilet?" Chase whispered in Tessa's ear then chuckled as he stood up straighter and surveyed the area.

"Something like that. They make me feel like an old warhorse."

He stared down his nose at her and bumped her shoulder. "You never have understood how beautiful you are, Tessa Hunter. You take my breath away even after all this time."

"If I had known you were a romantic at heart years ago, I wouldn't have been so afraid of you."

"I had to wear that armor to keep from losing control." He had turned solemn as his eyes continued to take in the surrounding area. "Besides, you liked all the macho rhetoric, whether you admit it or not."

"I liked the muscles and the guns."

He refocused on her. "And had I known then what I know now about—"

"Shish!" She pinched his arm. "Someone will hear you. Besides, what do you keep looking at? Is anything wrong?"

"See those two soldiers over there? They are keeping track of our group. One pulled our guide over to have a chat and nodded toward us. Our guide did a lot of nodding before they let him go to the transportation counter."

"Isn't it expected we'll be watched? I read where all adoptive couples found that to be true. They even had to sign some kind of a promise if they used the internet, they wouldn't give away national secrets or import porn to corrupt the Chinese youth."

"Yeah. Just paranoid, I guess. I can't emphasize enough how you stick out like a sore thumb here, Tessa. Be careful."

"I know, Chase. You've told me a hundred times." Tessa saw Mrs. Williams wave for her to come to the little souvenir shop. "I'll be right back. I think the other husbands need some confidence building. Try to be friendly instead of a scene out of Robo Cop. You look like you've crossed over to the Dark Side."

"You're mixing up your movie metaphors." She huffed a sound of impatience. "But I'll try."

Tessa wove in and out of a large number of people hurrying through the concourse and stopped several times to let an elderly person pass. Just as she reached the shop, a woman in a wheelchair dropped her purse and a small carry-on bag in front of her. No one stopped to help her with the contents on the floor. Tessa bent down and began picking up the few things that spilled and shoved them back in the woman's purse. To her surprise, once she got her squared away, the woman started yelling at her while hugging her purse with one hand and waving the other in the air. That's when she felt a hand on her shoulder.

Tessa turned to see a soldier who moved his hand to clamp firmly on her arm. He spoke to the woman in the wheelchair who continued to point at her and complain loudly. She tried to locate where she'd left Chase, but he was nowhere to be found. Mrs.

Williams came to her side but remained quiet.

The guard or soldier, whatever he was, grabbed Tessa's purse and started to open it. "What the heck is happening?" Tessa tried to take it back just as another soldier walked up. "I was trying to help her."

"She say you stole money from her things," he said in broken English.

"No. I didn't." The woman in the wheelchair jumped up and started to run. "She is escaping!" In seconds, the woman had disappeared into the crowd, but the two soldiers were fixated on her rather than the problem.

"You will come with us. We do not like criminal activity here."

"I'm not a criminal," she insisted. "I'm here to adopt a baby. I was trying to help her." Tessa quickly explained the situation, but they only narrowed their eyes and gave the impatient expression as if they had heard this excuse many times.

"Come with us," the first one said as he stepped aside and pointed down the concourse.

"I don't think so," came the voice of Chase Hunter.

The three turned to see Chase standing there holding on to the collar of a much younger woman who squirmed and continued to try and get away. He tightened his grip and showed Tessa's two captors a gray wig in his free hand. A rapid explanation in Chinese followed, catching the two soldiers off guard. They responded in kind and grabbed the woman and the wig.

She begged Chase with words Tessa couldn't understand as she became quieter and more submissive in the soldier's grasp. He responded to her in the gruff tone Tessa knew all too well. Whatever he said caused her to spit on the floor, which got her a smack upside the head then was dragged away.

Chase took Tessa in with one steely-eyed once-over as if checking to make sure she was in one piece. "You okay?"

Tessa pulled back her shoulders and lifted her chin in faux bravery. Inside, she was shaking like a leaf. She hadn't been in-country an hour, and trouble had already come knocking at her door.

"Thank goodness you caught her, Mr. Butler." Mrs. Williams laid a hand on her heart. "I do believe they were about to take your wife to jail. She was only trying to help that woman."

Chase's eyes darted to Mrs. Williams then back at Tessa. She knew what he was thinking: You didn't listen to me about being careful. "I know." She wanted to fall against his chest and feel his arms around her, but this was not the time or place to appear weak or guilty of something.

The Chinese guide, John, and the others joined them, worried and concerned. "Man, we saw you grab that woman as she ran into the bathroom. Did you see those women come running out?" Mr. Rickman laughed nervously. "I would have helped if it hadn't happened so fast."

"I'm very sorry this happened to you, Mrs. Butler," John offered. "This rarely happens here, so don't be afraid. I'm sure in the end they wouldn't have blamed you." He smiled again. "Shall we go? Our van is waiting for us outside. We have several stops I'd like you to see on the way to the hotel." He walked backward as the group followed. "We have a welcome dinner for you tonight. Beijing is a beautiful city, and I hope in the short time we're here you can enjoy it."

Tessa and Chase were the last to board the van. They found a seat in the back by the emergency doors. The fact that he took a position of escape wasn't lost on her. His head was on a swivel and his body grew tense, as he studied the busy crowds near their van. Someone caught his eye as he leaned closer to window. He clamped his hand down on her leg.

"What is it?" Tessa followed his line of sight. She spotted another soldier of some higher rank talking to the two men who had stopped her. The woman who had accused her of stealing stood with them, relaxed and calm. "Chase," she expressed nervously.

"They know we're here. It was a trap."

"Do you know the officer?"

"Yes. He killed my mother."

CHAPTER 9

The officer Chase pointed out to Tessa turned to search through the sea of vans and mini buses in their direction. He wasn't sure if a glare on the window would prevent him from seeing inside the minibus. The colonel's interest toward their ride heightened Chase's heartbeat for a few seconds. The woman, although young, possessed a hard edge to her face and stance. Either she'd lived a hard life or had military training. Either way, he sensed the beginning of a cat-and-mouse game with the Chinese government.

"Our cover was rock solid, Chase. How could anyone know our plan or who we were?" Tessa spoke softly as she also followed the suspicious activity near the minibus.

"My guess is we have a leak back home."

"A leak? But how? Who?"

"I've got a good idea, but you aren't going to like it."

"If you're going to tell me Honey Lynch is involved, I find that—"

"No. Not your crazy assassin friend. Someone much closer to the action at Enigma. Someone with a lot of connections to mainland China."

Tessa leaned back in her seat and frowned. She refused to say the name. The idea of a team member betraying them would be impossible for her to accept. When her bottom lip jutted out, he knew she had created a defensive argument. Leaning in, he kissed her temple to hide the whispered words in her ear.

"Dr. Wu. You know I'm right."

"Never. He wouldn't put us in danger. Besides, he's very patriotic and loves America."

"He's like the rest of us at Enigma: self-preservation then everything else comes after that."

"You're not like that and neither is the rest of the team."

"They are exactly like that, Tessa, and you refuse to see it. And yes, I am like that. The one difference is that you and our family are a part of me. If anything, I'm more dangerous than ever. I'm glad you can't see that in me. You have this uncanny way of only seeing good in people. I fear a day will come you'll see me for who I really am."

"I know who you are, Chase Hunter. I've always known. And you have a good heart or you would never have taken me and my wild bunch as your own. Not every man would have done that." She took his hand. "And not every man would have put his heart on the line when you took me back to the Tribesman, not knowing if you'd ever see me again."

He laid a rough hand on hers. "Hardest thing I ever did." He turned back to check the movements out the window.

As the minibus pulled away from the curb, the officer had started toward them. Relief washed over him that he wouldn't have to confront the man. Remembering how his mother had fallen only to be shot several more times by the monster who stood closer than he ever imagined possible, made it difficult to breathe. A plan formed to take his revenge, since he knew the man was alive. Now he needed only to find the other man who killed his father.

Retrieve this special baby as quickly as possible and escape to a safer place. Then he would come back to finish the nightmare that had plagued him since he was forced to leave his home. Maybe that's why he'd been so restless most of his life; unfinished business required his attention with extreme prejudice.

"This is our first stop," John announced. "To your left, you see the iconic picture of the founder of the People's Republic of China. He led our country from 1949 until 1976 when he died. Not only a politician but a military strategist, poet, and revolutionary who led our country into greatness."

"Think he believes all that nonsense," Mr. Rickman mumbled under his breath but loud enough Chase could hear him.

Chase tapped him on the shoulder. "Better keep that kind of talk to yourself, buddy. They have ears everywhere and don't appreciate freethinking Americans expressing their opinions."

He exhaled then popped his neck. "Right. I'll be more careful. Gotta get our baby and then home."

John continued, "And on your right, we see Tiananmen Square, which separates the city center from the Forbidden City. It is roughly fifty-three acres and has great cultural significance."

"Will we get to visit the Forbidden City?" Tessa asked.

"I'm sorry. No. Tickets are sold online. It is limited to 40,000 visitors a day. I tried to purchase tickets online but was not successful. I am so sorry. But in the morning, we will have an excursion to the Great Wall of China. I will let you off here to take photos under Mao's picture if you like or you can stroll around Tiananmen Square. Your rooms will be ready within the hour, so please do not go far."

Chase caught hold of Tessa's hand and pulled her back to slow her excited rush to leave for picture taking. He had no choice but to get in the group picture after John volunteered to snap the shot with several cell phones. He did his best to stand behind someone or pull his hand low over his brow.

Although he was a teenager when he left, and both his body and facial features had changed, there were ways to figure out who he was. He imagined each person in the group was undergoing such checks just to keep track of who was who and if they might pose some kind of threat. In his case, he was known in espionage and national security circles by several names, but mostly by reputation. There were very few pictures of him, and he wanted to keep it that way. He'd made a life being invisible and could live fairly free of worry someone would recognize him for the things he'd done over the years.

Did the butcher know he was still alive? Was he part of the plan to make all these children sick in the US? From what he remembered of the man, such an act would not have weighed on his conscience. Chances were good he only knew someone was searching for the child. All indications, according to his diplomat grandfather, were that after the investigation of his parents was completed, no further interest was shown in the children.

"Take my picture with Mao's in the background. It will be interesting for my students." Tessa tugged on Chase's hand. "My father might not appreciate it, but it will be fun to tease him a bit. What is this place anyway?"

Chase complied but kept his head on a swivel. Things could go wrong quickly here. "Gate of Heavenly Peace. It was a gatehouse."

Then he noticed the two soldiers he'd seen at the airport getting out of a PAP vehicle. These guys were part of the paramilitary wing of the Chinese Communist Party.

"Let's go, Tessa."

She followed his line of sight. "What's wrong?"

"Our friends from the airport just got out of that car. Turns out, they're more than just soldiers. Their job is to maintain domestic stability. In wartime, they provide support for the People's Liberation Army. Serious stuff. Looks like they've cornered John. Probably wondering where all of us are."

"In other words, us."

"That's my guess. We're not getting back on that bus. We've got about fifteen minutes before we should be back at the minibus."

He stopped a young woman on the street and asked her in Chinese to take a message to John, but to wait until the two military policemen left. Unfortunately, they didn't move that far away, but she was able to engage John casually to give him the message. Chase grabbed Tessa's hand, and they headed behind the structure that held the giant picture of Mao.

Tessa clung to him tightly but never questioned his decision to leave the group. He spoke Chinese fluently and could easily hail a taxi to take them to their hotel. Although their luggage was on the minibus, he didn't worry about it getting to the hotel. The soldiers didn't seem interested in anyone's luggage. He would explain to John later why he decided to go his own way. It wouldn't be the truth, but perhaps, if he were very apologetic, the guide wouldn't hold it against him.

Navigating the narrow passageways around the Heavenly Gate attracted a lot of attention, since there were few tourists that explored this section. He kept a tight grip on Tessa's hand, hoping she didn't let her curiosity slow them down. This would be just the sort of thing she loved in studying cultures. The visiting with locals needed to be avoided. These locals probably were not the friendly kind, since they appeared to be poorly dressed and a bit malnourished.

Glancing over his shoulder, he spotted one of the soldiers talking to a street guard who pointed in their direction. He shouted something, and he was pretty sure he was ordered to stop, but Chase didn't. Suddenly, a man stepped out in front of him, causing a collision that nearly knocked the man into the canal that ran alongside their path.

"Excuse my clumsiness, sir." Chase stopped and bowed his head for a second but managed to pull Tessa closer. The stranger eyed Tessa from head to toe in spite of wearing a disgruntled expression that made his mouth pooch out and his eyes squint. Chase spotted the soldier and the cop pushing through the crowd toward them.

"You must be careful," the Chinese man said gruffly. "This is no place for tourists. It is dangerous. What is your hurry?"

The man caught sight of the approaching officials. "We have some unfriendly soldiers trying to make an example of us. Can you help us?"

"Where did you learn to speak our language?"

"I grew up here," he answered hurriedly, not wanting to get into a history conversation about his life. "We are here to adopt a baby. We tried to help a woman at the airport, and she said we tried to rob her."

The man called a couple of thugs out of the shadows. Tessa's free hand went to his forearm and squeezed. "These men will get you to the other side. You are safe with them. Your woman is too pretty to be in a place like this. Her eyes are like jewels. She stands out. Wear sunglasses."

"Yes. I'll make sure she does. Thank you." Chase wasn't sure of the two bruisers who pushed through the crowd and motioned for them to follow. Maybe he could ditch them. Could he take them if push came to shove? "I owe you." Chase used the traditional form of greeting by making a fist with his left hand then covering it with the right palm.

The man did likewise and almost grinned but tightened his lips so that they formed a straight line. "Go. I will take care of them." He tilted his head toward the crowd behind him.

"Let's go, Tessa." He plowed forward where the crowded colonnade suddenly opened up for them to pass and just as quickly closed behind them. The two men ahead of him stopped and pulled them ahead then gave Chase a shove on the back to get him to move faster.

"That way. We will follow to make sure you go to taxi. Okay?"

Chase raised his chin in acceptance when he realized they were on a busy street. He could even see a sign for McDonalds in the distance. Spotting a taxi station in front of a restaurant, he hurried in that direction to secure a ride. It was easy enough to tell the driver the address of his hotel. Once inside the taxi, he watched his new friends turn and head back to the area where he'd collided with help.

"Was that one of your angels you're always talking about?" he asked his wide-eyed wife.

"Oh my gosh, I sure hope so." She sighed and leaned back in the seat. "My heart is racing."

Chase turned his attention to the driver and noticed he was stealing glances at them in the rearview mirror. "Tessa, how about you practice your Pashto until we get to the hotel."

His wife had become quite fluent in the language of Afghanistan, thanks to a man who kidnapped her several years earlier. His skills weren't that good, but he would manage if needed in this case. She squeezed his hand but said nothing as he pointed a finger toward the driver from her leg.

CHAPTER 10

Robert continued to enjoy the kids splashing in the resort pool as he periodically checked his phone to see whether Phoebe had sent the address of her uncle's ranch. Whatever took her away disappointed his expectations for the afternoon. She'd promised to be here for lunch to meet the kids. He enjoyed her company and hoped the kids would too.

Paying child support irritated him when he knew Tessa deposited it into a college fund for the kids instead of using it for necessities each month. That muscle head she married took care of things when needed. Maybe he would suggest starting some kind of IRA account for the kids. If he had access to it, then if he ran short of cash, the money would be there. The idea pleased him, thinking he'd pull one over on Mr. Knight In Shining Armor.

Was he jealous? Absolutely. How could she find someone after being married to him and having three kids? Well, maybe their marriage had been a bit of a sham, but he'd tried to make amends. But unlike Phoebe, Tessa was hardheaded to a fault. Whatever had changed her when she went to work for the university had led to her deciding she'd rather go it alone.

"Hi, handsome," came a silky voice followed by a kiss on his cheek. Long fingers traced his jawbone as Phoebe came to face him.

"You look fantastic." Her one-piece swimsuit showed off her beautiful figure. No extra ten pounds because of having kids there. Just a seamless, toned body he couldn't wait to explore if he could figure out a way to keep the kids interested in something other than him being a vacation organizer. "I thought you had work to do." He checked his watch.

"My client didn't show, so I thought I'd join you for a swim. You were deep in thought. I hope it was about me." She slipped on a pair of sunglasses then took a lounge chair next to him.

"It most certainly was." He raised his chin toward where the kids were climbing out of the pool and shaking off the water. "Here come my kiddos. Prepare yourself."

Robert handed them towels as they commenced their cautious head-to-toe exam of Phoebe who didn't waver under their scrutiny. After introductions, Phoebe took control, much to Robert's surprise.

"Have you tried the giant slide yet? You take a raft down tunnels and it's crazy fast."

"Dad doesn't like that stuff, and you have to have an adult with you." Heather frowned.

Phoebe jumped up and motioned for the kids to follow. "Well, you got one now! I love this slide. Come on, Robert. Don't be a spoilsport. Try it."

That was all it took for him to agree, and he ended up liking it enough to go several more times. An hour later, the wet and exhausted mob returned to him and insisted on being fed.

"Hey, I invited your dad and you guys to come out to my uncle's tonight for dinner," Phoebe announced. "I can show you around the ranch."

"A ranch?" Sean Patrick asked. "Dad, can we?"

"I also have horses. Heather, I bet you like horses. And I believe there is a new litter of kittens. I also have three Bernie doodle puppies left for sale. Hopefully, they are still there tonight. They sell fast."

"Dad!" the three kids begged.

"Okay. Okay. We'll go. Sounds like fun." He winked at Phoebe.

Phoebe wrapped a towel around her waist and picked up her bag. "I've got to run by work first so I'm going to change and head out. Robert, I'll text you with the directions. Sorry, babe, I forgot to do that earlier." She landed a kiss on his cheek. "Come early so the kids can feed the horses. You'll love it. Maybe I can even get you to buy a place out there." She laughed and tousled Sean Patrick's hair and pinched Daniel's cheek.

Heather leaned into him as if marking her territory. Women. Even at Heather's young age, she was appraising the competition. Probably learned that from her mother.

~ ~ ~ ~

"It's Ben, Tessa." Chase lifted the phone to his ear.

She applied some lipstick then came to stand next to him. "What's up?"

"Someone knows you're in China. I don't know how, but they do. Vernon is checking security footage, and Lazarus is hacking into other sources there. Strangely enough, there are no security cameras where you escaped from Tiananmen Square. We can see you running into that area, but then it goes dark."

"We have a leak. My guess is Dr. Wu. He still has a lot of contacts here and spouts all that Chinese proverb wisdom as if it will make a difference in the world. He also knows that scientist..."

"Jun Hie, you mean."

"Yes. Jun Hie and his family. Isn't that why we were chosen to come get his baby girl?"

There was a deep sigh on the other end of the phone.

"It isn't Dr. Wu. I'd bet my life on it."

"Then you're a dead man." Chase switched ears with the phone so Tessa could listen in. It was best they didn't have it on speaker in case the room was bugged.

"We even had the FBI check out Jun Hie to make sure no calls had left his safe house. Could be just a coincidence, and you raised suspicion at the airport, so an alert went out."

"We'll be on our guard."

"Now the bad news. Ten more adopted Chinese children have died."

"Where?"

"Eight of them were in the US. One in the Netherlands and a

ten-year-old in Germany. There were no clusters in the US. The news has picked up the story and run with it. The CDC has recommended anyone with an adopted child from Asia, whether it's China, Taiwan, the Philippines—any place, to go to their health care physician for tests. Needless to say, it is dominating the news, and parents are about to panic."

"Can't Dr. Jun Hie begin the process of creating a cure?"

"He has been provided a lab and a genetic engineering team that includes all kinds of brainiacs. But what we've discovered through his wife, who is extremely unhappy about leaving their baby girl behind, is that the baby holds the answers in her DNA and possibly her blood."

"Are you kidding me?"

"I wish I were. It's imperative you get that child here ASAP. She has become a political weapon between our two countries. To accuse the Chinese of yet another international incident like with COVID, could very possibly have long-range implications, one of which would be war. It would be a colossal insult to insinuate they would kill children for the sake of some unknown experimentation to manipulate power."

"So, what does your innocent Dr. Wu say about all this?"

"He believes it's a smoke screen for something bigger. We put a much higher value on human life than other parts of the world. These children who were adopted have been given a second chance in our eyes. To the Chinese, it was a solution to unwanted pregnancies when their population was too big to maintain."

"If that is true, then this has been in the planning for a long time. What is the age range of the children who have died?"

"Three to ten years, so far. Autopsies are pending on many of these, and the CDC is being as thorough as possible with the results. No two children have died of the same illness. Dr. Jun Hie is mute on the matter and refuses to explain until he has his daughter back."

"Any red flags as to what the Chinese are up to? Taking control of Taiwan maybe?"

"There is a lot of saber rattling there and has been for a long time. Nothing much has changed except the intimidation factor, especially when our politicians go over and make promises they can't or won't keep."

"What does Langly say?"

"They're meeting with the National Security Council even as we speak. The Pentagon is on high alert, because like Dr. Wu, they are convinced it's a smoke screen. The American public doesn't want to hear that with a war going in Ukraine and the Russians eyeballing the Baltic countries for invasion. Then there's Israel and Hamas, now Lebanon. Who knows how that will end? Add in Iran throwing tantrums, and we have the elements of a perfect storm."

"I hate to admit it, but Dr. Wu may be right on this one. It's a distraction for something bigger, but what? I still have him for the leak." Chase knew Tessa wasn't going to agree.

"I've got a call coming in from the president."

Without another word, Director Benjamin Clark clicked off.

Chase turned to Tessa. "I can't emphasize enough, you have to be careful here. We don't know for sure if they suspect us of espionage or just targeted us because we drew the short straw."

"I understand. I wish we could call home to make sure the kids are okay."

"Carter and the others said they'd keep tabs on them. Besides, Robert knows better than to screw with me."

~ ~ ~ ~

"Look at them with the puppies, Robert." Phoebe laughed and patted the mother Bernie doodle. "Why don't your kids have pets?"

"My ex didn't want another thing to take care of," he lied. "Money was tight for a long time, and we just didn't have the extra it would require. Tessa was a stay-at-home mom until a few years ago."

"Time to go, kids. Puppies are getting tired. You did a great job feeding the horses by the way. You're a natural. Maybe we can go riding the next time you come out for a visit." Phoebe leaned against the rail fence, impressed that the kids dutifully obeyed. "Good kids. They follow instructions well."

"Thanks. It's been a full-time job." He beamed. "And thanks for dinner. My compliments to the chef, and your uncle for allowing us to come, and your ranch hands for taking the time with the kids. Too bad your uncle wasn't able to be here. I wish we could have met him."

"I'll pass along your compliments. He is busy with his practice in Sacramento. He doesn't like to leave his patients. He also works at the University of Engineering and Technology, I think."

"That's where my wife, sorry, ex-wife works." He motioned for the kids to hurry. "We need to go. Getting late. I don't want your opinion to change when they start bickering. It's been a full day."

She pushed off the fence and slipped her arm through his. "I'll miss you. Why don't you come to a party I'm having at the resort tomorrow night? Lots of bigwigs, socialites, politicians, and connected people. I've created a marketing campaign for a group who is searching for a lawyer who can help them out. Do a little travel to DC and even in the Asian and Pacific market."

"Really? What do they do?"

"Investments, mostly. Planning to expand into natural resources and shipping. Big-time. Probably triple your income the first year. I'm sure they would sweeten the deal with stock options and end-of-year bonuses. It's been difficult getting anyone to travel since COVID. Everyone wants to work from home."

"Sounds a lot more exciting than family law. I'm pretty tired of that." He took a deep breath. "I used to do work like you're describing for a firm I worked for in Sacramento. They did some shady stuff, so I went solo."

Phoebe was well aware of the shady diamond deals that law firm was involved with and that Robert had been duped. How he got the FBI to bail him out remained a mystery, but she'd check into it. However, he had also brought a lot of money into the defunct law firm and was well respected.

"I already told them about you. Part of my job is to put ideas out there and make sure things work together to create an environment that is productive and legal, of course. This group needs someone full-time. I'm freelance so I have a number of clients." She hugged his arm. "Yes. I dug into your work history. Sounds like you were a rising star until the firm decided to cheat and steal. I admire what you did to bring them down." She kissed his cheek. "My hero."

Robert blushed as she wiped lipstick off his cheek.

"So will you come?"

"I got the kids."

"Sean Patrick is old enough to babysit them," she spoke through pouty lips. "Besides, we'll be at the resort."

"You're right. Of course, I'll go. Maybe we can even sneak away for some alone time."

Phoebe cooed softly into his ear. "I have a room already booked."

She waved goodbye to the Scott children and Robert as they circled the car to leave the ranch. The cell phone vibrated in her jeans pocket as a dust cloud from the road moved in her direction. Turning back toward the house, she activated the call.

"I wondered when you would call," she said drily. "Worried I might not be able to pull it off?" She listened patiently to the voice on the other end. "Of course he's coming. I'm very persuasive." A light laugh escaped her lips as she turned back to see Robert's car ease onto the highway. "You sound jealous. That makes me happy. Anyway, he's coming, so make sure you have everything ready. Late tomorrow night, he'll be in no position to refuse."

CHAPTER 11

The Red Dragon observed the two Americans stroll into the restaurant then be ushered into the private banquet room for those who were part of the adoption program. The thought of the abandoned infants who ended up on foreign soil did not always set well with him. Power agendas in China's favor often meant there was a hidden agenda.

The tide of abandoned baby girls leaving the country had slowed in recent years as the population decreased. The side effects of allowing so many adoptions resulted in consequences of gender imbalance and a shrinking workforce dominated by an aging population.

This was out of his control, nor did he desire to participate. What he did want to do was make sure the few babies who left China would be exposed to a better life than would be offered here. But the child he especially wanted to protect meant life or death for many already living abroad. He swore to protect the secret until the time when the puzzle pieces fell into place.

When the Americans ran through the street near Tiananmen Square, a rush of familiarity washed over him as the man turned to look back. For one second, their eyes connected and the memory of the long-ago night of mayhem found him. A taste of blood touched his tongue as he bit the inside of his jaw. Why wasn't he dead?

The investigation claimed the missionary children died in the escape over the mountains to Tibet. Buddhists monks died protecting them, and others swore they had seen their bodies. Soldiers found the badly decomposed bodies of two children, a boy and a girl. Lies and deception did not set well with him.

Even though the man had been a teenager on that nightmarish night, his Cherokee features still resembled what he remembered most about the teen. Those eyes had grown cold and hard. As a teen, that expression sent a warning to step lightly. The woman with him must be his wife. She was as fair as he was dark. Unaware of him, he studied them as they strolled into the banquet room. Could she be a weakness to be exploited? A corner of his mouth turned up in satisfaction imagining how the man might react. "I will soon find out," he mumbled to himself.

~ ~ ~ ~

Other than the hamburger Tessa ordered, which turned out to be goat meat instead of beef, there were no surprises. Their tour guide passed out an updated itinerary as to the following day's activities, which included a trip to the Great Wall, the Pearl Market, and a jade factory where he suggested everyone pick up souvenirs for their future baby girls.

"It will be something for them to treasure from their birth country, and you will also be contributing to the livelihood of a grateful people." His smile appeared sincere. An early breakfast in the common area of the hotel would be shared with other families here for the same reason; to pick up their baby. "It will be the last day with them until we meet up again in Guangzhou. There, your baby will receive her final physical exam, before being sworn in at the American Consulate as an American citizen."

The three American families present mumbled a kind of excitement. Tessa experienced that same excitement but knew the end result would be giving the child back to the birth mother. Poopy diapers and sleepless nights aside, it wouldn't take long for her to bond with the child. She'd even picked out a name for her.

Chase had flipped into soldier mode, and his excitement level became as endearing as a wet paper towel. The other future dads were downright annoying with sharing the things they'd done to the nursery back home. As usual, Tessa did a visual comparison of Chase and the other men in the room. She took a deep breath and let it out slowly, remembering their roller coaster life over the last few years. The man had captured her heart. He remained her adrenaline rush, and, hopefully, the father of another child.

Chase and the three potential fathers cornered John to interact. The sound of laughter reached her, a good sign. Her husband wasn't one of them, but he did manage a slight grin. The three women pulled Tessa to her feet while one announced to the men they were going to the ladies' room.

"Hopefully, there are no squatty-potties here. At least our room has a good ole Western-style toilet," giggled Mrs. Williams from Texas.

She slipped her arm through Tessa's and gave a squeeze. Tessa listened attentively—their baby chatter, what they had brought for the rest of the trip—just conversation that drove her mad with boredom. She had three kids already, and nothing they said or anticipated was even close to the transformation their lives were about to experience. *Just smile and nod,* she kept telling herself until she had to escape.

"I'll wait for you outside, ladies. I need some fresh air. I spotted a balcony off the main dining room."

Leaving the women behind, Tessa became acutely aware of her surroundings. Part of her training as an Enigma agent meant expect the unexpected. That's why she'd noticed a shadow as they entered the ladies' room. The outline of a soldier, maybe a security guard—no, something else. It was a flash of someone, but then it disappeared, thanks to the women who joined her, cutting off her line of sight.

Now she saw nothing. Maybe it was her imagination playing tricks on her because deep down she feared being discovered. The airport confrontation had shaken her more than she let on.

Stepping outside onto the balcony lined with plants, Tessa inhaled the cool breeze pushing against her face. The smell of rain perfuming the night crushed the oppressive stench of air pollution. The city lights sparkled, and the rumble of traffic was not so different than any other large city. For a second, she took it in, along with the distant music of the traditional stringed landtom.

"There you are." Chase stepped up behind her and circled her waist then pulled her close. "Enjoying the view?"

"Very much. Ready to go back to the room? I'm beat. It's been a long day and flight."

"I'm supposed to bond with the guys," he whispered in her ear. "Headed to the bar. One drink then I'll be up. I think the wives are already on the way to the elevator. I'll make sure you get to the room."

"Don't be silly. I'll ride up with the others." She turned in his arms and pressed against his chest. "Besides, they might need protection."

Chase chuckled. "I won't be long. Better hurry."

Tessa kissed him shortly and rushed out. She spotted the men waiting for Chase, laughing and most likely swapping exaggerations. She hoped Chase could try and enjoy this normal opportunity. Hanging out with people who didn't shoot first and ask questions later or saving the world on a regular basis, would be a good experience for him.

The three ladies stepped onto the elevator, followed by more couples. "Hurry!" one of them shouted, but the door closed just as she arrived. The second door opened immediately. Stealing a glance toward the men coming out of the restaurant, she lifted a hand toward Chase, jumped on the empty car, and pushed her floor number.

As it began to lift, the lights flickered and the car slowed. Tessa reached in her purse for pepper spray and remembered it wasn't allowed on the plane. She did have a small spray bottle of lavender water. No weapon. No alternative. Just experience and—fear. She willed it to keep going, to no avail.

The elevator bounced, followed by the lights going out. Before she panicked, she pulled out her phone to activate the flashlight. Finding the emergency button was a mystery since the buttons had Chinese characters, so she pushed each one. No bells or whistles went off, so maybe it was out of service too. Surely the ladies made it up, or could they be stuck too?

She decided to call Chase when the doors were opened by two leather-covered hands. Startled, she realized the elevator had stopped between floors, revealing a man's boots and legs. Falling back against the elevator wall, she dropped her phone. It hit the floor and slid across toward the opening just as a strangely clad man jumped down inside.

The man held up his hand to stop her from retrieving her phone then reached down to lift it. He stared at the screen then turned it off. Tessa couldn't make out his face because of some kind of head covering, maybe a helmet that had a metal piece down his nose but left large openings for the eyes and mouth. Because he dressed in black, she found it difficult to memorize anything significant. She remembered the lavender spray and jammed her hand in her purse, only to have him rush her and yank it away.

"I don't have much money. Take it."

He was close enough that she could make out dark eyes and a sudden amused smile. Just as quickly, it faded, and his eyes narrowed as they ran over her face and hair. When he reached to touch a curl that fell across her forehead, Tessa grabbed him by his leather vest and jerked him forward. At the same time, she jammed a knee into his groin, causing him to bend at the waist with a moan. Clasping her hands together in a fist, she brought it down on the back of his neck, a downward motion. Even though he hit the wall, not the floor, Tessa managed to shove him aside so she could try and escape.

Lunging up to grab the floor through the opening, she screamed for help. Clawing her way forward, a hand caught each ankle. He pulled her back inside then jerked her back into the elevator. Her knees buckled, but he slipped his hands under her armpits and shoved her up against the wall.

"Who are you?" he asked in broken English then repeated the question and emphasized his frustration with banging her against the wall before letting her feet drop back to the floor. "Who taught you to fight?"

"Tessa Butler. I took a self-defense class." She found it hard to breathe as fear took over her ability to plan her next move. "I don't want trouble. I'm here to—"

"I know why you are here. You aren't Tessa Butler. And you have found trouble."

~ ~ ~ ~

"What do you mean, you have some place to be?" Sean Patrick confronted his father who placed a pizza box on the kitchenette table along with the bowl of chocolate-covered strawberries, a box of Little Debbie brownies, a bag of popcorn and chips.

"I'm allergic to strawberries," Heather declared, picking up a piece of the fruit and smelling it.

Daniel grabbed it away from her and shoved it into his mouth while telling her to not do that.

"Allergic?" Robert gasped. "Since when?"

Heather shrugged. "Forever, I think."

"Dad, you can't leave us here. Where are you going?" Sean Patrick asked in shock as he pushed Daniel away from the food. "Don't drink that, Daniel. You know Mom doesn't let us have soda."

"Well, Mom isn't here, and I say it's okay. I've also accessed a couple of movie channels." Robert faked a chuckle. "Not too shabby, huh?"

"Mom isn't going to like it." Sean Patrick crossed his arms across his chest.

"Sean Patrick, my dinner is in this resort. It's a business thing where I'll be meeting some important people who may offer me a job that could be a game changer for me."

"What about us, Dad?" Daniel pushed his glasses up on his nose. "Will it change that?"

Robert put his hand on his son's shoulder. "No. Well, yes because there will be more money to do trips like this. Maybe even to places like Japan or Australia. That's cool, right? Phoebe says I'm one of the top candidates."

"You're leaving me in charge?" Sean Patrick continued in his military stance.

"Why not? Enjoy the movies, eat up, and make sure Heather doesn't eat those blueberries."

"Strawberries, Dad," the teen corrected.

"Right," he said absentmindedly as he admired himself in the mirror and straightened his tie. "How do I look?"

"Like a penguin," Heather admitted as she opened a chip bag. "But in a good way. Can I sleep in my clothes?"

"Sure. Whatever you want."

"Chase isn't going to be happy about this," Sean Patrick mumbled.

Robert pivoted and stormed toward the boy then pointed his finger in his face. "What goes on in this family is between me and your mother. It's none of Captain Muscle Head's business. Got that?"

The startled teen took a step back and dropped his hands down to his side. "Got it." He swallowed hard.

"Can you do this, or should I call the resort services for a babysitter? I would have thought you were too old for that."

"No, sir. I can do it. What time will you get back?"

"When I get back. Don't wait up." He smoothed his suit coat. "Give Daddy a kiss, Heather." She moved closer and held up her salty, barbeque-chip hands. "Nope. I'll kiss you." He landed a light kiss on the top of her head. "Listen to your brothers." He opened the door. "Be good. Have a good time."

CHAPTER 12

The kids devoured the pizza like a pack of wolverines that hadn't eaten all winter. The liter bottle of soda turned over on the table when the boys reached for the last chocolate fudge brownie. A rescue operation ensued but managed to drip onto the tiled floor. Accusations flew hot and heavy of who was the most responsible for the accident when Heather slipped in the puddle, sending her sprawling against the nearby sharp-edged coffee table.

"Blood," Daniel shouted as he rushed to help her stand.

Sean Patrick got a wet washcloth from the bathroom and applied it to the cut above his sister's eye. "Holy smoke, Heather. You whacked it good."

When she saw the bloody cloth, tears cascaded down her face. "I want Daddy."

"Daddy is at a dinner, Pookie. Remember?"

"Not him. I want Chasey. Now!" she insisted.

"What's this?" Sean Patrick pushed Heather's hair away from the cut and her neck. "Pookie, did you eat strawberries?"

"No. Just the chocolate off the top."

Daniel ran to the table, searched through the bowl of strawberries, and lifted one with the sides nibbled off. "I think she got some of the strawberry, Sean." He dropped it in the sink and came back for a closer inspection. "She's got hives."

Sean Patrick noticed her crying had turned into labored breathing. She'd never had this bad a reaction. "I'll call Dad. Daniel, check to see if there is a medical office here. I think we passed one near the pool door yesterday."

"My head hurts, Bubby." Heather always called Sean Patrick that when she was scared.

"We're going to take you to a doctor here at the resort. Okay?"

Her lip jutted out in protest, but when he lifted her in his arms, she laid her head against his shoulder. He managed to dial his dad, but there was no answer.

"They're about to close, Sean. Said they'd wait for us. I'll get the room key."

"I'll carry you, Heather. Okay?" Sean Patrick gently rubbed her back. He staggered a bit, but Daniel steadied him while shutting the door behind them.

~ ~ ~ ~

"You are a brave little girl, Heather," the nurse practitioner praised then butterflied the cut. "That inhaler should help with your breathing in a few minutes. Daniel, good job remembering to bring that. I gave her a low dose of Benadryl and it seems to be working. I'll get some for your dad to give again in five hours. Boys, does your sister need an EpiPen when she has an allergic reaction like this?"

"No, ma'am. This was the worse it's ever been."

"Where are your parents?"

"Dad's at a meeting or something here at the resort. He didn't answer the phone, so I thought I'd better not wait."

"And your mom?"

"Out of the country for work. Dad thought he'd take us on a little vacation."

"How nice of him. Well, you did a good job getting her here. See, the blotches are almost gone. Young lady, you'd better stay away from strawberries." She patted her knee. "Why don't you boys go get some snacks from the restaurant. Tell them I sent you. I'm sure they have some leftovers."

"Daniel, you stay with Heather. I'll go get something healthy this time." Sean Patrick hugged his sister and made eye contact with his brother who raised his chin in some kind of signal that meant he would take care of Heather.

Even following the directions the nurse had given him, Sean Patrick took a wrong turn. It wasn't that far from her office, but he got distracted by the swimming pool under the evening tiki lights and palm trees. He realized the mistake and turned down another corridor he thought might be a shortcut.

Stumbling over an untied shoelace, he'd bent down to fix the problem when he saw Phoebe come out of a side door near the kitchen with another man on her heels. He slowly pulled a push cart covered with a tablecloth in front of him. Her voice grew louder as she neared then stopped. Pulling the cloth back enough to take a peek, he saw black neck-length hair. The man in a dark suit was not his father.

Phoebe stroked the man's chest then leaned in to give him a passionate kiss, which he returned then pushed her back a step. If she was his dad's new girlfriend, why was she pulling him back to put her hands on his butt?

"You are one amazing recruiter, Phoebe. Our people like the prospect of that guy working with us. What's his name again?"

She stood on tiptoe and nibbled on his ear. "Robert Scott. Smart. Handsome. I'm thinking greedy as well."

Sean Patrick swallowed hard, wanting to ram the cart into their legs. Instead, he listened.

"I have to get back. He'll be searching for me. I promised some alone time."

He tightened his hold on her and squeezed until she groaned with pain and shook him off.

"You're taking this too far."

"I've got a job to do, and I'm doing it. Doesn't mean anything. I'm sure you've done the same kind of manipulation many times. Have you ever heard me complain?"

She turned and stormed off, her heels clicking as she went. The man followed close behind. It sounded as if he were apologizing.

Sean Patrick slowly stood when he thought the coast was clear. He ran back to the nurse's office and slid inside like he was doing an action movie. The nurse eyed him with surprise.

"Well, that was cool." She eyed him suspiciously.

"Kitchen was closed. Besides, I think we've had enough to eat for one night. Right, Daniel?" he asked, elbowing his brother who knew when to pick up on a hint.

"Okay. Well, I'm going to call security to escort you back to the suite."

"No. We got this. Thanks, though." Sean Patrick helped his sister into a wheelchair with a picture of a unicorn on the back.

"Hold on, young man. You're not in charge here. I'll go with you. Part of the job. I'd worry if I didn't. I want to make sure you are safe. I'll have security search for your dad in the meantime." She edged him out of the way and entered the hall outside the office.

They were almost to the elevator when Sean Patrick leaned in to his brother and whispered. "If she sees our rooms, she'll freak. Not only that, Phoebe is cheating on Dad. I saw it with my own eyes."

Daniel slipped his glasses into the pocket, which was part of the unicorn's head. "Oh no, I think I left my glasses in your office. My dad is going to have a meltdown."

The nurse appeared skeptical then caved. "No worries. I thought you had them on, but no matter. I'll go back. Where do you think you left them?"

"In the bathroom. On the sink."

She cocked her head as if she didn't believe him but turned the wheelchair around.

"I will be right back." She started to push the chair.

"You're making me carsick. Can I just sit here?" Heather sniffed. "Please, Nurse Gwen."

The nurse sighed and pointed to the boys. "Stay right here until I get back."

"Yes, ma'am." Sean Patrick added a salute.

The nurse ran to her office and disappeared inside. The boys slipped in behind her and shoved the rolling cabinet across the door then the desk and trash can with a skull and cross bones on the front. Since the door opened out, it would give them a few seconds to escape.

Running back to Heather, they found her with a smirk on her mouth. She raised both hands, palms out when the boys slapped each one and laughed. "Let's roll." He grabbed the wheelchair, and the three escaped to a different elevator down the corridor where he'd seen Phoebe.

The elevator opened to a busy corridor. Two security guards ran past them toward their room halfway down the hall. The kids eased forward.

Heather gripped the arms of the wheelchair. "Boys, as Chase likes to say, life as we know it is about to hit the fan."

~ ~ ~ ~

Tessa slid around the elevator as if doing so would put distance between her and the man. Each way she moved, he turned slowly to keep the distance from growing. Knowing it was futile, she gave up trying. He closed the gap between them, as if sensing she might try and fight him again. It gave her a chance to see him a little clearer as the overhead light flickered.

Her first impression was that he resembled a picture she'd studied of a Terracotta Soldier come to life and escaped from the exhibit in Xi'an. He wasn't as tall as Chase but just as intimidating, nonetheless. The glare he leveled at her as he cocked his head unnerved her. Maybe he was part demon or some kind of weird serial killer.

"I repeat. Who are you?"

"Tess—Tessa Butler. It's on my passport. It's in the zipper pocket of my purse."

"And the man you were with?"

"My husband."

"His name?" he growled.

Tessa could feel the situation spiraling out of control. She needed to calm down and get control of her rapid heartbeat and let the adrenaline fuel her chance at escape. She took a deep breath and slowly released it.

"His name!" he shouted, making her flinch.

When she didn't answer, he shoved her against the wall. He grabbed the front of her shirt. She immediately raised a hand on each side of his arms as if in surrender mode. It was a gamble he would expect her to knee him again, but he leaned away as if to make it impossible. However, she used her free hands as a weapon.

The elevator bounced and moved just as she slapped the sides of his head, hoping to hit his ears. But the helmet made of leather and metal, protected him. Without thinking, she jammed one fist under his chin, forcing his head upward. Then she punched him in the

81

throat, causing him to completely drop his hold on her as he stumbled back against the side wall.

The elevator jolted to a stop with the doors still ajar. She leveled a side kick to his knee as he lunged forward, stopping his momentum. Faster than her, he hit the button that closed the door. Moving in front of it, he took on the curious expression of amusement. His eyes raked over her with interest, but he didn't approach.

"I will be watching you, Tessa Butler, if that is really your name. Maybe we meet again where we can finish this in a—more interesting arrangement."

"That will never happen," she panted.

"Yes. It will. And you will not be able to do anything about it. Do not underestimate me."

"The same can be said for me." Her voice quivered, but she raised her chin in defiance.

"I can see that, Tessa. I look forward to our next—encounter." A slow wicked smirk played at the corners of his mouth as he stepped forward, but she stood her ground. He reached back and hit the open button then stood aside. "You may go."

Tessa barreled through the door and ran down the hall toward her room. Her hands trembled as she tried to open the door. The elevator pinged and she heard Chase with the other men exit the car. The room door opened, and she slipped inside.

She could hear them approaching as she leaned against the wall and tried to take deep breaths, but her heart continued to pound against her chest. Deep breaths, she told herself as Chase pushed into the room and turned the lock on the door.

"Tessa?" he said. "What's wrong?" He flipped on the light as she threw herself into his arms. He pushed her back and moved her hair out of her eyes. "Tessa, what happened?"

She'd opened her mouth to speak when the sound of someone clearing their throat drew her attention. On the other side of the room, a man lifted both hands in a kind of surrender.

"It seems I have come at a bad time."

~ ~ ~ ~

Robert Scott hurried to his suite to check on the kids and make sure they were already in bed. It was past their bedtime, at least for Heather. She needed a good ten hours sleep to keep her from being a handful in the morning. Opening the door, he froze at the sight of the room in disarray. He called for the kids with no response. He spotted a bloody cloth on the floor and a cracked glass on the coffee table. A wave of panic engulfed him as he grabbed the landline and called security.

"My room has been ransacked and there looks to have been a struggle. My kids are missing too. I need help now!" he cried in alarm. "Please. Hurry!"

CHAPTER 13

The man in their hotel room was clearly Chinese but spoke English extremely well. He had positioned himself where the bedside table lamps didn't shine directly on him. But, to his credit, he stepped forward revealing a surprise.

"You." Chase stepped in front of Tessa to protect as he confronted the man. "How did you get in here?"

He chuckled. "I have my ways, as do most people in my profession. Please." He pointed to the bed. "Sit. We need to talk." Chase led Tessa to sit down but remained standing in order to tower over the man.

"You're the man who helped us escape Tiananmen Square."

"Yes. I am pleased you had no further problems." He laid his hand on his heart. "I am Tan."

Chase didn't immediately respond.

"I am here to help you. The director of Enigma sent a list of some things you requested." He pointed to a backpack on the small desk in the corner.

"Open it," Chase demanded. He wanted to make sure it wasn't a bomb.

The man carefully unzipped the backpack and pulled out several weapons and other supplies. Chase quickly went to check things out then ran his hand over the interior of the bag to make sure there were no tracking devices.

"You are safe, Captain Hunter."

Chase cringed at the reference. "You must have me mixed up with someone else."

"My apologies, Mr. Butler." He sobered. "I have been working undercover here for about fifteen years. I am Chinese but was educated in the US for a period of time. Your CIA recruited me and on occasion, the very private and elusive Enigma has used me through Dr. Wu."

"That's not a roaring endorsement," Chase snarled. His eyes went to Tessa when he realized he'd totally forgotten her disheveled appearance. "What happened? You were shaking when I came in the room. Did you know this guy was here?"

"No. I had no idea. A man in the elevator attacked me. I took a different car than the other women because theirs was full."

"Did he hurt you?"

She shook her head nervously.

Chase kneeled beside her. "Did he…"

"No. It wasn't sexual. Just roughed me up a little. He wanted to know who I was." She quickly told him about the encounter and how she'd responded.

"Where are you hurt?" He ran his hands over her arms and then pushed her hair behind her ears.

"I'm not. I think he only wanted to scare me. Which he did. I don't think he expected I'd fight back."

"I should never have left you. We headed back when the other wives said the electricity was out on our floor."

"That outage was my fault," Tan admitted. "I programmed the systems to get up here without being seen. It's due to go off again in about twenty minutes. It will allow me to leave without anyone noticing. I'm so sorry Mrs.—Butler." He pointed to Tessa's neck. "There. On her neck. Please. Move her hair where I can see it better."

Chase carefully touched her neck and saw the red marks. "Are you bleeding?"

Tan leaned in and his eyes widened. "That is the mark of the Red Dragon."

"Who the hell is the Red Dragon, and why has she been

marked? It's not coming off." He pressed his thumb back and forth across the character. "I used to hear about a Red Dragon as a kid. Just a myth."

"The skin is not broken, and it is said that he uses some kind of dye to make the mark."

Tessa stood to examine it in the mirror. "I always wanted a tattoo," she said drily as she turned back to the men. "Am I somehow marked for life?"

"How did he do it?" Chase spoke calmly, knowing she didn't need him to go all Rambo over the situation.

Tessa shrugged. "Probably during the struggle. It happened so fast. I felt pressure—maybe once—on my neck, but no pain."

"Who is this Red Dragon?" Chase turned to Tan who seemed to have a lot of answers.

"Well, he shouldn't be here. He comes from the Gansu Province."

"We're headed that way day after tomorrow. First stop is the capital, Lanzhou. Again—who or what is he?"

"A myth. Legend."

"Psycho?" Tessa touched her neck as she gazed into the mirror.

Tan chuckled. "Maybe. No one really knows. It is the year of the dragon, so it makes sense that a Red Dragon would emerge. He protects the innocent, shows strength and strong character. Word is he is ruthless to those who are deceptive. The Chinese people have a rather strong affection for him whenever he emerges into a new generation."

"That wasn't my experience," Tessa reminded him. "I feel like I just received the mark of the beast from Revelations in the Bible."

"Not to fear. You did not," he reassured her and sat back down. "If he is in Beijing and you are leaving, it is unlikely he will follow without being detected."

"Unless he has two identities," Chase suggested. "Tessa, can you describe him?"

She proceeded to describe the costume and how part of the helmet had actually covered his face like some ancient warrior. "There was dark paint or makeup around his eyes too.

"Strange he knew exactly when the elevator would go down and the lights would be out."

"As I said, I manipulated the system. Those men who helped

you escape today are with me and waiting to do it again to make sure I escape undetected. You'll probably not see me again. My work is like walking a tightrope. I don't know who the Red Dragon is. Some say he's a ghost."

"He is not." Tessa pointed to her neck. "This is proof."

"Which would indicate he leads a double life. That might mean he is a person of power who can come and go as he pleases without detection or a discontent in the government, military, or wealthy business man who feels threatened." Tan shrugged. "Protesters and dissidents in China are nothing new. The causes bounce around between unpaid wages, environmental activism, and even land development. The last ones of any note were over COVID."

"I don't like it." Chase took a deep breath and checked the Glock he'd received. "How am I going to get this on the plane to Lanzhou?"

"You won't. When you leave here, stow it under the mattress. The room attendant will find it after you're gone. She works for me. When you get to your Lanzhou destination, someone will bump into you at the airport and pass off another weapon. Set your backpack down on the floor at the American Coffee Company."

"Coffee?"

"It has become very popular here among the young people. The barista will take care of everything. Be sure to order a caramel macchiato with almond milk and extra whipped cream. Can you order it in Chinese?"

"Yes."

"Perfect." Tan switched his attention to Tessa. "You are quite lovely and will cause a great deal of interest with curly blonde hair and blue eyes. People are generally very friendly to Americans because they are curious. Don't let your guard down. Be polite, but do not fall for tricks to lure you away from the group." He moved toward the door after checking his watch.

"Thank you, Tan," Chase said, following him to the door. "Anything else?"

"There is a traitor among your group here. I don't know if they've joined you yet, but be diligent." He gave the traditional palm over fist or Bao Quan to show respect. "I know you will. Your reputation precedes you." The lights in the hall flickered off as he opened the door. "Good luck." He stole one more glance at

Tessa then disappeared into the darkness.

Chase bolted the door then turned to Tessa. She stood hugging her arms in what he knew as an attempt at bravery. How could he have been so careless with her safety? "I'm so sorry, Tessa." He walked to her and hoped she heard the plea for forgiveness in his voice.

"I know. You couldn't have known, and I shouldn't have gotten on that elevator alone. I was seconds behind the other women." She touched his cheek with her fingertips. "I didn't mention this in front of Tan, but it sounded like the Red Dragon knows who we are."

Chase ran his hand up her neck to the red characters of the Red Dragon's handiwork.

"What does this mean, Chase?"

"I think it means he has marked you as his own."

~ ~ ~ ~

Phoebe rushed into Robert's suite as he tried to pick up some of the mess. The kids sat on the couch with the nurse practitioner. He came to stand in front of the kids after the hotel manager and the security people left.

"What were you thinking?" He tried to keep a low, controlled voice. The fire-breathing dragon waiting inside his mouth hoped Nurse Gwen would soon leave.

"Mr. Scott, I believe the same could be asked of you," the nurse snapped. "These children were left alone with no notification at the front desk that it would be advantageous to periodically check on them. Thanks to your quick-thinking sons, they got Heather to me for the help she needed. And if you check your phone, you'll see that they tried to reach you multiple times, as did I."

Robert raised his chin in stubbornness, flushing in embarrassment. "Thank you for doing your job." He snorted. "I don't appreciate your tone, however."

Nurse Gwen slowly stood and confronted him without batting an eye. "And I don't care what you appreciate, Mr. Scott. I'll be calling social services in the morning, so if you want to make a good impression when they come to check you out, I suggest you get this place cleaned up and your attitude in check." She turned to the children. "If you need me for anything else, just hit the intercom for help. I will notify the front desk you are of concern to me."

There was a lot of head bobbing, but Robert noticed they didn't commit to her offer. "Hold on—" he fumed.

"Mr. Scott, I don't like bullies, and you appear to be one. I also don't have any use for someone who leaves their kids alone in a strange place unsupervised. Don't try and threaten me, if that was what you intended to do." She turned her attention to Phoebe, which made him nervous enough to shift his weight to one hip. "Who are you?" the nurse demanded.

Phoebe stood and put on her best innocent expression. "I'm just a friend. Mr. Scott called me when he couldn't find the children. I rushed right up to help. He's a very loving and devoted father. This is a huge misunderstanding."

The nurse rolled her eyes. "I would love to have a dollar for every time I've heard that one." She turned back to the kids and winked. "Drop by to see me tomorrow, and I'll get you some of that pie I told you about."

"Yes, ma'am," the boys responded in unison.

Heather jumped up and hugged her around the waist then whispered, "I'm sorry."

Robert hurried to the door and opened it. "Thank you, Nurse Gwen. I can handle it from here."

The nurse stopped in front of him and frowned. "See that you do, Mr. Scott."

Robert slammed the door and turned to the kids who huddled on the couch. Heather sat in the middle, who reminded him of a squashed and scared rabbit. "You guys made the mess. Clean it up."

Phoebe stood and faced him. "I just made a call to housekeeping. They're on their way up. I'm moving you next door to a bigger suite. I've already taken care of the cleaning and damage, if there is any." She sent a sympathetic wink to the children. "Kids are kids. I'm sure this was just a playful misunderstanding. Kids get hurt all the time, Robert. Don't let this spoil your good news." She laid a hand on his chest. "Please. You're just scared of what could have happened. They are fine. I'll speak to Nurse Gwen in the morning. Come on. Let's get your things."

"What news?" Sean Patrick asked.

Robert cleared his throat. "We're moving to Washington DC."

"We?" Daniel snapped as he placed his glasses on his nose. "We can't leave our school and Mom."

Robert chuckled nervously as he let his eyes shift to Phoebe. "I mean Phoebe and I."

"You're getting married!" Heather gasped. "Does Mommy know?"

"No. We're not getting married. But we'll be spending a lot more time together for sure," Phoebe cooed.

"So, you're moving in together?" Sean Patrick wore a confused expression. "Can't you just do that here?"

"No. I'll still be here part-time." Phoebe rubbed Robert's back.

"Oh." Sean Patrick nodded. "At least you can still see that Chinese guy you were kissing downstairs earlier."

CHAPTER 14

When Chase wasn't mesmerized by the city lights out the window because he couldn't sleep, he evaluated his lapse in common sense in protecting his wife. He'd been all over the Middle East, Russia, Africa, Central Asia, and never given it much thought because he remained in control. Not here. This place was filled with clouded memories of another life as a child. It reminded him of both home and a prison.

Standing at the window, Chase continued to watch Beijing, a city that could have easily been Chicago or Atlanta. He became acutely aware how the country had morphed into a place he didn't remember. Gone were the monochromatic colors replaced by a vibrance that boasted of success and stability.

Only the sound of Tessa's heavy sigh as she rolled over caused him to refocus on her. How could she sleep like a this? It had always amazed him how she could just turn it off and sleep like a baby until she needed to wake up and carry on.

Dr. Wu had once told him her clear conscience and pure heart prohibited the evil of world from crowding in on her. Even when she had nightmares after Afghanistan, she could sleep. To his knowledge, those no longer plagued her, thanks to Dr. Wu. Sometimes he wondered if the man hypnotized her to keep her returning to him. They had become close friends. Chase didn't like it.

Why did the misfits of society, including himself, find themselves drawn to her? Having her in his life was like trying to prevent a toddler from crossing a busy street. But living without her might seriously cause him to go over the edge or fry what decency he had left. His mission in life involved protecting her and those mischievous kids of hers. Would this baby they were taking home test him to see if he could hack such a life?

After Tessa's miscarriage, they'd encountered some truths about their relationship and how to move forward. Her love, as always, was patient and endured the sense of betrayal that nearly overwhelmed him. In the end, her little girl, Heather, showed him life with the love of his life and three kids was the best gift God could possibly give a man like him. He certainly didn't deserve them.

"Chase?" came Tessa's soft voice as she raised up in bed. "Everything okay?"

"Yeah." He slipped back into bed and pulled her into the crook of his arm. "Just trying to figure out why this Red Dragon came after you." He felt her snuggle closer. "Well, and the fact we're getting a baby to take home. How hard can it be? Right?"

A soft chuckle escaped her lips then she kissed him on the chest. "This will be the hardest thing you've ever done, tough guy. She will force you to make all kinds of promises that will be almost impossible to keep and turn you into an overbearing, protective man. In a way, you've got part of that already covered. Heather is proof of that. Then there are the sleepless nights, diaper changes—"

"Wait. We never agreed to that." He pulled and frowned at her.

"That's why we're getting the big bucks. Combat pay."

"How hard can it be? Everyone pees and poops."

Another soft, patient laugh. "I can't wait," she admitted. "If it turns out you want to try again, I'm willing. Time is running out for us. That whole biological clock is not on our side."

"Here's an idea. Why don't we start practicing," he said, pulling her on top of him.

"Practice makes perfect." She kissed him on his neck and ear.

After their lovemaking, Tessa fell back asleep, but Chase

remained wide awake. All he could think of was why the Red Dragon may have targeted Tessa and the meaning of such an attack. Tessa thought he knew he was not Chase Butler. The only way that might be possible was if there really was a mole at Enigma, giving out sensitive information. His guess still focused on Dr. Wu since he was Chinese and had plenty of connections here.

Most people at Enigma didn't know that he and Dr. Wu had a history stretching back to their childhood. His parents had also been doctors who worked alongside Chase's. They didn't live in the village but came twice a month to help with surgeries or whatever needed to be done. Wu tagged along, and the boys would roughhouse and go on adventures.

At one point, he remained with Chase's family for six months to attend school. The Shaolin monks were just as hard on him as they were Chase. They got into mischief and often were punished with cleaning up animal pens and stalls. Wu remained with the Shaolin for six months. He traveled home after that and returned over the next few years to finish his training. Chase could still imagine him pranking after all this time. What had happened to make him a solemn, devious doctor who enjoyed exploring a person's darkest thoughts?

Tessa believed he was a kind healer and full of wisdom. Chase believed him diabolical, a witchdoctor and full of crap. The man could be a combination of all of that. But the big question remained, how did the Chinese know he was here? Did Dr. Wu have connections to the Red Dragon? It would be just like him to play both sides against the middle for one of his mind-bending experiments.

"Chase, we're going to be late. Wake up." Tessa shook him gently. "Do you know what time it is?"

He rolled over to squint at the clock then bolted upright. "Coffee," he moaned as he swung his feet to the floor.

"Here." She handed him a porcelain cup. "I used the instant we brought from home."

He held it between his hands for a few seconds then took a sip and let out an "Aww" that sounded as if it went on forever.

"I laid your clothes out for you. You've got time for a quick shower. Go," she demanded. When he didn't budge, she took the cup and placed it on the nightstand, followed by a grunt as she pulled him up. "Please, Chase. I don't want to miss the Great Wall."

He stretched then moved toward the bathroom. "The wall has been there 3000 years. It's not going anywhere."

"Ha. Ha. Very funny. Hurry up."

~ ~ ~ ~

To avoid feeling like a victim of some random attack, Tessa put on a brave face instead of acting like a scared rabbit when they walked out to the bus. It was ready to leave, but John, the tour guide, jumped off and motioned for them to hurry. When John appeared to scrutinize her, she wondered if he was the Red Dragon.

Was this going to be the new normal here? Every man she saw would be suspect? A threat? A danger to her and the child they were trying to take back to the States? What if the authorities already knew of their plans?

A man standing outside the hotel wearing dark clothing caught her eye. She hurried onto the bus and sat in the back next to the window, streetside, as Chase paused to speak to several of the men. Stretching her neck followed by twisting in her seat to try and find the mysterious man who spooked her, she decided it was just her imagination. Then he appeared at the corner of the building. Was it him?

He didn't dress like the hundreds of people filling the sidewalks and streets in a hustle to get to work or some other destination. His clothing resembled a costume from a movie about an unknown dynasty: part warrior, part lord. Although his features were not clear from this distance, his face appeared as a mask of indifference.

"What is it?" Chase drew her attention away from the street.

"I thought that might be the man from the elevator last night."

Chase leaned down to follow her line of sight. "Where?"

"He's gone." She gave a quick description.

He slid in next to her. "Probably one of the actors from the theater up the street. There's a long history of Chinese opera here. Might be an ad to come to the performance this evening. What about his face? Would you recognize him if not for all the distractions. Distinguishing features maybe?"

"No. Actually, he did favor an opera character I saw on a billboard yesterday."

The bus pulled out into traffic, and John began a speech on the history of the Great Wall.

"Maybe we could go to the opera tonight." She laced her fingers through his.

"It's not on the schedule," he said flatly.

"All the more reason to go. I'll probably never get back here. If anyone is checking our itinerary, wouldn't it be a good time to slip away for a few hours?"

"No. Not happening."

Tessa twisted her mouth into a pout.

"I know that look. No. Don't even think about it. We're not going out alone unless the whole group goes, including John. Understand?"

"So, there is a chance we could go."

Chase's warning frown shut her down. The dark side of Captain Chase Hunter might come to life any second. Sometimes she forgot how dangerous he could be even though past experiences had taught her many hard lessons on not obeying orders. Just because she became his wife didn't mean he stopped being in charge, especially when it came to matters of security and completing a mission.

Though traffic grew light after leaving the city, the trip still took almost two hours. Even with the throngs of people gathering to climb the narrow steps leading to the upper sections of the wall, Tessa loved every second of the experience.

The jade market had a restaurant that prepared a lunch for them. Several of the ladies were squeamish about the idea of all the serving bowls being on a large lazy Susan. They were filled with delicious foods both strange and diverse in textures and aromas. The waitress gave tiny spoons to dip into the dishes to encourage the reluctant guests to try it before taking a portion.

"But there are no extra serving spoons," the Minnesota woman whispered to Tessa.

The thought bothered Tessa until Chase dug in and offered her a satisfied grin. Fortunately, she was proficient enough at using chopsticks she didn't drop a dumpling on the floor like one of the future dads. It became a complete comedy of errors until the hostess brought them Western-style silverware. Chase and Tessa refused and continued with the traditional chopsticks.

"What is this?" she asked quietly.

"You don't want to know," he said out of the corner of his mouth then grabbed another bite.

Tessa pretended to be full and drank more tea. "I'm going to the restroom."

"I'll go with you," he said, putting down his chopsticks.

"Oh my gosh. You will not. I can take care of myself," she mumbled while the others were chatting and nibbling their food like they had eaten a green persimmon. "Maybe I should rescue the ladies. We can go shopping. Hope you brought your credit card. I noticed some pink jade when I came in."

"The green is the best," he said, taking her bowl to finish.

Tessa motioned for the ladies to follow. "Yeah, but it isn't pink."

The final stop was the pearl market in Beijing. Although late in the day, and the future dads failed to hide their boredom, their attitude turned to amazement once they entered the five-story building. The idea that the market had a lot more to offer than three floors of pearls and jewelry caught their attention since the ground floor sold MP3 players, digital cameras, DVD players, and other electrical items.

Since Chase could speak Chinese, the ladies followed them to the third floor that was divided into two halves. The first sold Chinese arts and crafts, while the second half began their exploration of the pearls that every woman needed, according to the vendors. Pearls covered the fourth and fifth floors.

"The higher we go, the more exclusive the pearls become. Keep that in mind when you are shopping." He waved them in closer, since they oscillated between timid and scared. When a large banner featuring a popular movie star buying pearls, they lost focus of why they were there. They pointed at another banner hanging over a pearl stall with a picture of the prime minister of England. He felt like he was herding cats with attention deficit.

"It's crazy loud and aggressive here but can be a lot of fun." He walked a little ahead, but the women quickly gathered close to hear him. "Prices start high, so bartering over price is important and expected. If you can't handle a little bartering, just walk away and say you can't afford it. Trust me, they'll come after you in order to make a deal you can't refuse. It's just business."

"Or maybe you can do it for us?" Mrs. Williams suggested sweetly in her Texas accent. The two other women chimed in on the idea.

Tessa covered her mouth as if trying not to laugh at his efforts to keep control. He was grateful when she stepped up to encourage them. "Well, we don't have a lot of time, so we should decide on what we're going to do."

"Right." Chase noticed several vendors had fixated on them, especially Tessa. Either they thought she might be of some importance or rich. They were about to spring into action so he decided to get control of the situation fast. "Ladies, you will find freshwater pearls, seawater pearls, coral, emeralds, gems, and other precious stones. It is easy to become amazed by the array of exquisite jewels. Decide right away what floats your boat. I believe these three vendors have a large selection. Let me introduce you."

Chase puffed out his chest and leveled a stern expression at the three men who stepped out to approach when he held up his hand for them to stop. He rattled on for a good minute, laying his hand over his heart at one point and bowing his head toward Tessa. Like a magic wand waved over ordinary men, they suddenly offered chairs to the four women as he stood behind Tessa with his feet slightly apart and his hands clasped behind his back.

The vendors were polite and spoke in a moderate voice as they offered various pieces and styles. Fortunately, Tessa's tastes were simple and it didn't take long for the pearls to be chosen for a necklace, earrings, and bracelet. Being a thrifty woman and having been on her own, she had only chosen earrings. Unknown to her, he ordered the other pieces, plus a ring with a huge pearl and several diamonds. Not once in his whole life had he spoiled a woman. Bribed them—yes, but never spoiled.

"I can't believe the deals we got," the Springfield mom marveled as she took her place on the bus. "Chase, you are amazing. I don't know what you said to those vendors, but they couldn't have been sweeter or more accommodating."

"Yeah, thanks, Chase," one of the future fathers moaned good-naturedly. "I'll be sure to send you a copy of my credit card bill when this trip is over."

Tessa leaned in to his ear when the bus began its journey back to the hotel. "What did you say?"

"I told them you were a princess with your attendants but preferred to stay under the radar."

"Chase," she said, shaking her head. "Better keep that to yourself. I kind of feel sorry for them for believing such a story."

"I'm always amazed how oblivious you are as to your beauty. Those guys were checking you out before I ever spoke up. They were not going to get pushy thinking I was your security and that you had other people with you. Those blue eyes probably wowed them." He chuckled. "Translating for all of you helped me practice. The only Chinese I get to speak these days is with Wu. And generally, that involves arguing and name-calling."

"I can't imagine Dr. Wu calling anyone names," she huffed.

"Oh, I do all the name-calling. He just gives me a bunch of Chinese proverb crap that infuriates me. I think that's why he does it."

"He's a good man."

"I swear, sometimes I think he's hypnotized you."

"You mean when he swings that little watch in front of my face and says 'repeat after me'?"

Chase jerked his head around in alarm until she elbowed him.

"I'm just messing with you," she laughed. "Just don't trash-talk him. I don't like it. He healed me, Chase."

"I know. I'm eternally grateful for that." He sighed and grabbed her hand. "Do you even know how many heads I've had to bust over you? I'm beginning to wonder if you're worth it."

"Humph. That's not what you said last night."

"Witch," he whispered in her ear.

"You'd better believe it."

~ ~ ~ ~

He observed the Americans disembark from their small tour bus, carrying bags of souvenirs. Their lackadaisical attention to people around them was comical, considering he could easily slip in and take their phones, wallets, or one of those expensive gifts from the pearl market without them realizing it until they got to their room.

Not so with the Butlers, as they called themselves. Their acute sense of surroundings kept him from moving forward. Both of them had their heads on a swivel, eyes constantly scanning the area. An outline of their security pouch with important papers and a passport was against the inside of their clothes. He wondered in that moment if the man also carried the weapon passed to him last night.

He felt amused when he watched the man called Tan leave their hotel room. The contact, a well-known arms dealer, worked for the CIA as a double agent. None of that mattered to him. Maybe Tan would tell him what he needed to know with a little—persuasion.

When the Butlers entered the hotel first, he eased toward the others and quickly passed through the middle of their conversation, putting his hand on one, two, then three people. He passed their tour guide, who locked eyes with him then quickly ushered his group toward the double doors. Turning back, he slipped a piece of paper into John's pocket before disappearing into the crowds.

~ ~ ~ ~

Chase noticed a nervous John pull an envelope from his pocket then head their way. "That can't be good," he mumbled to Tessa.

"Wouldn't they mail our pearls and jade home?"

"That was no problem. I'm talking about John. He's pale as a ghost and barely making eye contact at us."

John approached slowly, twisting his neck as if he were trying to pop it. He extended his hand holding the envelope. "This is for you, Chase."

Chase didn't try to take it. He could see his name on the outside. "What is that?"

"A man shoved it in my pocket."

"Did you see him?"

"Only as he walked away."

"Can you describe him?"

"I am sorry. No." He raised his chin then surveyed the area around him. "But…"

"But what?"

"It has the mark of the Red Dragon. I must check on the group."

He shoved it into Chase's hand and headed to the elevator to join the others.

Chase tore the envelope open and read the message written in Chinese.

"What does it say, Chase?"

He read it again to himself to make sure he got it right then aloud to Tessa. "I know who you are, Captain Hunter. Remember the words of Sun Tzu 'Know the enemy and know yourself in a hundred battles and you will never be in peril.'"

CHAPTER 15

"It's not what you think, Robert," Phoebe insisted as he followed her into the hall outside the new accommodations she'd provided. He stepped back from her as she tried to touch his chest. "I don't know what your son is talking about."

"It's not like Sean Patrick to make things up. If he says he saw you kissing another man, then…"

"Are you sure about that? Your kids, although bright and entertaining, are a handful. They are manipulating you because of your ex-wife."

"Leave Tessa out of this."

"Tessa. Tessa. Tessa. That's all I've heard since we've met. You complain about her, but the truth is you aren't over her. You're constantly throwing her in my face, making me compete for your favor."

"You're jealous."

"Absolutely," she snapped. "Besides, I can kiss whoever I want. It's not like we're exclusive, or at least you've never hinted that's what you want. So, screw you, Robert." She pivoted and planned to make a quick escape when he grabbed her arm and pulled her back.

"I'm sorry. You're right. I don't know what Sean Patrick saw and I guess it's possible they are a little jealous of my time with you. They didn't want me to leave them tonight, and maybe I shouldn't have. I just wanted to be with you and whatever you were a part of. You've been so great with them, and I appreciate that."

Phoebe let her shoulders sag in surrender. "I've enjoyed them. I admire your 'good dad' image, and it warms my heart."

"I'm crazy about you, Phoebe," he confessed as he pulled her into his arms. "I don't want to screw this up with us. I'm still shell-shocked from the divorce and being pushed aside in my kids' lives."

"I understand," she sighed as she let her hands trail up his arms to rest on his shoulders. "I thought we were starting a long-lasting relationship is all. I want to be a part of your future and everything that you're capable of." Phoebe raised her mouth to his, and he took it passionately. "I feel the same way about you, Robert. Let's start over."

"I'd like that. I'll start by talking to the kids about treating you with more respect."

"Thank you. I want to be part of their lives too. It means a lot to me." She sighed dramatically and ran her hands down his chest. "I guess our rendezvous will have to wait."

"Probably best since the nurse is going to be patrolling my every move for the remainder of our stay." He chuckled. "They sure have her hoodwinked."

"It's adorable really." She pushed away. "I'd better go. I have a few loose ends to tie up from the party, then I'm calling it a day. I'll touch base with you tomorrow. The Pacific Rim Consortium were so impressed with you. They'll most likely want to sign you right away. Are you prepared for that?"

"I will be. Just need to hear the particulars."

"Of course. I'll be there to support you and explain the ins and outs of international law."

"Thank you, Phoebe. For everything."

She rushed back into his arms and gave him a quick kiss. "You mean the world to me." She hurried away and left him standing alone. But as she turned back to see if he was watching her, the sound of a small sweet voice took his full attention from her exit.

"Daddy?"

"Something will have to be done about that," she decided.

~ ~ ~ ~

Phoebe opened the door to her temporary suite on the top floor. Flipping on the lights revealed a man standing at the floor-to-ceiling windows. His full attention appeared to be focused on the city and the desert beyond.

Dropping her things on the nearby sofa, she approached carefully. "What are you doing here?"

His hands were clasped behind his back. The clothes were his traditional black Chinese-style outfit that, to her, was dated and inappropriate in such a beautiful resort. His straight hair touched the lower part of his neck. Even though she couldn't see it from this angle, she knew there were gray streaks near his face and he wore an earring. His eyes were liquid obsidian, his expression a mask of indifference. Although he wasn't a tall man, or even muscular, she knew better than to underestimate his strength and agile speed to overcome an enemy.

She cleared her throat, as if he may not have heard her, although deep down, she knew he was gathering his words carefully, like an impending bank of storm clouds. Removing her shoes, she relaxed just enough to dare to move forward. Once she came to stand next to him, she raised her chin and followed his gaze out at the night lights that sparkled like jewels.

"Why are you here? If I knew you were coming, I would have prepared your favorite meal or told the staff at the ranch to expect you, Uncle."

He continued to stare out at the night as he spoke. "The staff know I am here. You have been busy."

"It is my job, Uncle."

"Not at my ranch it is not." His voice sounded low but firm. "You are no longer welcome there."

"But—"

He spun around, grabbed her by the neck with one hand, and squeezed. She did not resist, knowing it was pointless if he decided to kill her. "There are no regrets with you, so do not pretend." He slowly released her but continued to face her with his penetrating eyes. "What have you done to draw attention to yourself?"

"I'm recruiting for The Pacific Rim Consortium."

"Why?" he asked drily.

"I'm not sure why you have to ask." In spite of the fact he had loosened his grip, her voice choked as his eyes narrowed to slits. "I mean—"

He held up his free hand. "Enough."

The beat of her heart increased as it always did when she stood in his presence. Truth be told, she was afraid of her uncle. He was not a man to be undermined or left out of the family loop.

"You have secured a position for a man you've been keeping company with. Why?"

"He's a good fit. I get a recruitment fee and a few other perks."

"I understand there is a romantic element to this relationship."

"It helped to get him to come on board."

"I see. He has children."

She tilted her head in surprise. "How is it that you already know so much about my business?"

"How is it that you did not expect me to know? You use my ranch, eat my food, order my staff around, and work with people with questionable motives. What is the end game? Why this man to help you?"

She longed to sit down but dared not turn away until dismissed as he withdrew his hand from her throat. "His ex-wife has ties to the president somehow and periodically works for the State Department. Our country wants to know what they are up to. She is always in the wrong place at the wrong time. Afghanistan, Syria, Russia, and the list goes on. My people believe she may work for an intelligence group supported by not only Homeland Security but private investors to support their own agenda."

"I see. And you think by getting close to her ex-husband, you can manipulate information that would benefit the Chinese government."

"Exactly. If that doesn't go as smoothly as I hope, I mean, we hope, then perhaps we can persuade him with implied threats toward the children. He just needs to sign on the dotted line."

At this last comment, he raised his chin and stared down his nose at her. She wasn't sure if he intended to hit her or pat her on the cheek for a job well done. "You must stop this deal immediately." His voice grew flat, no hint of emotion or concern.

"This is dangerous and will bring down much trouble for you and the family. The mother is a loved member of the State Department and President Austin. You do not want to get on their bad side." His nostrils flared.

"How do you know this? Have you been spying on me? I thought you cared for me." She pouted.

"I know many things, and you are a spoiled, self-absorbed child who thinks only of your own material gratification. You dishonor me."

"But, Uncle—"

"What is the real reason you want this man?"

"I care for him and want us to have a life—"

He held up his hand again and sighed. Phoebe clamped her lips together tightly; her uncle had a short fuse. "Do not test my patience."

"Okay. Robert blabs about this ex-wife, and this is how I know she is in China. She is searching for a baby who holds the key to saving whatever is affecting these Chinese children dying around the world. She is traveling with her current husband who appears to have some suspicious connections. I won't go into that because most of it is cloak-and-dagger stuff."

"You are telling me that she confides in this—Robert?"

"No. The children tell him things because he can't stop pumping them for information. The man is still smitten by her, and I suspect he believes this will impress her or make her sorry for leaving him."

"I see. So, you really know nothing." He stepped away from her and turned to the bank of windows.

"I know the Chinese government is using this distraction with the sick children to move in and take over the Spatly Islands and perhaps even choosing this time to invade Taiwan. With wars in Ukraine and Israel and conflicts with Iran and Russia, it is thought the American people will have no stomach or interest in another conflict, especially when children are dying."

"I see. Your employer is using children, a housewife, and a bumbling ex-husband to make decisions on how China can become the most powerful country in the world. I wonder what will happen when they find out it is a ruse with an exaggerated attempt on your part to find favor with the Chinese government instead of the country who has made your life tolerable."

"You speak as if you are not on my side."

"I am not on your side because you have used me without my permission. This is unacceptable. If you continue down this road, I will personally punish you."

"Uncle, I'm sorry. I did not mean to dishonor you. I've sent word that Tessa and her new husband are in-country. General Sun Li won't let this fail. He has plans to reach higher in the government. There are other secrets to be discovered besides the baby they seek. Captain Hunter will soon find secrets that will be his undoing, Uncle."

"You may no longer call me Uncle. You have opened a can of worms that will destroy us all."

Phoebe cocked her head and dared step in front of him. "Fine. Then I will call you by your traitor's name, Dr. Wu. We'll soon see who is the failure."

CHAPTER 16

"Welcome to Lanzhou," John announced.

Chase had to admit the man remained in a good mood in spite of the speed bumps he and Tessa had created. After passing off the note to him the night before, John avoided interaction with them at dinner. He couldn't blame him. Crossing the Chinese government could change your life forever. Forever meant different increments of time depending on the circumstances.

The transport bus for the families drove slowly through the streets of Lanzhou. At one point, the Yellow River was visible. It overflowed from the recent rains and moved swiftly with muddy waves. Chase noticed her clamp onto the back of the seat in front of her, excited to see more of what she'd envisioned China to be. They pulled into a small parking lot that overlooked the river. A local vendor sold delicious-smelling noodles, but he cautioned Tessa to resist eating from these carts, not sure if the food would be safe.

Chase took her hand and led her to an observation deck to view the river. No guard rails or warnings to be careful here. A young boy with a boat tethered to the shore smiled up at the tourists.

"Chase, what is that boat made of? Surely it isn't a boat."

"It's a sheepskin raft with a wood frame. A big one can be made from 600 sheepskin bags. There is a tedious process to prepare the bags. The small rafts, like this one, are generally composed of around thirteen of them. These rafts are popular along the Yellow River in the Gansu province."

The boy waved and he called to them.

"What is he saying?" She took a step off the deck toward the narrow path leading down to the water's edge, only to feel Chase pull her back.

"He says you need to have your picture taken with him on the raft to tell your family back home you were on the Yellow River. No way you're doing that."

Tessa shrugged at the boy and shook her head no. He turned his attention to some of the others. One man from their group navigated the slick path to have his picture taken.

"Idiot," Chase whispered. "If he falls in, he's a goner."

Thankfully, the man never got in the boat but managed to have his wife use her camera phone to zoom in to take his picture standing near the raft with the boy. He walked away without giving him any money.

"You were supposed to tip him." Chase tilted his head toward the disappointed kid who was frail and skinny. He most likely could use a hot meal.

"Oh. I didn't actually get in the raft so I guess I'm good." He continued toward the bus.

Chase purchased a cup of hot noodles and navigated the slick downward path to where the raft wobbled in the water. He spoke to the boy whose eyes widened when handed the noodles. As an afterthought, he pulled a few bills from his pocket for the kid. It was received with much nodding and a smile that revealed some missing teeth.

When he returned, Tessa squeezed his arm. "And this is why I love you, Chase Hunter. You are my hero."

"That's what all the ladies say." He grinned. He patted her hand on his arm and landed a kiss on her temple.

Tessa laughed as he led her back to the bus where the guide waited.

The dread Tessa felt at traveling to China with a man who had suffered great tragedy here had been for nothing. If anything, Chase appeared rejuvenated. It was as if every smell, sound, and sensation brought a happiness to him when he shared the meaning or memory with her. Finally it dawned on her; he'd embraced coming home.

Maybe it was due to the fact of his fluency in Chinese that attracted people he encountered to strike up a conversation with such enthusiasm. Pride welled up inside her at his transformation. Perhaps he could finally bury the ghosts haunting him since witnessing his parents being murdered because they were Christians. No wonder he struggled with her spirituality.

"It scares me you are so dependent on your faith," he once admitted. "My parents gave their lives healing the Chinese people, and for what? In the end, they were killed because the communist feared the people they healed would no longer depend on the government but God."

"But no one knew they were missionaries."

"Someone knew. Whoever ratted us out brought down a murderous rampage and killed innocent villagers who only wanted to farm their land. That night, only a few Christians lived among us. My parents didn't share the gospel. They chose to live it. We were so poor, at times we barely had enough to eat because someone needed to feed a sick child, or aging parent. Many times, I was sent to take the place of an injured worker in the fields so the powers that be wouldn't find out."

"And the Shaolin monks? What of them?"

Chase chuckled. "I was a handful. My father thought a good dose of kung fu from the masters would keep me out of trouble. He was right there. I thought my teacher was an old man." He grinned. "He was about the age I am now. I'm sure he passed a long time ago. Life was hard for the monks. But they never complained. I admired that."

"Do they still take students at the monastery? Were you destined to become a Buddhist monk?" They found a seat on the bus and waited for the others to return.

Chase chuckled as he turned his attention back out the window to enjoy the river. "It's my understanding they are mostly there for tourists. The current generation, like in the States, do not have the discipline or desire to be much more than influencers. They serve their communities where they exist. But I've read most have disappeared, and the shines and temples may be more for show of a bygone era. They are protected and honored, but whether the people find solace there, I have no way of knowing."

He took a deep breath and turned back to Tessa. "You are enjoying all this, aren't you?"

"I love it. It's a magical place I've dreamed of visiting for so long."

"Spoken like a true geographer." He moved a curl out of her eyes. "I'm glad we're here together."

"How far was your home from Lanzhou?"

"Wuwei is about three hours north. Near the Mongolian border. That's a place you'd love. It's beautiful."

"Our baby comes from the orphanage there. Do you want to go back and see your home?"

"No," he said shortly. "There's nothing there for me."

"I thought maybe the survivors honored your parents by some kind of marker you could visit."

Chase put his arm around Tessa's shoulders. "I'm good. I'm at peace having come back. I can remember what was important. Everything has changed, yet stayed the same. My life was good after leaving here. I had a lot of opportunities, thanks to my fraternal grandfather and Director Benjamin Clark who became my commanding officer in the Army. Without them, I may have never met you."

"And your parents?"

"They believed in what they were doing. I have to respect that, even though I've never understood it. They are in a better place and with my sister. I can gain comfort from that. You helped me to remember the important parts of my life here. Part of the reason I was so hard on you in the beginning was because you reminded me of their eternal optimism, that goodness would prevail. It made me angry." He pulled her closer so that she could feel his breath when he spoke. "But you just wouldn't let me get away with that. I walked a path of self-destruction and probably would have ended up dead or in prison if you hadn't come along."

"You're welcome," she said, bumping his shoulder with hers. "If I could just get those other misfits at Enigma to listen to me, I wouldn't have to worry so much. Then maybe I could quit to get a normal job. Oh, John is about to give us more instructions. I'm ready to take a nap. Hope our tour is done for the day."

The driver turned over the engine, and their guide stood at the front, holding onto the floor-to-ceiling pole as the bus pulled out into traffic. He announced that the hotel was ready for their arrival, plus a surprise would be waiting after everyone checked in. An excited murmur drifted through the passengers as they hazarded guesses as to what he meant.

Tessa elbowed him, followed by the look, which meant he'd better pay attention.

"Sorry," he whispered.

Their guide continued, "I know you are anxious to meet your daughters and—"

"John." The Missouri dad yawned. "We're tired. The detour around the city was great, but some of us are ready for a nap. Can we do the sightseeing part tomorrow—I mean, if that's okay. We're all a little excited to meet our babies the day after tomorrow and want to be rested."

When the bus pulled up in front of the hotel, several attendants quickly unloaded their bags and moved them inside. The desk clerks waited like soldiers standing at attention. Tessa continued to feel impressed at how things ran in an orderly fashion in this country. They spoke English clearly and displayed a capable attention to detail.

The future father who had failed to tip the raft boy frowned and kept asking the young desk clerk to repeat herself. Finally, he threw up his hands in frustration. Since their guide was assisting another family who had left a bag on the bus, he was tied up.

"Can I help?" Chase stepped up to the counter. "I speak Mandarin Chinese."

"I wanted a room with a king-sized bed, but she says there are only twin beds in the rooms. What the hell? Do I look like I'll be comfortable in a twin bed?" Clearly, he was used to bullying people in the service industry and, in the US, hotels tried to comply with such requests.

"I see." Chase spoke to the young woman, who appeared to be a little worried. Someone might be tracking her ability to do her job with perfection. There was a good chance she put in long hours for almost nothing. He smiled at her and spoke in Chinese. "I'm sorry about this guy. He's an asshole." He chuckled, causing the young lady to blush and try to suppress her amusement. "Would you mind if I made up a story about the floor with the king-sized beds on it and why they are unavailable?"

"But, sir. We have no such rooms. I tried to tell him that."

"I understand. Let me scare him a bit, and he'll settle down."

"Yes, sir. Thank you." She stood at attention again and avoided making eye contact at the troublemaker.

"Well, what did she say?" Mr. Olson snapped.

"She is willing to accommodate you after all." Chase gave a thumbs-up but twisted his mouth in a frown.

"Great. Thanks. So, why the face?"

"It's under renovation. Something about black mold. At least, that's what I think she said. I'm a little rusty. You just have to be okay with that and be aware your baby won't be joining you there."

The man paled as the wife poked him in the side.

"I mean, you never know. If you're willing to take that risk, they may decide you are an unfit parent and give the child to someone else. There's a waiting list, you know. Tessa and I have waited nearly a year after all the paperwork and mind-bending things we had to do."

"Us too," the wife claimed. She leaned on the reception desk toward the clerk. "Twin beds will be just fine. It was a misunderstanding. I'm so sorry."

"Very well, Mrs. Olson. I do apologize for your inconvenience." The desk clerk offered a bright expression and tapped on her computer to complete check-in.

"Not at all." The wife waved her off and chuckled. "Men."

"Yes, ma'am."

Tessa slipped her hand into Chase's. He winked then again at the clerk. For a brief moment, the young woman made eye contact and nodded what appeared to be appreciation.

"You are a rock star, Chase Hunter." Tessa squeezed his hand.

"I'm afraid you've corrupted me into being one."

"Nonsense. You were charming me from the day we met. I've seen how you operate."

"I'm not sure I remember it that way. I'm pretty sure you

outmaneuvered me, letting me chase you until you caught me. I never had a chance."

He loaded their things onto the baggage carrier. The bellboy offered to take it to their room, and Chase accepted the offer since the tip would go a long way in making friends.

After unpacking the few clothes they brought for the trip, Tessa opened the suitcase full of baby things she thought they'd need until they returned home. Fingering the soft sleepers and freshly washed blankets reminded her of how sweet it was to hold a baby. Chase stood on the narrow balcony of their room and appeared to be studying the bustling city.

How would he react to a baby? He'd been an Army Ranger then a Delta Force officer who could disarm an enemy in the blink of an eye, get someone to safety when all seemed lost, and live off the land for weeks. But she'd seen how he interacted with her three children. He treated the boys like future soldiers, making them more responsible and respectful, but her daughter disarmed him at every turn. She adored him, and the feeling was mutual. But a baby?

"No big deal," he claimed on the flight from San Francisco. "How hard could it be?"

He seemed genuinely confused when she laughed out loud until tears squeezed from the corners of her eyes.

"I'm a soldier. Remember?"

"You're not on a military maneuverer, Chase. You're going to be a father of an infant who can do nothing but eat, poop, and cry. Forget sleeping. Oh, and expect to smell like puke once in a while."

"I know you're just trying to scare me. Again. I'm a trained Delta Force officer. I got this."

"You're a cupcake waiting to happen, Chase Hunter."

"Shish. Don't say that where anyone can hear you. I'm a deadly badass."

Tessa sighed and leaned against his shoulder. "We'll see who the badass is the first time you have to change a dirty diaper."

"I read a manual."

"There's no manual that can prepare you for that. Sorry."

A tap at the door brought her back to reality as Chase hurried to answer.

"Remember what I told you. Be careful. Always check to see who is there. We are not safe here. All that kumbaya feeling coursing through your veins isn't real. That's why we're traveling under false identities."

She gave a temperamental salute then cocked her head in irritation.

"Yes, sir!"

He narrowed those dangerous dark eyes at her as if she were a misbehaving Enigma agent or recruit. Not so long ago, such an expression would have turned her into a puddle of self-doubt laced with a heavy dose of fear.

He recognized John through the peephole. "It's our fearless leader." Swinging the door open he motioned for him to enter. "John. What's up?"

"Please make your way to the elevator so we can all go to the lobby together. The surprise I spoke of has arrived. Please. Hurry. The others have already headed downstairs."

Chase reached back and took Tessa's hand as he pushed the door shut.

The guide failed to suppress his lips from twitching as he led Chase and Tessa into the lobby where the others waited along with five other families who had joined the group. Surprises made him nervous and he'd just been promised one. Everyone was offered a glass of champagne. Grateful he was the first to be offered a drink, it lowered the chance of getting poisoned by whoever searched for them.

"Just let it touch your lips then dab it off onto the napkin," he instructed Tessa.

"What are we toasting, John?" asked Mrs. Williams who gulped her drink then took a second one.

"I have a surprise for you. But first, let's toast to a future of happiness and a long life for your baby daughters." Everyone followed his lead as he downed his champagne then set his glass on the tray. He slapped his hands together and chuckled. "Ready? I must tell you the surprise. If you'll follow me into the greeting room, you'll meet your babies for the first time. The orphanage decided to bring your little girls early. Come."

The lobby filled with a mix of gasps and laughter with a little jumping up and down by several of the women. Tessa's eyes filled with tears as she locked gazes with him and he took her hand in his.

It represented the baby they had lost early into her pregnancy. The dream shattered into despair and grief for what would never be. Here, they were pretending to take a baby and make it part of their lives. His dark heart exploded with regret at not being a better husband and support for her. Inwardly, he vowed to be the kind of man she deserved.

Why did the double doors swing open so slowly? And why did he and Tessa hold back as if they were marching toward yet another moment of doom and regret? How much pain must she suffer because of this career he chose? They eased into the room without the unrealistic expectations the others were displaying. Slipping an arm around her waist, Chase took a deep breath and felt a shiver touch Tessa's body.

Seated around the room were nine Chinese women, each holding a baby in her arms. Several had tears in their eyes. The information packet explained some of the workers often took babies home with them at night to make sure they were loved in a family situation. Chase watched several bury their faces against the child's body and embrace her one more time. What must it feel like to know the little creature they held would be taken from them after caring for them all these months?

A wave of pain washed over him seeing their faces streaked with sorrow, unable to hide the broken heart that might never disappear. Did these caregivers from the orphanage understand the generous gift they were giving these little girls? Did they realize the babies would be respected and given opportunities in America coveted by women all over the world? Would that make their pain bearable?

No. This gift they were giving to strangers would rupture their heart and soul as it had his when Tessa had a miscarriage. How much more desperate would this be to physically give a child away you'd grown to love?

Tessa pulled the picture of the child from her backpack as others had done. The photos were no more than a month old. Everyone searched for their baby. Each infant wore a name tag taped to the outside of their dingy clothing. The babies' heads had been shaved in case lice had been present at the orphanage. He had read about the practice in the adoption packet.

"Chase?"

He shifted his eyes to his wife's calm face as she offered him a weak smile. The tightening and release of his jaw caused by the realization he was forging through yet a new jungle called fatherhood caused him to take a deep breath.

"I'm ready," he whispered. This would be so hard for her. He would have to be stronger. "Let's find our daughter, Tessa."

CHAPTER 17

Chase took the picture from Tessa. Only two babies remained. The Minnesota couple stood in front of one as its caretaker rose to her feet and handed off the baby. The room echoed with happy tears among the Americans and low voices of the caretakers speaking Mandarin Chinese as if saying farewell to the life they'd lived for almost a year in some cases.

"That's her," he said, moving toward the seated caretaker who cradled the little girl in her arms, tears flowing down her cheeks. His heart ached for her as Tessa reached out and touched the baby's face. She startled and cowered against her keeper. Tessa slowly withdrew and offered a sympathetic smile.

Chase bent down on one knee before the woman and laid a hand on her knee covered in a typical gray uniform worn by such nurses and caretakers in orphanages. Her bloodshot eyes widened slightly at his touch. He glanced up at Tessa. "She is hurting. I'm going to offer her a Buddhist prayer."

Tessa knelt beside him and laid her hand on top of his as he spoke Mandarin.

"May you be free from sorrow and the causes of sorrow. May you never be separated from the sacred happiness, which is sorrowless. And I pray you live believing in the equality of all that lives." The caretaker lifted a hand to touch his cheek. He continued, "Bhavatu sabba-maṅgalaṃ Rakkhantu sabba-devatā. May there be every blessing. May all heavenly beings protect you. Sabba-buddhānubhāvena Sadā sotthī bhavantu te. Through the power of all the Buddhas, may you always be well." He pulled his hand free of Tessa's and laid it gently on the woman's cheek.

"You are the one?" she asked carefully. "The one who will save the lives of children?"

Chase nodded. "I am the one, good mother."

She smiled like an angel then tenderly kissed the baby girl then eased her into the strong arms of the Delta Force captain. "Pray, too, that we will be rescued from wicked and evil people, for not everyone is a believer. But the Lord is faithful; He will strengthen you and guard you from the evil one. (2 Thessalonians 3:2–3 NLT)"

Chase blinked at her New Testament words she spoke in Mandarin as his attention switched to the most beautiful baby he'd ever seen. His heart hammered with the familiar pain he experienced when Tessa walked into a room.

"She's perfect," he choked, focusing on Tessa for support.

But she stood and pulled the caretaker up into her arms. Together, they were crying and smiling. He continued to hold the child as if he'd discovered the Holy Grail.

"Ask her if I can take a picture of her, Chase. It would be nice to have that memory for her."

After he explained why he wanted a picture, she held up her hand and shook her head vehemently. "I think she's afraid, Tessa. Let's not push it."

A few words of reassurance were followed by her placing one last kiss on top of the baby's head. Turning away, she joined the other caretakers who made their way slowly toward the exit doors. A couple could barely walk as they sobbed and was held up by other women in the group.

Tessa laid her hand on her heart then swiped at tears rolling down her face. "That was the saddest thing I've ever seen."

"I know." He reached out to touch her wet cheek then back down at the baby girl placed in his care. "I've never felt like this." He gazed down into the child's face, puckered to cry.

"She's so—so beautiful." Tessa lowered herself into a chair

then patted the chair next to her. She reached up to touch the baby's bare feet.

He eased down in the chair, almost afraid he'd drop her, but couldn't stop staring at her.

"It's a miraculous kind of awe, isn't it?" Tessa accepted the baby from Chase. "I love you, Lotus. Already, you are my heart." A sob escaped as she bit her bottom lip. "Oh, Chase."

He slipped his arm around her. "I know, babe. I know."

Their heads touched as they wondered how this child might be able to save the world and just maybe, rescue them from the cloud of grief that had hung over their heads for too long.

~ ~ ~ ~

The Enigma team gathered in the conference room as Vernon pulled up the video feed of Chase and Tessa receiving the baby who could possibly hold the answers to saving the adopted children dying across the country. Director Benjamin Clark had to admit he'd been on pins and needles about this one. Would they be able to pull this one off without getting caught?

"Okay, Vernon, can you start the video Chase sent us about their unification with the child?"

"Yes, sir. Just activating the sound. There. Ready."

A few sat in chairs, and others stood or leaned against the table. Even Director Clark sighed with a sense of relief when the others cheered once the images of Chase and Tessa appeared on the screen. The captain never failed to demonstrate his confidence in what the mission demanded. Knowing Tessa was there to keep him grounded added a layer of security. Sometimes the director believed her superpower was keeping Chase occupied long enough to not search for old enemies and take revenge. She was the one person who could circumvent his shoot first mentality.

The video rolled. The scene had been set to music, adding a layer of emotion.

"Who added the tear-jerking music?" Zoric frowned at Vernon who was notorious for tweaking videos.

"It came like this, Zoric. Relax." The director leveled a no-nonsense glare toward the Serbian. "If you think you need a tissue, I'll grab a napkin off the coffee bar."

"Shut up and watch." Samantha crossed her arms across her chest and shifted her weight to one hip.

Director Clark studied his people as the story unfolded. It wasn't often they showed a reaction to situations. But this time a hush fell over the room. Like them, he began to experience the raw emotion as reflected on the faces of the caregivers and then the parents. When the camera turned on Tessa and Chase, the mood changed as the agents left behind found it necessary to suddenly sit. Their focus kept shifting away from the screen as if even they were affected by the idea of giving away a child. The director noticed how they cleared their throats or coughed in order to look away.

"All this time we were trying to toughen Tessa up and…" Samantha mumbled her disgust. "She's turned us into a bunch of marshmallows. I should be there to slap some sense into her."

"It's okay, Sam." Carter sat down next to her. "She'll be okay."

"But will the captain?" Lieutenant Ken Montgomery asked. "I've never seen him like that."

"Nor have I," the director admitted. "Maybe we should check on them. They've had the baby for about fifteen hours. Let's see how they did. Vernon, what's the time difference?"

"Seven a.m. to our four p.m. Dialing."

~ ~ ~ ~

Chase picked up the call on the first ring. "What the hell," he snapped. "Do you know what time it is?"

"Aw, there's the captain we all know." Lieutenant Montgomery chuckled. "You look like you've been on a drunk."

"Shish! The baby has hardly slept all night. I didn't know babies pooped and peed so much."

Everyone burst into laughter as Tessa slipped up behind Chase.

"Oh my gosh!" she moaned and pushed her hair out of her eyes.

"I didn't know you were so ugly in the morning, Tessa," Ken put in. "Dodged that bullet, I guess."

"You wish," Chase grunted. "Want to see the baby, I guess?" He carried the phone to where Lotus slept. There was a lot of cooing typical of people when they see babies. "Isn't she beautiful? So why are you calling?"

"Just got your video. Touching." Carter gave two thumbs-up while pretending to sniff back tears.

"Video? What video? We couldn't even take pictures to capture the moment. There's no video."

"Then we have a problem. Someone is very interested in your presence in Lanzhou. I'll get back to you."

When the director clicked off, he turned to Tessa. "We're in trouble, Tessa."

~ ~ ~ ~

General Sun Li stormed back and forth across the grounds overlooking the bustling city of Lanzhou. Five planes had landed in Beijing this week alone with twenty-five prospective couples adopting baby girls. Ten planes the week before with another thirty groups of parents. Time was running out to find the one baby that Dr. Jun Hie had left behind with the miracle antibodies in her immune system. Where was she?

Records indicated 100,000 children had been abandoned across China. That number didn't include children with disabilities. The true number of children was unknown due to rural bookkeeping and overworked caretakers and nurses who took care of the orphans. The child could be anywhere.

Abandoning a minor remained a crime punishable by up to five years in prison. The fact of the matter was the child, in many cases, couldn't be cared for and might have a better chance being left at an orphanage. The problem at hand was which of the 1576 orphanages hid the child, not to mention the matter of foster care for some of these children. That added yet another staggering number of places to hide.

The information on Dr. Jun Hie and his wife had mysteriously been removed from any databank. No doubt, he had planned his escape for some time and put protections in place in case he had to leave at a moment's notice. Whoever helped him was unaware the child left behind was the key to China becoming one step closer to world dominance.

He heard footsteps approaching on the gravel and turned to see Colonel Zhou Xiang. With an abrupt halt, the colonel saluted and waited to be addressed. He returned a lazy salute, followed by a nod of permission to approach.

"Sir."

"Good to see you, Colonel Zhou. It has been a while. I hope you have been well."

"Yes, sir. Excellent. Thank you."

"And your family?"

"Also, well."

The general locked his fingers behind his back and turned to take in the city of Lanzhou. "The Yellow River runs high."

"We have been blessed with a lot of rain. The last two years have been too dry."

"So, it has. And the Zhuanglang River? That is near your home? How does it fair?"

"That area is very dry, sir. Not much has changed."

"Oh, yes. I remember." He released a bored sigh. "There is an orphanage in Wuwei as I remember. Does your wife still work there?"

"Yes, sir. She volunteered after the last matron—passed away—unexpectedly."

The general cocked his head then faced his colonel. "Yes. A messy business. I'm sure she has provided good care for our most unfortunate children left to survive on their own. I should like to visit your home soon."

"We would be honored to share a meal with you."

The general admired the colonel's ability to welcome him in spite of hating each other. The night where both men had committed unnecessary murder continued to be a roadblock in getting the recognition he deserved. His superiors considered him a brilliant hothead who put too much at risk. That would soon change. The colonel would do his bidding, or his family would suffer the consequences.

"When will you be coming to Wuwei, sir? Is there a special objective to your visit?" Colonel Zhou continued to stand at attention.

"Relax, Colonel. Your stiffness is annoying me."

"Of course." He rolled his shoulders and popped his neck. "I assume since you asked about the orphanage that you would like to see the improvements."

It was impossible to keep from smiling. "Yes. As you may have heard, there are rumors of a child who holds the power to undo all we have done to distract the Americans while we set in motion the occupation of the Spatly Islands and even Taiwan."

"But why? Those islands aren't even inhabitable, nothing more than an exposed reef. Their diminutive size diminishes their strategic importance."

"True, but the islands sit in the middle of rich fishing grounds and next to critical maritime trade routes, which, if we controlled them, could cement Chinese dominance of the Western Pacific without engaging in a fight that would be difficult to win. We need more time."

"I know of this plan. I do not understand the role of an orphanage or one child."

"I have sent soldiers out to different provinces to search for this child. I decided to go to Wuwei myself considering we both have a history there."

"And you think my wife's orphanage might have this child?" he said in amazement. "Are you accusing her of something? She takes any child left at the gate then searches for the mother for two weeks as the law requires."

He held up his hand. "Of course not. She has been a model citizen. I know that you having a desire to continue advancement, would not fail to report activities that could reflect poorly on your reputation. I'm also sure the two of you would not want anything to reflect badly on your sons."

"My sons?" he repeated flatly. "They do as they are told and are loyal to our glorious country."

"And your wife who cares for the babies?"

"As you stated, she is loyal as well. You made it possible for her to have the job of running the orphanage. It has been a labor of love. I hope she'd made you proud. You will see when you come to visit."

"Excellent. There is another matter we need to discuss."

"Sir?"

"It appears that an American government agency has sent a spy among us to find the child."

"Do you believe him to be headed to Wuwei?"

"I am counting on it. Our American connection has said it is the child, now a man, Chase Hunter."

"He died."

"I thought so too. Apparently, we didn't convince the Shaolin how important it was to find them. I suspect he has come to take the child we search for, along with a good dose of revenge. Better be careful, Colonel. You have a target on your back."

"As do you." He smiled. "Karma is a bitch, it seems."

CHAPTER 18

Colonel Zhou called home to make sure all was well with his family. He had been blessed with two sons even under the one-child policy. Whether having a second child was a thank-you from the general or that the government had foreseen the tide of the policy changing remained a mystery. Fortunately, it had become common among those who possessed a little more money and could afford such a blessing.

His country had discovered disposing of so many baby girls in order to have a son had left the country without enough females to marry. Ten years earlier, a rash of kidnapping of potential brides in villages had forced the government to reconsider their stance.

By the turn of the new century, China's fertility was well below replacement level. To continue the one-child policy was clearly no longer defensible. China's gender ratio suffered because people preferred to abort or abandon their female babies, resulting in a labor shortage.

The new policy was announced in 2015. The Chinese government allowed all families to have two children, and in 2024, all married couples were permitted to have as many as three in an attempt to cope with an ageing population and shrinking workforce.

Hearing his wife's voice calmed his fears that something might be amiss at home. He gave her the bad news of the impending visit of the general. She was terrified of the man, expecting someday he would do to them what he had ordered against a defenseless village so long ago.

"It will be okay," he promised. "Tell our sons to be alert to any changes in our community and at the orphanage."

She promised to be careful but also vowed not to neglect the unfortunate babies needing a new home. The last few years, the number of babies had diminished because more and more little girls were being kept instead of abandoned. Although a blessing, his wife's life work would come to an end if the orphanage was closed. Would she be used as a pawn to control him? How much longer could he in clear conscience hide the truth of that awful night in the village? That worried him most of all.

He clicked off and stood holding the phone like it was a lifeline. What if it were true about the missing children of the missionaries? Could Chase and his sister have survived the dangerous trek over the mountains into Tibet so long ago? Would it be possible for the son to be in China and coming for him to seek revenge? What would become of his family without his connections and care? After all, wouldn't the American boy, now a man, believe in an eye for an eye? The truth would mean nothing to a man who had harbored grief and revenge for so many years.

Finding the American was going to be a top priority. He had to be stopped.

~ ~ ~ ~

Tessa picked up the baby who rewarded her with giggles after replacing the messy diaper. She bombarded the ten-month-old with kisses. Even Chase wore an amused expression watching their antics. Baby Lotus was fussy most of the night, and he had taken his turn without coaxing.

Robert pretty much refused to help when they had children, saying he didn't know how or what to do. Besides, all she did was stay home and play house anyway. Might as well earn her keep. That crushed her in so many ways, even though he tried to be funny. She knew it was the moment she'd fallen out of love with him. Yes, she had continued to love him, but the connection had been severed. The worst part was that he never noticed.

"Want to dress her?" she asked Chase as she handed the baby to him. He tickled Lotus beneath the chin. "You're really good with her," she bragged.

"You are the prettiest baby I've ever seen, Lotus," he declared in exaggerated words then switched to Chinese, which made her focus intently on him.

"Dress her in this," Tessa said, pointing to the denim romper. "She's probably going to wiggle, so be prepared to grab her as she heads for the edge of the bed." Tessa sat opposite them just in case he needed another pair of hands. And he did.

"Geez. Be still, Lotus."

Tessa, laughing, let him figure it out.

"There," he declared.

"You snapped it crooked. See? One leg is longer."

He frowned and had to retry two more times to get it right because she tried to crawl toward Tessa. Gently, he grabbed her feet and pulled her back to him then started the process again.

"Finally," he sighed. "I'm exhausted."

"It's called another form of birth control."

"I can see why." Chase lifted the child into his arms. "But it's worth it. Right?"

She scooted across the bed and rose on her knees to play with the baby's feet. "It is the best part of loving someone, Chase. The way you are trying so hard to be a good dad makes me fall in love with you all over again."

"And now I understand what a strong person you've been during these years we've known each other. I don't know how you managed. I'm in awe."

Tessa wrapped her arms around the two of them and kissed the chubby arms of Lotus. "This is going to be really hard to think about giving her up in a few days. You need to prepare yourself for that, Chase. I know you think you've done everything, fought the bad guys and won, lived through hell and survived, but you have never had to give up a child. And before you say anything, I know I haven't either. But not a day goes by without me saying prayers of protection for my children. A miscarriage was hard enough, but to lose a child I've brought into this world and loved would be my undoing. And now I love this little lost child because I know how she can bring a new dimension to my life. I'm going to lose her and it is already breaking my heart."

"I'm not going to get attached. I know where to draw the line."

Tessa took a deep breath. "You've already crossed that line. But it's all good. We'll do this together." She let her hand slip up his arm. "And when we get home, I want us to try for our own baby."

"I want that too." He leaned down and kissed her on the mouth only to receive a punch in the jaw. "Hey, kid. Is that any way to treat your dad?" Lotus let out a squeal of rebellion and won his complete attention. "She's jealous," he said, winking at Tessa.

"Another daddy's girl. I've seen how Heather manipulates you. Lotus appears to be working on her style to do the same."

"I can think of worse things," he admitted when a light tap on the door drew him to look out the peephole. He opened the door with one hand and propped it open with his foot. "John."

"I see you are settling in." He reached in and patted the baby's cheek. "Everyone is headed to the restaurant on the first floor. Please bring your supplies for the day. We'll be doing some sightseeing and won't be back here until midafternoon. I have some food already packed for the babies, and we will once again stop at a part of town where you can do a little shopping. We'll be served lunch by some monks at a nearby monastery that has a very colorful history."

"We'll be down in a couple of minutes."

"Very well." He turned and left.

Tessa shoved more supplies into the backpack for each of them, along with some bottled water the hotel had provided. "I'm ready."

"I don't think I took this much gear to be dropped in the wilds of Afghanistan."

Tessa could only laugh and pat his back. "Combat maneuvers and becoming a parent aren't that much different, I guess. Always alert. Danger is everywhere." She chuckled.

"I'm going to recommend we hire moms at Enigma from now on."

"Hmm. Interesting concept."

They made their way down the hall to the elevator and waited with the Olsons from Minnesota whose droopy eyes and shoulders reminded her how difficult a new baby could be on your system.

When the doors slowly opened, a man dressed in a high-ranking military uniform stepped off. Chase casually pulled his ball cap a little farther down over his forehead and eased onto the elevator, standing on the far side of Mr. Olson. As the elevator closed, Chase leaned his head back against the back wall and stared upward.

When he moved the baby close to his chest, Tessa's attention went from his expression back to the doors. What would be waiting for them on the other side? As the elevator slowed to a stop, Chase straightened and handed her the baby. He didn't have to say anything for her to know he had readied himself for an unwanted confrontation.

~ ~ ~ ~

Robert fretted over the evening's events concerning his children. Why hadn't he anticipated a problem? Heather could have been badly hurt. At least the boys knew to get help. After checking his phone, he realized they had tried to reach him several times and even left a message as to their plans. The ringer was set to vibrate, not the usual ringtone. He had focused on making a good impression with Phoebe's friends instead of his children's welfare.

The bombshell Sean Patrick dropped about Phoebe managed to make him feel ridiculous and more than a little bit of an idiot. The woman had mesmerized him and dangled promises in front of him to the point where all he could see was future success and a lot more money. He'd even convinced himself she was the woman for him: sexy, intelligent, successful, and interested in him and the children, or so he thought.

The thought occurred to him about the possibility she'd been playing him to get a headhunter fee as part of her job. Besides money, what did she have to gain by it? And who was the guy his son saw her kissing?

"Dad?" It was Sean Patrick.

"I thought you were asleep." He walked away from the floor-to-ceiling windows. "You okay?"

"I'm sorry about tonight."

"You did the right thing, Sean Patrick." He placed a hand on his shoulder. "I know you did your best. I should have checked on you guys. Things just got busy, and I forgot." The boy nodded and had turned away to go back to his room when Robert pulled him back. "Tell me about this guy you saw Phoebe with. Was it someone from the ranch?"

Sean Patrick shrugged. "I don't think so. He didn't look like a ranch-hand kind of guy. Kinda rich and important like Phoebe."

"You mean Asian?"

"Guess so. He was older than you too."

Robert bit the inside of his jaw. So maybe she had a thing for older men. Truth be told, she was a lot younger than him by about fifteen years. What was he thinking? "And you saw them kissing?"

Sean Patrick paused for a few seconds as if weighing whether to tell the truth.

"It's okay, Son. I need to know. Just tell me what you saw."

"I don't want to make trouble."

"You aren't." He placed a hand on the side of his face and realized how the boy's jaw had become sharper and more pronounced. The kid was growing into a man, and he'd never even noticed.

"I didn't see much, but they looked…"

"Yes?"

"Like they were a lot more than friends. He asked questions about you, and she tried to blow him off."

"Then what?"

"Not sure. They started speaking in another language. Maybe Japanese or Chinese. I don't know. Some weird words. Then she got all sweet and they did that thing Mom and Chase always do when they think no one is around."

Robert's heart sank. "You mean really affectionate and personal?"

"I'll say," he said, rolling his eyes and blushing. "Then they did the lip-lock thing several times and walked away. I couldn't hear them after that."

Robert turned away; he pinched the bridge of his nose and squeezed his eyes shut to think.

"Are you okay, Dad?"

"Yes. I'm fine." He turned back to offer a weak smile he didn't really feel. "Thanks for telling me. I'm sure it's all a misunderstanding. I talked to Phoebe about it. Nothing to worry about."

"So, are you going to keep seeing her? Take that job?" Sean Patrick approached him and frowned.

"It's a great opportunity. She wants it to work between us."

"She's lying, Dad."

"That's enough, Sean Patrick. You're too young to understand all the nuances between adults. It will be fine. Go back to bed."

"I want to go home."

"No. Go back to bed. You'll feel differently in the morning. We're meeting Phoebe for brunch at ten."

The boy's nostrils flared and his eyes narrowed before he turned and walked back to the bedroom. Why did the kid have to be such a handful? He was a lot like his mother in that regard. Since that muscle head was living with Tessa and the kids, his older son would probably try to imitate the jerk. Did he dare try and remove them from that environment?

Then he remembered the warning Chase had given him the day they headed out.

"Keep it in your pants, Bobby. If I hear Phoebe distracts you so that these kids get so much as a hangnail, I'm coming after you. Understand?"

Robert shivered. What would he need to promise to Tessa to keep himself out of the crosshairs of Captain Chase Hunter?

CHAPTER 19

A Chinese colonel stood in the hotel foyer, observing the new parents parade into the dining room for breakfast. Chase sensed the soldier in him jump-start the adrenaline rush that came when he went into a battle and later, a mission with Enigma.

A mix of rage, self-preservation, and revenge surged through his veins as he recognized the man who killed his mother. He first spotted him in Beijing, and now here. The image of her body lying in the dirt and his gun pointed down to finish her off still haunted him. If it hadn't been for the Shaolin monks, he would be dead too. Their courage was something superheroes were made of.

He could see that Zhou Xiang had risen in rank to a man with power. He couldn't help but wonder if that wasn't a reward for killing his parents.

"Who is he, Chase? Or are you just being careful?" Tessa asked as they sat down with Western-style muffins and hot tea. Before he could answer, the three other couples joined them.

The Williams couple tried to balance their baby and eat a muffin. They kept handing the baby back and forth. "John," asked Mr. Williams, "the place is crawling with military-type guys. Is that normal?"

"I am going to check. Please do not be alarmed. These things sometimes happen if there is a civil unrest difficulty. Nothing to do with us." His bobbed his head while displaying a frown then left the breakfast room as the other couples from the States and a few from Europe were entering.

"Civil unrest difficulty?" Mr. Olson chuckled. "Sounds like heads will roll."

"Shut the hell up, Olson," Chase snapped, causing everyone to freeze. "Don't say things like that here. It could be totally misunderstood that we were causing the problem."

"Oh." Mr. Olson paled and received a poke in the ribs from his wife. "Sorry. You're right."

John reentered, a little flushed. "Nothing to worry about, my friends. Just a report of a misguided thief preying on our new families. Stole some money and a camera from a French couple down the street. They're searching for him."

"With soldiers?" a German man from another group asked suspiciously.

"I understand the thief may have chosen a prominent official from the French government. China wants you and anyone who visits us to know that we take your safety seriously and will make sure your visit is filled with beautiful memories. We are very proud of our country." John continued to appear calm as the bus driver joined them. "Please gather up your things and follow me. We will be joined by the other new parents from yesterday." He fanned out his hand toward the doors. "Come."

Chase's head was on a swivel as they filed out into the lobby. Several more soldiers were posted at various places: the elevator doors, the front door, and another one walking around casually as if he had nothing better to do. They were in full uniform and more attentive than necessary, in Chase's opinion. The one at the front door made eye contact with him and quickly diverted his attention to Tessa. She beamed a smile at him and said hello, causing one corner of his mouth to lift slightly.

Nice job diverting attention from me, he thought. She lifted the baby's hand to wave at the soldier as she passed through the doors to the street, adding a nice touch. With her blonde ponytail swinging and wayward curls being played with by the baby, the guy couldn't take his eyes off her. Any other time, he'd probably give the jerk a death stare for ogling at his wife. Of course, it wasn't all that long ago he'd done a fair amount of ogling at her himself.

As he passed through the exit doors, he heard the elevator and glanced back over his shoulder to see the colonel who killed his mother meet the soldier who'd gotten off at their floor. Chase was a head taller than anyone else, so he stuck out like a sore thumb. He hurried with Tessa to get on the bus. They found a seat on the streetside to not draw attention as he pulled his hat lower on his forehead.

"Chase, that colonel guy is coming to wait outside the bus," Tessa whispered. "Lotus, I'm counting on you to be a good girl." She laid a free hand on his thigh. "Maybe he's really just watching for the thief, thinking he might sneak aboard."

"You don't believe that, do you?" he whispered back.

"No. Not really. There's no thief." She stiffened. "He's coming onto the bus."

John's eyes widened as the colonel entered the bus. He spoke quickly to their guide then the bus driver and proceeded to greet each set of parents either with a comment toward the baby or a pat on the infant's head. As he neared closer, Chase could feel the urge to escape closing in on them. He didn't like confined spaces, and trying to leave with a baby would be almost impossible.

The colonel stood one seat away when he caught sight of him and narrowed his eyes for a few seconds longer than was polite. Maybe the color of his dark-tanned skin had him wondering if he was a black man. It wouldn't be the first time someone got that wrong. He guessed he appeared even darker sitting next to Tessa.

"Morning. I hope your little daughter brings you much happiness," the colonel said smoothly as he tickled the baby's chin. Lotus perked up hearing him address her and cooed. Next, he spoke in Chinese to her, which made her reach for him.

Chase could feel his entire body go to fight mode as the colonel reached down and lifted the child into his arms. This time, his smile seemed genuine as he continued to speak in Chinese. Then his focus switched to him like a sharp knife cutting through the air as he continued to pat Lotus on the back.

"What are your names?" Although his voice sounded pleasant, his expression turned stern.

"We're the Butlers." Tessa gave her innocent-girl-next-door

expression that in all possibility launched a thousand ships in another place and time. She showed no fear. "We're going to name her Katherine."

"A good name," he bragged. "Will you call her by a nickname? I understand Americans like to do that."

"Maybe Katie. Not sure," she admitted.

"What about you, Mr. Butler. What will you call your little daughter?"

Chase tilted his head to eye the man he wanted to reach out and strangle with his bare hands. It took everything inside him to keep his temper in check. "Perfect. I'll call her perfect."

The colonel's face grew solemn as he leveled a stern gaze at him. Chase didn't like attempts at intimidation, but in this case, he thought caution would be the best path to survival.

A horrible stench followed a rumble from Lotus.

"Sir, I think our sweet girl just filled her diaper," Tessa declared as several dads let out a pew noise followed by coughing. "I see some brown on the back of her outfit. Maybe you should give her back to me so your uniform doesn't get soiled."

The colonel kissed the baby's cheek and passed her back gently. The baby reached for him and cried like she'd been stuck with pins. He checked his uniform and raised his finger to his hat as if saluting Tessa. "You have saved the day. I think I will leave you to it since this is not something I would know much about. Have a nice day, Mr. and Mrs. Butler. And congratulations."

"Tessa, there's an empty seat in the back to give you a little more room to clean her up," called the Texas mom.

Chase noticed that the colonel stopped, hearing Tessa's name. He turned back and followed her progress to the seat in the back. His eyes shifted to Chase. He didn't shy away from locking eyes with the colonel. The expression on the colonel's face was telling. His bottom lip jutted out as he slipped on a pair of sunglasses. They had been discovered.

~ ~ ~ ~

Colonel Zhou returned inside the hotel and called for the manager. A young woman quickly joined him and introduced herself.

"I want a list of all your guests who have checked in, in the last forty-eight hours, along with their room numbers."

"But, sir, we don't give out that kind of—"

Colonel Zhou tilted his head at her then straightened his posture to stare menacingly at her young face. "You are new to this position, are you not?"

"Yes, sir. I came here three months ago."

"Do you like it here?"

"Very much."

"Then, I suggest you do as I asked. We will also need access to those rooms."

"Of course. Follow me."

~ ~ ~ ~

What was Colonel Zhou doing here? The Red Dragon witnessed the encounter with the Butlers from the building across the street. Did he know who the American couple was and why they were here? There was little time to sort things out. He needed to lure them to Wuwei where he could take care of matters once and for all.

He remembered the encounter with the wife. Pretty but deadly. Trained but lacked a hard edge like the man she claimed to be married to. Maybe he needed to discover what made the woman so special. The smell of her lingered in his memory as did the softness of her skin and hair. Taking a wife had not been an option, but that could change. What would make her leave the military man? No. It would be the child.

CHAPTER 20

Instead of returning to the ranch, where he often went to recharge and become one with the universe, Dr. Wu had purchased a small cabin ten miles from Palm Springs. The views from the back patio faced west, allowing the magnificent sunsets to crowd out any stress he experienced from his job. The night sky offered a brilliant display of stars each night and he had often enjoyed it until the early morning hours.

Compared to the ranch house, the cabin was small, but here he didn't have staff to constantly ask about his wishes or try to impress him with their work ethic. The purchase was in hopes his parents would move from San Francisco, a city that suffered from urban problems in recent years. After COVID, he feared for their safety. But so far, they had resisted.

Phoebe, who wasn't a niece at all, but was the granddaughter of a distant relative. His parents had often volunteered to babysit her when he failed to produce an heir for them. Even as a child, she displayed a cunning gift of manipulation when it came to men. He quickly diagnosed her as possessing narcissistic tendencies. It didn't surprise him, considering how his parents and others catered to her. She had been a pretty child and was an even more beautiful woman.

The one person she knew read her like an open book was him. And he despised such tactics. She loved playing the damsel in distress, when it suited her, or the powerhouse who could get anything done. Trusting her to improve her lot in life was more of a sure bet than her affecting China's chances at becoming the most influential country in the world. She made life complicated for him.

Complications were things he'd learned to deal with long ago in a little village outside of Wuwei where the massacre happened. His family had been told to leave earlier that day by his uncle serving in the military under Zhou Xiang. It was difficult to believe his friend's family was in danger and so was anyone associated with them. His family escaped to Hong Kong, changed their names, and tried to be invisible. Three weeks later, his father was summoned to the American embassy to be questioned about what he knew concerning the attack.

"We have need to find Chase and Christina, Father," Wu insisted. "We must go to Lhasa. They are sure to come through there. They are our friends."

"No. We will be discovered or blamed for taking part. No way they could have survived. The grandfather is in Hong Kong hoping to receive word of their survival."

"But, Father," he shouted.

"Enough."

A message had been delivered to their tiny apartment several weeks later, slipped under the door. With no one there, Wu had opened it and seen that his friends, Chase and Christina had survived the massacre and the terrifying trip into Tibet. They were waiting at the Man Po Temple. Could they send help to get them to the American embassy?

Wu did not hesitate to make arrangements to find them and took half a day to reach the monastery. It took longer than expected because he needed to make sure he hadn't been followed. He could hardly believe his eyes when he saw his friends. Both were gaunt, dirty, and filled with a sadness he couldn't have imagined.

Christina had stumbled toward him and fell into his arms. He held her for a long time, remembering how sweet she could be with the singing voice of one of the angels her parents sometimes talked about.

Chase remained cautious and eyed him with those dark eyes that often frightened strangers in the village who might dare to pick on some of the other kids. While holding Christina, Wu extended his other arm toward Chase. He finally ventured closer, not to be embraced but to pull Christina from his arms.

"You could have warned us," he growled. "I thought you were my friend."

"I am. I wanted to warn you, but—"

"Is this a trap to catch us?"

"No. I promise. I would not do that. Why did you send for me if you thought that?"

"I didn't."

"Then who? No one besides my—"

"Your uncle? Zhou Xiang?" Chase hissed. "I'm sure he hoped we were dead. But just to cover his treachery, he put things in place with your father to catch us."

"I found the note under my door. No one knows but me. I will take you to the American embassy. Trust me."

Chase turned to the monk standing near him. "My grandfather is an American diplomat."

"If you call the embassy, they will know you survived and could endanger these monks. Please. Let me take you. Your grandfather is waiting for you. I contacted him before I came. He is waiting not far from here. We must hurry. A plane is ready to take you to America."

"If you are lying to me, Wu, I vow I will kill you."

"I am not proud of what my parents did to you. They told me you would be warned. I believed them. They too were in danger. Let me do this one thing," he said, straight-faced. "Christina, tell him I can be trusted."

"Chase, please. I want to go to America. I believe Wu. Besides, he spoke to Mom and Dad how he wanted to marry me someday. He made promises to our dad about taking care of me and would not dishonor that."

"We may have lived by the skin of our teeth in a backward culture, but Dad would never promise you to anyone. And I'm in charge now so that is never going to happen."

"Someday I will prove to you I am not your enemy." Wu took a deep breath and once again tried to remember that day and what happened next. The monks secured transportation for them and drove to a park several miles away where a black limo waited. It wasn't until a giant of a man exited the car that Chase let Christina out of his tight grip. She ran to their grandfather and watched him scoop her up in his arms. It was the only time he ever saw Chase tear up. He then turned to Wu and snarled at him.

"This does not clear you of not warning us. My parents could have made it out alive if you had not run like a coward to save your own skin. I will never forgive you, Wu. Never." He turned and joined his grandfather at the car.

Wu didn't see him again until Enigma sought his guidance in helping his team members with PTSD and other mental health issues. When he saw Chase, the soldier leveled a chilling glare he'd never forget. But a lot had changed in him, too and he no longer feared the missionary kid who made idle threats. Joining Enigma was an opportunity he couldn't resist. Loyalty had become a fickle mistress in his life.

Thanks to Phoebe, suspicion would once more catch up with him, and the life he'd managed to keep hidden could be exposed. Phoebe was a loose end that required a knot to be securely tied.

Tomorrow, he'd check on Tessa's children without anyone knowing. They were the most dangerous kind of leverage.

And the Red Dragon? It was his understanding that he'd made contact with Tessa. Who was he? Could he be a dangerous liaison created to find out what really happened the night of the massacre, or a beast hunting for his masters General Li and Colonel Zhou Xiang? Whichever way it turned out, putting Tessa in danger was not an option. They were dangerous loose ends. Enigma didn't like keeping secrets from them. And like everyone else on the team, he had many.

~ ~ ~ ~

Phoebe joined Robert and the children at the poolside Caribbean Café brunch buffet. The ambiance was a perfect match for the Turks and Caicos Islands. The music piped in to simulate that culture matched the Caribbean vibe. Although there were palm trees and plenty of tropical flowers, it couldn't compare to the real thing. She hoped Robert would be in a better mood and the children would not throw any more surprises at her.

Heather and Daniel talked to each other and only made eye contact with her when she directed a comment or question their way. They were being extremely polite and courteous, unlike Sean Patrick.

The kid reminded her of a sleeping volcano that had awakened to send up tenacles of smoke in warning of an intended eruption. He didn't shy away from her scrutiny and answered with a strong "Yes, ma'am" when answering her. The smirk he added forced her to admit for someone so young, he savored control like a military man. Didn't Robert mention he wanted to attend West Point someday? Maybe she could use that to her advantage.

"Robert, the Pacific Rim Consortium wants to talk business with you for a couple of hours. I know I told you I'd go with you, but would you rather I stay with the kids at the pool? There are some games and contests today I think they'd enjoy."

"Heather can't get in the water with that cut on her head," Sean Patrick interjected as he switched his attention from her to Robert. "That water is full of germs."

"Sean Patrick." Heather scowled. "I'll be fine."

"I promised I'd watch after you, and that's what I'm doing."

Robert chuckled nervously. "Wow. Sometimes I forget how responsible you are." He turned to Phoebe. "I'm going to have to find someone to stay with them and make sure they are safe."

"Seems to me, Sean Patrick is more than qualified," she cooed, tilting her head toward the teen.

"Sean Patrick, I don't want to leave you with all this responsibility. Maybe the resort has a chaperone we can use."

"I don't know who these chaperones are, Robert," she said, reaching out and touching his hand that lay on his thigh. It drew his gaze downward then up at her eyes. "Let me call my assistant to come and stay with them. The game room will be open in about thirty minutes. I trust her completely." She was already pulling out her phone to call. "I'll step outside so you guys can decide."

"Thanks, Phoebe."

The cell phone rang three times before anyone picked up.

"Hello," came a masculine voice.

"I need a favor."

CHAPTER 21

The rain came as a heavy mist by the time they left the zoo. Tessa felt sickened at seeing the tiger pace in an outdoor enclosure no bigger than a sixteen-by-sixteen room that included a raised concrete platform for him to lie on away from the damp floor. Getting her picture taken on a Bactrian camel turned out to be the highlight of the day.

The handlers provided a purple robe made of velvet and trimmed in gold. Chase said they commented she must be a princess from Mongolia. She figured that was a reach since there hadn't been a Mongolian princess since Genghis Khan's empire began falling apart. Besides, no one could possibly mistake her for Asian.

They were being kind. Chase tipped them a little extra, which caused a great deal of glowing expressions and head bobbing, especially when they realized he could speak their language.

Their next stop included a temple near the Yellow River. John suggested the new parents might want to receive a blessing from one of the Shaolin monks who agreed to visit with them on their new journey as parents.

A few parents remained seated, saying they were too tired to climb the steps and their daughters had just fallen asleep. Tessa quickly slipped out into the aisle and reached for Lotus who was wide awake and playing with Chase's bottom lip that he made funny noises with.

"Another memory to remind me of my childhood," he said, gathering their backpacks.

"You've been here?" Tessa asked as they exited the bus.

"No. But there was a dedicated Shaolin Temple and monastery in our village. They were very curious as to what my parents were doing and often came to dinner. I would hear them talking to my parents into the night."

"They must have had a lot to talk about, considering they were both in the religion business."

Chase shrugged. "Maybe. I didn't pay much attention. I figured if I pretended to be asleep, then I wouldn't be called on the carpet for screwing something up at the temple that day," he chuckled. "But the Shaolin were part of the reason I survived. If it hadn't been for them, I'd never have made it back to the US." He took a deep breath.

"You love China, don't you?"

He raised his chin and blinked. "Yes. There are so many good things here that are beautiful and spiritual."

"I didn't think you were much on religion?" she said, stuffing Lotus into the front chest carrier Chase slipped on his body.

"Maybe not religion, but something bigger." He grinned at her. "You taught me that. Ten minutes with you, and I believed in angels."

Tessa poked him in the arm. "Now you're just sweet-talking me."

"Is it working?"

"Oh yeah," she said, tickling Lotus's ear. "Guess I'll have to keep you after all."

He gave that low, wolflike laugh, deep in his throat, that always managed to thrill her. The baby on his chest and ball cap pulled down low over his forehead gave added fuel to the fire that burned inside her when she observed him like this. How did she get so lucky?

Climbing the seven sets of stairs was not an easy task after a restless night, and a visit from the Colonel Zhou character that nearly pushed Chase over the edge. The rain dripped off what appeared to be some kind of pine tree. When the stone steps became slippery, Chase took her elbow from time to time to navigate the uneven stairs that had seen centuries of pilgrims coming to be blessed.

John ushered them into a large open-air courtyard that reminded Tessa of a movie scene with a towering pagoda and young men practicing kung fu. The smell of incense grew strong as several priests attended locals on a wraparound-porch structure that protected them from times of rain or summer sun.

Several priests entered the courtyard, dressed in red robes. John explained a donation would go far in continuing the work of the Shaolin here as they helped the poor and educated those who couldn't afford to attend school. The group dug deep in their pockets and gladly handed John crumpled handfuls of bills.

When it was their turn to receive the blessing, the priest fixated long and hard on Chase. His white beard and a cloudy eye hinted of his age. The priest had a couple of missing teeth and a few age spots on the side of his face. His shaven head glistened from the mist. However, his posture reflected a strength and confidence that reminded her of Chase.

"Would you follow me?" the priest asked in English.

Chase nodded as the elder instructed the second priest to tell John he wanted to give them a private tour for a special blessing. The second priest took care of the request. John wrinkled his brow at the request then bowed his head in acceptance. She hoped he would join them in case of a problem, but Chase didn't appear concerned.

"Follow me," the old priest said.

Once inside the building, an explosion of color greeted them. Their footsteps echoed as they moved toward the front where an altar held a large gold Buddha. Chase appeared calm as they stopped in front of the beautiful statue.

"No one can hear us in here, Chase." The priest removed Lotus from the chest carrier and handed her to Tessa. The next thing she knew, the two men were embracing each other. When they parted, the priest had tears running down his cheeks. "My son has returned."

Chase pulled him back in his arms as if he was afraid the man would disappear. "This is Shi Yen, my old master," he told Tessa with the biggest grin she'd ever seen. "I didn't know you were still alive, Master. I am so glad to see you."

"And I you, young Chase. You are a grown man."

"How did you know it was me, Master?"

"I could smell you." He sniffed then held his nose, making Chase laugh. "Americans smell funny, but you—you have the smell of a tribal man. An American Indian, I think. Your blessed mother was Cherokee, was she not?"

"Yes, sir. And what of the village?"

"After the massacre, it was burned down. No trace of it today. The people who survived escaped to the hills or caves, emerging only to farm their crops in the day. The soldiers didn't bother them there. Even I had to escape."

"And the temple and monastery between the village and Wuwei?"

He sighed. "It remains, but only because so many tourists come to see it. Several movies have used the site to show the old Shaolin way. I don't think we were ever so good-looking as the movies try to copy us." He offered a sly grin.

"And the others? The ones who helped us escape?"

"Ahh. They remained in Tibet. The people there have no love for the Chinese and wanted to protect them. After a while, the soldiers stopped searching. Bodies were found the following spring in the mountains. For some reason, the authorities believed you were dead. I left that same night."

"I remember you telling me to be brave when we came to the monastery."

"It was the wish of your father that if things got bad, we would help you escape. I think he knew someone was plotting against your family. Your parents brought peace and good news to the people for miles around. It was not something that pleased the communists at the time. Today, that might not be the case. But still, you need to be careful."

"I guess if you recognized me, someone else will too. I saw Colonel Zhou this morning. He was a lieutenant, maybe a major, back then. I still see him kill my mother."

"Even with one good eye, I recognized your walk, young Chase." He turned to Tessa who felt mesmerized by the moment. "And you have a pretty wife. Welcome."

"Thank you, Master Shi Yen."

"You must be careful," he warned. "You are a problem that was never fully resolved for General Sun Li. If he finds out you are here, then trouble will follow. He has convinced the government the massacre was started by those who hated the work of your parents and their teachings."

"I'll be careful, Master. What do you know of the Red Dragon?"

"I know he is active again. I believe it to be a new dragon. The dragons come and go. Since this is the year of the dragon, we are hopeful that he will bring prosperity and peace. But it could be just the opposite."

"Who is he?"

"Who knows these things? A dragon comes alive whenever he chooses. Sometimes he is a man, and sometimes he is a monster."

"A man claiming to be the Red Dragon found my wife and frightened her in Beijing. He knew who we were."

"If you are still alive, then I would say either he is a friend or…"

"He wants something?"

The old priest stared up at the ceiling then back to him. "Red Dragons in human form may want something that belongs to you since…"—his eyes went to Tessa—"your wife did not suffer harm… He should not be in Beijing."

"What do you mean?" Tessa asked, stepping closer to Chase.

"The Red Dragon inhabits the caves outside of Wuwei. He has been seen there many times. The people believe he is there to protect them, so they do not complain. He brings good fortune. But even a dragon needs companionship. He wants something from you. Be careful, my son."

Another priest hurried inside and whispered into Shi Yen's ear.

"You must follow Bataar. He will take you the back way to meet with your people. They have also been guided to a new location. It has been suggested to John that he deliver all of you back to your hotel."

The old priest reached for Chase who was gathered in the soldier's strong arms. Tessa also wrapped her arms around the old man, even as the baby protested.

"If I don't see you again, Master Shi, I will lift prayers of protection for you and your work here," Tessa said as she filled with unexpected emotion.

"Thank you, my new daughter. Now go." She stepped back, but he caught her hand. "If you are pure, there is no need to fear the Red Dragon. Remember, when everyone contributes wood, then will the fire burn brightly."

She covered his hand with hers. "My friend Wu once told me that. I admire him greatly."

"Let's go." Chase pulled her away.

John waved them onto the minibus with an expression of desperation plastered on his face. There was an empty seat behind the driver where they easily slipped in just as their guide tapped the driver on the shoulder. Instantly the vehicle moved out of what appeared to be an alley then slowly merged into a parking lot with other tourist-type vans and buses.

There was also a presence of military vehicles. Tessa spotted the colonel who had come onto the bus and taken Lotus from her. Her heart had nearly jumped out of her chest. He ran up the steps of the temple, stopped, and searched the back of the parking lot. Fortunately, their minibus had navigated to the side of a much larger bus with tinted windows. She could no longer see the colonel, but as they moved out of protection, she noticed him continue up the second tier of steps just as a cloudburst sent torrents of rain on the crowd and the colonel.

"That was close," she mumbled.

John sat across from them, frowning. The sound of a few fussy babies and private conversations masked the attention being shown to them. "Excuse me, Mr. Chase Butler, but there always appears to be a great deal of unwanted attention wherever you and Mrs. Butler go."

"Your point, John?" Chase spoke cooly as he turned his attention to the side mirrors on the outside of the bus.

"I don't want any trouble."

"That makes two of us. Don't worry about it."

"Colonel Zhou Xiang is an important man. He is searching for someone."

"How do you know this?"

John leaned in and whispered, "The hotel contacted me while you were with the Shaolin. Old Master Shi is known to speak his mind about the heavy-handedness of the military. He and Colonel

Zhou Xiang have not always gotten along."

Chase's jaw tightened and released. How much did John need to know? "Isn't that what the military does—scares the ones who try to make life better for the powerless and sick? I'm just guessing. I used to be in the military myself and, wherever I served, there was always a dictator who controlled the masses with a bully."

"Bully? I do not understand."

Tessa snuggled Lotus who had fallen asleep on her shoulder. "A bully is someone who likes to intimidate a person they see as weaker than themselves."

"Ah. Yes. That happens here when certain people do not fall into line," John admitted. "However, Colonel Zhou Xiang, although tough and intimidating, is known to be fair. Although he did not always get along with the Shaolin, he protected the monastery you just visited when General Sun Li tried to convince The Central Committee of the Communist Party, it hid enemies of the state."

"Good to know," Chase said flatly. "And the colonel managed to save them?"

"Yes. Some say it was the Red Dragon who convinced The Committee. This was many years ago. Then the Red Dragon disappeared. In the year of the dragon, he has emerged again. I don't know who to be more afraid of, the military or our honorable dragon." John bowed his head as if showing respect. "And he has sought out your wife and left a message for you. I am wondering why."

"Just lucky, I guess." Chase smirked. "I'd like to meet this Red Dragon. Think you can arrange that?"

John's eyes widened. "I do not understand why you think I could do such a thing?"

"Maybe because you are never far away from where he is. After all, he gave you the note for me. He knew Tessa was alone when she got on the elevator. Out of all the hotels in Beijing, he knew where we were."

John's face morphed into a hard mask as an eyebrow lifted. "I am sorry. The Chinese like to say you should dig the well before you are thirsty."

Tessa thought of Dr. Wu and what his response might be. She interceded on Chase's behalf. "The best time to plant a tree was twenty years ago. The second-best time is now."

"And the meaning of your words, Mrs. Butler?"

"Don't put things off. If you want success and growth in the future, the best time to act is now. The Red Dragon wants something. We need to know what and why. We are ordinary people, John," Tessa insisted. "Why us?"

"I wonder the same thing. I repeat. I do not know the Red Dragon. No one does." He stood and picked up the microphone. "Families, we have returned to our hotel. I've been notified we need to gather in the reception room for instructions about the rest of our trip."

~ ~ ~ ~

Chase noticed how the friendly staff avoided eye contact and turned away if approached. The Minneapolis man grumbled that they were rude and he planned to post this attitude on a number of travel sites. They filed into the reception room where all the chairs had been turned upside down on the tables. A vacuum cleaner remained plugged in as a housekeeper shuffled out.

John was bombarded with questions as soon as he walked in. He held up his clipboard and laughed nervously. "This will only take a few minutes. We have been notified today that the paperwork from the Wuwei orphanages has not been sent in the packets you require to get your final visas in Guangzhou. It is required to swear your babies in as US citizens."

A lot of grumbling from the families, followed by a sense of disappointment mixed with fear filled the room.

"Those of you who arrived yesterday from Hong Kong and accepted your babies, have nothing to worry about. Those children came from Xi'An in the Shaanxi Province. I am happy to say you will proceed day after tomorrow to Guangzhou. There, you are scheduled for physicals for your babies, as is required. Then you'll have time to shop and see some of the sites. Someone from my office will make sure everything is in order. I will join you later. But, for now, get some rest. Your itinerary will be slightly different for a few days. I will slip a new schedule under your door tonight."

A few of the parents who were in the clear meandered out, tired but relieved. Chase sensed the proverbial shoe was about to drop.

"John, you look like you're about to give us bad news." The Texas dad had folded his arms across his chest and took a General Patton stance.

"I'm afraid there has been, how do you Americans say, a hiccup?"

"What kind of hiccup?" Chase was momentarily distracted when Lotus reached for him. He gently took her from Tessa.

"I am sorry to say the rest of you who arrived from Beijing did not receive the important papers needed to go to Guangzhou. The orphanage is in Wuwei—"

"Wuwei," Chase snapped. "That's three hours from here by train."

"Yes. I am so sorry. The orphanage is shorthanded and unable to provide anyone to return so soon to Lanzhou with the necessary paperwork. Things do not work at the speed of light here in China. I'm sure you found this out when applying for adoption. Normally, this would take months to fix. But if you are willing to travel to Wuwei, you will be able to secure these papers from the Office of Government Permits. They will be expecting us tomorrow afternoon. The train leaves in the morning. I do apologize."

There were questions about cost, food, and other things, until Chase finally held up his hand. "Just let the man talk. He didn't cause this."

John bowed his way. "Thank you. I will have the necessary information for you within the hour. Please. One of you from each family come back here, and I will have what you need. Then we can discuss any concerns over dinner later tonight."

"That will be fine, John. Thank you." Chase led Tessa to the door, and the others took the cue to follow. He opened the door and let them pass through first. He turned back at John who nodded his thanks.

"Isn't this a little suspicious?" Chase adjusted Lotus in his arms as Tessa rubbed her back.

"Yes. The soldiers searched everyone's room while we were gone. Colonel Zhou forced the staff to hand over the keys. They had no choice. Still think Colonel Zhou is a good guy?" Chase asked.

"From what I understand—you know a great deal more about that than I ever will."

CHAPTER 22

Enigma headquarters was located at the Sacramento University of Science and Engineering. A medical school and a law school was part of their diverse programs. It ranked as one of the top-rated universities in the country. Many of the law students had made their way into the FBI or the Department of Justice after having spent internships at the Supreme Court, in various states. The Geography and Social Sciences Department covered everything from archelogy to geopolitical conflict.

The director of Enigma, Benjamin Clark, was also the Dean of Geo Sciences and had expanded it to subjects that encompassed everything from physical geography to climate change and oceanography. But his primary interests were cultures and how that affected the geopolitics of the world. Tessa Hunter had been instrumental in making that subject come alive in her research and classes. They were always full and, thanks to Tessa, some even managed to secure internships at the State Department in Washington DC.

He had prepared an update on the adopted children from China for Chase whenever he called in. At least they had the baby and would be coming home in a few days. There was more good news to share as well. Several team members joined him, expecting the phone call to let them know everything was going as planned.

"Shouldn't they have called in already?" asked Zoric. He was a dark personality and hard to understand sometimes with his Serbian accent. His job involved interrogating suspects or prisoners. Some at Enigma admitted he enjoyed his job a little too much.

"Incoming call from Dr. Wu." Vernon put the call on the big screen to include everyone.

"Good afternoon." His voice came across as dry and apathetic as was his style. "Have you heard from Chase and Tessa yet?"

"Still waiting. What do you have for us?" The director motioned for everyone to sit down.

"Not much. The Pacific Rim Consortium is making a job offer to Robert even as we speak. He'll be hard-pressed to refuse it."

"How do you know this, Dr. Wu?" Samantha asked skeptically. "And where are you?"

"I saw the offer. I'm in Palm Springs."

"Are the kids okay?" The director was aware that Carter felt a certain responsibility toward them, since Chase had put him on alert. He also didn't put much trust in Robert.

"Yes and no." He went on to explain what had happened the night before and that thanks to Sean Patrick's fast actions, Heather was okay.

"I like that kid." Lieutenant Ken Montgomery grinned.

"Yes, he is remarkable—like his mother, it seems." Even when Dr. Wu spoke, he never lost his no-nonsense frown.

"Vernon picked up some chatter at the resort," began the director, "about the woman called Phoebe. I believe she is dating Robert Scott. We believe her to be a spy. She is involved with some heavy hitters from China. Although she was born and raised in the US, she has ties to mainland China. A man was spotted leaving her suite at the resort last night."

"I believe, besides Robert, she is seeing a man who is a Chinese American by the name of Matthew Yu. He is a wealthy investor in the stock market and a bit of a narcissist. Phoebe, besides being his mistress, is a power broker who recruits influence in DC. He has benefited from her underhanded dealings." Dr. Wu's voice remained even and unemotional.

"Yes, the FBI is well aware of Matthew Yu. He, too, is hunting for our scientist, your friend, Jun Hie. We are hoping he will slip up and give the FBI a reason to arrest him." Director Benjamin Clark sighed. "He is very careful."

"Why not let us go in and encourage him to come with us. I can be very persuasive." Samantha offered one of her Cheshire smiles.

"Except, if Tessa's children saw you, your cover would fall apart, not to mention Robert still believes you and Tessa are best friends." Dr. Wu's sinister way of looking down his nose when he raised his chin usually had the effect of making a person feel stupid when he addressed them. "I'm sure you already know this."

Samantha's lip curled in a snarl and she raised an eyebrow.

"I told Chase I'd go get the kids at the first sign of trouble." Carter was a former astronaut who didn't mind getting in the thick of a bad situation if needed. "Might be interesting to meet this Phoebe."

"I'm sure she's just your type, too," Samantha snapped. They'd had an on-again off-again relationship for a while.

"That's enough." The director tired of their bickering and leveled an impatient scowl. "Let's stay focused. Dr. Wu, about Matthew Yu being the one who left Phoebe's suite late at night—it was someone else. Yu was under surveillance by the FBI. Any ideas?"

Dr. Wu barely blinked. "I'll see what I can find out. Any chance Robert left the children alone again to seek her out?"

The director checked his notes then addressed Dr. Wu. "He wasn't under surveillance, but the man leaving made it a point to cover his face. He was also shorter than Robert and had a steady and confident gait."

Dr. Wu paused a few seconds then continued. "The woman has a number of admirers and, after seeing the guest list from the party at the resort last night, I can only assume she is buttering up other clients. I am currently concerned, given Robert's current lack of confidence since Tessa has remarried, that his love of money may tempt him to do something uncharacteristic in order to impress the family. It's no secret that Captain Hunter pushes the man's buttons every chance he gets."

A wave of laughter floated across the room with a few insulting remarks made toward Robert Scott. The man had made life hell for Tessa for a number of years, causing Enigma to secretly handle some embarrassing situations.

Director Clark continued. "Thank you, Dr. Wu. I will make the Ervins aware the children may come home early to spend the rest of their vacation with them. Fortunately, they live next door and understand how things work here."

"I'll be in touch, Director. Although I am not on the Pacific Rim Consortium board, I have connections there, as you know."

"Anything you can pass our way will help in this situation. And some good news I need to share with all of you since Wu is on the phone. No deaths of adopted Asian children have been recorded in the last few days. The CDC has managed to vaccinate hundreds of children against childhood diseases, including polio in the last seventy-two hours."

"But none of the children died from any of those," added Zoric.

"True, but they all had weakened immune systems. According to Dr. Jun Hie, this disease with the deadly formula consisted of a cocktail of viruses that had been eradicated. The children were injected with different combinations until one was found that could be used as a time bomb in their system. He relented on waiting to get his daughter back to start the process of creating the serum. The CDC is working with Dr. Jun and are convinced the inoculations will give them more time. We also have his wife to thank for the change of heart. She couldn't watch another child die. Let me be clear. Dr. Jun has assured us that this can be successful."

"That is great news," Dr. Wu confessed. "Excuse me for saying so, Director Clark, but I find it troubling that now he thinks he can recreate a vaccine to protect these children no one wanted except foreigners. A month ago, he said he needed his baby daughter to break down the formula."

"You don't trust him?" The director rubbed his forehead out of concern.

"No. This is why. Although he is a brilliant man with an eidetic memory, such a scientist would still require his notes to validate what he already knew to be true. He may be stalling or even make mistakes in creating this new serum. I would check with the men and women at our university medical school to see what they say then voice your concerns with the CDC. I'm concerned he may still be working for the Chinese. It would not be like the CDC to skip steps either."

"As always, Dr. Wu, your help is invaluable."

Dr. Wu nodded then clicked off.

"How did he come to be in Palm Springs?" Carter asked in confusion. "Heck of a time to take a vacation. Any chance the old stick-in-the-mud is one of Phoebe's clients? I mean that in the most inappropriate way."

"What other way is there with you?" Samantha mumbled.

The director explained. "I thought since the Pacific Rim Consortium were holding meetings in the area and also recruiting, it would be prudent to have someone there who had connections. This whole business with the children dying is a distraction. Our China contacts have given us information that confirms they are planning on invading Taiwan to control the semiconductors industry. Currently 90 percent of those conductors are used throughout the world. Japan, Germany, and Israel occupy a significant place in the semiconductor industry. With Israel focusing on their security and the US backing them up, it is a given we are concerned. To make things worse, only 12 percent of integrated circuit manufacturing takes place here in the States."

"With our focus on finding a cure for these children, the American people and the news outlets, as you would expect, are covering this to the max," Samantha fumed.

"Correct," agreed Director Clark. "But on the flip side of that, we can do what we do best."

"Create our own diversion and mayhem?" asked Ken Montgomery. "Because I'm all in for that."

"I'm sure you are, Ken. Thanks for always making my blood pressure act up."

"My pleasure." He chuckled good-naturedly.

"Anyway, our contact in China has given us a great deal of information in the last year. The cost of that will be to get his family safely out of China. He feels it is only a matter of time until he is discovered."

Vernon pointed to the screen. "Director, there's a call coming in from Captain Hunter."

"Connect us, Vernon."

Only a couple of seconds passed until the image of a proud Captain Chase Hunter holding baby Lotus appeared. He took her hand and waved to everyone, just as Tessa slipped in and beamed her happiness.

"Morning everyone," Tessa chirped and lifted a cup of coffee. "Our sweet baby girl actually slept two four-hour shifts last night."

"We feel recharged." Chase chuckled as he kissed the baby. "Right, Lotus?"

"I think I'm going to be sick," Samantha moaned and ran her hand over her face.

"Aww, isn't she cute," Carter chimed in. "You're a natural, Chase. Taught her any curse words yet?"

This made him laugh. "Only in Chinese." He leaned into the camera. "Tessa doesn't know."

She slapped his arm and took the baby. "She needs a change before we leave. Better hurry it up."

As she turned away and disappeared off screen, Chase sobered. "We've had some unexpected changes to our schedule. Our papers to leave the country with Lotus are missing. The orphanage failed to send important information for each of the babies in our group."

"What's the plan?" The director leaned forward in his chair.

"We're all traveling by train to Wuwei. I'm not sure what to expect. We've been told it isn't a big deal."

"I believe there is a power play being put into place, Chase. You need to be constantly aware of your surroundings. Your contact may very well be your way out, so don't burn any bridges."

"Who should I be looking for?"

"I don't know. Wish I could tell you. It's all cloak-and-dagger. He wants to leave China with his family."

"Now?" he fumed. "No. It's too dangerous."

"I suspect it's the only way you'll be able to get those papers you need. According to our sources, General Sun Li knows someone from here is searching for the baby. He has learned you survived the massacre and of your connection with Dr. Wu. I don't believe he is aware you've located the child or where you are."

"Big surprise there," he growled.

Director Clark tilted his head toward the door. "Give us a minute. I want to talk to the captain alone. Vernon, that means you, too. I can handle the phone."

One by one, they left the room without saying another word. They knew when to remain silent. After the door clicked closed, Director Clark turned back to the screen.

"Dr. Wu had nothing to do with your parents dying. You know that. He has been a great asset to Enigma. His advice, therapy, and medical expertise has been exceptional."

Chase pursed his lips and narrowed dark eyes.

"Where is Tessa?" the director asked.

Chase glanced over his shoulder then back at the screen. "In the bathroom cleaning up Lotus. Why?"

"I sent Dr. Wu to Palm Springs. Mostly to keep tabs on the Pacific Rim Consortium, but he has discovered Robert is making a deal with the devil. I nearly pulled the children out last night after Heather was injured."

"Is she all right?" Chase spoke in a controlled voice.

"Yes, thanks to Sean Patrick." He filled Chase in about the kids, along with Robert's new love being a spy trying to sign him up to do their bidding. "We suspect, in the end, she'll use the children as leverage. Dr. Wu has the Ervins on speed dial, and Carter most likely has already filed a flight plan to get them."

"I don't like it. Do it now."

"Robert has told this woman all about your trip to China. She, in turn, has funneled that information to the Chinese."

"And you trust Wu?"

"I do. And I suggest you don't tell Tessa."

"Not happening. That would be breaking the trust between us." Chase checked the time. "I gotta go. Call you tomorrow."

CHAPTER 23

Deception. Dr. Wu had mastered it long ago in order to pry information from those suffering from PTSD. It was what made him good at his job. Everything he heard from his patients was given in confidence. At that point, he was able to begin a plan of healing and transitioning them into their new normal.

Only Captain Hunter had refused to participate in his sessions, even when the man needed help. To make matters worse, he'd jaded his team's opinion of him, calling him a mind-bender and not to be trusted. If they had a problem, bring it to him. He'd fix it, smash it, or kill it. Director Benjamin Clark still insisted they take their turn talking to him. Only Carter seemed to enjoy the sessions, but he was also the least damaged by the work they did.

Things changed around the office the day Tessa walked into Enigma, reminding him of a scared rabbit, laden with way too much information about things that jeopardized national security.

The organization took advantage of her and abused her sensibilities and innocence to get what they wanted. Yet, she prevailed and remained optimistic. Being the gullible girl-next-door type, she believed everything they spoon fed her until they had hooked her into working with them. Threats of bodily harm transitioned to an addiction to walking a thin line between right and wrong.

Since that time, he had secretly observed her and used his gifts to explore her psyche. Little Miss Sunshine had a dark side, too, which made her perfect for Enigma. At first, Captain Hunter refused to issue an offer she couldn't refuse, but the captain had an Achilles' heel. She was that weakness, and the battled-hardened soldier knew it.

After being kidnapped in Afghanistan by a man who was both villain and hero, the woman needed therapy to heal. She suffered from Stockholm syndrome, and Captain Hunter would let no one but him help her. For that, Dr. Wu was grateful. Unbeknownst to her, she healed him too. They had become good friends, and there was nothing he wouldn't do for her, considering what a pure heart she possessed.

They still met weekly to work in his small greenhouse full of orchids and lilies. But the idea that she saw something wonderful in Captain Hunter, who had killed many men in his career, helped him begin to see the man in the same way.

Now here he was, caught in the middle of things he wanted no part of, thanks to Phoebe. Due to his profession as a psychiatrist, he preferred to hold judgment until he had either all the facts or more information. But he possessed enough to know she was betraying the US to China.

The secrets he kept from Enigma might destroy the only peace he'd found since coming to this country. He'd gone into psychiatry to help those who carried guilt, ghosts, and regrets like ticking time bombs. Helping others had been a kind of therapy for himself.

He had taken an oath of no harm and had always practiced it religiously. When he thought of Phoebe, something cruel and vindictive ate at his reasonable side. If harm should come to those children or even Robert, he would make sure she suffered a slow death.

The thought of instilling fear in her gave him pleasure. Maybe he wasn't so different than the others at Enigma. All he could do was keep track of her and measure the success she pretended to already wear for China to see.

~ ~ ~ ~

Chase spotted Colonel Zhou Xiang exiting a government vehicle. It was near the offices where the parents were to get their final papers to hand over when and if they made it to the American Consulate in Guangzhou. Without swearing the babies in as American citizens, they wouldn't be able to take that final flight home. Although it would be weeks before the documentation arrived to have in hand, the consulate would be able to stamp a passport for them to continue the last leg of their journey. Time was of the essence in getting Lotus to her parents so the doctor could complete the lifesaving formula for hundreds of children.

Their small bus pulled into a lot at the end of the street. While John took care of the parking charge, several of the men stood and stretched their legs. The train ride had been three hours after a quick breakfast on the go. Babies were tired, and parents were getting cranky.

"Did you see the colonel?" Tessa whispered.

Chase grunted a quiet reply. "He didn't waste any time getting here. Probably diverted us to Wuwei because he keeps a home nearby. My guess is he made those papers disappear. I would bet money he recognized me."

"You sound like you personally know him," Tessa said in surprise. "How do you know that? I thought it was only because you saw him murder your parents."

"He used to come to my parents' clinic sometimes. My parents healed his son, who, by the way was a good friend of mind—just like Wu."

Tessa turned stiffly in her seat to face him. "What? Wu lived here too? How could you have kept that from me considering my relationship with him?"

"Because you needed him, and I…"

"You used me to spy on him for yourself," she accused hotly. "How could you?" she huffed and turned away from him. "How could you?"

"He's the best at what he does. You deserved the best, Tessa. And, let's face it, he likes you," he said flippantly. "But like it or not, he's a snake in the grass. He could have saved my parents and didn't."

"How do you know that? You escaped. There could be others who made it out. So, were they all out to get you? Seems to me you need a little therapy to deal with all these paranoid passive-aggressive emotions swirling around in that head of yours." She let Lotus go to him as she reached for his face.

"I don't need you to psychoanalyze me. You knew I was damaged goods when you married me. That is never going to change. Better get used to it," he growled as he kept checking the area around them through the windows.

"Get used to it?" she snapped. "I don't have to get used to anything you dish out, Captain Hunter. I've taken men down like you several times, and you are no big deal. So, get that through your thick skull. I lived a long time without you, and I'm sure I can manage to do it again," she hissed. "So, you'd better get used to that."

"Why do I feel like a praying mantis who just had his head bit off by his mate?" he asked, amused at her temper and how her eyes had turned violet. They hadn't done that in a while. "Let's talk about this later. I'll catch you up to speed."

"Humph," came a sullen response then she stared out the window.

"Women," he sighed. She turned toward him, wearing a mean scowl. He decided it was best to just shut up. They rarely crossed swords, but he had the distinct impression she wasn't going to let this go.

Why he wanted to keep it from her was a mystery even to him. Maybe if he told her, she'd realize how truly broken he'd been until she walked into his life. Until this moment, she'd seen him as some kind of freaking hero with superpowers. She idealized him, thinking the sun rose and set in him. He was good with that even if it wasn't true.

One of his greatest fears was that she'd discover he wasn't good enough for her. There were several others waiting in the wings to fill his shoes, but they were no different than him. Like him, however, they were good at keeping secrets about their past and wouldn't want her to know who they really were on the inside. She attracted those kinds of men like a magnet. Maybe he should ask Dr. Wu about that someday.

"Everyone, gather your backpacks and other personal items.

Our driver will remain with the bus, so there's no worries about your luggage. We'll be spending the night here at a nearby hotel. Everything has been taken care of for your convenience. However, we cannot catch a train back to Lanzhou until tomorrow evening." Groans and complaints immediately started. "At that time, we'll join the other families who remained behind. We'll continue with an abbreviated schedule."

"But we had tours lined up, John," complained the Springfield family.

"Yes. We will be doing a tour here tomorrow to a beautiful part of the country. You will enjoy it. I promise. At the end of that tour, you'll be taken to the train station. A delicious dinner will be prepared for you on your way back to Lanzhou." He held up his hand as questions flew his way. "I know you are disappointed, but I have planned a wonderful day for you tomorrow. And tonight, the Gansu Dancers are performing, and you will be their guests, thanks to the honorable General Sun Li and Colonel Zhou Xiang. The general provided his box seats for you because of the inconvenience." The continuous smile John displayed had begun to irritate Chase. "Let's proceed to the office to get your papers. I've called to let them know we are on our way. After that, we will go to the hotel for you to rest. There are street merchants nearby and some shops with traditional Chinese goods if you'd like to visit there before dinner."

How quickly the group could be appeased. Americans and their shopping would be their downfall. Thankfully, Tessa wasn't one of those. She'd had to account for every penny when she was married to Robert. Little did he know, she was socking away the money she made from Enigma. She managed to accumulate a sizeable savings, which Enigma accountants invested for her. It didn't take long to triple her earnings. Most things she bought were on sale or from thrift stores. Nothing pretentious about her; another reason he adored her.

The group filed off and unfolded the umbrella strollers purchased once they arrived in China. They had already been given a workout. The babies fell fast asleep as they made their way to the Office of Documents.

~ ~ ~ ~

Colonel Zhou Xiang observed the Americans from a distance. They waited patiently behind other families from Europe trying to obtain papers for their new daughter. Their expressions were a genuine reflection of love and hope as they lifted the children from strollers to be weighed and measured. Questions were asked pertaining to the parents' country of origin. The Germans and French, Colonel Zhou noticed, were impatient and rude to the clerks. He turned to his assistant.

"Make sure the Europeans have to wait. Turn the air conditioner off and open the windows in their waiting room."

"Sir, that is on a street side. It will be noisy for the babies." The soldier straightened as Colonel Zhou frowned at him. "Yes, sir. Right away. And the Americans?"

"See that they are well taken care of."

"Of course."

Colonel Zhou remained standing in front of the one-way mirror to observe the Americans but focused on Mr. and Mrs. Butler. The man appeared cold and hard to be married to such a delicate flower. At first glance, he would not have given him another thought. With the alert an American courier had arrived for the baby girl, the general was desperate to find him. It would certainly circumvent China's plan to distract the world from their own devious attempt at world dominance. Because there was something familiar about Mr. Butler, Colonel Zhou imagined the man as a young teen.

"Did you install the age cam on the tablet?"

His assistant assured him he had. "However, the picture you provided was worn and a bit faded. I'm not sure how accurate it will be, sir."

"Thank you. I'll take it from here." The colonel dismissed him.

The facial features intensified as if going from teen to man in a flash and, for the first time, he could identify who stood among the other Americans. There had always been something unique about the boy: taller than the others, darker, demonic eyes that could penetrate a bully's self confidence in a blink of an eye. His son learned from him and also became a champion of the underdog to this day.

He replayed the age cam one last time and erased the video. Mr. Butler who stood nonchalant with a baby girl folded in his arms was that boy.

His own son had been best friends with the American. They had gotten into plenty of mischief back then, forcing both families to place the boys with the Shaolin for a time. The training cemented their ability to be fearless and attempt the impossible. However, the Shaolin possessed a way to channel that energy into discipline and strength. The two boys became a force to be reckoned with among their peers.

Chase Butler had to be the boy Chase Hunter that lived in the village where the massacre occurred. The Shaolin aided in their escape. The irony did not escape him that Buddhist priests forged a partnership with Christian missionaries and worked alongside them to make a better place for the people on the outskirts of Wuwei.

He could still remember them walking together through the countryside to lend comfort and healing to those in need. At the time, he had been both confused and impressed by their devotion. Even he had fallen for the goodwill the missionaries spread in the community. Hadn't they given his first wife comfort until her death and later saved his son's life? Then he'd given in to the ultimate betrayal.

The boy was a man; a man with the appearance of a hardened warrior. Why send him to do this thing that could affect his country? Revenge? Or did he seek closure? This presented a whole new set of problems he wasn't sure could be resolved in a timely and uncomplicated manner. Flashbacks of that night still haunted him. There was always the idea that someday the massacre would come back to wreak havoc in his life, destroying the penance he'd paid.

~ ~ ~ ~

Chase froze at hearing the name of Sun Li who'd orchestrated the massacre in his village. He wondered if the massacre had propelled both men to achieve their higher rank. What other evil had they committed to obtain such a position? Apparently, Zhou Xiang was still doing his bidding. Nice to have both pieces of Satan's spawn in one place. If only he had a gun.

He felt a surge of satisfaction deep inside his gut, knowing he didn't need anything but his hands and opportunity to take down both men. He studied what he presumed was a one-way mirror. Raising his stubborn chin, he tried to level one of his fierce expressions at whoever was on the other side of the mirror and mouthed a promise, hoping the person could read lips. "I'm coming for you."

CHAPTER 24

Robert cocked his head at the limo waiting outside the resort to take his children to a new location. After Phoebe told the kids about the GameARama Adventure Experience, they were all in. He didn't like the idea of so much unsupervised activity away from the resort.

"This does not solve my problem, Phoebe. I'm not letting them out of my sight again. Unless I have a person I can trust to supervise them, it's still a no." Robert felt good about standing up to the woman who in reality was probably not a safe bet to leave in charge of his kids.

"Dad, it's GameARama!" Daniel insisted. "Laser tag, bowling, video games, and there's even a snack bar."

"A nurse is on staff if Heather should need anything." Phoebe toyed with his collar and smiled at the kids.

"No. I screwed up last night. No. No. No. I can't risk it." He noticed his oldest hadn't said anything when Daniel and Heather made a fuss about going. "Sean Patrick, I'm asking your opinion."

Sean dropped his arms to his side. His face brightened. "Not a good idea. I can't keep up with everything they'll want to do. Daniel doesn't like me to boss him around and, well, Heather is a whiner. She'll drive me crazy until I give in. You know how she is.

It works on Chase, but it just makes me mad."

The mere mention of Chase rubbed him the wrong way.

"Robert, the Pacific Rim Consortium is expecting you within the hour. Are you really going to blow this?" Phoebe snapped. "I went out on a limb for you."

"Kids, how about I drop by the concierge and let them know I'll be in a meeting for a few hours and need someone to monitor your whereabouts, although Sean Patrick is capable of taking care of things. No swimming because of Heather's cut. I'll request that the nurse drop by or send security every half hour. When I get back, we'll go to GameARama Adventure. How does that sound?" Phoebe shifted her weight to one hip and pursed her lips tightly. "Maybe Phoebe will join us."

She walked over to the limo and opened the passenger side door and leaned in to address the driver. "Plans have changed. Come back in about three hours. I'll call you first." She slammed the door a little harder than was necessary, giving Robert the idea she didn't like her plans being circumvented. Good to know.

"Sounds great, Dad. Thanks." Sean Patrick nodded then shifted his eyes to Phoebe who had zeroed in on him coldly, which made him chuckle.

Robert took Heather's hand. "Let's go talk to that nurse friend of yours. I'd like for her to check your head before I leave. Daniel, you and Sean Patrick check out the gift shop to see if there are any puzzles to work while I'm gone."

Daniel didn't have to be told twice. He ran toward the gift shop, nearly bumping into one of the hotel workers. Sean Patrick held back, waiting for Phoebe to join him.

"Sorry you went to so much trouble, Phoebe. Appreciate the effort."

"I bet you do," she said coyly. "You don't like me much, do you, Sean Patrick?"

"I don't want my dad to get hurt is all."

"It's sweet of you to try and protect him. But I think I'll be doing that after he accepts this job. You won't have to worry about him."

"Maybe he won't accept the job."

"It's a wonderful opportunity for him."

"He won't want to go off and leave us."

She reached over to push his hair off his forehead, which made the boy jerk away. Her quiet laugh reminded him of Ursula from Little Mermaid. "Don't underestimate me."

"I was thinking the same thing about me, Phoebe."

"Does your mother know how you act?"

"Yep. Who do you think I get it from? And when she gets back, I'll be sure to tell her all about you. That should put an end to my dad thinking you're the best thing since peanut butter and jelly. I know the truth. Chase taught me enough Chinese to know what you were talking about to your boyfriend who is old enough to be your grandpa."

"That's enough."

"I'll say." He hurried ahead and joined his brother in the gift shop then stuck his head out. "Aren't you coming, Qin ai de?" He really didn't know much Chinese. But Chase had taught him how to say sweetheart and a couple of other nice things to impress the girls at school. Seeing the expression on Phoebe's face was worth getting chewed out the previous night.

Phoebe stopped in her tracks and decided she didn't like Robert's oldest smart-ass son. He was old beyond his years and fearless in many ways. He took the anger his father dished out to him last night and didn't blink an eye. Could the stepfather be the influence? It certainly wasn't Robert. And how much Chinese did the kid really know?

Her phone vibrated. She recognized the number and shivered. "Yes, Uncle? I mean, Dr. Wu. What do you want?"

"Rescind the offer from the Pacific Rim Consortium for this man named Robert. His wife is trouble."

"So I gathered. How do you know this?"

"The same way I know everything, Phoebe. I am connected to powerful people."

"Then you tell your people that my people have already made an offer and there is no turning back. If you really cared for China, you'd stay out of my business."

"The Red Dragon is involved."

"I care nothing for the Red Dragon. It is a myth. Nothing more."

"He is making plans for the mother of those children. It would be wise not to cross him."

"Or what? You'll spank me? I'm not a little kid anymore."

"I have plans of my own, and you are to stop whatever you think you are doing so I can continue. I am in charge. Not you."

"Well, Uncle," she fumed. "We'll see about that." She clicked off and slipped her phone back in her purse. Uncle Wu had become a threat to everything she'd ever tried to do. Her whole life there had been nothing but secrets and hidden agendas. People in their community in Chinatown both feared and respected him. His work had made him wealthy. She wasn't sure how he'd accumulated so much money but suspected it was illegal.

Robert returned from seeing the nurse as Heather scampered into the gift shop with her brothers. From outside the large wall of windows, he could easily keep track of their movements. "I'm sorry about the limo. If I had known you were planning something, I could have stopped you. You should have said something."

"I wanted to surprise the kids. It's fine. And I would love to tag along later if all the loose ends are tied up. Why don't you take the kids back to the suite, and I'll meet you at the conference center in the west wing of the resort. I'm going to make a few calls to check if everything is ready."

"You are amazing. I'll be down in thirty minutes."

"Make it twenty." She squeezed his arm.

A frown toyed with the edge of his mouth.

"That way I can give you a few hints about how things will go. I'm pulling for you." Her hand went to his cheek and stroked it.

"Right. Good idea."

Phoebe waited until the four of them reached the elevators. All turned to wave goodbye, except for Sean Patrick. He lifted his chin and grinned. She chewed the inside of her jaw, a nervous tick she had when things didn't go her way. The brat was trying to intimidate her. First item on her list of things to do was study this creature, Tessa. Who was she really?

~ ~ ~ ~

Box seats near the stage on the second floor of the Gansu Theater were spectacular. Although the box belonged to General Sun Li, Tessa didn't feel guilty. She was too excited knowing they'd secured premium spots to enjoy the Gansu Dancers. Considering there was plenty of room for the four families plus John, it stood to reason the general would not be included in the night's festivities. For that, she felt relief. John assured her there would be no one else joining them.

"This is beautiful." Tessa couldn't keep the awe out of her voice as she twisted in her seat to see the extravagant décor in red and gold. "Wonder how old this place is, Chase?"

John jumped in to answer. "Not very old at all. Construction began in the early twentieth century. With world wars and economic collapse, completion came shortly after World War II. By Chinese standards, this is practically brand new." He chuckled.

"Smells a little like mildew to me," the Plano mom complained as she wrinkled her nose. "Probably the upholstery."

A rejected expression filled John's face. He'd tried so hard to make the best of this bad situation.

"I love the upholstery. Think of the amazing men and women who have sat here." She sighed as she placed a hand on her heart. "You wouldn't like my chairs at home. I love faded fabric." She winked at John. "Thank you so much, for making this happen for us. It was so kind of you."

His face brightened. "You are welcome. I will pass your comments to the general and Colonel Zhou. They were most adamant that you take their place tonight."

"Oh my. They were supposed to be here? How gracious of them," the Springfield mom interrupted. "The people here are just so nice."

Chase frowned as his eyes surveyed the theater. He was searching for a quick escape if needed. Although no one seemed to notice, she knew Chase was also listening to every word. Generally, he could turn on the charm and fit right in with a group.

Of course, that group usually was up to no good, and he often planned to take someone out. Did he even know how to act around normal people? From his cool treatment of the other parents, she would guess that was a big no.

Of course, she'd spit a little fire at him earlier. There had been no time to clear the air. The obvious fit of temper she'd displayed barely registered with him as he fixated on finding the colonel and maybe even the general. Sooner or later, it was going to hit the fan, as her dad used to say about trouble coming.

"John, is there a restroom where I can change my little one? She doesn't like to be wet, and I don't want to have to get up during the performance."

"Of course. I'll show you the way."

She quickly informed Chase of her plans, and he nodded once she told him John was going with her.

Once out in the corridor, Tessa also put her full attention on the comings and goings of people. She spotted only a few Westerners and determined from their conversations they were European college students. There were a few others, also with babies wondering around with a tour guide. The crowd had thinned as John led her down another corridor at the far end of where their box seats were located.

"There on the left. I'll wait for you here"—his phone chirped—"after I take this call."

"No problem. I can find my way if you need to get back."

Lifting the phone to his ear, he gave the okay sign then turned his back to her. She noticed he only listened instead of speaking. Maybe it was a recorded call or spam he didn't wish to acknowledge. Did the Chinese even have spam calls?

Tessa pushed open the tall door decorated with painted flowers and trim. Inside, the restroom was a combination of Chinese and Western culture when it came to using the facilities. Fortunately, there was a baby station where she could easily change her squirming daughter. It was impossible not to shower her with kisses and praise. At that moment, she thought of the baby as her own. The child had stolen her heart, and she had no intention of surrendering her to someone she didn't know back in the States.

She sang to Lotus, knowing it always got her attention. Besides kicking and cooing, she'd smiled up at her, mesmerized at whatever song she chose to sing. This one was something she'd learned when her children were little. It was in Japanese. The words were magical to her children and, apparently, Lotus felt the same way.

Suddenly, the lights flickered and dimmed. The baby pushed out her bottom lip and turned her head toward the door. Tessa followed her line of sight but saw nothing.

"No worries, my sweet girl. It's okay. See the lights are all on again." She lifted her into her arms and grabbed up the diaper backpack awkwardly to one shoulder. "Should we go see Daddy?" Another kiss to her cheek did not cheer her up this time. She continued to stare at something. "Are you going to be fussy? Are you scared?"

She pivoted and fell back against the baby station. The lights flickered again and dimmed to nearly dark when a figure clothed in black leather and metal stepped forward. The lower part of his face was covered, but the top was painted bloodred. His black hair hung below his helmet that resembled something from a bygone dynasty. A sword was sheathed at his side.

The Red Dragon.

"We meet again, Tessa Hunter."

She squirmed away as he approached and reached out to her.

"Give me the child."

CHAPTER 25

Tessa opened her mouth to speak, but nothing came out—not a scream, sob, or a cry for help. The man had just appeared, like a ghost. Why hadn't she heard him? Lotus certainly did. He took one more step and cocked his head to eye her head to toe.

"I repeat. Give me the child. You are in danger."

Maybe it was because she was scared or that his English carried a heavy accent, but she found it difficult to respond. When his eyes narrowed, much like a dragon might do just before he set you on fire, she pulled Lotus to her chest and placed a hand on the back of her head.

"She is my child, and I love her. I'm going to start screaming if you don't leave this instant."

Even though she forced herself to be brave, he wasn't buying it and jumped in front of her then whirled around as he lifted some kind of small shield from his back and positioned it to protect them. A pistol shot ricocheted off the piece of equipment, and he lunged away from her toward two men who had entered the restroom. They dressed like thugs in bulky clothing.

They aimed their guns at the Red Dragon. He managed to somehow jump in the air and kicked one in the face, causing him to drop his weapon and slide toward Tessa.

He disarmed the second man so quickly it felt like a blur. By grabbing his pistol hand of the second the attacker, Red Dragon let out a growl then snapped it back. Tessa heard the bone pop as the man screamed and fell to his knees. He continued to immobilized him by landing a foot upside his head, rendering him unconscious.

The first man he relieved of his weapon rallied and raced to get the gun at Tessa's feet. When he bent down, Tessa rammed a knee under his chin as he tried to stand, sending him backward. Before the man could roll out of the way, the Red Dragon stomped on his face, sending a spray of blood from a broken nose. The Red Dragon pivoted toward Tessa to meet her gaze. She lifted the gun from the floor and pointed it at the ancient warrior. The man she managed to knock down pulled a knife from his boot and scrambled to stab the Red Dragon in the back.

"Look out," she yelled as she fired at the man who already had his hand in the air to penetrate the Red Dragon's neck. Blood splattered as she watched in horror as he crumpled to the floor.

"Give me the gun," he ordered but took it from her before she could surrender it willingly.

"Is he…dead?"

"Only grazed his pride. We must leave. I will return and take care of them." Once more, he extended his arms. "Give me the child. I will not hurt either of you."

Tessa handed him Lotus. He moved to the last stall and opened the door. Taking the bottom of his fist, he pounded on the wall three times, opening a door into darkness.

"Follow me. I will take you back to your seat. Your guide is still talking on the phone. He cares nothing of your safety."

"Okay." She stepped into the darkness, swatting frantically at a spiderweb that touched her face.

The Red Dragon stopped and spun around to confront her. She thought he would be angry for her ninja moves against a spiderweb, but instead he gently touched her cheek and removed the invisible threat she felt. His hand lingered a little too long, and she pushed it aside. "I'm fine."

He turned back and grabbed her hand with his free one as he moved among rafters. Something scurried across her foot, drawing a shiver and soft cry from her.

"Just a rat. Do not worry."

"Oh. Well, if it's just a rat. Good Lord Almighty," she mumbled.

He stopped and handed Tessa the baby. "I leave you. Tap here"—he took her hand and placed it on what felt like a button—"and the door will open across from your box seats. "Thank you for saving my life, Tessa Hunter. We will meet again soon."

"Oh goodie." She knew her response sounded sarcastic. "I can hardly wait."

"I am glad to hear that. I feel the same." He stepped too close for comfort.

"I was making a joke, so don't get the idea I like you." She tried to step back, but he followed.

"Do not get the idea you have a choice in these things." He took her arm then shoved her toward the button that would let her escape to a lighted corridor.

She sucked in her breath then turned back to thank him, but the Red Dragon had disappeared.

When they stepped out into the brightly lit corridor, Lotus buried her face in Tessa's neck. She adjusted the diaper backpack on her shoulder and surveyed the area around her to make sure no one was around to notice her coming out of a random wall like a ghost. Apparently, everyone had taken their seat. Cautiously, she moved toward the maroon curtains that framed the gold-painted door. As she reached for the handle, the door swung open, and Chase crashed into her.

A sob escaped from deep in her chest as she fell against him, careful not to smash Lotus.

His arms went around her and the child. "Tessa," he whispered in her ear, voice edged in panic. "You gave me a scare. Where is John?" He pushed her at arm's length. "Tessa? What's wrong?"

"Two men…" She dared sneak a peek down the corridor and saw John running toward them. "Take me to our seats, Chase." She sniffed back tears. "Please. Now."

"Okay. Let's go. The show is starting. Watch your step. There are some lumpy carpet places you could catch your foot." He turned on the flashlight from his phone and helped her. Reaching over, he took Lotus as she sat down. "Just tell me you're okay," he insisted.

She could only nod like an anxious toddler and leaned against his shoulder. "I think I killed a man."

Chase jerked his head around as tears cascaded down her cheeks. "Do we need to leave?"

"No. Everything is being taken care of."

"What? By who? John?"

The curtains opened, and they sat in darkness as the stage was flooded with pink-and-purple light. Beautiful dancers in sparkly costumes gracefully floated onto the stage as the orchestra began to play. Tessa let herself cry through the first two numbers. No one would notice, since she and Chase were in the last row of chairs and the rest of the group sat wide-eyed by the magic the Gansu Dancers created.

By intermission, Tessa had pulled herself together and Lotus slept peacefully cradled in Chase's arms. Although he rocked the baby, his eyes were constantly scoping out the theater for changes, danger, and an unusual amount of attention directed their way.

"Tessa, where is the restroom?" The Minnesota mom stood holding her baby.

"Yeah. I gotta go too. Hopefully, we don't have to use one of those ridiculous squatty-potties like at the airport." The Plano, Texas mom handed the baby to her husband. "Let's go."

Tessa stood and felt Chase rise too.

"I'll go with you ladies. It's late, and you can't be too careful."

"Me, too," the Springfield dad volunteered. "That green tea goes right through me." His wife hushed him and rolled her eyes in embarrassment.

John waited outside their box seats in the corridor talking to men dressed in black uniforms with guns holstered at their sides. He held up a hand to stop them and pointed to the two men with him. "These are the people's police, Mrs. Butler. I am so sorry I couldn't walk you back to your seat earlier."

"You were still on the phone. I didn't want to interrupt you or miss anything."

"Again, I apologize. These officers said there was some kind of accident and wondered if I noticed anything near the restroom. Did you see anything?"

"What kind of accident?" the Springfield dad asked.

"A misunderstanding between some guests. I suspect it was a family matter." The police walked away, one making notes as John let his breath release. "Someone said they saw a man walk out with blood on his face and another had broken his wrist. Strange."

"The floor was slick in the ladies' restroom," Tessa lied. "Maybe the floors were the same way in the mens, and they fell."

"Aww. I never thought of that. That happens more often than you can imagine. They want tourists to be so impressed with the shine on everything that they fail to see how dangerous it is." He pointed down the corridor. "Right there. It's safe to go." As the others moved in that direction, John stepped in front of Chase and Tessa. "I don't want to know why things keep happening when you are around. But you are putting everyone in danger."

"It is not our intent to do that, John."

"I waited for you to return, Mrs. Butler."

"You were on the phone."

"I was not."

Chase switched to Chinese and leveled a dangerous scowl at their tour guide. "Lao Tzu once said, those who know, do not speak, and those who speak do not know. Careful what you remember, my friend."

John stepped aside and fanned out his hand toward the end of the corridor. "You are a wise man, Mr. Butler."

"And you are as well."

~ ~ ~ ~

Taking in the city from the window of their hotel room toward the vastness, he knew what lay beyond and the dangers it held. Chase wondered if he could take Tessa and Lotus and escape now rather than wait as planned. He still didn't know who he was supposed to meet and make arrangements to leave. Was that even possible? To the north was Mongolia. He had no connections there these days, or at least not close enough to assist him. There wasn't even a way to contact them. For all he knew, they had moved on or died.

He could take a train to Jiayuguan, once a military fortress that overlooked the Gobi Desert. It had been used to be on alert for invaders. Like many things in China, it had become a tourist destination, and the city around it had grown by leaps and bounds.

It would be easy to get lost there but also easy to stick out like a sore thumb without backup. Add a wife and baby, and it sounded ridiculous to expect help there. He knew for a fact Enigma or any other US national security group had no assets there.

He remembered seeing the Qilian Mountain range for the first time when he and his sister escaped the massacre. Back then, the Buddhist priests had contacts across the land. Those mountains were treacherous, vast, and the altitude alone would be impossible for a baby to tolerate.

The Tribesman came to mind as he toyed with ideas. Of all the people in the world to trust, it was Tessa's former lover who could get them to safety or contact someone who could. Chase had no idea where he was, though, or how to reach him. It would be just like him to be in some hellhole at the end of the world, where he felt most at peace. Maybe the director could reach him. Then again, time was of the essence.

He turned away from the window and spotted Tessa curled up on her twin bed with Lotus in the crook of her arm. Even though the room was mostly dark, the streetlamps outside shone in enough for him to see that she'd stuck her leg out from under the covers like she always did after her dream cycle began.

He walked over to his bed and sat on the edge, watching the two of them. He wondered about the practice of twin beds in the hotel rooms, but if you were getting acquainted with a fussy baby, it didn't matter. You couldn't sleep with your partner.

Never would he have imagined his heart could feel this way when looking at a woman. Until Tessa, they were mostly a matter of one-night stands or encounters with his job. He didn't want attachments, complications, or emotions that might cloud his black heart. Then she stumbled into his life, swinging a rolling pin and smelling of chocolate chip cookies. Even now, it made him smile to think of that day.

Damn, she was so innocent and pretty, even if she was covered in flour and held what he thought was a bomb. Looking back, he considered it the beginning of the end to him being satisfied with living alone. He plotted excuses to keep her at Enigma. Figuring out what to do with all that bubbly sunshine she emitted that made grown men stupid, continued to be a problem, even today.

At one point, he wondered if he could weaponize whatever she had to bring those he hunted under control. She attracted trouble like a heat-seeking missile, and he spent an enormous amount of time getting her out of messes.

Now, here he was married, a thing he said he'd never do. The other thing he promised to never do was return to China. And the last thing he promised to avoid like the plague was become a parent. Being a stepfather was a lot more intense than he'd imagined, and all he could think about some days was having a child with Tessa. *Three strikes, you're out!*

He stood and reached over to lift Lotus away from Tessa's embrace so she could rest. The urge to kiss those chubby cheeks was too great to resist as he carried her to the crib provided by the hotel. Why did this little girl make him feel so happy and scared at the same time?

"Everything okay?" Tessa mumbled, trying to open her eyes as he got into his bed.

"She's sound asleep. No worries."

Awkwardly, she pushed the covers back and joined him in his small bed. Pulling her to his side, he let her lay her head on his chest until she fell back asleep. He touched her hair as he tried to figure out her story concerning the Red Dragon.

Why was he stalking them? Did he work for the government? Tradition would say no. He was a myth of the people, a kind of Chinese Robin Hood. From Tessa's accounts, he didn't sound much like the Robin Hood he remembered as a kid, in movies. Was this just another actor who'd spotted Tessa and, like the other villains she encountered, taken an interest? If so, this was not the place or time for him to go commando on a Chinese Nationalist who had some kind of psycho-deceiver complex.

"He knew those men were coming, Chase," she'd explained earlier. "If he hadn't been there, they would have hurt me to get to Lotus."

"And you just followed him into a dark attic space with no weapon, no way to contact me? You let him take your weapon instead of defending yourself."

"I had Lotus," she snapped. "They were clearly going to kill him then come after me. And yes, I followed him. There was a dead guy lying on the floor, or I thought he was dead, and another unconscious one. How would I have explained that?"

"Well, although in bad shape, the dead guy apparently walked out on his own leaving no sign of anyone else. My guess is they were working with Mr. Red Dragon."

"You weren't there. It wasn't like that."

"Did he in any way make his intentions known as to you coming with him or me being a problem?"

"Just he wanted me to give him Lotus, which I refused to do."

He knew she was lying since her eyelashes were blinking rapidly. She couldn't control that tick. "At any time, did he touch you?"

"No."

Another lie. But why? His thoughts ran to the Tribesman. And there was another dangerous lowlife who had fallen for her and continued to be a thorn in his side. But that was beside the point. He trusted the Tribesman; this so-called Red Dragon was another matter entirely. Tessa being Tessa would believe there was a spark of good in him just because he saved her from two thugs, who may or may not have been real.

There was a light tap at the door. Chase checked his watch. 2:30 a.m. Not good.

He gently laid Tessa's head against the pillow and picked up the base of a lamp he had removed the shade from earlier, in case he needed a weapon. He stared out the peephole at a man standing with John who appeared wide-eyed and a bit frazzled.

"Tessa," he snapped in a normal voice. She sat straight up in bed and kicked the covers off. "Push the crib against the wall and stay down. Someone is at the door with John. Be ready to grab her up and cover her with your body."

He waited for her shadowy form to follow his directions without question.

"Ready?"

She didn't answer, but he knew she was.

Another tap at the door and he again used the peephole.

CHAPTER 26

R obert took a deep breath as he pulled the black leather envelope toward him after hearing about what they expected of their new liaison for the Pacific Rim Consortium.

"Welcome aboard, Robert," the CEO of the company declared as he extended a hand of friendship, and the other eight around the conference table applauded. "We are excited for you to work alongside us as we make strides into more productive advances in shipping, and universal commodities exchange among likeminded countries." He was Asian Australian with a slight accent. Phoebe mentioned he'd traveled a great deal with his family growing up until he attended boarding school in DC. His new boss appeared older than himself but moved like a man much younger with his toned and athletic body.

"This position is a surprising advancement I hadn't considered until I met Phoebe." He nodded her way. "I will, of course, look over the contract, prospectus, and stock options."

"We would expect nothing less, Robert. The yellow document concerns your stipends for travel, living arrangements, and membership fees we cover. I think you'll find the package quite generous. Phoebe has real estate contacts in the DC area. She's available in the next week, I believe, to take you to check out a place to live. I'm sure you'll be interested in a few private schools available as well. That too is included in your bonus package. And we can help with the sale of your Grass Valley property."

"Insurance?"

"The best." He grinned. "Right, gentlemen?"

There was a lot of head bobbing.

"Let's have a drink to celebrate, shall we?"

That appeared to be some kind of signal because two young men dressed as waiters entered with a cart of champagne and glasses. Robert wasn't much of a drinker and rarely touched it. Another thing he'd had to get used to with Tessa. She didn't want alcohol in the house unless it was to cook with or make some kind of fertilizer for her garden. What a stuffy old stick-in-the mud. Bet Phoebe would never do such a thing.

"To a new beginning," the CEO toasted.

Everyone echoed the sentiment and toasted him with what appeared to be genuine pride. They made him feel like he was king of the mountain. Finally, a little appreciation for his hard work ethic.

"Phoebe, can I have a word, please?" the CEO asked as she set her glass down on the cart.

Although several of the men tried to include him in their conversation about playing golf later in the day, Robert was more focused on the CEO talking to Phoebe. He definitely was standing too close and leaning in even closer when he spoke.

She kept pushing her hair behind her ears and biting her lower lip seductively. Once, she laughed softly when he arched an eyebrow and smirked. He reached in his pocket then palmed something to her, which she took nonchalantly and continued to speak quietly. The CEO appeared to be focused on her mouth painted bright red.

Sean Patrick was right. Damn it. The woman claimed to be interested in him and the kids, but why? What did she have to gain from him working with this group? He would study the information and reach out to some contacts he had about the organization before signing on the dotted line.

"So how about that golf game, Robert?" the man next to him asked. He tapped his watch. "I've got a tee time in forty-five minutes. Join us."

Robert had taken only a sip of his champagne when he set the glass down on a tray the waiter held out to him. "Sorry. I promised my kids a trip to GameARama this afternoon. It's a vacation trip for us. Their mother is traveling for work, so I get the fun part."

"Good for you. My kids love that place. I hate it," a second man confessed. "Too much noise and not enough booze. Once a year is about my limit. Fortunately, the boys also like golf, so I do that instead. The wife likes to go shopping anyway."

"Isn't that the truth?" The first man rolled his eyes in irritation. "Maybe another time, then. We look forward to working with you."

"Thanks." As he moved toward the door, the CEO approached with Phoebe at his elbow.

"Leaving? Phoebe tells me you are headed to GameARama with the kids. I'll call down and leave some tickets for you. Those places get expensive. Besides, my father-in-law owns the place."

"That's convenient." Robert chuckled. "Appreciate it."

"I'll expect a call from you in a day or so, Robert."

He extended his hand, and Robert took it firmly. It was then that he noticed Phoebe slip something in her jacket pocket. Whatever the CEO palmed her had been tucked safely away in her pocket. He walked Robert to the door and held it open for him.

"This is a great opportunity for you, Robert. I know this partnership will be beneficial for both of us."

Phoebe followed him into hall then looped her arm through his and hugged it affectionately. "I'm so happy for you." Her voice carried a tone of excitement. "I'm guessing you'll want to go over your information tonight. Can we have an intimate dinner, just the two of us?"

"No. I promised the kids I'd be in tonight. Even though I'll be working, I'll be present. That's what they really want, I think."

"Oh." She removed her arm from his and waited to speak until they were on the elevator. "Robert, you do understand this job will require a lot of travel and long days. There are going to be times when you aren't going to be with your kids. The consortium provides excellent schools where students can live on campus or choose to be home when you are. I thought you knew that."

"Tessa would never go for that. I have to promise to donate a kidney to get my kids as it is. I guess they won't be living with me.

I'll hardly ever get to see them unless Tessa follows me there." He sighed. "That might be possible, since she works for the State Department."

Phoebe cocked her head. "Really? What does she do there?"

"No idea. She's a geographer. She's buddies with the Secretary of State. I think she does data on cultural awareness or something."

"Interesting. That would be perfect, then. I bet you love to pick her brain about her work. I sure would."

"According to her, it's equivalent to watching paint dry. Never talks much about it because—"

"It's top secret," she interrupted with excitement.

"Ha. Heavens no. The woman is scared of her own shadow and thinks spiders should be considered a terrorist threat. The Secretary of State is single and invites her out from time to time so they can have a girls' weekend. She did get invited to the White House a couple of times."

The elevator door opened. "Wow. Why?"

"Once because her uncle was receiving the Medal of Honor. I don't know. We get a Christmas card every year. I think the Secretary of State has her tag along with her sometimes if she has a meeting, especially if there is a culture thing to explain."

"Sounds like to me she might enjoy living in DC."

"Since she married that military jerk, I doubt it. He's a professor who teaches French literature, if you can imagine. Boring stuff. He went with her to China. There again, her buddy asked her to go for her. I think she's bringing back a baby for some high-profile dude in San Francisco. Guess they were too busy to go themselves. Probably wealthy and could afford it."

"Probably. Have you heard from her since she left?"

He stroked her arm that was looped through his. "Are you jealous?"

"A little." She jutted her bottom lip out in a pout. "How long will she be gone?"

He shrugged. "I have to get back to work, so the neighbors will take care of the kids until she gets home. They've become like grandparents to them. I'll pick them up after work. The boys have a couple of ball games, and Heather has dance lessons."

"They'll have the best in DC."

"Hmm." He stopped to pick up the tickets for GameARama and

noticed how her eyes had glazed over. "Still want to go with us this afternoon?"

"I think I'll pass. You should be with the kids. Call me later. Maybe we could go out to dinner as a family."

He leaned in and kissed her. "I would like that." She stepped back to leave. "Oh, what did the boss palm your hand with?"

"What?" she asked as she tilted her head.

"You put it in your pocket." Robert pointed to her jacket. "A date for later?"

She reached in and pulled out a card, read it, then handed it to him. "Business card for some Realtor in Georgetown in case you don't want to live in DC or Bethesda. Very upscale. Why?" she said, frowning. "Now, who is jealous?"

Robert read it and felt like a fool. "Sorry. Guess I was." He shook his head in disgust. "Forgive me?"

"Maybe." She batted her eyes and kissed him on the cheek. "Depends on later." She blew him a kiss and left.

~ ~ ~ ~

Leaving the lobby, Phoebe made sure Robert had exited then reached in her pocket to pull out the business-card-size key card to the CEO's apartment in the office building where he worked. They had a standing date every Wednesday after one of these board meetings. At least that nosey little brat of Robert's wouldn't catch her this time.

The only other thing she needed to consider was her uncle Wu. He wouldn't approve of her sleeping with a married man and one who had connections to China. Maybe this would be the last time unless she played the really-bad girl tonight and convinced her boss Wu had outlived his usefulness. She chuckled as she slid under the steering wheel. But first she'd stop by Naughty Nights Boutique for a little something special for her performance.

CHAPTER 27

Chase stepped back when the door handle turned with the help of the person on the other side of the door. There was a click to access, but the dead bolt prevented entry. In one quick motion, Chase released the dead bolt and swung the door open. He reached out and grabbed an arm that was still attached to the handle and jerked him inside. A second man jumped back and held up his hands in surrender.

"Easy, man," came a familiar voice.

Chase motioned for him to enter, shut the door, then slammed the man he knew as Tan up against the wall and held him around the throat with one hand. He turned his attention to their tour guide, John, sending a powerful message with rage written in his expression.

"It's me," Tan choked as he pawed against Chase's hand, which only tightened.

"Please, Mr. Butler. This is my father. Remember he helped you escape Tiananmen Square in Beijing. He has come to talk to you and poses no danger." John's voice quivered.

Chase weighed the situation and made eye contact with Tessa. She lifted Lotus from her crib while making sounds of irritation. With a pat on her back, she bounced her gently then laid her back down. He slowly released Tan, who started rubbing his neck and shaking off his fear. But Chase spun him around and once more shoved him into the wall as he dropped his lamp weapon. Frisking him provided a loaded Glock 19, preferred weapon of the CIA. Chase released him and held him at gunpoint.

"Are you always so rough with your guests?"

"When they come sneaking around my room in the middle of the night, I am."

John stood nervously hugging his arms. He wore pajamas, and his unruly hair indicated he had been surprised as well.

"John?" he growled. "What's going on?"

"I'm here because—" Tan started.

"I didn't ask you, Tan. I asked him. He's scared, and I want to know why." He raised his chin and stared down his narrow nose at the tour guide. "Is Tan really your father?"

"Yes. Doesn't always like to come and go like normal people."

"Probably because he'd get his head shot off for being a subversive to the Chinese government." Chase pointed to edge of his bed. "Sit down. You'd better start talking, Tan, because I haven't had much sleep since I became a dad, and I've got a bit of a short fuse."

Tessa grabbed her robe and joined him. He hoped having her at his side might make them let their guard down. Even in the dappled light, her appearance created interest with blonde curls resembling Medusa.

"Keep your voices down. The baby is a light sleeper," she warned in a whisper.

Both men accepted her request and nodded like a couple of school boys dragged before the principal.

"Eyes on me," Chase snapped and decided Tessa needed to move back to the crib in case he had to bust a couple of heads. A tilt of his head delivered the message.

"Sorry about being so late. Took me a while to get here," Tan admitted. "I brought that gun for you."

"Sure, you did." Chase knew his voice was like ice.

"And to make you aware General Sun Li knows you're alive, Captain Chase Hunter. He considers you a loose end and doesn't want that to come back to haunt him."

"I'm the least of his worries."

"Not true. He also knows you're here for a very important baby. We don't get much news here that's of any importance or true, but my sources in Hong Kong say there's a new epidemic of disease that hits only children of a certain age. The Chinese do not want to be a part of that problem like COVID."

"Too late. The US already is considering it's the adopted Chinese girls who are dying."

"Wh-what's so special about this baby?" John stuttered.

"We're just here to adopt a baby. Everything else is just a coincidence."

Tan started to stand, but Chase jerked up the Glock and pointed it at his head. "Sit down."

He eased back down and held up his hands. "The chatter is that there's a baby with some kind of immunity that can be reproduced to save a child from the sickness."

"If that were true, I would think the Chinese would be all over themselves to save the day, considering what it did to their standing in the world with COVID. Who knows how that disaster happened? Well, I guess someone does, but the truth will probably never be told." He lowered his gun. "Relax. Back to General Sun Li. Let's say there is a special baby that holds the cure or at least some solutions to this problem. How does the general play into this?" Chase continued to tower over them in a show of intimidation.

"He plays a part in the program to make China the number one economic power in the world. His responsibility is to create a way to make China's power grab happen. Semiconductors are Taiwan's baby, and the States do not plan to let anything take that away from them." Tan's voice had turned low and serious.

"Old news. We know that."

Tan continued. "Right now, the shipping channels are being slowly eaten up by Chinese strong arms in the military, inch by inch. Soon they will have control, along with more economic say on who gets what and when. China also makes 95 percent of the world's shipping containers."

"France, the Swiss, and Denmark own the largest cargo ships," Chase admitted.

"And they're going to want access to those Pacific shipping routes. Do you think they're going to let the US tell them what to do? Nope. So, create this little diversion, or sleight of hand as you Americans like to say. Add the wars in Israel and Ukraine with Russia throwing tantrums, and you have a perfect storm. Americans have never been good at geography."

Tessa had made studying the subject her life's work. "He's right, Chase. The dominoes are set up to start falling. There won't be anything we can do about it because we're trying to save adopted Chinese babies. Who knows how long they've been trying to infect them."

Tan took a deep breath and let it out slowly. "Anyway, my point is the general wants that baby and the real father who created the virus or whatever it is. He wants both of them dead. If the world finds out about yet another Chinese problem engineered to hurt children, taking over the world will have to halt." He shrugged. "They will be spending all their time doing damage control."

"And you think our baby is connected to this?" Chase asked carefully.

"No idea. The general searches everywhere. But someone alerted him to your true identity in the States. Your background story is solid. Nice touch changing your name because you wanted to move on with your life. But apparently, someone you know spilled the beans, as you say. Someone with connections here."

"Do you know who it is?"

"All I know is it's someone with an ax to grind with you." He pointed a finger. "But you did not hear that from me. Unsubstantiated and unreliable intel on that part."

"So, why take a chance and come to me with this?"

"I'm a really good guy." Tan shrugged.

"Of course, you are." Chase spoke slowly, shifting his attention to John, who had taken on a whipped-puppy expression. "John, how do you play into this?"

"I don't. When my dad saw that I was your tour guide, he decided to keep an eye on me. He…" He shook his head and huffed as if he became tongue-tied. "He works for the US. He keeps his distance from my mother and me to keep us safe."

"Are you the one I'm supposed to take to the States?"

Tan frowned. "No. Absolutely not. The only reason I'm here is because of my family. I can get them out whenever I want. I don't need you. They won't go though. I've tried."

Chase arched an eyebrow. "John?"

"He's right. My mother refuses because my grandparents are old. Someday I would like to go. But I can't leave my family. When my father is ready to return, we will go together."

Chase raised his chin and squinted as if by doing so he could think clearly. "Someone is trying to leave here and should be contacting me."

"No idea who that could be. Maybe it's the Red Dragon. From what I hear, he's taken a liking to Mrs. Butler," he said, staring at her. "Can't say I blame him. Blonde and blue eyes are pretty rare around here. People might be rude to get their picture taken with you."

"John, did you see the Red Dragon enter the restroom where I went to change the baby?" She came to stand in front of him. "You knew I was alone," she accused.

"I-I wasn't sure."

"Bullshit," Chase snapped. "From what Tessa tells me, that getup he wears pretty much makes him stick out like a sore thumb."

"I was on a call. I had to take it."

"From who?" Tan asked in surprise. "You didn't tell me that. You knew he went in after her?"

"I believe it…it may have been General Sun Li. At least that's the name he gave me. Said he had men in the building searching for a deserter, and I wasn't to interfere."

"John." His father threw his hands up in exasperation.

"I clicked off and started that way when I saw the Red Dragon. Two thugs from nowhere rushed in. I thought they were after the Red Dragon and would protect Mrs. Butler. When she didn't come out, I worried. Next thing I knew, the two men were coming out, bloody and bruised. By the time I went in, Mrs. Butler had disappeared." He ran his fingers through his hair as his mouth twisted in guilt. "The police came quickly. Everything was cleaned up as if nothing happened."

"You should have come to get me," Chase snarled. "That outlaw could have…" Chase pulled her behind him.

"I know. I'm sorry," John stuttered. "There are dangerous forces here. The general, if that is who it was, asked about my mother and grandparents. I didn't know what to think. When I realized there was nothing I could do, I did come for you." He swallowed hard. "I was greatly relieved to see you safe, Mrs. Butler."

Tan stood slowly, holding his hands up to calm Chase down. "I, too, am sorry. My son is just trying to do a job. The general is a devil and power hungry."

"And Colonel Zhou Xiang? Is he still the lap dog of the general?"

"Considering he had those papers held up for the baby's visas to get sworn in as American citizens, searched your room, and is strutting around like a peacock—yeah, I'd say he's still a lap dog. You know him?"

"He killed my mother," he said drily.

Tan lowered his hands, shock apparent on his face. "You're the one who escaped the massacre of those missionaries."

"I'm surprised you know of it."

"Only because the CIA gave me the info years ago when I decided to come here. It nearly got Sun Li in front of a firing squad. Somehow, he managed to convince the higher-ups it was someone else who quickly was sent to Hell. It wasn't that the Chinese cared about two missionaries, but who they were related to."

"My grandfather was an ambassador and a career State Department diplomat to places all over the world. He had the ear of several presidents and was director of the CIA for several years. I suspect he knew things they didn't want to be connected to them. My sister and I made it out only because of the Shaolin monks in Wuwei. Some of them paid with their lives for doing that."

"Sorry about your family. All the more reason you must be careful." He walked over to the crib and reached down to pull a cover over Lotus. "They all resemble little dolls at this age. No wonder the world wants our babies that people have given up so freely. You are lucky to make the cut. Did you request a certain area?"

"No. Why?"

"I thought maybe since you lived in Wuwei or at least near here, you wanted a child who brought back memories."

"We didn't get to choose the location of babies available, Tan." Tessa joined him at the crib. "We waited eighteen months to hear if we had been accepted. We would have taken any child." Chase admired how Tessa could lie so easily. She had tricked him several times with that gift.

"Of course," he said quietly. "I know she will have a better life in America."

"Anything else?" Chase grunted as he walked to the door. "I need some sleep. We have a bus tour to Jiayuguan Fort then head to Guangzhou tomorrow night."

Tan snapped his fingers and motioned for John to join him. "Almost forgot. Don't go. It's a trap."

CHAPTER 28

The sun poured through the window of their room as Tessa finished getting dressed. She'd packed their bags while Chase played with Lotus. From time to time, she shifted her attention to him when he laughed and teased. This warmed her heart. For such a badass, he could sure turn on the charm with kids. His presence in her kids' lives meant they had a role model to admire and imitate, instead of Robert. Although she knew Chase had broken laws, killed evil men, and walked a thin line of right and wrong, she preferred him to the man who was the birth father of her three little monsters.

"What did John say when you called him about not going with them today?" Tessa zipped her bag then carried it to sit atop of the bigger suitcase.

"Considering his father said it was a trap, he wasn't surprised. I think he's going to just say Lotus had a rough night and we were exhausted. Our train leaves at seven. Hopefully, the train will get all of us there on time. I'm going down in a few minutes to load our luggage on the minibus they're taking."

"I packed both our backpacks for what we'll need today. I'm actually glad we're not making the trip today, although the brochure made it seem like my cup of tea."

"Better safe than sorry. We're on the outskirts of Wuwei, and there are plenty of small shops and parks to visit. We don't have to hurry and check out. There's an outdoor space where we can have breakfast. I've been craving more of that congee."

Tessa wrinkled her nose. "Just toast and coffee for me." The baby reached for her, and she managed to say a few words in Chinese that made her wiggle happily.

Tessa decided the transition of being alone with Lotus and quiet was just what she needed. The outdoor space gave Chase a chance to read the paper in Chinese. He poured over it like it was a copy of *USA Today*. The smells and sounds of the tree-lined street gave her a chance to relax—a little. There was no time to let her guard completely down.

Could the Red Dragon be nearby? Was he watching? Would he make good on his threat to come get her, or was he just trying to intimidate an American? She should have told Chase about the threat, but he would have gone all Rambo on her and thumped anyone who got within three feet of them. Besides, he seemed harmless for the most part. If he wanted to harm her, last night would have been the perfect time.

He had an earthy aroma that reminded her of wood smoke and pine. The worn leather of his gloved hand felt cool as it touched her cheek and hair. Those dark eyes pierced her soul as they bored into her, but they held interest more than threat. A shiver came over her.

"What's wrong. Need your sweater?" Chase poured himself another cup of coffee.

"No. Just caught a chill when the breeze hit me."

"Let's go across the street to the park. It's nearly noon. I need to stretch my legs. Then we can hit a few shops if you want." Chase stood and stretched out his long legs then opened the umbrella stroller for Lotus.

After crossing the street, Chase kissed the baby girl and chuckled when she cooed at him. "I never thought I'd feel this way, Tessa." He ran his hand over the head of the child then down her cheek. "She's beautiful."

"I'm so in love with her. How can we give her up?" She gave a few rapid kisses to the baby's cheeks, causing her to wiggle with delight. "That's right. I. Love. You." She turned the child around and up to her shoulder, where little arms circled her neck then grabbed a fistful of curls.

"Stand over there by that flower bed so I can take your picture."

Tessa carried the child so easily, unlike him, who thought she might break with the slightest sudden movement. He resisted strapping her to Tessa or himself when carrying her. She assured him the baby carrier was perfectly safe and secure. When she started to move off, he helped her place the baby in a forward position.

Several times, Tessa made silly expressions or kissing sounds at him in the way that caused his heart to pound like the first day they met. Only now, did he understand that was a reaction to falling in love; something he'd never experienced.

"There. Nice and secure." He stepped closer to make one more adjustment, but Tessa pushed him back and laughed.

"She's fine. You may have cut both our circulation off, Chase."

A frown crossed his face. "Then let me fix—"

Tessa reached out and pushed on his chest. "I'm kidding. You are definitely going to be a helicopter dad. Poor Heather! What you must put her through."

"Heather?" he asked. "I think it's the other way around. That kid has taken ten years off my life already. She's manipulating, bossy, sneaky, too smart for her own good, and—"

"And you love her desperately. Stop complaining."

"The boys are so much easier to deal with," he moaned, motioning her to stand by the flowers.

"That's why, someday, women will rule the world."

"I agree. Behave and flash those pearly whites of yours" He spoke his next words in Chinese, making the baby flap her arms and giggle as he snapped pictures.

Just as he felt unsteady on his feet, he heard Tessa call out to him. Was he having a seizure or a case of vertigo? He nearly dropped his phone when his eyes went to Tessa and the baby. She was staggering and clutching at the child.

"Chase," she called again as he tried to step toward her.

The rumbling sound started as screams from people walking on the streets and cars screeching or plowing into each other made this new reality crash into him: this was an earthquake. Trees swayed, and a pagoda nearby tilted then collapsed.

He tried to move toward Tessa as she fought to stay upright, throwing her arms out as if walking a tightrope. Without warning, the pavement cracked and split apart, swallowing Tessa and the baby. As quickly as it had begun, the shaking stopped.

His legs felt like rubber, but Chase managed to stumble toward the opening about eight feet in diameter. Fortunately, it wasn't too deep, maybe six or seven feet. He could see nothing through the gray dust except chunks of concrete.

"Tessa!" he yelled. He finally spotted her.

The baby's cries drew his focus toward Tessa. Her hands were on top of the child's head as she struggled to sit up. Sitting up, she lifted a hand toward him.

The rumble of an aftershock caused more chaos around him. But the hole sank another foot. When he tried to ease down inside, debris rained down, and she covered the baby again with her hands and arms.

People staggered while others eased off the ground. Sirens wailed and bystanders stumbled to help others. A young man rushed up to him and offered to help.

"I need a ladder, rope, anything to throw down to her. She has a baby with her."

"I will be right back." He scampered off, leaving Chase to call down encouragement. "Can you stand up? Help is coming."

"The ground feels loose, Chase. I'm afraid it's going to sink. I need to try and climb out. It isn't that far."

Tessa struggled to stand and nearly toppled over with the baby but managed to brace herself on a slab of concrete.

The youth ran back holding a rope. "The man in the shop"—he pointed to an elderly man limping toward them—"will come to help."

Chase thanked the boy and made a lasso to throw down for Tessa to slip around her body. Just as she secured it, another aftershock rumbled, shifting the debris in the hole. A piece hit Tessa, knocking her off-balance. He tightened his hold and kept her upright but could see blood on her face. She shook her head and dropped her hands from the baby for a few seconds.

"Tessa, look at me."

Her hands returned to the baby.

"Tessa! Tessa! You've got to try to climb out. It isn't far. I'll pull you up. You need to hurry. The hole is going to collapse."

She nodded and grasped the rope. Lotus continued to cry, adding to the distraction and confusion. The first few steps were slow as she climbed like an awkward toddler learning to walk.

Both men and Chase pulled the lifeline, only to have it catch a couple of times. The fear she'd slip out of the loop worried him. She was hurt and couldn't tighten it.

"Chase," she moaned. "I. Can't. Do. It." Tessa gazed up, covered in gray dust and blood, tears filling her eyes. "I love you. Forever."

"Damn it, Tessa. Shut the hell up and try. I need you. Our family needs you. That baby will save a generation. Do it."

"I'm not strong enough."

Chase yelled for help in Chinese, and the younger of the two men ran at several men on the street. They quickly joined him, caught the rope, and pulled. It was all it took to give her a lift up the crumbling wall over a twenty-foot hole. Finally, he could reach down and grab the noose. With the help from the young man, he managed to pull her body from the hole into his arms. The momentum caused him to fall backward with Tessa and the baby landing on his chest.

A cheer rose up at the success. Chase propped her against a toppled bench and thanked his helpers who had stepped in at the last minute. The old man remained, as did the first who came to the rescue and kneeled to have a closer look at Tessa and the baby.

He motioned for the young man who was first to help. "She needs a doctor. Check the clinic," he said as Chase helped him stand. "Yona, bring water too. There are bottles in my cart outside the store."

He started backing up. "I'll bring the doctor to help. She is across the street. I see her now."

Chase squatted by Tessa and removed the baby who had stopped crying. She looked sleepy. He hoped that was a good sign. When Tessa smiled, his heart skipped a beat. Reaching out, he cupped her chin in his hand.

"I thought I lost you."

The old man tapped Chase on the shoulder. "I will rush my friend along. I might have a first aid kit. I will bring it back to you."

Chase got to his feet and bowed politely. "You saved my family. I will offer blessings for you forever."

The old man returned the bow. "Yona will be back soon. I will find the first aid kit."

Chase watched in confusion as he hobbled back to his shop. The young man stopped and spoke to the old man then hurried back to them.

Tessa tried to adjust her position. "What is it, Chase? I think I'm okay. Just a bump on the head. Can you help me up? Maybe if we flip the bench over, I can sit down."

Chase reached down and pulled her up with one hand since he also held Lotus. She wrapped her arms around the two of them then laid her head against his chest while patting the baby's back.

The young man named Yona set four bottles of water on the ground to help Chase with the bench. Once it was secure, Yona took Tessa's hand and offered a shy smile. "The big man and I will help you."

He spoke perfect English.

"What did the old man call you?" Chase asked.

"Yona." He touched the baby's feet. "She lost her shoes in the fall. Yona means—"

"Bear. It means bear," Chase said suspiciously.

Yona straightened and stared at Chase with narrowed eyes. Chase experienced a wave of confusion then quickly asked the young man a question. Yona's eyes widened and he began to back away then bolted away into the park. Chase tried to call him back, but he disappeared among the people. trying to make sense of what just happened.

"What about a bear?" Tessa asked.

"He said his name was Yona."

"Does that mean bear in Chinese?" she asked, leaning back on the bench.

"No. It means bear in Cherokee, the language of my people."

"How can that be?"

Chase sat down next to Tessa until Yona emerged from the park, this time leading an older woman who carried a medical bag.

"What did you say to him?" Tessa asked.

"I asked him where I could find a doctor, in Cherokee. I have no idea if he understood me or not."

"Chase, the excitement, this place—it has you upset and confused."

"You're probably right. This"—he let the baby go back to her—"just made me relive that night long ago when I lost so much."

Yona tried leading a woman to them, but she would stop and check an injured person. She resisted until he pointed their way and made a great number of hand gestures. Whatever he said made her squint their way.

Chase studied them as they approached, transfixed by the woman. He rose slowly to his feet.

The woman was skinny, dressed in baggy pants and a long black tunic. Her hair, black peppered with a great deal of gray, fell over her shoulders in two long braids. She didn't resemble the Chinese, considering how dark her skin was and the shape of her cheekbones.

"How can this be?" he whispered.

The woman stopped some ten feet from him and blinked in disbelief then covered her mouth as if shocked. A wail of pain escaped from deep inside her.

"Chase? Do you know her?"

He took a step toward the woman. "She's my mother." He wanted to cry out her name, but the words stuck in his throat. Then she was running to him, crying, with outstretched arms. Catching her tiny body up in his arms, he lifted her feet off the ground.

CHAPTER 29

"Let's take a peek at you, little one." Chase's mother, Nora, placed the baby on a diaper-changing station she kept in her small house at the orphanage in case she needed to keep an eye on a baby throughout the night. "Then I will bathe her to make sure there isn't something I missed. I knew I would see you again, my little ka-ma-ma."

Chase translated for a very confused Tessa. "That means butterfly."

"It pleases me you have not forgotten your native tongue or the language of your youth." His mother lifted the baby and carried her to a plastic tub of warm water in the kitchen sink. Let's get all this off you," she cooed. She refocused on Tessa. "There is a shower in there." She nodded toward a door. "I want you clean to examine. Chase, can you bathe my little granddaughter while I get my new daughter-in-law some clean clothes?"

"I've done harder things," he admitted, stepping up for the job.

"And I want to hear all about that. Come with me, Tessa. I'll get you some clothes."

Chase whispered to his wife, "Answer no questions. I don't trust her."

"She's your mother."

"And she's more Chinese than American by now. Who knows what has happened to her over these years? She could easily turn us in to protect whatever is going on here. Nothing important as to why we're here or what we do. Understand?"

Tessa faked a smile as his mother rejoined them.

"I'll be right back to help you, Son." She sighed. "It feels so good to finally say that again."

The damage from the earthquake was localized. Most of Wuwei had not suffered more than you'd feel in a slight aftershock. Two people were missing and almost one hundred people had been hospitalized, most of whom had already received treatment and been released. Chase realized again how lucky they'd been to escape a horrible tragedy. If not for the young man, Yona, this could have turned out differently.

Yona had come and gone in the house a number of times, recognizing the young man was older than he'd originally believed. Each time he came in, he appeared to be measuring Chase carefully, as if surprised he was still here.

"Who is the kid?" he asked his mother after examining Tessa.

She patted Tessa on the arm and pushed curls away from her face. "You had a cut on your head. I cleaned it. Have you had a tetanus shot?"

Tessa assured her she had.

"Very good. I don't have any antibiotic cream."

"I have some in my backpack. We were told it would be a good idea," Chase admitted.

Yona came in once more and whispered something to Chase's mother. "Yes, of course." She exhaled then hugged each of her guests. "He wanted to know if you would be staying for dinner. We have noodles and some cucumbers tonight. It isn't much, but very filling."

"We should probably get back to the hotel."

"Chase, no," she begged. "Don't leave me so soon. There is so much to say and to learn about you. Please. Besides, Yona says that the hotel restaurant is closed because of a gas leak, and part of the building was damaged. I doubt it will be fixed by nightfall, especially if the hotel had many guests. I beg you. Stay."

He shifted his attention to Tessa who held the baby. He was hoping for a way out or at least a little guidance since he didn't trust himself at the moment.

"I think that's a wonderful idea, Nora. Thank you. Besides, I'd love to hear about this little ka-ma-ma since you were at her orphanage."

"And I want to hear about my daughter. What is Christine doing since you left?"

How do you tell your mother that her daughter was murdered after surviving such a hard life in China? Or that her son had turned into nothing short of an assassin for the president's problems that needed solving with extreme prejudice? Would she want to see the scars on his body from the many misadventures he'd survived in his life? Most of those were mental.

"Oh, and what of your father's parents. Are they still alive? And of course, my father, my brothers, and where do you live?" She laughed happily and sat down in a wooden chair. She slapped her legs and pointed to Tessa. "And where did you meet this beauty? I want to hear about your family too, Tessa. Our families have become one." She reached out and pulled Tessa down into a chair next to her. "I am so happy." Tears flowed down her cheeks. "I prayed every day that God would let me see my children one more time."

Chase came to stand in front of her and pulled the slim woman to her feet and wrapped his arms around her. "Mom. I'm sorry you had to live here alone all these years. I saw them shoot you and Dad. The monks came back to search for you and were given the news you didn't survive."

"Your dad died instantly," she said, putting her bony hands on his cheeks. "You are a big man like him." Then she ran her hands down his neck and down his arms. "But you are Cherokee like me. I am proud. Do you have pictures of Christine?"

"Not with me."

"Maybe you can send me some."

"Send you some? What are you talking about? I'm not leaving you here. You're coming home," he said in astonishment.

"I cannot." Her voice was heavy with sorrow as she shifted her attention to Yona. "My work and home are here."

"No. Your home is in North Carolina. Your father needs to see you one more time. He is in his nineties. The whole family needs you, especially my family. We are moving not far from there soon.

What is so important you can't leave?"

"You don't understand."

"Explain it to me," he fumed.

Her eyes widened as if startled.

"I'm sorry, Mom. I just want to understand. You can't honestly believe I'd be okay with that."

Yona came to stand behind Chase's mom and leaned down to speak softly in her ear. "Are you leaving us?"

She patted his hand then timidly looked at Chase.

Chase pointed to the young man helping around the small house and wondered who this Yona person was to carry such an important name among his people. Why did his mother call him Yona? Was it to remind her of him, since that had been his nickname as a young boy? She used to say he reminded her of the black bears that roamed the Great Smokey Mountains, her home.

He leveled a hard look, he was known for, with the young man. It caused him to stop and lay a hand on his mother's shoulder. His mother, unaffected by his rising temper, reached over to touch his wife's hands that held Lotus securely. She rocked back and forth to lull the baby to sleep. Chase thought maybe he was dreaming. Could this be yet another nightmare? He decided to just concentrate on Tessa, his anchor to all things normal. She seemed to sense this was getting the best of him and sent a silent signal with her warm eyes to calm down.

"Yona, thank you again for helping us. Without you, I may have lost my wife and child."

Yona nodded, but did not offer a comment.

"You knew I was Cherokee. I think you knew who I was." Chase tried to sound even-toned instead of like an interrogator.

Again, Yona bobbed his head and patted the bony shoulder beneath his fingertips. "Growing up, she spoke to me in Cherokee. Said she prayed every day you would return so that she could see you one more time. She had a picture of your father and said you might resemble him except for the color of your skin."

"Most of the pictures were destroyed in the village where we lived. The one I had was damaged in the fire. I could only guess how you might change," she said. "So, I taught him our native tongue and called him Yona. If you came, hearing the name would bring you to me." She reached over and lifted the baby's hand to kiss. "And to think my youngest son brought you to me is such a blessing."

Chase could feel his chest tighten as he shifted his attention to Yona then his mother. Now he could see it. He wasn't full Chinese. His skin was darker, and the eyes were more rounded. "What are you talking about?"

"Yona is your brother." She gazed lovingly up at Yona as he bent to kiss the top of her head.

"Brother?" he said, confused. "What are you talking about?"

"I married your mother," a male voice came from a man in uniform standing in the entry doorway. He removed his hat and carefully hung it on a hook next to the door. "Yona is our son." His voice lacked emotion as he raised his chin in what appeared to be stubbornness.

Tessa rose to her feet and grasped the back of Chase's arm as he slid in front of her.

"You?" He jerked his head around to frown at his mother who rose and quietly went to stand next to Colonel Zhou Xiang.

Next, Chase focused on the second man coming through the door dressed in a traditional Chinese-style shirt. He was the colonel's older son, a good friend of Chase's growing up. The dark hair was longer than most Chinese men he'd seen so far. The wire-rimmed glasses failed to hide his menacing eyes leveled at him. The penetrating stare reminded him of the kind of confrontation he'd experienced with rebels, terrorists, and corrupt soldiers across the world.

It was difficult to measure the man's strength under the loose clothing. Although he was taller than his father, he did not match Chase's six-foot-one height. The only other man brave enough to level that kind of challenge to him was Tessa's ex-husband, Roman Darya Petrov, a wild tribesman from Afghanistan.

"What is he talking about, Mom?" Chase blurted as she took the colonel's hand in hers.

"He is my husband, Chase. Yona is our son."

She stepped in front of the oldest son, named Hao, his childhood friend. His eyes shifted to her. Slipping her arm around who might be an enemy, she gave him a slight squeeze then stepped away. Was she defusing a volatile situation?

"You have two brothers, my son. They have brought me great

peace and pride in their accomplishments."

"You sound Chinese," Chase said flatly, still keeping an eye on Hao, whose expression still remained sinister.

"That's because she is Chinese," Hao insisted. The voice was much deeper than he expected.

"She's an American." He shifted his attention to the colonel. "If you think I'm going to accept this, you're wrong. I was there when you shot down my parents with another officer. Then you stood over them and shot them again as they lay in the mud. How many others did you slaughter that night?" He walked up to the colonel and stood inches away from him.

The older son stepped closer, only to be pushed back by his father.

"After all my parents did for you," Chase growled.

"Stop it," his mother ordered. "I know you were terrified that night. What you saw and the reality are two different things. Zhou saved my life, that night."

"I was there. He shot you." He continued to snarl at the colonel. "My father saved your son when his appendix burst. My mother nursed him back to health because your wife died. And then you turn on them?" His voice had morphed into an intimidation tactic he used on enemy combatants, but he was careful to keep it low. You never knew who might be listening.

The colonel's nostrils flared. "I did not kill your father. Colonel Sun Li, now a general, did that."

"And my mother?"

"He did shoot me, but in the leg. I fell next to your father. He died instantly, as I told you." His mother rubbed the colonel's arm. "That awful man sent Zhou to shoot us again to make sure we were dead. He kneeled down by your father…" Her voice caught in her throat.

Colonel Zhou broke his hypnotic intimidation tactic at Chase to put his arm around his wife, Nora Hunter. "Your father had the death stare. I knew he was gone. But I saw your mother's fingers withdraw from your father's hand when she opened her eyes. Since I was given the task to shoot your parents again, I shot your father two more times. To do that to the man I respected haunts me to this day. But I knew he was at peace. Sun Li believed I'd shot both your parents. I was put in charge of mopping up his mess."

"Zhou took me to his home in Wuwei and took care of my leg." She reached back and pulled the grim-looking soldier forward. He finally smiled down at her then returned to a sour expression once he connected to Chase.

"My son and I searched for you and your sister," Zhou admitted. "But the monks didn't trust me after being at the village where so many had been hurt or killed. They believed I was trying to trick them when we told them your mother was alive." He sighed and crossed the room where his other son stood stoically. "But you were gone. The monks said they didn't know if you survived or reached Tibet via the emergency route your parents had planned. They had much to lose. Several of the monks lost their lives when Sun Li sent soldiers to get answers."

"You killed them too?" Tessa said, putting her hand on her heart.

"I did not. I tried to warn them, but they would not listen. The next time the soldiers came, I had time to warn them."

"I was heartbroken," his mother admitted. "I lost all that was dear to me. Having me in his home put Zhou and Hao in danger too. I prayed they would be spared because of their kindness."

"And your mother's prayers were answered," Zhou Xiang said matter-of-factly. "Then Sun Li was promoted and transferred. He and I did not see eye to eye on how to deal with the people of Wuwei and surrounding communities like your village. He left me behind. Six months later, I was in charge and promoted. A year after your father's death, I asked your mother to marry me. It was in name only. My son needed a mother to watch over him. I had to be gone so much that I worried he would get into trouble. I felt responsible for her unhappiness. I needed to know she would have a home until I could figure out a way to send her back to the States."

"So, what happened? You decided to help yourself to my grieving mother?" Chase's words released like venom.

Tessa came to his side and pulled him away from his new stepbrother. "Chase, that's enough. Let them explain. You weren't here. They're trying. This can't be easy for them either. Please."

"Okay. I'm listening. This is all just a lot for me to take in. If I had known you were alive, if Grandfather Hunter had known, he would have pulled out all the stops to rescue you."

"Once Sun Li found your mother was alive, I was blacklisted. That was another reason I asked her to marry me. It was a way to protect her. Then, one day when I returned home from a two-week deployment, I found her laughing with my son. They were playing some kind of game. I realized in that moment how much I loved her. She let me pull her up from the floor where she sat with my son. When my arms went around her, she told me how glad she was that I had returned home."

Tessa sighed. "Aww. That's so romantic." Chase glowered at Tessa, causing her to blush and whisper, "Sorry."

"Chase, I don't have to justify what I did to survive to you." His mother's voice grew stern as her body went rigid. "I never thought I'd find love again after losing your father. But I did. I wasn't much older than you are now when I discovered I was pregnant with Yona. I began putting my life back together and have lived as God planned."

"You think God planned to separate us? Because if He did, no wonder I have a hard time with all this religion stuff. Do you think God planned for your daughter to be murdered if we had stayed together as a family and gone home together?"

"Chase!" Tessa snapped.

His mother's mouth opened as her hands fell to her sides. "Christine is dead?"

"I'm sorry," Chase's voice softened when he stepped toward her. "I didn't mean to tell you this way. Mom, I'm so sorry."

She turned and ran outside, the screen door slamming behind her.

Everyone focused on Chase with anger and looks that could kill. He hung his head and shook it with disgust. When the whisper of the baby girl drew his attention, he took her from Tessa.

"I am sorry for your loss, Chase," Zhou said quietly. "You and I must talk more about this, but please, go talk to your mother. Then come talk to your brothers. You must stay here tonight. It is not safe on the streets with cleanup crews, debris in the roads, and so many people choosing to sleep on the streets tonight until their homes are secured. There have been a number of aftershocks."

"Thank you, Colonel. I don't mean to sound ungrateful."

The colonel bowed slightly. "I know. Please. Go talk to your mother. She has prayed for this day since that awful night. Do not spoil her joy. She is a good woman and has been a gift to these people."

Tessa took the baby again and tilted her head toward the door. Hesitation slowed his exit into the tiny yard that smelled of wet grass and herbs. His mother's shoulders shook in sadness, her head bowed in prayer or perhaps under the weight of being despondent. He finally had a second chance at dissipating a nightmare that had plagued him for years.

He moved closer to touch her shoulder until she turned toward him. Those lovely dark eyes, like his own, glistened with tears. Tessa's kids had made him a father. The thought of losing them was beyond his comprehension. His fingertips touched her smooth brown face, and she covered them with her own wrinkle-free hand.

"Mom, there is something I've wanted to tell you for all these years."

A weak attempt at joy tried to crease the frown she wore. "What is it, my son?"

"I love you."

She fell into his arms as his body let go of the pain and agony that had shackled him for way too many years.

CHAPTER 30

The sound of the movie Robert rented for the kids kept getting louder. Rather than tell them for the hundredth time to turn it down, he decided to take his work to the bedroom. Rubbing his eyes, he momentarily focused on the lights of the city spilling their temptation through windows. A fleeting thought of Phoebe waiting anxiously for his call toyed with his senses, knowing how their togetherness would escalate. Blinking, he shook his head and refocused on the business at hand.

The salary was three times his current income. Adding in stipends, insurance, and club memberships, both in DC and California, made it closer to four times. Reading the job description, he'd decided he would be a glorified lobbyist influencing lawmakers and other political powerhouses to throw their support behind the Pacific Rim Consortium.

"What the hell for?" he asked out loud.

There was an entire page on him traveling to China to observe the culture and its progress over the last twenty years. He wondered why Taiwan and Japan were not included in his visit. Their names were listed as members of the consortium, along with the Philippines, Singapore, South Korea, and Australia. He found it curious that China was the only one trying to educate him on its importance.

His thoughts went back to the meeting earlier in the day. Something felt off. Maybe he was still reeling from the idea Phoebe was leading him on or that Heather had been hurt the previous night. Maybe it was because the others seated at the table weren't actually Asians but white men who looked like him. Rich white men at that.

Why him? His law business, a mix of family law and an occasional criminal case, dealt with IRS problems or retirement accounts. Several years earlier, he'd earned a great deal of admiration for his work ethic and promised a lot of potential with his law firm. When he went solo, he spent a great deal of time building his client list but had yet to match his former salary. Thankfully, Tessa hadn't insisted on child support, which remained a mystery to him. He needed only to contribute to the kids' college fund and give her the house. Done.

He kept reading the fine print. The DC thing bothered him. In the initial interview, they'd asked a lot of questions about Tessa and her job. He reassured them, although divorced, they had a mutual-respect relationship. Were they concerned she had friends at the State Department? Or did they hope to use him to gain access to those friends of hers?

Walking to the windows, he drank in the glitz and false hopes of a city and found himself wishing he could discuss this with Tessa. Always Tessa.

Why had he screwed things up so badly? There had been a time when he couldn't wait to be her everything. He'd developed a habit that ignored what she needed and took advantage of her goodness. Never did he count on her strength to stand on her own.

Even though he knew something was amiss with her the last few years, secrets she never shared, he didn't care enough to find out what they were. It never occurred to him she'd leave him. Even with Phoebe in the wings, all he really wanted was to talk to Tessa. What did she think? Would she miss him? What about the children? Did this sound like a good idea? Tell him what to do before he signed on the dotted line.

"Tessa," he whispered then closed his eyes against the distraction of the city below. Maybe if he took this job, she'd see that he really deserved her attention and respect. Maybe.

The chirp of his cell phone broke his reverie of days gone by, and he reluctantly answered.

"Phoebe. I was just thinking about you," he lied. "I wanted to take a break. Kids are restless. They've been wanting to go for a swim with the colorful lights at the Caribbean pool. Why don't you join us? Some adult company would be just the ticket for me."

"I'll order some snacks," she offered softly. "See you in thirty minutes. I'm just leaving a meeting at the downtown office. I miss you," she added.

"Ditto."

The phone call ended. Why didn't it feel this was real?

~ ~ ~ ~

Phoebe turned to her boss who had just stepped out of the shower. Wrapping a towel around his midsection, he ran his hands through his dark hair while gawking at her.

"I need to go. Robert sounds a bit melancholy. I'm meeting him at the resort."

His eyes narrowed as he pulled her closer. "I hope he's worth it. I don't like competition, Phoebe."

Jerking the towel away as he pressed against her, caused her to catch her breath. "Trust me, he isn't who you should be concerned about." Taking a deep breath, she reluctantly stepped away. "Once we give him work to do, and he sees his first paycheck, he'll be too busy to have much time for me. Will that make you happy?"

"You act a little too fond of him for my liking. Text him and say you're running late." He pulled her robe open and began kissing her on the neck then worked his way down her body.

~ ~ ~ ~

Chase and his mother were deep in conversation as baby Lotus began to fidget and fuss. Tessa tried bouncing her while digging in the backpack to get her some formula.

"Let me help you," Hao, Zhou's oldest son offered as he reached into the backpack. Hearing his voice quieted Lotus. He reached for her. "Let me hold her. I think she remembers me."

"Of course. I'll fix her bottle if you'd like to feed her." Tessa

211

had to admit her arms hurt from the fall, and exhaustion was quickly taking over her ability to think clearly. Yet, the excitement of finding Chase's mother and the discovery who her husband was kept her too anxious to try and sleep.

"Father, could you make Chase's wife some tea?" Hao called.

The colonel stood at the screen door, engrossed in his wife and Chase's reunion. He failed to respond to Hao.

"I'll do it," Yona spoke pleasantly. "Do you like cream or sugar? I have heard Americans like it that way."

"No. Just tea will be fine. Thank you, Yona. I appreciate both of your kindness." She handed the bottle to Hao, who appeared to feel comfortable feeding her while standing.

Yona bowed his head then moved to the kitchen area that joined the tiny living room. She turned her attention to Hao who cooed at the baby. "Did you help your mother at the orphanage?" She tickled the baby's feet and received a giggle and a kick.

"Sometimes. This one was special."

"How so?"

"She grieved for her mother and was very upset most of the time. We all took turns holding her and trying to comfort her fears."

Hao's eyes met hers. There was nothing shy about his attention as they narrowed and reminded her she should be careful, even if he was family. Something about him warned her he might be dangerous. Was it the lift of his chin or the fierce way he studied her with open interest? Stepping back, she took a deep breath.

"Were you in the army?"

"Once. But it has been a while. I sometimes help my father."

That's when she noticed his hair reached his collar. "What do you do besides help your father?"

"Are you interrogating me?" he asked cooly as he bounced the baby.

"No. I mean—I'm just interested. Chase mentioned a friend from when he was growing up. I didn't know that…"

"My father protected his mother from being killed. Because of that, it has not been easy for us. Whether Chase believes it or not, my father loves her and would die for her if necessary. We all would."

Tessa flinched at his harsh tone. "I'm sorry. I'm just trying to understand, Hao. I believe what you say. I meant no disrespect."

His features softened. "We have a garden next door. Do you feel up to seeing it? Tomorrow you will be very sore. Maybe some fresh air will do you good. Bring your tea, and we can sit and enjoy the small fish pond Yona made."

"I never say no to a garden. Let's go," she answered enthusiastically. No way did she want to make an enemy so soon. Even so, she couldn't help but be leery of being with a strange man who held her baby. But Chase was nearby if she got into trouble.

"You are uncomfortable with me," Hao observed as they sat down on a bench near the rocky pond. "Why are you afraid?"

"Because of your father, I guess. And, well, everything is just so unexpected. Chase rarely spoke of his life here. I think it was too painful." She shrugged. "This kind of changes everything."

"My father says your passport identifies you with a different last name. Why?"

"Could we just talk about something else? Changing his name years ago seemed prudent since he once lived here. His grandfather suggested it." Lying to him felt wrong. He nodded as if accepting her answer then chuckled at Lotus who had fallen asleep.

"Would you like to know more about Chase when we were growing up?"

"Let me guess—he was a rebel."

"Yes. We both were as was our other friend Wu. The three of us constantly got into trouble. I have not seen Wu for many years. He left the day of the massacre…" His voice trailed off. "I lost two best friends that night. To this day, I don't understand why the soldiers wanted Chase's parents killed. My father also refuses to talk about it."

"I got the impression your father was searching for someone— maybe us."

He shrugged. "Maybe. You can ask him yourself." He handed her the bottle and placed the baby on his shoulder. "I am glad to know Lotus has a good home to go to."

Tessa straightened. "How did you know her name was Lotus?"

CHAPTER 31

"Good news," Phoebe chattered matter-of-factly as she studied her manicure. "Robert is signing the contract. We had a long chat last night, and I managed to clear up any concerns he had about working with us. He wondered why China was the lead on this and not some of the other Pacific Rim countries, Japan in particular. He was also concerned that North Korea played a part in this. I assured him it was mutually exclusive to all the Pacific Rim countries and that Washington was in agreement. I gave him a few names to contact if he needed verification."

"I've got another call coming in from China. I think we're zeroing in on Tessa and Chase Hunter. My last contact said they had the baby and were being monitored closely. Call you back in a bit."

"Speak." She propped the phone between her ear and shoulder as she dug in her handbag. There was a pause. Next came the sound of traffic noise in the background, along with voices and crying babies. "Well?"

"There's been an earthquake. The target is missing along with her escorts."

Phoebe pulled the phone closer and asked the contact to speak again. When she absorbed the shock of the information, she fumed at the person on the other end. "Maybe they're dead. What's the problem?"

"Our tour guide said they were staying at another location since our hotel was slightly damaged and there's no restaurant. We were supposed to take a train back to Lanzhou tonight then a plane to Guangzhou to the American consulate to get the babies sworn in as American citizens. That has been delayed while the authorities inspect railroad lines for problems."

"What about taking a plane?"

"Flights are few and far between out of Wuwei. We've been told our best bet is a train. Are you sure this is your target? They seem so normal—like us."

"Well, you aren't normal people, are you? You knew what you were signing up for when you agreed to do this. You have a fat bank account because of it."

"But—"

"No buts," she huffed. "Do your job, or that baby you're toting around will go back to the orphanage or perhaps become sick with the same virus other Chinese children in America are suffering."

"That is cruel."

"Better decide right this instant, or I can easily have you accidently step in a sinkhole after an earthquake."

"No problem. I'll keep an eye on them. I want this baby."

"And we are footing the bill for you to be a parent plus a little extra. So, next time you call me, you'd better make sure you have information instead of whining about a guilty conscience. Understand?"

"Yes."

Phoebe clicked off and closed her eyes to compose herself in the rooftop garden of her condominium building. The sound of water dripping from several Zen-inspired fountains calmed her long enough to relax from the strain of dealing with stupid people.

"Problem?" came a male voice behind her.

She turned slowly to see her uncle. "Dr. Wu. I didn't hear you enter the garden."

"So, it would seem." He walked to the edge of the roof and calmly observed the area over the iron railing to the street below. "It is a long way down."

Phoebe shivered. "Why are you here?"

"Checking on your well-being. It appears you are playing with fire again, and I would hate for you to get burned."

She came to stand next to him. "I am doing my job. I can serve China and the US."

"You cannot. You must choose."

"And what do you choose, Uncle Wu? Sorry—Dr. Wu?"

"That is none of your concern. This is my home. I have a life here. It is a delicate balance."

"You play both sides against the middle, just like me and so many others."

He slowly moved away from the edge as if he were admiring the garden. Phoebe followed.

"Tell me, Dr. Wu—how have you accumulated so much wealth with just being a doctor and teacher at a university?"

Wu's thin smile unnerved her. "Investing in the things that are important."

"It's my understanding that you are a double agent and make it a point to turn some of your more important patients into robots for the greater good of China."

His lips thinned to a straight line but he said nothing.

"I, on the other hand, am just trying to connect people with others to make money. That is the American way. Wonder what would happen if word got out about your methods?"

"That is something you will never know."

"And why is that—dear, dear uncle?"

Amusement filled his eyes. "Because you would be dead."

"You would kill a family member?"

"No. But I have disowned you. So, whatever you're up to, stop. This is your final warning. I don't want my life disrupted because you are careless and a greedy, self-indulged child. This Robert you are grooming is not a good fit for this Pacific Rim job you have managed to secure for him. Why him?"

"I'm not sure I should tell you," she hissed then thought better of it when his gaze iced over. "Okay. Here it is. Robert's ex-wife has contacts in Washington. From what I gather, she also has the ear of the president. The State Department uses her from time to time to gather data. Nothing big, just small stuff. I convinced the consortium that it could lead to bigger things if she thought her family could benefit or maybe—be at risk."

Wu raised his chin and pretended to study the sky. "I see."

"I'm glad you do."

"I see that you are a fool. If you had done your homework, you would know that woman is married to a very dangerous man who would rain terror on us like no one has ever seen if something should harm her. Her interactions, though innocent and nondescript, have managed to endear her to powerful people. It is too risky."

"I have that covered. Once we get control of the shipping channels in the Pacific, we can move in on Taiwan and take charge of the microchip industry. Things are falling into place, Uncle. I have found the baby with the key to saving the sick adopted children from China. If we destroy the child, the world will be focused on finding a cure, not the stealth movements of taking over the Pacific."

"And what makes you think you have found the child?"

"I have a contact in the group of parents with Tessa and her husband, Chase Hunter. Turns out, he is known in certain circles there and may be seeking his own form of revenge on the men who killed his parents. I have that on good authority as well. The child they were given is the child of the scientist who can make a new vaccine."

"You would let Chinese children die for your own personal gain?" he asked calmly.

"For China's gain. Not my own."

"But you would benefit."

"And you could as well, Uncle Wu—I mean Dr. Wu. Besides, you've been on the edge of respectability a lot longer than I have. Admit it."

"This is your last warning. Robert Scott is a time bomb, and I want no part of it."

"Very well." She pouted. "I will do as you wish."

Wu turned and walked away from her. Once she heard the rooftop door close, she pulled out her phone again and dialed her boss. It rang only twice.

"Yes?" came the voice of her boss.

"You need to report a traitor to the FBI. Do it today."

~ ~ ~ ~

Tessa blinked nervously at Hao and waited for him to answer. "Hao, how did you know her name was Lotus?"

"My mother called many of the babies by that name depending on the day of the week or month they were found. It is a common name."

Tessa zeroed in on his voice for the first time. Something about it made her feel uneasy. Was it that or the chord of familiarity in his voice?

"I like how your eyes turn violet when you are angry." He leaned in to get a closer look, forcing her to take a step back. "I did not notice this earlier…" The corners of his mouth tilted up slightly.

"Earlier? Earlier than what?"

"I apologize. My English is lacking at times. I meant when we first came home to find you here. I was not standing close to you but I sensed your anger."

"Oh. You and your father did frighten me. I was terrified actually."

"It was not our intent. My mother and brother mean everything to me."

"Will you sacrifice our safety for theirs?"

"I understand the Red Dragon would not like harm to come to you, Tessa." His eyebrow arched as his eyes narrowed. After passing her the baby, he stood and let his eyes roam over her hair and face. "I must find your husband. We should talk. There is much to discuss and plan for your safe return to America."

"How do you know the Red Dragon wouldn't harm me? How do you know we have met?"

"I did not know. I have heard rumors that came to my father."

"Will the Red Dragon help us?"

"I cannot say for sure." His eyes softened as he continued to study her from head to toe. "I would not count on it."

CHAPTER 32

Dr. Wu returned to the resort later in the day to check on Tessa's children. He joined in a tai chi class, followed by a late lunch near the pool where he could see Robert and the three children. They knew him, of course, so he stayed back, not wanting to bring unnecessary questions that would be answered with lies. His main purpose was to see if Phoebe followed instructions, which he already knew was impossible.

Rather than check his watch, he used the position of the sun. He tipped the waiter for a salad that had seen better days and headed toward the circular drive outside the entrance to the resort. The sound of birds and rustle of dry flowers did little to give him peace at what most likely was going to happen. From the corner of his eye, he noticed security comparing him to what appeared to be a photo. Without hesitation, one of the security guards lifted a house phone and made a call. Yes. Soon, his life would change again.

A tourist pointed at three black SUVs coming through the stone gates flanked by stone saguaro cacti sculptures. Turning into the circle drive, they screeched to a halt as he turned to stride away slowly. The sound of opening car doors failed to hurry his steps. *What will be, will be,* he decided.

Hurried footsteps echoed behind him.

"Dr. Wu," a familiar voice called.

Yet he kept walking calmly away as if the name meant nothing.

"Damn it, Wu, halt!"

More hurried footsteps, and this time he glanced over his shoulder to see four FBI Agents swarming in his direction followed by an older, more determined agent.

"Don't make me shoot you, Wu," came the familiar voice as he circled around to confront him.

Wu narrowed his eyes and measured the abilities of the young agents as his body gauged the outcome of his attack on them.

"I am unarmed, Agent Dennis Martin." He spoke calmly as he charted his next move.

"What the hell have you gotten yourself into?"

It was intuitively obvious to Wu that Agent Martin was the only one of these men who comprehended the seriousness of what a threatening move toward him could mean. "I repeat. I am unarmed and therefore no threat to you."

A smirk toyed with the corner of Agent Martin's mouth. The man was familiar with Wu's ability to take out the other four and leave his self-respect in place.

"I want you to put your hands behind your back, Dr. Wu."

"With all due respect, Agent Martin, I will not do that. What do you suspect me of doing?"

"Espionage. Money laundering. Oh, hell. A bunch of other stuff I don't want to get into out here in front of God and everybody."

Several people were recording him on their phones which were seized by a capable agent left back at one of the cars. "The Scott children are inside with their father."

"I sent two agents in an hour ago to make sure they didn't wander out and see their mother's best friend getting hauled off in handcuffs."

"I am grateful, Agent Martin." His head tilted slightly as he once again measured the men who had their weapons pointed at him.

Only Agent Martin stood at ease, dangling handcuffs off his index finger like a piece of fine jewelry. "You're not going to try some of that kung fu crap, are you? I really hate that stuff." When Wu did not respond, he continued, "How about I toss these to you, and you slip them on so no one gets hurt."

"I'm inclined to say—no."

Agent Martin sighed and chinned a signal to the other four who rushed Dr. Wu like bulls in a china shop. One by one, he put them down easily. If they tried to stand, he landed a sidekick or punch to the kidney, rendering them helpless. The moaning, embarrassed Agent Martin exhaled and pinched the bridge of his nose. Several other agents jumped out of the cars and headed for the fray, only to have Agent Martin raise his hand for them to stop.

"Guess I'll have to add assaulting a federal agent to that bad-boy persona you just demonstrated." He motioned for Wu to join him, but he did not. "Okay. I'll come to you if you have no objections."

Dr. Wu turned his back toward the agent and placed his hands behind him. "Thank you for not shooting me, Agent Martin. You are a wise man."

He turned him around to face him. "I get that all the time. Let's go, Bruce Lee."

A great deal of nervous activity followed them to the second SUV when another agent opened the door for them. Dr. Wu peered in first then turned to Agent Martin. "I see you brought back up."

"Get in the car," a temperamental voice ordered.

Dr. Wu slid inside with Agent Martin moving to the passenger side in the front.

"Dr. Wu, was it necessary to disable all those men and crush their confidence?"

He turned his hands to get the cuffs removed and, once free, he rubbed his wrists. "Director Benjamin Clark, I am pleased to see you. And how are things going at Enigma?"

~ ~ ~ ~

The smell of rain perfumed the air. Heat lightning flickered in distant clouds resembling a light show he'd seen in St. Louis long ago. Chase had made peace with his mother; she had to survive. Hadn't he done things to survive? To all appearances, Colonel Zhou Xiang had taken good care of her and brought the light back to her eyes and life. Knowing he had a brother, complicated things. When Director Clark told him there was a family who needed to escape, he had no idea it would turn out to be his mother and her new family. Apparently, she hadn't known anything about it. The question circling in his head: Did the director know his mother was alive all this time?

"Let's sit down and talk about this, Chase." Zhou pointed to the table on wobbly legs. He made a mental note to fix it before he left.

"Why escape at this time? Surely, you had ways of leaving the country?"

"I did. But I was never able to take your mother with me." He reached over and took her hand. "Hao was in the army for a time and he traveled, but if he strayed too far, there were questions." Shifting his eyes toward Yona, he continued. "My youngest son will soon be serving active duty in the army."

"I thought China had gotten rid of that practice."

"Males in China between the ages of eighteen and twenty-two must register for twenty-four-month compulsory service, but enough volunteers exist that no draft of compulsory service was enacted. Even so, we were notified six months ago that Yona needed to report to begin his service. I believe it to be a way to control me. General Sun Li despises me and knows I can expose him at any time. This has been the only way I have been able to protect my family."

"How were you able to reach out?"

"Two ways. We agreed to take Lotus in the event that Dr. Jun Hie needed to escape quickly. That time came, unfortunately, when he was working in the lab in Wuwei. He knew me many years ago and was a friend to a Dr. Wu in the States. He was sure the man could help him once there. Wu is a common Chinese name and I had no reason to believe it was the boy that was part of your life. I lost contact with his family the night they escaped."

"You knew of Jun Hie's work on the virus?"

"I knew he was working on something important for the government. I did not piece it together until he left and the news leaked out about the China children dying of some unknown virus. But I believe the CIA and the FBI had intervened in that operation to get Jun Hie out of China only because he managed to inform the proper people. I made a deal to take my family to America for helping in the event Lotus would need to escape without her parents. By leaving Lotus with us, her parents were assured she would be returned to her rightful parents."

Tessa stroked the baby's head and sighed. She'd fallen in love with a child she couldn't keep.

"Did they tell you who would come for Lotus?"

"I do not believe they had that information. The fewer people involved, the more likely she would remain safe."

"How did you know when to send her to Lanzhou for the handoff? Wasn't it possible that General Sun Li found out and waited for her?"

"There was no guarantee, of course. That's why I showed up there. I wanted to make sure she got to the right people. When I saw you, I did a little digging."

"You recognized me after all these years?" Chase eyed him suspiciously.

A narrow smile crossed his lips as his eyes diverted to his wife who was lifting the baby from Tessa's arms. "You resemble your mother. I heard you speak Chinese as well. Of course, the general had already received word someone had found the child and there was a good chance it was you because you had the background and training to pull off such a feat."

"And you didn't tell me?" Nora frowned and withdrew her hand from his.

"I wanted to be sure. Giving you false hope when both of us believed your children died during the escape was too cruel to chance it. Forgive me."

"Someone in the States tipped him off?"

"Yes. I know it was someone you know. A person with connections. The general has plans to visit me any day. He doesn't trust me and I have too much to lose to stay. It is time we leave."

"And you had no idea I survived the crossing into Tibet all those years ago?"

He shook his head and frowned as he dredged up the past. "I was so ashamed of that night. I tried to warn your parents they must leave. They assured me they would—but they waited one more day. Even I did not know Sun Li moved up the timetable."

"And what of the Wu family. Did they know?"

"Yes. Of course. I also contacted them because they had worked so closely with your parents and traveled with them to the various villages selling their healing herbs. I told them your parents were leaving and would join them in Hong Kong."

"So, Wu didn't know we were in danger?"

"I cannot say for sure because he was working in Wuwei at his job. The family took nothing with them. When I checked on their whereabouts several days later, they were gone. The neighbors said that young Wu argued with his parents about making sure all of you had left, and they assured him you had."

The contempt and disrespect he'd shown Dr. Wu all these years flashed before his eyes. "I'm not sure I believe he was so innocent."

Hao interrupted. "Believe it. He was in love with your sister and wanted to make sure she wouldn't be harmed."

"In love? She was fourteen."

"He didn't tell you because he knew how protective you were of her. He was seventeen, I think. He even got up the courage to tell your father his plans to marry her when she was of age. He promised to finish medical school and provide for her." Hao laughed. "She had followed him around like a puppy since she was eight years old. I wondered if he knew she survived the crossing."

A flashback of how his sister had run to him after they reached Hong Kong finally made sense. Why had he not come to him later when she entered college? Did he know she had died? Was that why he had never married? His hatred for Wu had always clouded the ability to make a connection as he had with the other team members.

"He knew," he growled. The group grew quiet as they avoided eye contact. "I need some air." He addressed his mother when he remembered the lesson his father taught him. "Thank you for a good meal, Mom. It was delicious."

She blew Chase a kiss when the baby reached up and patted her cheeks. Pushing through the screen door into the dark yard, he heard his mother tell Hao to join him to reconnect. Chase wasn't sure he wanted any part of that. Although Hao had not participated in the massacre or warned him, he mostly likely hadn't known what was coming. When Hao's father was away, he spent nights with the Hunters. He remembered Hao had been excited a few days earlier that his father was home and wouldn't be around until he left again. Hao's father planned taking his son fishing and to practice archery while he was home on leave.

"I guess we are finally brothers," Hao teased, arriving at his side. "Then again, I thought of you as my brother when we were kids. Your mother was my mother even then."

Silence welled up between them until Chase shook his head in confusion. "I thought the same of you, Hao. But your father…"

"It feels like a betrayal," he said coolly.

"Yes. Why didn't he reach out to my grandfather? He was a diplomat and could have brought my mother home."

"I have asked myself the same thing many times. Your mother was very ill after the attack, and we believed she would not survive. A doctor who admired your parents secretly came to treat her. It has been the only time I saw my father pray."

"Pray? Your father?" Chase snorted. "I find that hard to believe."

"Me too since it was the only time I witnessed it. I was a kid and worried we'd be found out. So I didn't ask about it. From what little I've managed to piece together, my father converted privately and promised to protect your parents and the work they did while he served God undetected. This, I only found out after Lotus became part of the picture and my little brother was drafted into the army."

"And what do you think about leaving China? Will you come?"

"And what would I do there? America blames us for COVID, and we have heard how violence against Chinese Americans has been increased. I speak English poorly and have a short temper."

"So, I remember." Chase chuckled. "Mostly when I beat you at stick fighting and sword play."

Hao joined him in the laughter. "I have missed you, Brother. And my father tells me you are a real warrior for your country. What does that mean?"

"I was an Army Ranger and a Delta Force officer."

"Ah. You have fought the demons in your life for many years."

"True. And you? Not married at your age?"

"I have little to offer a wife. You have a pretty wife, Brother. Keep her close. Some men would take her for their pleasure, and you would never find her."

Chase sobered. His old friend had lost his friendly demeanor. "Someone like you?" Hao didn't answer. "Mark my words, I will kill any man who touches her and threatens her happiness. She is an innocent caught up in a series of terrible tragedies involving baby girls from this country. Her heart forced her to come and find Lotus. We will leave tomorrow to rejoin our group."

"Your group left hours ago for Lanzhou." Hao's attention shifted to the lighted kitchen and Tessa standing at the door. "Guess my father forgot to mention that."

"I thought the trains were down."

"Turned out to be more of a problem to the north. They should be nearing Lanzhou." He continued to watch Tessa outlined in the doorway. "We are happy to have you here."

"I'm going to find a way to Guangzhou in the morning. That is the final destination then we'll head home." Chase followed Hao's line of sight and noticed how lovely Tessa appeared between the shadows of light and dark. Lanterns were lit inside the house creating a soft glow. "Any suggestions about how I can get out of here, Hao?"

"Dig the well before you are thirsty."

"What the hell does that mean?" Chase moaned.

"Plan ahead. Prepare for the eventuality so when it occurs, you can avoid any unwelcome scenarios." Hao's attention did not deviate from Tessa as the evening breeze pushed through the screen to move her hair.

"What do you know of the Red Dragon?" Chase said cautiously.

"That he is dangerous and sees beyond the mountains set to block his way."

Chase pushed in front of him to block his view of Tessa, forcing him to shift his attention to him.

"If the Red Dragon touches my wife one more time, I will hunt him down and cut off his head."

"And it is said a dragon's treasure is not measured in gold, but in the warmth of its fire; a fire that burns from the heart."

"Meaning?" Chase didn't like where this was headed.

"Do not chase the dragon's tail; walk beside it and learn its dance. The dragon is not your enemy."

"Then he damn well better stay away from Tessa."

"I doubt the Red Dragon would listen to me—if I knew him."

"In that case, I'll give you your own advice."

"And that would be?"

"Prepare for the trouble so when it occurs, you can avoid any unwelcome scenarios. In other words, be careful." Chase turned back to see Tessa still standing in the doorway. "Just saying." With that, he gave a light punch to Hao's shoulder and joined Tessa in the kitchen.

CHAPTER 33

The three black SUVs sped through Palm Springs to a location in the desert where Dr. Wu had been staying since his arrival. The doors of the lead and last vehicles opened upon arrival. Several agents entered the premises as if they'd discovered some threat to national security. At the intensity of their pulled weapons and search, Dr. Wu wondered if he might have overlooked an obvious problem. A female agent returned to the middle car where he sat with Agent Dennis Martin who powered down his window.

"All clear, sir. No listening devices, cameras, or explosives."

Agent Martin grunted when he stretched his legs and stomped his feet after exiting the vehicle. He moved like a tortoise with a limp after having been given his freedom from captivity. The director of Enigma slid out on his side while Dr. Wu remained seated until Agent Martin opened the door for him.

The agent slipped on his sunglasses then leaned down to offer a pooched-out frown. He tilted his head for Wu to get out.

"Ya know, Wu, I always figured you to be the normal one of that Mad Max bunch at Enigma." Agent Martin slammed the door behind him then moved around the rear of the car to join the director. "I can't wait to see how you're going to get out of this." The agent offered a sinister chuckle and held up his hand. "I mean—you aren't going to get out of it, but it will be entertaining to see you try."

The director kept walking as he engaged the agent. "That's enough, Agent Martin."

"Thank you, Director," Wu spoke low and threatening.

But Agent Martin continued to grin at him, taunting him into becoming violent. It didn't happen.

"Leave us," the director ordered the FBI agents.

As they filed out of the house, Agent Martin stood his ground even though the director arched a stubborn eyebrow in his direction. He continued speaking to the director but he focused on Dr. Wu. "With all due respect, Director Clark, I'm not going anywhere, and you don't have the authority to tell me to get the hell out." He sized up Dr. Wu head to toe, when he put his hands on his hips, revealing a holstered weapon. "Besides, I would be remiss if I left an important man, like you, Director Clark, unprotected from a possible terrorist. Why, the president would never forgive me."

Dr. Wu took a step closer to the agent, who dropped his hands down at his sides and stiffened.

"Careful, Wu. I know you're lethal, and I won't underestimate you like the young agents you kicked ass earlier. And I won't hesitate to introduce you to Smith & Wesson." His voice had turned icy, his hand resting on his holstered weapon.

"Agent Martin, if I had wanted to harm you, I would have snapped your neck so fast you would have become a human Pez dispenser."

"Ha. Ha. Ha. Good one. So, you have a sense of humor. Must be smoking a little happy weed too. Guess a few more charges wouldn't hurt."

"Well, if Yosemite Sam and Bugs Bunny will dispense with the theatrics, maybe we can allow Dr. Wu to get back to business." The director poured himself a glass of saki he found in the refrigerator and gulped it down then gritted his teeth. "No wonder the Japanese lost the war," he mumbled as he examined the glass. "Sit down."

Both men complied. Dr. Wu admired the director and did not want to show disrespect. Agent Martin, however, was a federal bully, much like the other agents at Enigma. His loyalty to Enigma was in place only because he'd screwed up a security detail with President Austin a few years back and Enigma made it go away without him losing his job. The trade-off was he did whatever Enigma needed without question or complaint. That part had never happened. Dr. Wu desperately wanted to evaluate the man, but since he technically didn't work for Enigma, he couldn't request an interview.

"We wiretapped your niece's phone and—" Director Clark started.

"Technically, she is only my niece by an unfortunate hookup by a promiscuous relative on my mother's side of the family. I have disowned Phoebe."

"Your timing is suspect, Wu," chuckled Agent Martin. "Guess everyone has a black sheep in their family."

"Perhaps you'd like to discuss yours at some point, Agent Martin. I'm sure you have a lot to get off your chest. It could be very therapeutic."

"Tell ya what. I'll make an appointment when you're in federal prison. You probably won't be booked up or need to adjust your schedule to fit me in."

"Nobody is going to prison, Agent Martin," soothed the director. When the agent opened his mouth to protest, he glowered at him. "This is all very amusing, gentlemen, but let's get down to it. Chase and Tessa have been discovered by General Sun Li, which is what we did not want."

The director informed them of the unexpected discovery that Chase's mother was alive and well in Wuwei and had been the one caring for Dr. Jun Hie's baby girl. "Neither party involved knew of the relationship between Chase and the caretaker from the orphanage."

"She is alive." Dr. Wu sighed as he bent over and put his face in his hands.

The other two men remained silent as Wu tried to control his emotions, something he rarely needed to do. Finally, he lifted his head and leaned back in the chair. The director poured him some saki, and he gulped it down. "Such a coincidence is mind-boggling, Director Clark. Tessa would say angels were at work on this one."

"Agent Martin, I understand you may not know the whole story here, so I've prepared a file outlining the events of Captain Hunter's family and his connection to Dr. Wu." He pushed a file across the table."

"Director, may I have a moment?"

The director nodded.

Dr. Wu stood and moved toward the kitchen window. Outside lay the barren yet beautiful landscape with the mountains as a backdrop. Yet he saw a little village outside Wuwei where he fell in love, made two best friends, and learned the ways of the Shaolin. It had vanished in one night, and now he was informed someone survived.

Wu wasn't sure how long he stood there. Director Clark had grown sensitive to his people's feelings over the years, an improvement only since Tessa had joined the team. It pained him to think she was in danger.

Agent Martin came to stand beside him. "You okay?"

"I will be," he said coolly. "I take it you've read the file."

"Buddy, you tell me who you want me to arrest and consider it done. Hell, you want me to shoot 'em, I might even do that."

Dr. Wu pursed his lips together as if resisting a smile then placed his hand on the agent's back. "I'm afraid if you did that, then you'd have to be my social secretary in federal prison." He turned back to join the director in the other room. "Let's see how we're going to fix this."

"To continue, after wiretapping your—ex-niece's phone, we learned that someone in the adoptive parents' group that travel with Chase and Tessa is working with the Chinese. They have been able to track the group from the beginning."

"How did the Chinese know to do that?" asked Agent Martin.

"We believe there were several groups being tracked, but this one had a couple leaving from Plano, Texas, which has a large Asian population. After backtracking their internet history and whereabouts over the last six months, we inadvertently discovered they had a number of contacts with people of concern, under surveillance. One of those contacts was Phoebe. Dr. Wu was able to fill in some blanks for us."

Dr. Wu caught Agent Martin up to speed about the job offered to Robert, along with the ultimate goal of the consortium. "It sounds like they believe they can have a better access to the State Department, and what better way to do that than to threaten Tessa's family. They, of course, have no idea who Enigma is or what they're dealing with."

"Also because of Phoebe's involvement with Robert," the director continued, "she was able to discover that Tessa worked for the State Department from time to time. Their hackers could have found out a number of things through Robert's sloppy internet footprint."

"She seduced him and, since he is still unaccepting of the divorce from Tessa and uses the kids as pawns, he was easy pickings for someone like Phoebe." Dr. Wu's shared frown deepened. "Robert has spilled his guts about Tessa and Chase on several occasions. Enigma became aware of the relationship about a month ago, and we began following areas of possible espionage."

"And what did little Miss Perfect think about the new girlfriend?" Agent Martin asked cynically.

The director leaned back in his chair. "I felt it wasn't anything to concern her with since Robert dates a lot of women. There was a chance this was just another fling to soothe his bruised ego. Chase is so protective over those kids that I decided to wait. It wasn't until Chase and Tessa left for China that we realized Phoebe posed a problem and planned to tag along on Robert's vacation with the kids in his care."

"I believe we should step in and let Robert know who he is dealing with, and get the hell out of Dodge." Agent Martin jammed his index finger into the tabletop. "Sooner rather than later."

Director Clark shoved a transcript of a phone conversation alerting the FBI of him, over to Dr. Wu. "She is the one who started the wheels rolling and turned you in, Dr. Wu. I'm sure you already suspected this."

Wu took a deep breath and exhaled slowly.

The director continued, "As a precaution, I have requested that the FBI post several of their agents in different capacities to make sure the children are safe and that Robert doesn't do anything—"

"Stupid?" Agent Martin snorted.

"I was going to say unexpected. But your choice of words may be a better fit. He has no idea what he has gotten himself into.

Therefore," the director continued, "Agent Martin, I want you to have what Tessa calls a 'come to Jesus' talk with him about his situation. I also want him to carry on as if he has no idea what is going on."

Dr. Wu interjected more information. "Use caution, Agent Martin. The men Robert saw at the board meeting are not the real board members. They prefer to stay off the radar and use satellite technology to observe the meetings."

"There is another hiccup I'm afraid." The director exhaled. "It appears that Chase's mother has remarried and had another child in that union." The director shifted his focus intently to Wu. "She married Zhou Xiang."

Dr. Wu clenched his fists on the table.

"Who is Xiang?" asked Agent Martin.

"The man Chase thought killed his mother. And this is the family wanting to leave China and come to America as political refugees. Xiang has a lot to offer us in the way of intel. There is still a lot to be discovered about his sudden change of status, but no doubt it has to do with Chase finding his mother. Dr. Wu, do you know anything about the Red Dragon?"

"A talented or powerful individual is often referred to as a dragon among humans, meaning, he is a leader of an exceptional group—perhaps workers or followers." Wu shrugged. "That person may be considered a head of a group of dragons. This is the year of the dragon in China. It is a powerful creature many revere. But in today's world, a man can pose as a dragon in spirit to claim power and recognition."

"Our concern is the trade corridor in the Pacific Rim."

"Considering the dragon holds immense symbolic power in Chinese culture, and represents imperial authority, the Chinese government might feel that this is the perfect time to exert its influence in that region and take control of the trade routes." Director Clark leaned forward in his chair. "And as you say, it is the year of the dragon."

"In the old days, dragons were closely tied to the emperor, and the throne was called the Dragon Throne. In the last year, there has been a greater visibility of pictures, stories, and symbolic references to dragons," Dr. Wu spoke matter-of-factly. "Who doesn't enjoy a good dragon story?"

"And this new Red Dragon? Chase says he is stalking them but only makes contact with Tessa."

Agent Martin chuckled and rolled his eyes upward. "That woman can get into more trouble. Is she in danger?"

"I'm beginning to think 'danger' is her middle name. It depends on the dragon," Wu admitted. "Dragons of long ago were good. There is plenty of evil in China these days. Chase knows all about dragons and their power. If the dragon makes a move to stop him with the child or tries to take Tessa, it is my guess we'll have a headless dragon to explain to the Chinese government."

"Damn, Wu. I didn't know you were so much fun." Agent Martin raised an eyebrow. "I bet you're a hoot telling bedtime stories to Tessa's kids."

"I have never been given the opportunity to tell her children bedtime stories of dragons of long ago."

"Why is that?" Agent Martin asked.

"Chase sees me as a dragon and has often hinted he dreams of beheading a dragon someday." This made him display a rare smile. "He just hasn't gotten around to it yet."

CHAPTER 34

The nice thing about a dry climate and a gentle breeze was one didn't mind the heat, especially while bellied up to a bar near a swimming pool that resembled a tiki hut somewhere they'd probably never visit. At least, that was Agent Dennis Martin's attitude as he sipped on his soft drink and pretended it wasn't watered down. He caught a glimpse of himself in the mirror behind the bar and felt amused at the image. Dressed in a tropical shirt and khaki shorts with aviator sunglasses to hide his roaming eye, he felt more like Magnum P.I. than an FBI agent.

The pretty new agent, wearing a black swimsuit, was stretched out on a lounge chair near the shallow end of the pool where Tessa's kids had joined a game of keep-away with other kids. Where were those honeybees when he was a young agent? He swiveled his barstool toward the area to keep tabs on his target.

Finally, Robert appeared poolside with a tray of burgers and fries then called for the kids to join him at a table with a turquoise umbrella. With laughter and a certain amount of shaking their wet heads like dogs at their father, their laughter floated across the open space. He pretended not to appreciate it but ended up joining in the fun when he pulled out a loaded squirt gun and blasted the kids in the face.

The agent wondered for the thousandth time what the hell Robert had done to tick Tessa off so bad she kicked him to the curb. It would have been just like that Enigma bunch to frame the sap to help with the shove out the door. They clearly wanted Tessa all to themselves since she was a magnet for the kind of trouble they craved and destroyed. It made their jobs easier.

On second thought, she deserved better anyway, not that Chase Hunter was a move in the right direction. But women tended to go for those macho types who played the bad-boy routine. And he was as bad as they got, in his opinion. He didn't begrudge the man for a little hero worship from a babe like Tessa. The entire Enigma clan were dangerous, and he just didn't want to see her get hurt. Even though he gave her a hard time, she'd become the closest thing to family he had.

"Three apple juices and a Dr. Pepper," Robert ordered. He tapped the bar with his finger and turned to check on the kids still giggling and throwing an occasional French fry.

"Fancy meeting you here," Agent Martin said as he lifted his drink with one hand like a toast then set it down on the bar.

Robert's eyes widened as he pulled his shoulders back. "Agent Martin. I—I didn't recognize you. On vacation?" he asked timidly.

"Actually, I'm working undercover," he said then tilted his head at the bartender who moved farther down the counter to serve another customer.

"Is he an FBI agent too?" He gawked in bewilderment as the man kept refocusing his attention their way.

"Oh yeah."

"Nothing dangerous, I hope. I got the kids this week." Then he thought better of his comment and soured. "Did that muscle-headed troglodyte, Chase Hunter, send you to spy on me? See if I was taking good care of the kids? He's the kind of guy who likes to emphasize each word with a blow to the head. I don't know what Tessa sees in that ape."

Agent Martin smirked and drained his drink. "Muscle-headed troglodyte… Hmm. I like it. I couldn't agree more."

"Really? I thought you guys were friends."

"Hardly," he chuckled. "I just pretend to like him because I got the hots for Tessa."

"Now, wait a minute," Robert snapped.

"Just yanking your chain, Robert." He landed a soft fist bump to his arm. "In my line of work, you make friends with the devil from time to time and, well, Captain Hunter is someone I have to deal with in that regard."

"Oh." He leaned in. "What exactly does Fred Flintstone do besides teach French Renaissance literature no one cares about? I mean, I know he served in the military, but—"

"Right. Once a soldier, always a soldier, I guess."

"That doesn't answer my question, Agent Martin."

"I think he helps out with Veteran Affairs and is a speaker about PTSD at those meetings. Goes down to Belize to help out at a camp for vets to heal. Comes across as a Boy Scout, you know. Makes the wife all giggly and swoon worthy." Making the ex irritated and uncomfortable was more fun for him than for Robert.

There were a few moments of uncomfortable silence as the bartender returned with the apple juice boxes and his soft drink. "Well, good luck with whatever you're here for." Robert was stepping away when Agent Martin propped an elbow on the bar.

"Why don't you deliver the drinks and come back for a chat."

"Got the kids. Need to keep an eye on them, or Tessa will have my hide."

"Yeah. Probably wouldn't like hearing about Heather having a fall when you were out trying to get laid by China's version of Mata Hari."

"Excuse me?" Robert froze.

"Deliver. The. Drinks, Robert. That pretty lady over there in the black swimsuit is one of my agents. She'll keep an eye on the kids after you eat your lunch. Then you come back over and let me explain how things are going to be for a couple of days. Don't tell the kids I'm here." He tilted his head. "They call me Uncle Dennis, you know. Think you can do that?"

"Is this some kind of a shakedown?"

"Shakedown? You've been watching too much TV, Robert. This is the freaking Federal Bureau of Investigation telling you to get your ass back here in ten minutes." He frowned. "Tick. Tock." He pointed to his watch.

~ ~ ~ ~

Tessa got up with Lotus several times during the night. Cuddling and humming a lullaby as she tiptoed through the small house had her resting after only a few minutes. But the activity of being the mom of a baby again left Tessa too exhausted to sleep.

The mattress was a double at best, and their bed at home was a king. Chase was a big man and required plenty of room even when he didn't toss and turn. And tonight, his restlessness had lasted far longer than normal. His concern about their safety, along with the sudden explosive revelation of finding his mother, weighed on him.

But she, too, felt restless. Her body hurt from falling in the sinkhole. Chances were good she would be hobbling around like an old lady by morning. After laying Lotus down in a dresser drawer made up as a temporary crib, she went to the living room area and let her eyes take in the yard. Soft rain pinged against something metal, and a low rumble of thunder rolled across the sky. The breeze coming through the open door quickly chilled her feverish body. The house was small and had no fans or air-conditioning. Putting her hands on each side of the doorframe, she closed her eyes and lifted her chin to feel the heat leave her body.

She didn't know how long she stood there, but mist began to tease her as the breeze increased. Sighing, she dropped her hands to her sides just as a flash of lightning lit up the yard. In that second of daylight, she caught sight of someone still as a statue. In the next burst of light, the figure began to walk toward her. In that instant, she recognized the clothes and the gait of the Red Dragon.

Grabbing the doorknob, Tessa slammed the door shut and locked it securely. Her heart pounded as she pivoted to press against the frame. She pushed off and hurried to check on Lotus when she ran into Chase's hard body. She circled his waist with her arms and held on tight.

"What is it?" he yawned. "What are you doing out here?"

"The Red Dragon." She looked back at the door. "He was standing in the yard watching me."

Chase pushed her aside and unlocked the door.

"No, Chase. Don't open the door."

Chase grabbed a fireplace poker and pulled the door open. He pushed the screen door open with his foot. Lightning again turned night into day as he flipped on the porch light. Backing into the living room, he locked up then faced Tessa. "I didn't see anything. Maybe it was just a bush moving or something blew through the yard."

Tessa hurried into the bedroom to check on Lotus who slept snug in her makeshift crib. Tears rolled down her face.

Chase wrapped his arms around her and kissed her temple. "It's been a long day, Tess. You were hurt and—"

"I could have died. Lotus could have died."

"But you didn't." He slowly turned her around. "You're traumatized with good reason and exhausted. Come lie down. I'll hold you until you fall asleep then I'll sleep on the floor so you can have more room. You're going to be sore in the morning. Okay?"

With a shiver, she climbed into bed and pulled him in beside her. "I miss our family. I want to go home. How are we going to get your mother there?"

"We're not."

"You're leaving her? But, Chase…"

"My first priority is getting you and Lotus back to the States. I'll come back for them."

"Come back?" she moaned. "They'll be waiting for you to do just that. I can't do life without you, Chase. Not anymore. You've given me a new beginning and I see how our life can be together. Find another way. Please."

Chase wrapped her in his naked arms and pulled her closer. "Xhou said he'd help me find a way to meet the rest of the group in Guangzhou." He ran his hand down her shoulder. "Sleep. The next few days are going to be hard in order to get out of here."

"Do you trust him?" She yawned.

"No. But he's the only option we have right at present." He rolled her onto her back then waited until her eyes closed. "I'll take care of Lotus if she gets up."

She nodded off. The woman could sleep through a hurricane. He had come to believe it was because she had a pure heart—and maybe an angel following her around.

When her breathing changed to a relaxed state, he stood and checked on Lotus. Her rosebud lips made sucking sounds. What a perfect little creature. He wanted to lift her up and carry her around, letting her finish out the night on his shoulder, but resisted.

Heather, Tessa's youngest affected him the same irrational way: a state of constant overprotectiveness and what-ifs. The boys were worrisome only because he knew what kind of mayhem boys could get into. They were often easy to outmaneuver and stop before the police got involved or amputation was required. But little girls were different. He came to stand over Tessa, and he saw her similarities to Heather: stubborn, manipulative, and dangerously beautiful with absolutely no idea how terrifying the world could be.

But something outside had frightened her. Was it the Red Dragon? Had he followed them to his mother's home? If so, why? Too many unanswered questions in this house and this trip as a whole. The sooner they got out of here and on a plane, the sooner they could put this baby situation behind them once and for all.

No matter what Tessa thought, he would return for his mother and take her home where she belonged. If the rest of the family wanted to come, he'd make it happen. If not, so be it. But, for now, he would get the two most important people in his life to a safe place.

Yona, his new brother, left him a little shell-shocked at the moment. He favored his mother rather than Zhou, his father. He had mixed feelings as to how he wanted to process the relationship. All this time, he'd hated Zhou Xiang because he believed he'd killed his mother.

The truth left him a little off-kilter. Ignoring Yona was easier than figuring out how to respond. Part of him wanted to believe he was just another Chinese person who helped them during a natural disaster. The truth disturbed him. Of course, he should come to the States. That might be the only way to get his mother to agree to return.

He strolled out to the kitchen/living room combo and pulled back a lace curtain to check the backyard. The rain had stopped, and the moon bounced along puffy clouds that appeared eerie and threatening. Movement caught his eye, when he refocused on two men standing near the back building connected to the property. Yona and his father had moved there so Chase and Tessa could have the main bedroom. His mother took Yona's twin bed in the second tiny bedroom. He wasn't sure where Hao spent the night, although his mother mentioned he did not stay with them.

The clock on the wall indicated the late hour. Pretty late to be having a family meeting. They stopped talking when something distracted them near the seven-foot gate entrance to the yard. They both took a step back from whatever was cloaked in darkness until a figure emerged dressed in dark clothing. He stood with his back to Chase, prohibiting any kind of recognition for later recall.

The figure emerged, but Zhou didn't appear to be frighten. Yona was pushed behind him. The young man reached around his father by putting his hands on each upper arm as he peered over his shoulder. Zhou pointed toward the gate and mouthed words Chase couldn't make out.

Should he make his presence known?

The door was easy enough to open without being noticed, but the screen door squeaked, causing the stranger to spin around to confront him.

It was the Red Dragon.

CHAPTER 35

The shadows hid the features of the Red Dragon. Tessa claimed he sometimes had worn a mask, but only part of his face appeared to be painted. Clearly, he didn't want anyone to know his identity. This was his first contact with the elusive Red Dragon.

"Chase, stay where you are," Zhou ordered, holding his hand out. "Please."

"Red Dragon?" Chase asked calmly. "I don't know what you want with us, but leave my wife and child alone. We are no threat to you."

When the Red Dragon spoke, Chase realized he wore a covering over his mouth to change his voice. The Red Dragon continued to speak in Chinese when he took one step closer. Chase dug in his heels and doubled his fists.

"You are causing much trouble among the people here." The Red Dragon stood with his feet apart like a man getting ready to attack.

"How can that be? I only just arrived."

"General Sun Li's devil soldiers search for you. People will get hurt if they do not hold the answers he wants to hear. He will soon come here to visit this man." He turned his head slightly toward Colonel Zhou. "His life could be in danger because he protects you. I came to warn him. And your wife loves a child who does not belong to her."

"Americans adopt Chinese girls all the time."

"This one is special."

"They are all special."

"Not like this one. I will take her—and your wife, if you cannot protect them."

"Then we should work together."

"I work alone." He raised his chin in defiance.

"You can trust me."

The silence thickened. Without warning, the Red Dragon pulled a sword from the sheath attached to his back and pointed it at Chase.

Remaining transfixed by the situation was not in Chase's DNA. He wanted to use the element of surprise and spring into action against the enemy. His hunch was that the man wanted to intimidate him more than attack.

"Let me be clear. I will take your woman if you cannot protect them. And you will never find them. This is my warning to you— do not stand in a dangerous place trusting in miracles. There are no miracles here."

"And I will tell you this Arabian proverb: never trust a fool with a sword. And. I. Don't."

The Red Dragon chuckled satanically and held the sword in front of his painted face as if in salute. "We will meet again, Captain Hunter. Be sure of it," he said in broken English. "And then we will see who is the fool."

The Red Dragon backed toward the gate and disappeared into the darkness as mysteriously as he'd arrived. Chase turned his attention to his stepfather and Yona. The older man had his hand on his heart.

"Are you both okay?"

"Father?" Yona asked as his father leaned into him.

Chase rushed to him and took his pulse. "Let me help you inside the house. My mom can help you."

"No. It's just my blood pressure acting up. I ran out of medicine several days ago. I will get it tomorrow."

"He's lying," Yona asserted. "He needs his other medicine. I'll get it." In seconds, he returned with water and a medicine bottle.

Chase took the meds and read the label. Thankfully, his Chinese abilities hadn't lessened over the years. "Zhou, sir, do you have a heart condition?"

"I don't think so? Why?"

"This is for congestive heart failure. Who prescribed this for you? One of the military doctors?"

"Yes. General Sun Li's personal physician."

"Does my mom know?"

"I didn't want to worry her." He took a deep breath. "I'm better now. Thank you. I was afraid you would be hurt, Chase. Your mother would never forgive me, and I couldn't bear that." With help from Chase, he managed to stand. "Thank you. I will be fine."

"Where is Hao. Does he not live here too?"

"No. He has his own place near the school where he teaches."

"Yona, can you help your father into bed?"

"Yes. Thank you, my brother," he said timidly.

Chase met him eye to eye and raised his chin in acknowledgment. "You are welcome—little brother." He grinned. "Promise to watch after him for a while and come get me if he seems to be struggling. Understand?"

"Yes." He pulled his father toward the small building. "We will see you in the morning. Will you help me explain to our mother about the medicine?"

"Yes. She'll know what to do."

~ ~ ~ ~

Tessa finished her bowl of congee and decided she was starting to like it. After helping Chase's mother clean up and dress the baby, she heard the front door open.

"Hao." Nora turned up her cheek for a kiss from her stepson. "Have you eaten?"

"Yes, Mother. I was wondering if Tessa might like to go to the park and do tai chi with the neighbors. It is cool this morning because of the rain."

"Oh, I would love that, but I have Lotus and—"

"I will go with you and play with my granddaughter." She smiled as she lifted the baby in her arms and addressed Hao. "Chase left early this morning with your father to find transportation to Guangzhou."

"It is a short walk to a little park. The earthquake didn't do much but turn over a few flower pots in the garden and down a few tree limbs that have already been removed. We should have a good crowd." Hao leaned in and tickled Lotus's cheek to get a noisy giggle. "I'll get the stroller for you, Mother."

Tessa enjoyed the exercise and discovered she was quite good at it. Thanks to Dr. Wu's lessons, she didn't have trouble fitting in and actually felt more relaxed when they returned. Nora said she had some chores to do at the orphanage and maybe some exams for the babies soon to leave. When Tessa offered to tag along, Nora shook her head.

"I do not want you there, my daughter. It is sad to see these babies in such a place. Although our orphanage is much better than most, it is not pretty like you imagine and does not always smell as fresh as Americans want. Fortunately, here, there is one attendant to four babies. In years past, in many orphanages, there was a one-to-twenty ratio. That does not always make for good care. But today, there are fewer babies leaving and care has improved. But still, I wish to go alone."

Tessa accepted her explanation as she reached out and stroked the woman's arm. "I am glad you are here, daughter. Thank you for loving my boy." She quickly left as tears appeared in the corners of her eyes.

Hao and Yona went outside where they twirled bamboo poles. Dr. Wu had tried to teach her this technique, too, but she'd struggled to get the hang of it, mostly because he was not a patient teacher when it came to martial arts.

Since the baby had decided to take a morning nap, she moved the dresser drawer to the kitchen where she could hear Lotus if she cried out. Pulling her hair up in a messy bun, and pushing up her sleeves, she slipped outside and dared ask to join. Their expressions were amused as they agreed and tossed her a pole. She caught the five-foot pole in midair like a pro.

"Dr. Wu has been working with me, but he says I'm about as graceful as a panda falling out of a tree holding a rubber hose."

Both men chuckled and took up a fighting stance with each other, leaving her out. Their sparing grew loud and aggressive, while she stood there in awe and a little miffed that they weren't including her. Without warning, they pivoted toward her and charged, letting out a blood-curdling yell. Startled, Tessa fell back into a stack of flower pots, knocking them over as she hit the ground. Next thing she knew, they were standing over her, laughing.

Humiliated, but mostly irritated, she rolled to her feet, feeling the sore spots she'd received from the accident the previous day. While still laughing, they turned slightly, ignoring her just long enough for her to swing her pole and make contact with Hao's back. He staggered and jumped around, returning to attack mode. She swung again. This time, his pole came off his shoulder and met hers with fierce aggression. But she remembered a lesson Dr. Wu had taught her.

In one swift motion, she raised her pole from the ground to meet his grip, blocking his attack, and pushing him back. The advances brought a faster and harder blow. Somehow, she managed to counter it, mostly to protect herself. Hao sidestepped to let Yona have a crack at her. It was apparent by his smirk he had underestimated her scared rabbit expression, allowing her to stop his advance by running her pole between his ankles and twisting so hard, it spun her around. When she righted herself, Yona lay on the ground trying to scramble up, red faced and angry.

Both men advanced on her. Those poles were going to whack her hard enough she'd know her place in a matter of seconds. At the last second, she pretended to stare past them and faked a haughty smile of satisfaction.

"Chase, thank goodness you're here!" she yelled.

Both men stopped and turned to check behind them, discovering too late, it had been a trick. She slammed her pole against Yona's shoulder, causing him to drop his pole, then ran at Hao with a scream of a rabid she-wolf. Her moves were far from graceful, but her strength kept him stepping backward until he neared the fence. In a surprise move, Hao spun around, clamping on to each end of the pole, then shoved her into the fence with more strength than she expected, causing her to drop her pole.

Both were panting, and Tessa could feel disgust at herself falling for such a trick. He stepped closer, pressing the pole against her chest. The pressure continued to increase, and the fight was no longer in fun. This only made her angrier as she tried to push free, but he clearly had the upper hand.

A diabolical expression touched his lips as his eyes darkened, reminding her of someone else. Tessa raised her chin and tried to appear seductive.

He leaned in. "I see your eyes have turned violet, so I must have struck a nerve."

Tessa planned to take full advantage of his distraction. She reached out and gathered the fabric of his jacket in her hands.

Tessa spoke through clenched teeth. "Time for me to strike a nerve in you." In a fluid motion, she jerked him to her then jammed her knee in his groin. He howled and fell back as the pole fell from his grasp. Tessa caught it before it hit the ground. Swinging the pole with both hands, she made contact with his side, knocking him into a mound of dirt.

Tessa held out the pole to Yona. "Anything you want to try, little brother, or are you good to go?"

Yona burst out laughing. He bent over and pointed at his bigger brother who wobbled to his feet, covered in dirt.

Hao dusted himself off and rubbed his privates as he approached Tessa. "Wu has trained you well. You misled us, I think, at your capabilities." He bowed his head and gave her the hand-over-fist move.

She returned the Bao Quan. When Yona picked up the poles, Tessa tilted her head at Hao. "This is the second time you've mentioned my eyes changing color. I feel you already knew this. How did you know my eyes turn violet when I'm angry?"

Hao sobered. "You ask too many questions. It is not a good thing for Westerners to be too interested in the things we do here."

"I'll take it up with the Red Dragon the next time I see him," she snapped. "I don't especially like being scared out of my wits or stalked by him or a pretender." She pushed Hao aside.

Chase, holding Lotus, opened the screen door and took in the scene. "You didn't let Tessa talk you into fighting with poles, did you, Hao?"

"She tricked us." Hao morphed into a good-natured man again. "I will not fall for this a second time." His eyes diverted to her like slits of fire. "Thank you, Tessa, for teaching me a lesson I will not soon forget."

Those words most likely had a double meaning she also would not soon forget.

CHAPTER 36

囍

Chase handed off Lotus. Tessa changed her diaper, fixed a bottle, sat in a rocker, and relaxed with the baby. Yona continued to laugh as Chase held the door for him. He seemed to enjoy teasing Hao for underestimating Tessa and even made fun of himself. The easy camaraderie between the two left Chase a little envious that he hadn't experienced this part of family over the years. The thought that Hao, his best friend growing up, was now his stepbrother and Yona a blood brother, felt satisfying.

"Where's my father?" Hao's eyes searched the room.

"I think he went to get your mother. Apparently, you are having an important guest tonight."

"Who?" Yona asked with youthful enthusiasm. "I hope they have a daughter." He chuckled and posed in front of a cracked mirror on the wall. "I'll need to get ready."

"No. I believe it is General Sun Li," Chase said drily. A heavy silence fell on the room. "Your father found a message on his phone when we went out."

"You shouldn't be here with the baby," Hao said sternly. "He'll take Lotus and kill her."

"Chase?" Tessa struggled to stand up holding Lotus, when Yona rushed to help her. "Can we leave today? Do we have a way out."

"Not until tomorrow afternoon. There's a puddle jumper to take us to Lanzhou airport then on to Guangzhou. I've already got tickets. We'll get to Guangzhou late, but I was able to contact our boss who will have someone standing by to take us to our hotel. We're not that much off schedule with the others."

"But tonight?" Tessa asked. "Where can we hide and be safe?"

"I have a small place near the park." Hao stepped closer to Chase and put a hand on his shoulder. "I could do nothing as a boy when Sun Li destroyed your life. My father believed you had left and wouldn't let me go."

"He told me. I appreciate the care you gave my mother. It is hard for me to understand why he didn't try to reach the American embassy or consulate to let them know she was alive."

"I think in order to protect me and, later, Yona, he had to appear apathetic toward her well-being. There has never been a time when we were not under suspicion. Although we were told you were dead, our mother never gave up hope or stopped praying she would see you one day."

"Yet now, he decided he needed to try and escape."

"Lotus provided that opportunity. I think you know how the pieces started to fit together to make that possible. We were left in the dark for most of this, but the man called Tan assured my father things were in place to escape. Yona must not serve in the military. It is yet another way to manipulate my father to do his bidding. And we feel he will also make sure that Yona serves in the most dangerous assignments."

Yona was a fit young man and could serve the US in so many ways. It wouldn't be easy to transition, but with Chase's help, maybe this could be a good thing. "Yona, how do you feel about leaving China?"

"As long as my family can stay together, I am willing to make a new life. I have read about the opportunities in your country. I am strong and smart. I will adjust. You will be proud of me. I promise."

Pride welled up inside his chest. "I already am. Hao, what about you?"

"It is not something I have considered. I thought my life would always be here. It seems you came to change everything we thought was true. When my father wanted to escape, I went along with the idea, only to give him hope. I do not believe it will happen. You will leave without us to get Lotus back to the US to save the China dolls of this country. While we wait—"

"I'm coming back for you," Chase insisted. "I will get you out. Plans are already underway to make that happen."

"I want to believe you, Brother, but it is possible that only Yona can make any journey over mountains or desert you have planned. My father is not in perfect health, but strong. Even so, to fight his way out or live with the danger of waiting for your return might be too much for both my parents."

Chase gritted his teeth because Hao was right. "I have to try. I want my mother home where she belongs, deserves to be." He reached out to Yona and slipped an arm around his shoulders. "I have a brother I need to know and help. And you and I can start over—together. I want you to be a part of my family, Hao."

Hao slowly nodded acceptance. "I will wait and see but promise to get Mother and Yona back with you."

"And the colonel? My mother loves him and will not leave without him."

"You would take my father after all the pain he's caused you?" Hao said.

"Tessa"—he sought her out and noticed tears in the corners of her eyes—"has taught me many things over the last few years. Two of those things is faith and forgiveness. It's a struggle for me, but I am trying. I am not like my mother by a long shot."

"We want you with us, Hao," Tessa said. "We've just got to get this child to the States or more children will die, and we need your help."

"Let's go. Gather your things. Yona, make the house appear as if nothing has changed. No signs of a baby. Understand?" Hao gave orders like his father.

Yona quickly set about the tasks to be completed.

Chase helped Tessa in the bedroom and kept an eye on Lotus who was playing with a squeaky toy that also rattled. She was happy as a clam, he thought, and couldn't resist picking her up. When he did, she pushed her face in his at an attempt at a kiss, which made him laugh.

"I love you too," he said softly then hugged her. "Tessa?"

She came to stand next to him and laid her head against his arm. "I know. That feeling is overwhelming, isn't it?"

"Yes. So helpless yet so powerful."

"Do you still want to try again for a baby?"

"More than anything." He kissed Lotus on the top of the head then gazed down at Tessa. "More than anything," he repeated. "When we get home, we have a lot of decisions to make about leaving Sacramento and moving to Tennessee, baby and…"

"Leaving Enigma for good?" Tessa asked hopefully.

"Absolutely. It's time to let others do the heavy lifting for the country. I don't want to miss out on one more thing I never believed in."

"Thank you." She stood on tiptoes and kissed him.

Hao rushed in. "Just got a text from Father. We don't have much time. The general plans to surprise us by coming early. We need to go now."

~ ~ ~ ~

"Agent Martin, thank you for getting back to me so soon." Director Benjamin Clark spoke matter-of-factly as he put his phone on speaker. "How did it go with Robert?"

"Not well. He tried to argue with me about Phoebe's innocence."

"At least you didn't shoot him."

"Not yet, anyway. I really wanted him to bolt or pretend he had a weapon. The weasel just wanted to call me names like stormtrooper and macho-pinhead."

Ben couldn't help but chuckle. "And those names don't at all describe you."

"I can tell by your tone you may find this a little amusing. He's a major asshole. What did Tessa ever see in that jerk?"

"Love is blind. Or so I hear. Tessa has a propensity to find the good where there is none. Robert is a smooth talker, and she was a country girl without much experience, from what I have gathered. Captain Hunter kind of blew that up, as we know."

"Yeah. Then she goes and gets involved with that Tribesman character and marries Chase. I'm starting to think she doesn't have enough sense to come in out of the rain." His voice was flippant, laced with a snarky growl.

"You may be right, but it is what it is and she has been invaluable to us. I plan to keep her as long as possible. Now, about

Robert…what is the plan?" the director asked.

"I was able to pull some video Dr. Wu had up and show Robert he wasn't the only cowboy in the rodeo."

"I can do without the colorful metaphors." The director had begun to sound bored.

"Right. He was shocked—I think. He did say he felt something was off with their relationship and mentioned her boss," Agent Martin continued.

"Yes. Edmond Yu, a capitalist who has his fingers in shipping, steel, and mining. He convinced China to sign the UN treaty about seafloor mining several years ago. Currently, they are the leader in that endeavor. We, on the other hand, have refused to sign it because the UN has their fingerprints on it. So, that, too, could come back to bite us in the ass."

"Robert is smitten with this Phoebe woman and I have to say, she is easy on the eyes, but dirty through and through. Dr. Wu says she is a narcissist and sees her role as an influencer rather than what it really is: someone who needs admiration while believing others are inferior. Her lack of empathy is leading her down a dangerous path." Agent Martin switched ears for his phone. "I, of course, gave him a digital file on her and left any Enigma associations out of it. Wouldn't want him to know his helpless ex-wife runs around with assassins, rogue warriors, con men, and people with a shoot-first mentality. He thinks she's a wimp."

"We've all been a victim of that false assumption at one time or another. Will he sign the contract as we directed?" the director asked.

"Yep. He's all in. Told him we'd make it up to him—provided he lives through it. He even made me put it in writing. Lawyers. Can't live with them and can't kill them."

"Don't you have a law degree, Agent Martin?"

"Well, you don't have to rub it in, Director. I've been at your beck and call for a while. I'm totally corrupted and get that warm and fuzzy sensation when I get to work with you guys."

"I detect a note of cynicism. Keep an eye on him. I have a feeling he'll drop the ball. And the children?"

"Taken care of. No worries. I just need you to have Carter at the airport when I make the call."

"Done."

CHAPTER 37

General Sun Li exited his four-wheel vehicle. He pretended to adjust his sunglasses, but, in reality, surveyed the surroundings outside the orphanage. Built on the edge of town when it was still a farming community years ago, it did boast of a beautiful valley below. Years ago, it claimed to be a stop along the Silk Road. In recent years, it had become a drab, patched building with a clean exterior.

A few pots of flowers sat outside along the front of the covered porch. The double front doors bore faded images of a laughing Buddha playing with children and colorful birds in native trees. The yard had been closely cut, and the sound of hammering from a nearby shed meant some kind of repair was taking place. These places always needed more care than they were worth.

He took a deep breath and pivoted to take in the city nestling below this high point. Next, he turned toward the northwest, knowing it bordered inner Mongolia and would be a perfect route to escape. The people and the monks were friendly to those in need.

Tourists still wanted the experience traveling the Silk Road, as if following their romantic dreams would come true. These kinds of people were common and, if Chase and his family wanted to disappear, that would be the way to go. He turned to his aide. "Is Wuwei Si Temple in operation?"

"Yes, sir. The grand master there is old but still has disciples to run the Shaolin-style kung fu school. I hear these days they do not accept foreigners."

"Nevertheless, I don't trust them. The Hunters were well-known throughout the Gansu Province, and there has been a certain amount of contempt for the military since the so-called massacre years ago."

"Yes, sir," the aide added drily, causing the general to make eye contact with him.

"Perhaps suggest that their monastery remains open at the goodwill of the government."

"Yes, sir."

"That would be a perfect place for the Americans to evade us." The general removed his sunglasses and made an effort to clean them.

"I will notify the local authorities and insist they alert us to unusual activity around the monastery, especially involving American tourists. But, sir, if that is their corridor of escape, traveling that road into Mongolia is difficult even without a baby."

"Which makes it easier to find them," Sun Li said coolly.

The clank of iron locks opened the doors of the orphanage followed by Colonel Zhou Xiang who came to salute the general. Their eyes locked as if friends, but they were adversaries.

"Welcome, General. It is a pleasant surprise to have you visit today. My wife has already made my life miserable for not alerting her sooner." He smiled. "She wanted things to be perfect, as always."

"I am sure it will be fine. I wanted to see the progress she has made here. It has been a few years since my last visit."

They began their stroll toward the entrance. The sound of a baby crying drifted outside as Nora appeared. Dressed in a clean black smock over her clothes and with her braids pushed to her back, she offered the Bao Quan greeting and lowered her chin in submission.

In spite of a difficult life with heartache and discomfort, Nora remained a lovely creature. He wondered if all Native American women retained such beauty as they aged. Her skin remained clear and youthful; only the creases around her eyes displayed aging. Threads of gray hair were woven throughout her braids and, for some reason, he wanted to touch them.

A fleeting thought surfaced at taking her after he disposed of the colonel. But then again, having him alive and knowing he could do nothing about it was a much better form of revenge.

"Welcome, General Sun Li. I am pleased you came to visit our little orphanage." She stepped aside to let him see the wide hall and how clean the floors were. "We are preparing four babies to travel to Lanzhou tomorrow. One is even a boy this time."

"A boy? How can that be?" It was hard to imagine giving up a son.

"The child has a cleft palette and a deformed foot. No one wanted him. He is eighteen months and needs a home. A couple from Australia arrives tomorrow. They are more than happy to accept him since their wait would be another year for a baby girl. We are so glad to make this happen."

"And the others? How many are left here?"

Nora's steps slowed and she stared down at her feet as if pondering what to say. "We have ten baby girls, ages two to ten months."

"That is not very many." The general exhaled and shrugged what appeared to be indifference.

They entered the nursery where several babies were being rocked or fed.

"Most of these will be gone by month's end. That is a good thing." Nora fanned her hand out for the general to follow as she tried to make eye contact with her husband.

"Do you have enough money to run this place? It is very expensive, I think."

"Yes. It is expensive. The adoptive parents always give a donation of $5000 in US dollars to help us out with expenses, but when there are many babies to be placed, there is not enough money."

The general walked over to a crib where a baby slept, then peered down in curiosity. "How many attendants stay to take care of these children each night? Seems like a waste of resources."

"No, sir. Because we have so few babies, the attendants take the children home with them at night to love and care at their own expense. Some come back and forth each day, and others, if there is a grandparent in the home, care for the baby. It is very difficult for them to give the children up when the adoptive parents arrive, even though they will be given good homes and advantages not available to an orphan."

The general cut his eyes sharply to Nora. "There is not much need for so many orphanages like twenty years ago. We allow families to have two, even three children these days. I see no reason to continue the practice."

Colonel Zhou took a deep breath. "Although this is true, sir, we need to make sure the ones that are still abandoned recklessly and without thought of their future have a place and excellent care. This orphanage is proud that they have one attendant for every four babies. That is not true in other parts of the country."

The general clasped his hands behind him and moved away from the crib. "It is an unnecessary luxury for baby girls that no one wants. I will consider this."

"Sir, it means so much to future families and to me. I've worked hard to make this a place China can be proud of."

He stopped and admired her long and hard. "I'm sure you would be willing to do almost anything to continue your work here."

Zhou Xiang quickly came alongside his wife, not missing the general's insinuation. He was unable to voice an opinion when Nora raised her chin in defiance.

"I would do anything for these children and the good people who work with them. They depend on me."

He tilted his head. "I am glad to hear your devotion is as strong as your obvious common sense. I am sure we can come to some kind of—arrangement, Nora." He shifted his focus to his colonel and narrowed his eyes then walked ahead of the two, leaving them to stand paralyzed with dread.

~ ~ ~ ~

"Dad, is something wrong?" Sean Patrick wondered out loud that his father seemed distracted playing miniature golf. "You haven't said a word since we started."

"No. No. Just planning out my next move. You guys are getting too good at this game. Maybe I should get you a golf pro to give you boys some lessons. What do you think?"

The boys agreed that might be fun, but Heather rolled her eyes and admitted she'd rather have more dance lessons.

Robert had clicked through the digital content he'd transferred to his phone that Agent Martin left him along with the paper file. Those papers were shredded in the office center as instructed. He poured over it twice to make sure he read everything carefully.

A spy? Phoebe is a spy? How could that be? Even if it wasn't true, her association with Edmond Yu suggested illegal activity. He'd let himself trust Yu because of his own desire to be rich and important. Maybe he let himself believe in the dream because of his own need to prove to Tessa she screwed up by letting him go.

He wanted her to regret leaving him. The idea of her having to beg him to take her back—which he gladly would—might have become a reality. That thought surprised him because he had convinced himself he was falling in love with Phoebe.

He reevaluated their time together and realized there had been hints of things too good to be true. The woman stroked his ego a little too much, seduced him with fancy parties, introduced him to powerful men, and a ranch with horses that impressed his children. Add in the expensive suites, including a sexual appetite he found impossible to resist, he'd become a sitting target for espionage. Peddling her influence to secure him a job in Washington DC had connotations that could permanently destroy his career.

~ ~ ~ ~

Agent Martin studied Robert with his kids and wondered what was going through that head of his. Earlier when they had that come-to-Jesus talk, the director had suggested he might want to embellish the truth. He hoped Robert could buy how important the good will mission Tessa had been given by the Secretary of State, really was without giving away the life and death reality. He tried to make it sound innocent and mundane at first.

"You have put your ex-wife in danger, Robert."

"How? I would never do that," he insisted.

"Be that as it may, you have. She was asked by her friend, Secretary of State Bonnie Finley, to bring back a baby from China who belongs to a very important man. Once the baby arrives, the party involved will sign a treaty that will protect Taiwan for the next ten years."

"How did I hurt her?"

"You told Phoebe her whereabouts at every turn, plus who her husband is. He is former military, plus grew up in China. They don't really like being shunned, outwitted, or shown the door, as we say. Besides, the Department of Defense likes to keep their former bad-ass special forces a secret. You kind of blew that. They are aware the baby is the key to the success of this exchange."

"I can't believe Tessa would be part of such a thing."

"I doubt she knows of the importance. It was a simple trip. Visit the Great Wall, check out a few temples. Pick up the baby. Come home. Easy. No big deal. You changed that and made it sound like the State Department was a bunch of buffoons playing with national security."

"What kind of danger is she in?"

"Since there is a connection with the baby and a Chinese diplomat, they could be arrested and sent to prison or worse."

"Worse? What does that mean?"

"It means, you'll never see her again."

That seemed to take the wind out of his self-absorbed sails and he promised to do the right thing. Agent Martin wasn't proud of lying about most of what he'd told Robert, but he wouldn't lose any sleep over it either. If anything happened to Tessa, he would personally see to it the guy never practiced law again and lost custody of the kids. Then he'd kill him.

The thought suddenly occurred to him—he'd become just like the Enigma agents he claimed to despise. Somewhere along the way, his sense of law and order for the collective good had flown out the window.

A willowy creature in a tight-fitting red dress approached Robert and kissed him, which seemed to snap the man out of his reverie. He gave a low whistle, knowing Robert could hear him through his earwig. "She is mighty fine, Robert. Relax. You got this."

CHAPTER 38

"Thank you for an excellent meal, Nora. It is not often I get a home-cooked meal as fine as this one." The general dabbed his mouth with a cloth napkin that may have been repurposed from a faded dishtowel. "Be sure to tell Hao I missed him at dinner."

"You honor me, General. Hao will be disappointed that he missed you. He comes and goes. He volunteers for several schools at night for whoever needs tutoring." Nora began clearing away the dishes as her husband led the general outside to a lighted patio space with two chairs. Yona brought them a pot of hot tea with Nora's best china. In spite of having a chip on one cup and a hairline crack on the other, the feeling of elegance remained.

Zhou remained calm during the evening, managing to keep his anxiousness from affecting his blood pressure. Fortunately, he was able to get a new prescription, thanks to his wife, and had it filled earlier in the day. He was convinced the general was attempting to slowly kill him. Nora checked him over at Chase's insistence. Did her son finally believe he had nothing to do with the murder of his father? Or did he just want to get out of the country and was using him to make that happen?

The important thing was to get Nora and his boys out of China. It grew more difficult to continue pretending he could effectively

259

do his job and cover for the general time and time again. Chase might be the only way to make that happen with whomever he worked with in the US. He didn't really care if it was the CIA or some other security organization that promised to help him.

"The earthquake did some damage to the old quarter of the city, I noticed. I understand an American couple were injured."

"I was notified by the local authorities. Several of the couples who were adopting babies from Nora's orphanage were finishing up paperwork to be able to get visas from the American consulate in Guangzhou. I checked the hotel listed on their itinerary."

"And?"

"They had taken a tour of some temples. They were to leave by train but were delayed due to the possible disruption of damaged tracks."

"There was no damage."

Zhou took a sip of his tea. "Yes. The hotel contacted me and informed me the group had left. No one reported going to the hospital. Nora happened to be on scene when it started. Nora," he called.

She appeared at the screen door drying a plate. "Yes?"

"Did you assist any injured people yesterday after the earthquake?"

"Yes. Several. Why?"

"The general thought an American couple had been injured."

"A woman was injured in that sidewalk cave in, but she was from South Africa. I administered first aid and offered to call an ambulance, but they refused. I worried about the baby, so they did let me check her out."

"Was it one of your babies?" the general asked.

"No. They used the orphanage in the northwestern part of the province. It is much larger than the one here. They came to visit the sites with their group. I thought they should get examined, but they were in a hurry to leave. I considered it odd, but I needed to get back to my babies to make sure all was well. Is there something wrong?"

Zhou waved her off. "No. Just speaking of recent events."

She nodded and disappeared back into the kitchen.

"Were you thinking it might be the American couple you spoke of earlier?" Zhou Xiang said nonchalantly.

"I followed them here to Wuwei. They are using passports under the name of Butler." Sun Li took a sip of tea.

"Ah. Yes. I remember. I met them in Lanzhou. The man was rather a brute and rude." He leaned in and whispered, "He did not appear to be Native American, nor did he recognize me. I do not want Nora to hear of this. She has been through so much as you well know," he said through gritted teeth. "There is no need to give her false hope. Whoever this man or couple might be are not from the past."

"I see. You are sure?" Sun Li asked.

"As sure as a person can be in this situation. Many years have passed, and the boy and girl who escaped on the night of the massacre could not have possibly survived that trip over the mountains. The Shaolin buried them during the crossing of the mountains into Tibet."

The general shrugged. "And you buried the Shaolin who helped them escape."

"It was to save my own reputation that I did so, General. There is no trace of that night, except for Nora." He stole a quick glance back over his shoulder into the kitchen. "She is happy here, serving the people of China. There are not enough doctors here, and it gave her a reason to live."

"You took advantage of the situation." Sun Li smiled wolfishly. "I cannot say I blame you."

Zhou's hair stood on the back of his neck. "She saved my son's life when he was very young. I owed her that much when I discovered she was still alive."

The general leveled a disgruntled expression Zhou's way. "You disobeyed a direct order."

"I followed your orders, and then you left me to clean up your mess. I took most of the blame for that night. Not you. That is why I took pictures, recorded testimonials, and videotaped the fires set by your men."

The general's face darkened.

Zhou went on, "What is done is done. I do not need an American in my city to destroy what I have created for myself or expose the truth. It would be devastating for both of us."

"Blackmail. I could just have you killed, Zhou."

"Yes." Zhou smiled. "But then the evidence would be released to both our government and the Americans who were told a pack of lies concerning the missionaries who had ties to one of their diplomats."

"I must be going." He stood and glared down at the colonel. "This has been good. I am glad we are on the same page, Colonel. It appears that neither of us has anything to worry about."

Zhou stood. "Correct. It has been my pleasure to share a meal with you, General Sun."

"Where did you say your son Hao is tonight?" He moved to exit through the iron gate on the side of the house where the garden grew.

"I did not say, General. My son has his own life. I do not keep track of his whereabouts."

"Pity. Tell him I would very much like to talk to him about—an opportunity he won't be able to refuse."

Zhou pretended not to care. "Of course. Thank you for sharing your valuable time tonight."

~ ~ ~ ~

Tessa tried to entertain Lotus in Hao's dark, two-room apartment at the back of a storefront. There was a small yard he used to access his place. A tool shed with one film-covered window had been converted into his office. The apartment was sparsely furnished. The kitchen and living area were about the size of her patio porch back home. The bedroom had a twin bed and a bamboo table that had seen better days. Each room had one window and although the temperature outside was cool, inside felt like an oven. Lotus became fussy.

"Can we sit outside, Chase?"

"No," he snapped as he peered out the window. "And keep the lights off. Hao texted me that the general is prowling around with his henchmen."

"He'll find us."

"Colonel Zhou is coming to take us to a safer place where we'll catch the plane tomorrow."

"I feel like we don't have enough backup, Chase, and that we're flapping in the wind as to our safety." She bounced the baby to soften her fuzzy attitude.

"With any luck, this time tomorrow we'll be in Guangzhou." Checking the small clock over the door, he realized how late it was. Sounds in the storefront put his senses on alert. Five minutes passed, and Yona came through the back door. Chase had raised his weapon to take action and quickly lowered it. "I could have shot you."

"Sorry," he whispered anxiously. "We must go."

"I heard something in the storefront."

"It was me. I stole some supplies and put them in Father's car. Please. Hurry," he repeated, motioning them to follow. "We don't have much time."

"Tessa?" Chase fastened the baby in the carrier on her chest. "If we get separated—"

"Separated?" she gasped.

"If we get separated, get to the airport outside of town. I put the address in the baby's bag. It's also in your phone in code."

She took a deep breath. "Okay."

They had slipped outside, each carrying a small duffle bag and backpack, when men sprang over the tall fencing. They were dressed in dark clothing, but the only weapons they brandished resembled four-foot poles. Chase guessed they didn't want the sound of gunfire to alert the neighbors but didn't rule out the possibility of them having guns. One started to rush forward when Tessa screamed and backed into the house for protection.

"Give us the baby."

Yona took a fighting stance after picking up a garden rake. Since Chase had placed his weapon in a side pocket of his backpack, there was no clear way to retrieve it without losing precious seconds. Instead, he snatched a hoe propped near the back door.

The four attackers were quick as lightning, and there was little time to guess who they were. The odds were two against one, but Yona had no problem holding his own. He had mastered the art of the pole, and using the rake actually gave him an advantage when he dragged it across one man's face and back ended it into the other man's teeth.

Chase abandoned his concern for his brother and fought the two beefy attackers coming at him. Because of his own strength, he matched them well and managed to disarm one causing him to lunge forward, knocking Chase off-balance. This gave the attacker a second longer than he needed to pick up his pole and slam it against Chase's rake. When he fell against the house to break his fall, Chase's hand clasped a hedge lopper, which he swung up and made contact with the attacker's head.

Considering the force with which he connected to the man's skull, he no longer wasted valuable concern on the man rousing to another attack. The guy left standing twirled his pole like a high school pom squad captain. Although he couldn't twirl the lopper, Chase could block the rapid blows meant to kill him. When the man stepped back and narrowed his satanic eyes, Chase opened the jaws of the lopper just before he rushed forward. He managed to clamp onto the pole and twist so hard that it threw the man into a flip. As he struggled to get up, Chase hit him in the kidney, followed by a killing blow to the back of the head.

Yona had one man down and advanced on the other. When he let out a yell that sounded like a Yeti in heat, the man blinked and stumbled over the hoe Chase dropped then stepped on the blade, causing the handle to fly up and smack him in the nose. Yona finished him off by laying him out in an unconscious state.

Both men were panting as they entered the kitchen of the little apartment.

"Tessa," he called. "Tessa?" Chase searched the little dwelling and even pushed open the bathroom that wasn't much bigger than a closet. The door that led into the entrance to the storefront stood ajar. It had been locked from the other side. He kicked it open and found the room dark except for a flickering nightlight. "Tessa!" he yelled louder than he intended.

Yona approached him carefully holding something in his hand near the nightlight. "Chase, she is gone." He extended his hand with what appeared to be a Polaroid picture.

The selfie revealed the Red Dragon holding Tessa back against his chest as he extended his arm to take the picture. Her eyes were wide, and the baby was crying. He flipped the picture over to find a message.

I warned you I would take her if you could not protect her.

CHAPTER 39

"**D**id you have a fun day with the kids?" Phoebe waved to them. "From their smiles, I'm guessing they are enjoying the miniature golf. Hope you used sunscreen because their faces are a little rosy."

Robert ignored the fake concern. "Your message said you wanted me to meet with your boss?"

She rubbed his back with a gentle hand. "Edmond wants you to sign the contract first thing in the morning. It will be just us." She hugged him. "I'm so proud of you. He is just over the moon impressed with you, Robert." When he didn't respond, her voice lowered in concern. "What's wrong? You're not having second thoughts, are you?"

Agent Martin spoke in the earwig. "Easy, buddy. Women are like sharks. They can smell blood in the water."

He took her hand and kissed it. "With you at my side, how can I go wrong. I would do anything to make you happy." He pulled her closer.

"I can't wait to share this new life with you." She stroked his face then the side of his head gently.

"So, what exactly will I be doing? The documents I went over were kind of vague about that."

"You'll represent the consortium's economic interests, push for change in Washington, wine and dine the big shots, and help them come to a mutually acceptable agreement."

"On what?"

"Robert, don't overthink this." She slipped her arm through his. "This is a jewel of an opportunity. Your salary will triple, and you'll get to travel, meet important people, and help make policy."

"Sounds like a dream come true."

She slipped her arm through his. "It really is. And I'll be there right beside you."

"But everything is all legal, right?"

"Of course. That's why we wanted a lawyer. I bet once Washington gets to know you, you'll be on the fast track for the attorney general job." A light chuckle escaped her lips as she cut her eyes toward the kids headed their way. "When will you tell the kids?"

"Not right away. Don't want to worry them or spoil our vacation."

"Such a good dad."

Agent Martin spoke to him again. "You're doing great, Robert. Ask her about Edmond. Just like we rehearsed."

"I read a few things about Edmond. Born in China, immigrated to Australia then to the US and finished Harvard Business School. Does he also work for China's interests?"

"Don't be silly. Besides, his goal is to blend both China's and the US's goals into one, so both countries will succeed. Is that a problem?" she asked cautiously.

He let his eyes explore her expression for the first time and saw the person Agent Martin had described. "No. He's paying me almost what I'm worth. I'll make sure he notices that."

"Perfect. A man after my own heart."

"I got a sitter tonight. Late dinner? The Desert Oasis? It's five star and here at the resort. I don't want to be too far from the kids. I've decided to send them home tomorrow after the signing. Then I'm all yours."

"I like the sound of that."

"I have a very important question to ask you." He kissed her quickly as the kids ran up.

"I can hardly wait."

She turned to the kids and started asking questions about the golf game. Heather was animated and excited to share. The boys hung back to listen but kept diverting their attention to Robert.

Funny how they had tried to tell him they didn't trust her. They saw what he couldn't. What did that say to him about his priorities? He just wanted to get them home and away from this mess in case something went wrong or he did anything more to damage his relationship with his ex-wife.

The idea Tessa might be in danger for just picking up a baby in China was a little hard to believe, but she did pal around with that woman who had become Secretary of State. He could see where that might put her in danger. She had never had much sense when it came to the friends she made. The guy she married was proof of that. The marriage was destined to fail, and when it did, he would swoop in and pick up where he left off.

"Earth to Robert," Agent Martin said in his earwig. "You're zoning out on me. Snap out of it. You've started out strong. The big magic show in the special events room is about to start. I've got someone there who will escort you to premium seats. Lucky you, your lady friend got the best seats in the house. That should make her look like a rock star to the kids. Try to have a good time. It's Las Vegas-style fun."

Robert twisted his body enough to spot the agent sitting at a table holding a book. He wondered how the man and Tessa became friends. Was it after he screwed up with his law firm and got involved in that whole conflict diamond business? Just another time when he became the victim—like now. It all worked out though. This would too.

"Come on, kids. Phoebe has another surprise for you. I think you're going to like it."

~ ~ ~ ~

Robert drank in Phoebe's lacy black cocktail dress and her slim toned legs as she pulled him out of a chair and toward the balcony. They overlooked the beautiful gardens, lit with lanterns, and the shadow of the Native American deity Kokopelli in the center of a rock fountain. For an instant, he thought of how Tessa would like the gardens and that Kokopelli might be present. She was a sucker for that kind of thing. All in the past. Phoebe meant the future.

"What did you want to ask me tonight?" She laid her head against his shoulder as his arm went around her waist. When he said nothing, she straightened and pulled him around, her forehead had creased and her mouth turned down as if she was concerned. "Robert?"

Reaching inside his suit jacket, he withdrew a small velvet box and went down on one knee. Her eyes widened as he opened the box. "Phoebe, you have changed my life in so many ways. Will you marry me?"

~ ~ ~ ~

Chase jumped into the colonel's car and let Yona drive since he had no idea how to navigate in this part of the city. Things had moved so fast earlier; he hadn't had time to pull up a map. This had to be the quickest way to get away. They had managed to retrieve the one backpack and duffle bag dropped in the yard, needed to escape one more time. Tessa must have the one with the baby's things.

"I saw a motorcycle when I broke into the store. I don't see it now but students come and go in this area. Even my brother has one." Yona dodged cars like it was the Indie 500.

"Where is he tonight?"

"He had a class and then planned to help at a tutoring center."

"Are you sure?"

"No. But I do not know his exact schedule. He told me when we were trying to leave my house and you were packing up. Said not to worry if he did not come around for a few days."

"What does that mean, Yona?"

"Said he would go into hiding so the general would not search for him."

"Why would he do that?" Chase thought it sounded odd.

Yona had picked up speed and laid on the horn several times to keep the traffic from blocking his escape.

"Hao is not trusting of the government and hates the general. He has not always been one to show he feared him. Even tonight, the general asked to see him. He wants to offer him something."

"Like what?"

"My father thinks it will be a threat of some kind to make him fall in line. He plans to close the orphanage too. Mother will be heartbroken, but admitted it was time to leave."

Chase didn't like that Hao was missing. "Where are the colonel and my mother?"

"They are hiding too. I came to check on you because he worried the general might find where Hao lived since he showed interest in him."

"So, Hao just left us back there to be attacked?" he fumed.

Yona became quiet for a few blocks. "He had no way to know the general was asking my father about his whereabouts. I think he went to get the Red Dragon."

"He is friends with the Red Dragon?" He turned in his seat and banged a fist on the dashboard, causing Yona to flinch. "He knows I sent him a warning. I guess he is not my friend after all."

"Yes, Brother, he is. He is trying to help. Please. Do not be angry. You will see."

"Take me to him."

"I cannot."

Chase pulled his weapon and jammed it against his brother's head. "Are you sure about that?"

~ ~ ~ ~

Tessa had tried to find a hiding place in Hao's tiny apartment and realized she had to get out. She decided to escape through the store that joined his quarters. Remembering the door had a loose clasp on the other side, she pushed it to see if it would break. The door felt stuck, but after jerking on it several times, it opened. She checked the yard one more time. Chase and Yona fought for their lives. She had to believe they would be okay. Her orders were to leave and get to the airport. What she would do between now and then was still a mystery.

She sucked up her courage and turned her attention back to the open door into the store. One step inside, she ran smack into what felt like a wall, except this wall put his hand over her mouth so she could not scream. When she stumbled back, he caught her in his arms and pulled her close.

"Red Dragon," she gasped when he pulled his hand away

enough for her to breathe. "Please. I am only trying to get home with my child. I need your help." His eyes bored into her, and the thought occurred to her that he meant her harm.

His leathery clothes were warm, and his scent reminded her of wet grass after a cleansing rain. From his cheekbones to his chin, he wore a loose-fitting black mask and under his eyes appeared to be red streaks of makeup or paint. It was a strange impression at a time like this, but Tessa thought he was rather beautiful. She found herself mesmerized by the danger.

Instead of speaking, he nodded acceptance and spun around, jerking her after him. Cautiously, they approached the front door of the store. He pointed toward a shadow outside then held up his hand as if she must wait.

"Okay," she whispered then caught his sleeve to stop him.

He whirled around, his eyes creasing in confusion.

"Be careful."

He lifted his hand and laid it on the baby then on her cheek. He then slipped outside like a phantom.

The man was both ghostlike and stealthy as he moved, and she could barely see him in just a few seconds. What she did see was a man dressed like the others in the backyard. He ran toward the Red Dragon, holding a machete with both hands. There were no bloodcurdling screams or loud footsteps, only the deadly speed of an assassin. Tessa swung the door open and screamed, "Red Dragon!" as she pointed.

The attacker moved so quickly that Tessa feared she was too late, but the Red Dragon spun around in time and landed a roundhouse kick to the man's head. Although the attacker went down, he jumped up like he had springs attached to his body and swung the machete violently.

The Red Dragon jerked back then let out a yell that would have awoken the dead. Chills ran over her body as he pulled his long sword from the sheath on his back and swung with both hands. This time, the man did not get up. It appeared as if a large part of his neck had been severed. Bending over, her body rebelled as she gagged back her impulse to vomit. When she straightened, the Red Dragon had disappeared, leaving her to spin in circles.

A motorcycle roared up and screeched to a halt. The Red Dragon swung his leg over the side almost in the same instant he put down the kickstand. Tessa felt frozen in place and relieved he hadn't abandoned her. When he rushed up to her, tears of relief trickled down her cheek.

"You saved my life. Thank you." Red Dragon was matter-of-fact in his thanks.

"I-I thought you left me," she choked.

"Never. I am your servant always. Come. We haven't much time."

"But, Chase..." She stared back at the building as he tugged her to the motorcycle and helped her mount.

"Warriors find a way. We go."

He swung his leg over and, in a split second, they disappeared into the night. Was it a good decision? Probably not, but what choice did she have? Lotus must be saved at all costs. She had to pray for Chase's safety and that he would meet her at the airport tomorrow as planned.

Frightened and overwhelmed with the fear of failure, she wrapped her arms around the Red Dragon and laid her head against his back as Lotus relaxed and dozed off. His leathery glove lay gently on her hands for only a second. It gave her the strength to endure the next few hours.

~ ~ ~ ~

Robert unlocked the door of his suite and stepped inside to see the sitter asleep on the couch. She was also an FBI agent and stayed with the kids all night. The sun was up, and here he was sneaking in like he broke curfew. She roused quickly and stretched then nodded his way. After giving him a rundown of the evening and how things went with the kids, she took her leave.

He activated the Keurig coffee maker and headed for the shower. For once in his life, he felt extremely dirty, and he wanted to wash off the smell of Phoebe. Standing under the rain shower, he hoped he could also wash off the memories of her touch mixed with lies. How could he have gotten roped into this situation with her?

Their meeting had been an accident, or so he thought. Given this new scenario, he didn't know what to think, except Tessa had somehow generated the invitation with the Pacific Rim

Consortium. That still was a nonsense idea that his ex-wife could have that kind of influence in Washington.

She was a geography professor, for crying out loud, a nerd with way too much geopolitical research floating around in her head. Nobody cared about that. Yet, according to Agent Martin, they wanted him because she had connections. The only connection she had was a Christmas card from the president. They had met because of her uncle receiving the Medal of Honor. No mystery there.

Drying off, he decided he'd try the coffee then take a quick nap. One thing he had to admit about Phoebe; she was fully engaged when it came to sex. But even that repulsed him, knowing he'd committed to something that could brand him a traitor to his country. How was he going to explain this to Tessa?

Sitting on the couch, he sipped his coffee that hit his stomach like a bomb. He felt hot and cold at the same time. Repulsed and anxious to get this next part over with, Robert checked for messages from Agent Martin. There were none. Twisting the earwig back into place, he waited, hoping to hear a word of encouragement or praise for a job well done.

The anticipation of a few minutes of time crashed and burned as his three kids staggered into the living room yawning and stretching. Heather climbed up in his lap and laid her head against his chest. The boys sprawled on the couch like lazy lions. Why did he fight this feeling of responsibility of being a parent? Most of the time, it wasn't so bad. It was better when Tessa was there to carry the bulk of the load, but still. This certainly taught him how hard it could be.

"When did you get home, Dad?" Daniel asked.

"Late," he said, adjusting Heather on his chest. "You were asleep. Did you like your sitter?"

"She was cool," Sean Patrick admitted. "Said she'd come back today if you had any meetings. Maybe take us to the pool. Going to be some games and an acrobat demo, she said. So, do you? Have meetings, I mean."

"Yes. I already made arrangements for her to come back in a couple of hours. Got to meet with the CEO of the company I'm thinking of working for."

The kids remained silent, and he wondered if they cared what he did. It wasn't like he'd been Dad of the Year. "You guys good with that?"

Mostly he got shrugs and sighs. What did he expect? Actually, a little crying and rage would have been a nice touch.

He ordered breakfast for them, and at least then they had quiet conversation and recapped the evening's events, mostly games and a Christmas movie they'd seen a dozen times, no matter the time of year.

The sitter was waiting for them downstairs in the lobby and had made an itinerary for Robert who read over it quickly and decided he'd rather be going with them than what he was about to engage in. After he said goodbye and walked outside to have a valet retrieve his car, Agent Martin strolled up in a suit. The mirrored sunglasses were a little much.

"Just a tip, if we ever do this again, Robert. Take your earwig out if you're going to get down and dirty with a Chinese spy. Just sayin'."

Robert moaned and realized he probably was on tape and could be blackmailed into doing the FBI's bidding for the rest of his life. "Go to hell."

The agent chuckled. "You remember what to say today?"

Robert nodded and avoided eye contact.

"Sign that document and let them give you your first assignment. Ask a few questions that make them nervous. Just go with the flow. You'll figure it out."

"Go with the flow. Great," he snarled. "And what if their heads explode or something?" he asked sarcastically.

"We can only hope," he said with a smirk. "I won't be far away. Several other agents are already on scene. Don't sweat it. Here comes your car. Drive safe, pretty boy."

Robert paused outside the driver's side of the car and pointed at the agent when he spoke to the valet attendant. "Told him you'd tip him a fat fifty for his service. See ya." When he slipped behind the wheel and drove off, he checked the rearview mirror to see the agent fishing money out of his wallet. "Well, that was worth it."

CHAPTER 40

The Red Dragon helped Tessa up the narrow path to his cave house. Tessa sent some pebbles off the side and could hear them tumble a long way then hit what sounded like water. It was so dark she could barely make out his body. He had managed to tie a small flashlight the size of a ballpoint pen to the front of the carrier for Lotus. With a tight hold on Tessa's hand, he moved forward, apparently not needing a light for himself.

At one point she shivered. The path was getting steeper and narrower by the second. Where was he taking her? Would she ever see Chase again? Had she taken too big a risk this time? She gasped for breath. He stopped and pushed her against a rock wall.

"We are almost there. You are safe. I will not let you fall. It is better that we keep moving." He reached down and turned off her light. "From here, you must trust me. I will hold your hand. You must hold to my belt with the other. I do not want anyone to see light moving along the top of the ridge." The Red Dragon pulled her to his chest so that he could see her face. "Look at me," he said quietly. The baby moved at the sound of his voice. He took a moment to stroke her little face and speak something melodic in Chinese. When she stopped moving, his eyes seemed to smile. Maybe it was her imagination in the darkness, but suddenly, she wasn't afraid.

"I'm ready." She nodded nervously, but with a deep breath she repeated, "I'm ready."

When they entered a cave, Tessa realized it was actually living quarters. She stumbled in relief, but he caught her in his arms to steady her. He lit two small LED lanterns. He came back to her and unfastened Lotus then laid her in a basket like the one she imagined baby Moses had floated in the Nile River to protect him from the Egyptians. He turned to remove the carrier as if he might be unfastening body armor. Then she saw blood on his side.

"You're hurt," she said in alarm. "He sliced you with the machete." She tried to turn him to check the seriousness.

"Can you repair the wound? I do not think I can do it at this angle."

"I will do my best. Do you have a first aid kit?"

He took the baby carrier and laid it on a table and searched through a trunk for supplies. When he handed her the kit, she spotted the bed.

"Maybe you should lie down. It might be easier for me to work on you if you are still."

He began to undo his leather armor but seemed to struggle, so Tessa helped him undress from the waist up and sucked in her breath at the gash on his side.

"Red Dragon, you need a doctor," she said, helping him to lower to the bed.

"You are enough, Tessa. I will tell you what needs to be done. I have had training."

She started to ask where and when, but it didn't matter at this point. He needed her help, not a hundred questions. Step by step, he told her how to clean the wound then how to anesthetize the area. "At least you won't hit me if I hurt you—accidently, of course."

His eyes creased as if he might be smiling as she kept working.

Luckily the first aid kit had sterile gloves for her to use. He grimaced when she cleaned the wound. Even through the pain, he managed to tell her how to suture the wound properly and then apply a bandage in case it continued to bleed. She found some over-the-counter pain meds in the kit plus a case of bottled water next to the trunk.

"Take these. It's going to hurt like crazy soon. And this may keep a fever down too."

He tried to sit up, and she quickly put her arm behind him to assist.

"You should rest," she said, kneeling down by the cot-like bed and resting her hand on his knee that still bore the leather armor. It was strange to have him this close and looking at her with feverish eyes. "I'm going to wash your chest. It will cool you down and remove anything I left that might infect the wound. Okay?"

She filled a bowl with water and found a sponge in the kit to run gently across his chest. Tattoos colored his shoulders and down his arms. When she moved to wash his back, she discovered a large tattoo of a red dragon from his neck down to his waist. She stroked the dragon as if it were alive. It was so beautiful; she couldn't help but trace it with her fingers.

"You are giving me...I think you call them...goose bumps." He straightened and turned his head to see her.

"Oh. Sorry. That was rude of me. I just have never seen such a beautiful beast on someone."

"Dragons are here to help man, not scare them."

Tessa stood and returned the first aid kit to the trunk then walked to the opening of the cave to take in the view. She could see lights below and in the distance. "What is this place?"

He pushed off the cot and stood. She rushed to put her arm around him so he wouldn't fall. Leaning into her, he walked to the mouth of the cave.

"This is a cave house called a Yaodong. They are built into the side of a cliff along this valley. They avoid the wind and maximize the use of sunlight and water for the people to farm. I chose this cave because it has a vaulted room with clay walls. I have several rooms and you can see they are peppered with stones on the outside and arched openings. I keep the basics here, but not much else. Neither dragons nor warriors need things that would make them soft and unprepared."

He still wore the mask, and it had to be uncomfortable.

"Come, sit down." She led him back to the cot and held on to him as he lowered himself to sit. "I'm going to remove your mask so you will sleep better. I'll sit by you to make sure you do not start to bleed. Then, in the morning, you can take me to the airport to meet Chase and Colonel Zhou Xiang." When he didn't respond, she came to kneel by his bedside. "You are taking me to meet them. It's the only way I can protect Lotus and get her home where she belongs."

"I will protect you, Tessa," he said as his eyes closed. "I do not wish to reveal my face. I just need a few minutes to rest. Then we will talk about the future." He let her help him lie back down.

Future? The only future would be to get out of China and back to her children. The only future was making a baby with Chase and starting a new life in Tennessee where she belonged.

"You must not try to leave. It is dangerous. I will help—you." And then he was asleep.

She waited a good thirty minutes before she untied his mask and slowly pulled it away. She jumped to her feet and covered her mouth so that she didn't cry out at the wounded warrior. Then she knelt down again and laid her hand on his heart.

"Hao!" she exhaled. "All this time you were the Red Dragon and I never suspected. My husband's best friend and stepbrother. You are a good man. No wonder you knew how to dress a wound. Your stepmother has taught you well." She wanted to laugh and cry at the same time but decided to attend to him for the rest of the night.

Several hours had passed when she decided to check out the cave dwelling. She found a journal stored in a crack of the wall in the second room. She thumbed through the pages, examining his transformation in sketches of what must have been his life as a boy and growing up. She recognized Chase, the Shaolin, his sister, and much more.

Somewhere along the way, he must have known he was destined for this secret identity. She couldn't read the words written in Chinese, but the sketches spoke volumes. After going through it several times, she closed the book and held it against her heart then hid it back in the crevice in the wall.

She found another cot and placed it near the Red Dragon in case he needed her. A silk robe and a sheet were in the trunk. The robe was warm enough for her and she hoped the sheet would be enough for him. Lying there in near darkness, she studied his face until her eyelids became too heavy to resist sleep. She allowed the dragons in her imagination to protect her the rest of the night.

~ ~ ~ ~

It was a ten-minute drive to the offices of Edmond Yu. To his surprise, Phoebe waited at the entrance where he was told to park. He turned the engine off. She joined him inside the car.

"Plans have changed." She leaned in and kissed his cheek.

"Why?"

"Didn't ask. Didn't think it mattered. I'll give you directions."

Robert tapped his earwig when Phoebe turned to look out the window. He tapped the earwig a second time hoping to hear a comforting voice. The silence forced him to adjust it only to pull it out. When Phoebe suddenly turned back, he panicked and fumbled with it, only to drop it on the floor. A wave of panic washed over him.

Phoebe continued to give him directions. Maybe it was the early morning sun affecting his ability to think straight. Did he actually finish that first cup of coffee? The idea Agent Martin wasn't reassuring him each step of the way both annoyed and worried him. When Phoebe tried to engage him in conversation laced with laughter, it reminded him of a baby rabbit screeching when an owl snatched it from its mother.

The destination turned out to be a small cluster of buildings designed to resemble adobe-style haciendas. Flowers were in abundance along with tourist traffic. She pointed out a restaurant that had indoor and outdoor seating. People were already going in for brunch. He wasn't sure he'd be able to eat again without vomiting. His stomach was already in knots.

Entering, Phoebe led him to a private room that opened to a room full of people. The applause grew louder when they walked to the center of the room. Startled, he realized it was a celebration for him joining the company. Agent Martin might have it all wrong. There was nothing sinister going on here.

Phoebe escorted him to a table where Edmond Yu waited with more applause and the contract. There was no question that he would sign it.

"Welcome to the family, Robert." He handed him a pen and shoved the contract his way.

Maybe he could just run. Instead, he signed the agreement and held it up for everyone to see.

While food was being served, Edmond took him outside. He congratulated him on the engagement to Phoebe and said he hoped they'd be very happy in Washington DC. Robert began to relax in spite of not being connected to the FBI. Earlier, he'd noticed the obvious attention Edmond gave him during moments with Phoebe, a contorted expression, as if in pain. She made a big deal of her joy as she pawed him and flaunted her engagement ring. Thankful he didn't have to pay for it, he wondered if it was even real.

"Robert, I've sent some documents to your hotel for you to go over. I know it's your vacation, but I'd appreciate you weighing in on the legality of them. It concerns making a few deals with China that are outside the realm of government oversight."

"Our government?"

"Of course. We represent the interests of the Pacific Rim countries of Asia. That is our first priority. No worries. The US government is well aware of us and what we do."

"So, I'm working for China?"

Edmond took a sip of his champagne. "Among others, but yes. I thought lawyers always read the fine print."

Robert followed his line of sight to Phoebe. "Guess I was distracted."

"I'm sure she's worth it." He set his glass down and disappeared into the crowd, shaking hands and chatting like this was no big deal.

After several hours, the party broke up and he drove Phoebe back to get her car. She insisted on following him to the hotel so they could tell the children they were engaged. All he wanted was for this to be over. Nothing had been said or done to indicate there was a threat to national security. He located the earwig and placed it back in his ear. Even after tapping it and saying Agent Martin's name, there was no response.

CHAPTER 41

Tessa's eyelids fluttered open to see dappled light. For a good twenty seconds, it didn't dawn on her she was in a cave or that she had a baby to tend to. Stretching like a feline, she wondered why coffee wasn't teasing her to engage with the morning. Then her eyes fell on the empty cot next to her, and the whole previous night came rushing over her like a tsunami.

Throwing the silk robe off, she swung her feet to the uneven floor to see a man standing a few feet from her, holding baby Lotus in one arm and a dangerous knife in the other. He was still dressed in his leather armor, except for over his chest where he had sustained a wound. Shoulder pads were in place as were the shields on his arms. The paint remained under his eyes and across his nose to his cheekbones. With the mask gone, his face was fully exposed.

"Hao—I removed your mask last night so you could breathe easier."

"You did what you thought best."

She approached him slowly and noticed how Lotus reached her arms out toward her, causing her heart to warm. "Did you find food for her in my backpack?"

"She has been fed."

Tessa reached toward his bandage, but he flinched and stepped away. "I am fine."

"Let me change your bandage. I want to make sure you aren't bleeding. How do you feel?" She moved to touch his head, and once more he moved. "What is it? What's wrong."

"You know who I am. Does that not disturb you?"

"Ha. If you knew what I've been through in the last few years… What I'm saying is, your identity only surprised me. What disturbs me is what Chase is going to do when he finds out. Please, let me check you out." She took the baby and set her on the cot and pointed for Hao to sit next to her. Her wide eyes and squeal caused Tessa to laugh.

Hao tilted his head at her. "There has never been laughter in this place. It is—good."

Tessa kneeled down and removed the bandages. The baby cooed and tried to clap her hands. "I think the stitches held and no signs of infection. Your skin is cool."

"Are you still frightened of me?"

"More angry than frightened. You deceived Chase and me. I don't like that."

"It was necessary."

She stood once again. "We're supposed to meet your father at the airport. Take me there now," she demanded coolly.

His dark eyes narrowed.

Unsettled, she cleared her throat and picked up Lotus. "Do you have a problem with that? I asked you to help me last night, and I appreciate that you did without thinking of your own safety, but it is time to go." Tessa tried to use her authoritative haughty voice, which only resulted in him lowering his chin and staring down his nose at her then rose to his full height.

"I will decide when we go."

"Okay. When do we go?"

He grabbed up the backpack and baby carrier. "We go now."

Tessa sighed in exasperation. "Men," she mumbled as he slipped the carrier over her head.

"Thank you, Tessa, for taking care of me last night." He slipped the baby into the carrier.

She held her breath when he invaded her space more than she liked. "I guess we're even."

He stepped aside and pulled on the leather shirt before relieving her of the backpack. "Think what you will. This may be fate without destiny."

"What does that mean?" Tessa felt confused.

"It means that a man and woman may be fated to become a couple but not destined to stay together."

"Good thing we're not a couple."

The Red Dragon's eyebrow arched as his lips pushed together as if resisting amusement. "Then again, fate is hard to predict."

"Not this time," Tessa said sternly.

"You have much to learn, Tessa Hunter."

~ ~ ~ ~

The air felt warm and stuffy inside the hangar where Chase had spent the night tied to a chair with one leg shorter than the others. His younger brother's head bobbed as he slept, also tied to a chair. The previous night swam up to him as he shook his head to clear the cobwebs. His ribs hurt and suffered from a pounding headache. Yona appeared to have a trickle of dried blood just below a cut under a swollen eye.

Having defeated General Sun Li's men, he ran back to search one more time for Tessa, even though he knew the Red Dragon had taken her. With blood on the sidewalk outside the storefront and two men badly injured, he guessed the Red Dragon had fought his way through to escape with Tessa and the baby. Hopefully, some of that blood didn't belong to her.

He remembered Yona driving like a bat out of Hell and being angry at what he was being told about his stepbrother leaving them unprotected.

"We need to leave. The authorities will be here any minute." Yona pulled at his arm, but the wail of sirens had already begun.

The realization he'd held a gun to his brother's head like he was a third-world terrorist sickened him. The kid was only trying to help him and save Hao's reputation. Lowering the weapon, Chase complied with his brother's request to be patient.

"Okay. I'm sorry. I mean no harm to you, Yona. It's my wife and child I'm concerned about."

"Hao will find a way. Trust me."

In another instant, they were surrounded by flashing lights and military police-style vehicles. The only option was to pull over or crash into innocent bystanders. Men swarmed out, guns aimed at them. They were ordered to drop their weapons, and Chase could see that Yona's hand twitched in a move to refuse. He grabbed the boy's weapon and put it on the ground. When they raised their hands in surrender, a police car door opened and a familiar man stepped out, straightened his jacket, and approached them slowly.

"General Sun Li," Chase said.

"We meet again, Chase. I believe you go by Captain Hunter, although you are listed on the tour as"—he extended his hand toward the driver who had joined him and handed him a piece of paper—"Chase Butler. Charlie for short, if I read this right."

Chase surveyed the number of men protecting the general. No way he could take that many, even with Yona's help. These guys didn't have poles but guns that would put a hole in them the size of a golf ball.

"You grew to be a big man like your father." The general eyed him top to bottom as if measuring his strength and potential for attack. "You should have died when you crossed the mountains with the Shaolin." He turned to the security team. "Restrain them. And don't take chances. I understand Captain Hunter has a lengthy resume of kills for those who cross him."

"Always room for one more."

"Where is your wife and the baby?" The general's voice turned icy.

"Not here," Chase answered sarcastically.

General Sun Li landed a fist on Chase's cheekbone, but it failed to stagger him. "Try again, Captain Hunter. Where are your wife and the baby?"

Chase spat blood on the ground. "My wife has failed to max out my credit card and heard there was a great sale at—"

This time, the general landed a fist to his gut, followed by one to his lip. "Try again, Captain Hunter."

"With all due respect, General, sir, go to hell."

This time, a man in uniform stepped forward and struck a baton on his shoulder, side, and thigh, causing him to topple like a redwood. Yona begged for mercy as another man beat him when he heard the general yell, "Enough. Bring—my guests." He nodded toward his car.

In seconds, one of his men opened the back passenger side door and stood aside. Colonel Zhou Xiang eased out then turned to extend his hand to another person. His mother appeared fragile and small in the evening light of the flickering streetlamp as she emerged.

"I see now you needed encouragement to answer my questions in order to understand the gravity of refusing me. Interrogating a big man such as yourself could take a while. Time I could be doing other things. However"—he walked over to Colonel Zhou Xiang and eyed him—"the colonel is fit, but his age may not be conducive to giving me what I need." The general reached out and lifted his mother's chin then turned to Chase. "Such a beautiful flower."

"Get your hands off her," Colonel Zhou Xiang raged. A guard stepped up behind him and slammed a baton in his lower back, dropping him to the ground.

Nora shoved at the general's chest, begging for her husband's life.

"Okay!" Chase shouted. "I don't know much, but I'll tell you what I know."

The general returned to stand in front of him. "I'm listening."

Chase told him about his attack failing and finding the note from the Red Dragon. He even produced it to prove he was telling the truth. "Our plan was to meet at a small airport not far from here and fly to Guangzhou."

"That wasn't so hard, was it? Why would the Red Dragon take your wife and the child?"

"He's been following us since Beijing and has isolated her several times."

"Romance is in the air." The general chuckled. "So even the Red Dragon has a weakness. You'll never see her again, I'm sure. And I guess you want to kill him."

"I do and I will."

He turned back to the colonel. "Where is your son?"

"I told you earlier tonight. This is his home. He should have been home by now. If he is not, then he spotted you and won't return. He, like Captain Hunter, has reasons, as you know, not to trust you."

"Since Captain Hunter is at your son's house, I can assume he is helping him escape as well. Not a good day for your family." He turned to his men. "Take them to the airport." He took one of Nora's braids in his hand. "Except for you. You will ride with me."

"No." Zhou Xiang struggled to get to his feet.

"No harm will come to her."

The soldiers forced Nora into the car. Chase and Yona tried to save her, but both received a beating for the attempted escape.

When they reached the hangar, the general emerged from the car with bloody scratches on his face and a fat lip. Nora was dragged out, fighting like a warrior. That no-nonsense attitude of his mother probably saved her from whatever the general had planned for her. He didn't catch all the words she shouted in the Cherokee language, but he was pretty sure the man was going to roast in Hell.

Having pieced together the previous night, Chase wondered where Zhou and his mother had been taken. At least he could keep an eye on his brother. The idea that Tessa and the baby were out there facing danger alone was almost too much to bear. Images flashed before his eyes at the possibilities—none of them he would be able to live with if she came to harm. Was it too late to learn to pray like she did all the freaking time? Did his mother practice praying when her heart and spirit were broken? Was that how she survived? No. He remained too angry to forgive and forget.

A movement in the rafters caught his attention. The diffused morning light coming through the hangar doors didn't expose whatever large object kept moving across the beams. At first, he thought he was hallucinating, but whatever it was, it had a leathery skin. When it disappeared, he tried to look around the room and saw nothing unusual. Then he felt a breathy whisper on his ear as a leathery hand clamped down on his shoulder. Chase started to turn his head, but a dagger was laid against his cheek to stop him.

"Will we fight together as Shaolin warriors, or will you seek vengeance against me?" The Red Dragon moved the dagger slowly against his cheek.

"Where is Tessa?" Chase hissed.

"Safe."

Chase felt the bands that held his hands break after the dagger withdrew. "If my wife has suffered no harm, you need not fear me."

"The general is outside. Pretend you are still constrained until we attack. Yona watches us. I have already freed him. He will wait for your signal." The Red Dragon tapped him on the shoulder again with the dagger. "I would not fear you anyway—Brother."

CHAPTER 42

Once back at the hotel, Robert didn't wait for Phoebe but hurried into the lobby and picked up his package of documents. He'd hoped to see the place crawling with FBI. Had they set him up? He inquired about his children, and the concierge informed him they were in the shade garden. To his surprise, he found them doing tai chi with their sitter and one more person in traditional Chinese clothing.

The teacher had his back to him, but his long hair hung down past his collar and, even from here, he appeared extremely fit and toned. He guessed he might be no more than five ten, but exhibited a larger-than-life presence. As the teacher slowly turned, Robert noticed a streak of gray framing his profile and recognized him as a martial arts instructor for the kids back home.

"Look, Dad," Daniel shouted and waved. "Master Wu is also vacationing here this week. Can you believe it?"

Robert waited for the lesson to conclude. Dr. Wu turned to make eye contact with him. He seemed to remember Tessa saying he was some kind of therapist at the university. All he knew for sure was he taught his kids kung fu. He decided it was another creepy friend of Tessa's. The sitter stepped closer and extended her hand to him, and he bowed over it as he took it.

"We have never met. I am Master Wu. I know your children from their kung fu class. I was surprised to see them here, so we took a few minutes to work out. I hope you don't mind."

"Of course not. Tessa has said they love their classes with you by the way."

"They are hard workers."

In Robert's experience, most of the time, they complained about so much as taking the trash out.

The sitter excused herself and waved goodbye to the kids. Wu bowed his head slightly to her then moved back through the garden explaining about various plants. The kids tagged along, hanging on the man's every word. They motioned for their father to join in, but he held back.

In that moment, Robert heard a gasp and turned around to see Phoebe staring at him menacingly. He walked over to take her hand, but she pulled back.

"How do you know Dr. Wu?" Her voice sounded like she'd been gargling razor blades.

"Master Wu? I don't, really." He explained about the lessons and that he worked at the university with his ex-wife. She shifted her attention to the kids and Wu. "What's the problem?"

"The problem is, I wouldn't let my pet boa constrictor be alone with him. He's a dangerous man who manipulates people's minds."

Robert's body went on high alert.

"He will steal your children and turn your ex into a zombie. You need to get them away from him this instant." She was backing away when Wu turned to face her. His hands fell to his sides, and his eyes narrowed.

"How do you know him, Phoebe?" A rush of panic filled his chest as he tried to stop her.

"He is a hitman for the consortium. He uses all kinds of mind control." She teared up. "I beg you. Please get the children. I'll meet you out front with the car. We must leave."

~ ~ ~ ~

She pivoted and disappeared so fast he couldn't ask another

question. Hitman? Why would the consortium need a hitman?"

He tapped the earwig. "I'm in trouble here. Where are you?"

Agent Martin strolled out of nowhere and came alongside him, still wearing the suit and Terminator sunglasses. "Stop tapping that earwig. You're giving me a migraine."

"Hitman?" He pointed to Dr. Wu. "I thought you were supposed to be watching after us."

"Oh him? Hitman? The man is a pacifist. He won't even step on a cockroach. Raises orchids and helps soldiers with PTSD." He pushed his glasses up on his nose with his middle finger. "Besides, my agent was with them. Just between me and you," he whispered, "I think she has a crush on the guy. Go figure, when she could have me." He shrugged.

"I'm sick of your snide remarks and lackadaisical attitude toward this whole mess."

"Just tell me how you feel, Robert. Get it out. Maybe, when this is over, we can set you up with my buddy Wu over there. One thing I like about him is that he doesn't say much. Always a plus. Well, and he and Chase Hunter don't get along. I really enjoy that angry back-and-forth between them."

"He knows Chase? Great."

"Chase knows everyone. The guy gets around." He folded a piece of gum into his mouth. "I heard Phoebe went to get the car and whisk you away to a safe place."

"At least she's looking out for me."

"Nope. She's setting you up. When she saw Wu, my kung fu wizard friend over there, she realized he had made good on his promise to eliminate her. You didn't hear that from me," he added. "They're related or something. Not sure of the details."

"Not sure? Isn't the FBI supposed to be sure!" he fumed.

"More or less. I'm kind of a free spirit. You got some kind of package of documents while you were out. I'll take that," he said, slipping it cautiously away as if it might hold a stick of dynamite. "While your fiancée was running like a scared rabbit out to her car, she managed to call her boss."

"Edmond?"

"Yes. Told him about Dr. Wu being here, involved with you, and I'm not sure, but she might have seen me. Some say I have FBI written all over me. What do you think?" He raised his chin and turned a profile to him.

"She knows you?"

"I mean, do you think I look FBI?"

Robert wasn't sure if the man was toying with him or he was an idiot. When he tried to meet the man's eyes, although invisible through those stupid glasses, his hard expression with the tightening and release of his jaw indicated this was just his style of intimidation and distraction. The man might be as dangerous as Chase Hunter.

"I'm getting my kids and leaving."

"No. You're going out to the car and leaving with Phoebe. Tell her the kids are back with the sitter. Get her to tell you what is going down right now and why Wu scared her. I've got people to examine this packet. I'm sure she's going to want these back."

"My kids…"

"You're not taking them anywhere. This is it. Go for a drive. No worries. Her car has a tracking device, and be still my heart, we can hear everything you discuss. Just please don't discuss last night. I don't think I'll ever get that picture out of my head. The sitter's on her way back, and Dr. Wu would die for those monsters of yours, so chill out. Damn. You're a mess. Get going."

"How can I trust you with the kids?"

"Hell, Robert, if you can't trust the FBI, who can you trust?" He touched his ear then lowered his glasses slightly. "She just pulled up in the circular drive. Ticktock. Move it."

~ ~ ~ ~

Robert ran to his kids first and told them the sitter would be coming back. He made eye contact with the straight-faced Dr. Wu. "I love my kids."

He arched an eyebrow. "It is a good thing you do." He spoke with enough frost to cool down a desert at noon.

"Bye, Daddy," Heather said, catching Dr. Wu's hand and swinging it back and forth as she skipped away with him in tow.

Robert loosened his tie as he ran to exit the building and jump in Phoebe's car.

"Where are the kids?" She pulled out and sped toward the

highway then pulled into a parking garage.

"I left them with the sitter. What is going on?"

"Dr. Wu is a powerful man in Hong Kong. He has connections on the mainland. He warned me to stay away from you," she admitted frantically.

"Why? Why did he warn you? Is my family in some kind of trouble?"

She steered the car into a parking garage. "I need you to tell me who you are working for while I can still help you."

"I'm not working for anyone."

"Where are the documents Edmond sent you? They are important and could cause me and the others in the consortium a lot of trouble."

"I-I don't have them. They are back at the hotel." He couldn't help that his speech slowed as if laced with doubt while covering his tracks.

The passenger side door opened, and a stout Asian man reached in and pulled him out by the collar as Phoebe freed him from the seat belt. She exited the car and walked around.

"Where are the documents, Robert?"

"I already told you. I haven't picked them up. I was told they were sent to my suite." Another Asian man appeared and sucker punched him in the gut so hard he puked. "Phoebe, what is happening?"

She jerked her chin toward the exit. "Go get those documents." The beautiful woman he admired had morphed into some kind of she-devil. Finally, he could see how he'd been played.

"Why me?"

"Your little domestic diva of a housewife is playing a dangerous game with the Chinese and messing up our plans."

"What plans? Tessa is about as dangerous as paint drying. She's a teacher and a mom. That's it." Sweat ran into his eyes.

Phoebe smirked and ran her hand down his cheek. "She is playing a dangerous game by bringing back a baby that will spoil our plans for economic dominance in the Pacific. Up until she got involved along with her husband, we've had a diversion with an illness killing adopted babies."

"I-I don't understand?"

"That baby holds the key to saving the children from a disease no one has yet identified. While the world focuses on that problem, we are moving in to take Taiwan and the Spatly Islands. It will be done with barely a shot fired. This country cannot focus on more than one problem at a time and finds war distasteful."

"Aren't you afraid I'll tell your plans?"

This made her chuckle. "Seriously? Do you think I'll let you go? You're a dead man if you don't help us."

"Maybe I'm working with the FBI," he bragged as he shook the stout guy off him.

Her face soured. "Check him." It only took a few seconds for the brute to run his hands over him.

"She didn't say give me a colonoscopy, pal," he fumed, trying to squirm away.

The brute shoved his head sideways and dug in his ear and pulled out his earwig, which he handed to Phoebe.

She spoke into the device. "Whoever you are, we have your little informant. You'll be able to pick him up on the side of the road soon. Just so you know, Dr. Wu is bringing me the kids in case I don't get those documents back. I'm sure you have them by now."

Robert tried to call out for help when Phoebe dropped the earwig and crushed it with her high heel. She stepped close enough he could feel her breath as she studied his face. "I really did like you, Robert. We would have made a good team."

~ ~ ~ ~

Agent Dennis Martin gritted his teeth and reached out to tech support. "Earwig is down, and the tracker isn't working. Last indication was that they're in a parking garage about five miles from here. Sending support."

His next call went to Agent Carter Johnson. "Are you at the airport yet?"

"Just landed. How bad is it?"

"Bad enough. Lost contact with Robert. They're after the kids."

"I'll fuel up, then we're off. Get the kids here."

He moved to the entrance to the garden and kept track of Dr. Wu, his agent, and the kids, as they approached. The boys saw him first and stopped. Their faces scrunched in confusion.

"Hello, boys," Agent Martin said matter-of-factly. "You doin', okay?"

Dr. Wu joined them, and Heather lunged at the agent and hugged him. "Uncle Dennis, what are you doing here? Want to go swimming with us?"

He laid a hand on the top of her head. "Can't today, sweetie. Take a rain check?"

"Sure. Why are you here?"

"Sir, I was wondering the same thing," Sean Patrick asked, a slight shake in his voice. "Are Mom and Chase okay?"

Dr. Wu came to stand next to the agent who said, "Last I heard, your mom is wowing the Chinese with her chocolate chip cookies. May have to negotiate some kind of release to get her back. They really like those cookies, and she won't give up the recipe." He shook his head and planted his hands on his hips.

Heather laughed. "Oh, Uncle Dennis. You're so silly." She gave him another hug.

"Really, sir, why are you here? Clearly, you're not on vacation." Sean Patrick surveyed the area, frowning.

"On business. And because of that business, Dr. Wu and I are going to send you home. Your dad is going to help us out here, and it's pretty important he stay for just a little while. This was your last day anyway, right?"

The kids nodded.

"Great. And guess what? Carter Johnson flew his plane down to pick you up."

The kids did a high five and began smiling again.

"I've sent a couple agents to collect your things, and we're good to go. I even have one of our fancy FBI black SUVs sitting out front to escort you to a small secret airport outside of town. How does that sound?"

Daniel and Heather could hardly contain themselves. Sean Patrick, on the other hand, hung back as they walked to the front entrance. "Agent Martin?" When had the kid gotten so much taller? "What's really going on?"

"Nothing you need to worry about. Your mom is safe, and so is Chase. They'll head home in another day or so. Your neighbors, the Ervins, are buying out all the ice cream from the grocery stores, from what I hear." He shifted his attention to Dr. Wu who was a little too quiet for his liking. "Hop in the car. Buckle up. We'll be on our way in a minute."

Once he'd checked to see things were secure with the kids, the agent turned to Dr. Wu. "We've lost contact with Robert. Last thing Phoebe said was that you were bringing the kids to her."

Dr. Wu said nothing as his eyes went to the back seat of the car.

"Just another thing to get Robert to cooperate."

"We've got the documents, and that's what they want back." Agent Martin was handed the new packet. "They've been swapped out and resealed so that they appear unopened."

"I will take them and get him back."

"I'm going with you," Agent Martin announced as he noticed the kids motioning for him to get in the car.

"It is better I go alone." He held up his phone. She has already texted a place to meet."

"She thinks you'll bring the kids."

"My niece thinks a lot of things. One of those things is that she will get away with this. She has a target on her back for screwing this up. Edmond is a dead man. He protects her. He cannot protect her from me."

Agent Martin handed him the packet as Dr. Wu's car was brought around. "Good luck. We'll be listening and right behind you."

"Get the kids to Carter. I need to know when they are safe."

"Done."

CHAPTER 43

Chase could see a Learjet taxi past the open hangar doors toward, on what he guessed, a runway. It powered down, but the sound of the engines still hummed. Relief sank in when he realized it most likely was his plane to Guangzhou. Since this airport flew the wealthy, political elite, and military brass on a regular basis, the soldiers milling around exhibiting little interest in the plane, gave him hope they still had a chance at escape.

Yona nodded toward him. Already, he felt protective of this new sibling in his life. In some ways, his features were similar to his own. Maybe that was just what he wanted to see. But the hatred he'd carried for Zhou Xiang for all these years had gone from a raging fire to warm embers that showed signs of dying out. All this time, he'd taken care of his mother, loved her, and provided a home for her. Whether that was out of guilt or love, he did it with honor.

Orders being shouted, soldiers hustling back and forth in front of the hangar took the calm atmosphere to a sudden burst of activity. Several soldiers entered looking stiff and dangerous in their camo fatigues and carried a bullpup-style assault rifle. They leveled their steely-eyed focus his way, ignoring the approaching threat behind them as they moved in his direction.

The Red Dragon tapped the two soldiers on the shoulder. They spun around and each received a quick blow to the head with some kind of club and a jump kick to their chests in rapid succession. They fell back and hit their heads on the concrete. Either they were dead or had major concussions. Either way, they were no longer a problem.

Yona rushed to help Red Dragon pull them off to the side behind a stack of boxes then returned to his chair. Chase could see the Red Dragon pull two swords from the double sheaths on his back then pointed one toward Chase, then slid it behind a metal box. Chase acknowledged the gesture as he watched him back into the shadows.

General Sun Li marched into the hangar, followed by five guards. His downturned mouth and red face indicated trouble. He stopped a few yards from Chase. Apparently, his reputation gave him cause for concern. "It appears that my prisoners have escaped. Would you know anything about that?"

"I know that you're a loser and a piss-poor general to let that happen—sir."

"Yet you are here all alone without any means to freedom."

"Things are not always as they appear—sir. You of all people should have learned that years ago when you thought you'd killed me and my family."

The general turned his head and, for a split second, looked concerned. His eyes appeared to frost over with rage as he pulled his baton and lunged toward Chase.

Even though his body ached and his muscles were stiff, Chase managed to grab the baton on its way down to his shoulder and jerked it away from the general as he pushed himself off of the chair.

With wide eyes, the general jumped back. When the general struggled to pull his weapon, he ordered the others to attack. His men swarmed forward, allowing him a successful retreat.

Yona stood then swung his chair to smack the pistol from his attacker, but it didn't stop him from grabbing the chair legs to attack the younger man. The younger man held his own with plenty of loud yells and name-calling that startled the soldier, slowing him.

The Red Dragon had intercepted two of the soldiers by using

vicious sword play that hindered them from pulling a weapon. Chase raced to retrieve the second sword hidden behind the metal box. At first, he felt clumsy due to being tied up for so long. But the weight of the sword in his hand and the adrenaline pumping through his veins invigorated his will to survive. He sprinted into the fight with the Red Dragon who had been surrounded by three soldiers.

Together, Chase and the Red Dragon fought like the Shaolin warriors they had trained to be, only their skills were not being used to defend a temple from bandits, warlords, or invading forces. They were servants to a baby girl who would save the world from the perils of another pandemic that may lead to war.

Yona disabled his attacker and joined the other two. However, Sun Li's protector also joined the fight. Although these men had fighting swords, they were no match for the modern Shaolin warriors who were battle tested against the evils of the world.

The quick actions of all three warriors prevented any of the remaining soldiers from pulling a gun after receiving a deadly stab wound. They fell to the floor, barely alive.

"Where is Sun Li?" Chase surveyed the area, cautious of a second sneak attack.

"Gone," a soft voice said behind him.

Chase pivoted in alarm then realized it was Tessa standing with outstretched arms. He dropped his sword as she ran to him. Catching her up in his arms, he delivered a hard kiss to her lips. When he set her feet back on the ground, he remembered the baby.

"Lotus?"

"Right here, my son," his mother said, cuddling the baby in her arms. Zhou Xiang limped beside her. Even though his uniform was ripped, crooked, and bloody, he carried himself with pride and his chin up.

Chase went to them and ran his hand down Lotus's face until she giggled and reached for him. Turning his attention to Zhou, he pulled his shoulders back and saluted the man. "Sir, I am sorry I misjudged you. I hope that someday you can forgive me. My mother chose a good man. Thank you for taking such good care of her all these years."

Zhou put his arm around her waist. "I think we took care of each other. And you and I have much time to live in peace. But, for now, we must get you on that plane."

The Red Dragon approached carefully and stood several steps away from Chase as he surveyed the united family. Chase noticed how he observed Tessa as she took the baby from his mother.

"Hao. Or should I call you the Red Dragon?" Chase shook his head in disbelief and laid a hand on his friend's shoulder.

The Red Dragon removed his mask and waited. His adopted mother covered her heart with her hand then ran to him with open arms. His father limped forward, eyeing him from head to toe.

"Hao? My son? I suspected you were involved in dangerous activities. But not this."

"I did not want to deceive you, Father, but it was for your protection and Mother's."

Yona's pride shone in his eyes. Chase realized the kid knew from the beginning the identity of the Red Dragon. He had been as much his protector as the Red Dragon had been for the others. At that moment, Chase was so proud of this family.

"I would feel better if I knew where the general was," Chase offered.

"He was slipping off like a Chinese krait snake when we came in. If I had a gun, I would have killed him," Zhou growled. "But no matter. You must go."

CIA Agent Tan rushed in and motioned them to hurry.

"Don't tell me you're the pilot?" Chase said, moving his family forward to the Learjet outside. "Is there anything you can't do or provide?"

"I am pretty amazing. With all due respect, Captain Hunter, shut up and get on the plane." He pointed to the Red Dragon. "I am not taking him. Too dangerous."

"Not an option. He goes with me."

"No." It was Zhou Xiang. "You must go without us. We will slow you down. Others will be looking for us too."

"I got your back, Captain Hunter, but not these guys." Tan shook his head.

"No way. They're going. Mom, get on the plane."

"We'll discuss this when we're in the air," Tan grumbled then helped Nora to the plane. He turned, and a twisted grimace of horror crossed his face. "Get on the damn plane now!" he shouted.

Chase spotted what he saw. General Sun Li walked at a good clip, loading his rifle without even checking his progress. The Red Dragon stood his ground until Chase jerked him so hard he lost his footing and fell on the stairs, just as a shot rang out and snapped at the ground where he had stood. The general lowered his rifle then lifted it again.

As the next shot rang out, Zhou Xiang pushed in front of Chase and took the bullet in his chest.

His mother screamed inside the plane.

Zhou Xiang, his former enemy collapsed into his arms, and Chase struggled to lift him. Lumbering up the few steps to get inside, Hao jumped up to cover his retreat. Yona ran down the steps carrying a Glock, which Hao grabbed out of his hands and aimed at the general. Tears were running down the younger version of himself and knew there was no way a shot would hit the enemy.

"Get on the plane," Chase ordered. "Take your father." He handed him off to Yona and accepted the challenge.

Chase backed up the steps, shooting a weapon he'd taken from one of the downed guards. The roar of the Learjet engines drowned out any distraction from inside the plane. The general took cover instantly.

Chase felt hands on his collar, jerking him inside the plane. Nothing mattered but getting back to the colonel who lay bleeding on the floor of the plane.

Tessa kneeled beside his mother with her arm around her sobbing body. His wife gazed up at Chase with bloodshot eyes in a déjà vu moment. Not so long ago, it had been her sobbing over the body of Roman Darya Petrov, a man she deeply loved and married to get out of Russia. He too, had taken a bullet for him. This man had done the exact same thing, and he could only imagine it was to pay back for the pain and suffering he'd caused him and his mother.

The tilt of the plane and wheels locking into place verified they were safe, at least for a little while. The sight of the Red Dragon falling to his knees next to his father and Yona holding his father's head in his hands broke his heart. Chase kneeled next to the colonel and placed his fingers on his neck then reached across to his mother.

"Mom, he's gone. I'm sorry. He saved my life, and I did not deserve it. If I had known what he was trying to do, I would have stopped him."

She laid a hand on his that rested on her face. "He knew I could not lose you again. It was his last gift to us. I loved him so much. I wish you could have had more time together."

A great remorse welled up inside him. "I do too."

"I know that like your father and sister, I will see him again someday. It is a joy I can take comfort in, Chase."

Tessa continued to hold his mother when she offered words of comfort to him. "You were meant for great things, Chase. Many lives depend on you, as it always has. I know it is hard to understand and see that. But I see it."

He nodded and stood. Assisting his brothers, he moved Colonel Zhou Xiang to the back of the plane then assisted his mother into her seat. Yona sat next to her, holding her hand and rubbing his thumb over the back of her fingers as his eyes glazed over in what Chase assumed was grief. Tessa took Lotus and found a place to buckle in as he and Hao moved to the cockpit to talk to the pilot.

"I filed a flight plan that takes us to the northeast corner of Inner Mongolian Province. I left a lot of hints how we planned to land and escape across the border into Mongolia. With any luck, the general and his band of cutthroats will head that way."

"And where are we going?" Chase asked.

"We'll go to Guangdong province and park the plane about fifty kilometers from Guangzhou. I have a ride for you, but not for everyone."

"I told you—"

"Brother, I will take care of Mother and Yona." Hao laid a hand on Chase's shoulder. "I have a safe place for them. Tessa can tell you. Then, when you are ready to come get us, send word to our Shaolin Master, Shi Yen. He has connections and will find us."

"And you will come too, right? Don't make me come find you."

"I will bring them to whatever destination you plan. I cannot promise I will follow. There is much work to be done here. One of those things is taking care of General Sun Li."

"I am sure my mother will have plenty to say about that, Hao. You are her son and she will not leave you behind," he reminded him sternly. "Do you feel up to dealing with that?"

The Red Dragon turned back to find his mother leaning into Yona. He continued. "I need to bury my father. For now, she will grieve. Yona and I will make sure she is safe and is ready to leave with you. Yona will do as I say. Trust me."

"Tan, what will you do with my family who remains?" Chase tapped him on the shoulder.

"Don't worry. I have a safe house and then my people will let the Red Dragon take the lead."

"You're a good man, Tan." Chase clamped him on the shoulder, causing the man to cringe then shook him off.

"Well, it certainly has been interesting."

~ ~ ~ ~

The car made enough turns that Robert became confused as to how far they had gone. Car sickness was about to take over as sweat beaded up on his forehead. Once, he asked for the AC to be turned down, and the brute driver slammed on his brakes, throwing him onto the floorboards. Phoebe peered over the seat at him and clicked her tongue.

"Sorry, baby. Won't be long. Wu is meeting us up ahead. I told him to bring your kids." She pooched her lips in a kiss toward him and reached back to touch him, but he repulsed away from her touch.

"Can I keep the ring? I'm assuming the wedding is off." She twisted it on her finger.

"It's fake anyway. Like you."

She held it up in front of her to get a better look. "You worthless piece of—" Biting back any further comment ended when she pointed to a small house. The car jerked to a hard stop before Phoebe exited the car. Robert tried to roll himself back onto the seat. The brute opened the door, grabbed him by the ankle, and dragged him out onto the ground.

Phoebe motioned for Robert to be helped to his feet as Dr. Wu pulled in front of the house.

"Where are the kids?" she asked.

"Asleep in the trunk."

"No!" Robert shouted followed by begging. "Please. Don't do

this. They're just children. Take me. Do whatever you want."

"Oh, shut up, Robert," Phoebe moaned.

"They'll suffocate in there, and it won't take long in this heat." Robert was on the verge of tears.

Dr. Wu held up the packet of documents. "Is this what you want?"

She snatched it from his hand. "I will get this back to Edmond. I know he will appreciate your cooperation."

"The two of you have made a mockery of the Pacific Rim Consortium. It was once a peaceful way to work side by side with other Asian countries so that together we could grow strong economically. But Edmond had to rule the world and tried to do so with the aid of Chinese powermongers."

"You lack vision, Dr. Wu."

"And you lack a conscience."

"My kids!" Robert screamed.

"I will take Robert to the desert. Know that I don't like cleaning up after you, Phoebe. I will come for you soon."

The fear of death leaped to her eyes as Dr. Wu walked Robert to the passenger side and buckled him in.

"Please, Dr. Wu. My kids. I'll do anything you ask. Don't let them die."

Dr. Wu leaned in and snapped the seat belt as if to test it. "Shh. They are safe. Agent Martin has taken them to the airport. They may be already in the air." He closed the door and walked to his side, noticing that Phoebe and her goon had started up her car and backed out of the driveway. She stuck her hand out the window and gave a condescending wave to Robert.

When she was out of sight, he headed out on Red Canyon Road. This was a longer way back, but he wanted to make sure Phoebe hadn't created a trap for him.

"Where are we going?" Robert asked nervously.

"To a safe house."

"And my kids?"

"Safe and soon to be back home." Dr. Wu adjusted his mirror and realized Phoebe and her driver were following them. He sped up, and so did they. "Here they come. Brace yourself."

Phoebe's driver started to pass them and rammed them on the

driver's side. Dr. Wu was fighting to control the car when Phoebe stuck a weapon out her window. As she fired, he let off the gas, and the bullet hit the front tire, causing him to swerve and lose control then slam into the red bluff alongside the road. The airbag deployed violently against him. He fumbled to find his weapon under the seat. But it didn't matter. Phoebe didn't bother to stop to see if they were dead. Robert was badly injured and the car was crushed against the red wall of rock. The smell of gasoline hit as smoke billowed from under the hood.

"Robert! Robert!" he called as he tried to open his dented car door. "Wake up. We have to get out of here."

CHAPTER 44

It was late afternoon when the plane landed outside Guangzhou and remained only long enough to refuel. Chase said his goodbyes to his mother and brothers, not knowing for sure if he'd ever see them again. Two men waited for them in a limo with tinted windows. They were dressed like a rich chauffeur and a personal bodyguard. The license plates were government issue.

"Are you sure this is a good idea?" Tessa eyed the two Chinese men standing at attention. They tilted their chins up in a greeting before speaking.

"No one will mess with us. We look pretty legit, don't you think?" He introduced himself as Jimmy in a New Jersey accent. "We're taking you straight to the American consulate for your papers then to the White Swan Hotel. The other families you traveled with are there, except for one."

"What happened?" Tessa scooted into the backseat. "The Plano couple were in touch with someone on the mainland and were feeding them information on your whereabouts. That's how they narrowed the search down in the first place. They are being held at the consulate. The Plano baby has been given to another couple who have already been cleared and sent home."

"What will happen to them?"

"Not known. My guess is sent home to stand trial for treason or maybe a lesser charge if they cooperate. They were suspect from the beginning because they lived in Plano, an area with a large Asian population. It seems someone reached out to them and promised a baby if they helped with finding the China doll you were to pick up. Their guide, John, overheard them talking and notified his father. The rest, we took care of."

"These guys know what they're doing. You can trust them. They're the best the CIA has. They are more Chinese than the Chinese." Tan chuckled and shook their hands. "I need to get the rest of your family to a safe place. Chase, it's been a pleasure. Let me know if you need me later."

"I will be in touch. Thanks for everything."

~ ~ ~ ~

The baby whimpered with irritation. Tessa's eyes closed in exhaustion then snapped open. Chase might as well have been wearing camouflage for guerilla warfare the way he kept double-checking their route. She knew he continued to be hypervigilant and hated surprises that might be out of his control.

Although the trip into Guangzhou had been noneventful without even getting stuck in five o'clock traffic, the driver entered the American consulate with his buddy only to emerge in a few minutes.

"Boy, did they appear relieved to see us. They were nervous as a cat." He passed the paperwork back to Chase in a sealed envelope. "Okay, folks, we're off to the White Swan. Lots of people there just like you. Buzz and I call it the Crybaby Hotel because of so many little girls leaving China."

"Mrs. Hunter." Buzz turned back to offer a patient smile. "It's beautiful and very clean. The food is top-notch. Last chance to get souvenirs."

"I think I'll just take a nap."

This made the man chuckle. "I don't blame you. It's been a rough trip."

The sun had dipped behind the skyscrapers by the time they checked in and unloaded in their room at the White Swan Hotel.

"We're set to have dinner with the other families at seven. You're going to love this. It's the Elvis Americano Good Vibration Restaurant. How American is that?" Chase announced in amusement as he walked around the room rocking Lotus in his arms as her eyes drooped toward sleep.

"Please tell me they have steak," Tessa said, falling on the bed. "I'm starved."

"I suppose you could get eel or scorpion, if that was your jam."

"Steak and mashed potatoes are my jam right now."

"Take a nap. Then I will. Tonight is going to get intense for us."

"Wake me up if I'm still asleep in an hour."

But he didn't. He let her sleep instead, and it would prove to be the right thing to do.

~ ~ ~ ~

Dr. Wu limped down the hospital corridor to meet Agent Martin who stood talking to the director of Enigma. "Where is he?"

"Surgery. Thanks to that good Samaritan who stopped and got the two of you out of that burning car, he's going to live another day to annoy people." Agent Martin smirked. "How are you?"

"Sore. He took the brunt of the crash." Dr. Wu had been examined and released. "The children?"

"Back home. We aren't telling them about the accident just yet. We haven't even told Tessa. Of course, we have no idea where she is. That Red Dragon character decided he'd step in and be a hero. Apparently, we are missing her and the baby."

"Time is running out," Dr. Wu admitted.

Director Benjamin Clark stepped out of the shadows and clicked off his phone. "I have Ken Montgomery and Zoric at the Ervins' home just in case there are more problems," the director said confidently. "We're searching for Edmond and Phoebe. They are MIA."

Dr. Wu limped away. "I assure you there will be no more problems from them. You can count on that."

"Wu, if you know where they are, let us handle it," Agent Martin advised.

He failed to acknowledge the agent and kept walking.

~ ~ ~ ~

"Look who it is," shouted Mr. Olson from Minnesota. He motioned for them to join the conversation area with the two families left plus John, the guide. "Where have you guys been?"

Mrs. Rickman put her arm around Tessa. "We were so worried. John said you were caught in the earthquake and were delayed."

"I'll say," Tessa moaned. "Couldn't get our luggage even after waiting and had to leave most of it. Missed our train then our flight. So, nothing to do but wait."

"I told them my contact there helped you find a place to stay." John grew pale.

"Yeah. Thanks, on that one," Chase interjected. "It was small but clean, and the food was decent. Anyway, we're here now, and I understand tomorrow is a tour of some gardens and the Chan family home. Think Jackie Chan will be there?" This brought a round of humorous comments to lighten the mood.

"I think we're traveling with those folks over there," Mrs. Rickman added. "Sweet group. From the Northeast. Boston maybe."

The small talk continued as they all moved to the buffet line where steak and mashed potatoes were served, along with watermelon, green beans, and apple pie. It was a taste of home. Tessa and Chase moved to a table that overlooked the Pearl River. They could see the people on the small fishing vessels that navigated quietly along the dark waters, lit only by the lights from the skyscrapers on the opposite shore. The others also sat at individual tables with their babies to enjoy the night air and the bobbing of boats.

"I think everyone has had enough of people and want to be alone," Chase said between bites of steak. "How's my girl?" he cooed to Lotus who played with the Cheerios Tessa had brought from home. He pointed at Tessa's plate. "You need to eat because—"

"I know," she snapped. "I'm sorry. Just a little nervous."

He reached across the table and took her hand. "I got this. Just like always." He turned to observe the river, seeing a patrol boat stop a boat and board. He felt sorry for the people on board. The police soon emerged and returned to patrolling the river. He wondered how often they stopped the boats.

The Elvis Presley song "Love Me Tender" started playing, which made Tessa laugh. "Can you believe we are eating steak and listening to Elvis Presley in this ancient country?"

He grinned and stood. With a new kind of dad finesse, he managed to wipe the cereal away from Lotus and lift her out of the high chair. "Come on. Let's dance before the world turns crazy again." He reached down with one arm and helped Tessa to her feet. A surprised expression lit up her face as he hoped it would, and she walked with him to the dance floor where several couples were slow dancing.

Having his arms around both of his girls gave him a sense of calm. Tessa laid her head against his shoulder and sang softly, along with the song. Lotus kept reaching out and touching her. He had always remembered, to an extent, China being home. He realized that Tessa had become his home. The state of Nirvana meant the paradise she'd brought into his life. Now he planned to thrust her into another dangerous situation, but hopefully for the last time.

"Tessa?" he said, kissing the side of her head. She didn't respond. "We should go." He could feel her sigh and knew the beginning of the end had arrived.

Chase and Tessa excused themselves early, saying they were exhausted. The others vowed not to be far behind after such a big meal. Once their room door closed, they laid Lotus down on the bed since she had dozed off. Both remained quiet as they repacked backpacks with a few supplies that had been left in their room for them. Whether it came from John or the two who had driven them from the airport, the supplies were most appreciated.

Half past ten, Chase pulled Tessa to their small balcony and kissed her on her neck then made his way upward. She quickly fell into the rhythm of making love and started to explore his body.

"One last time," she breathed seductively into his ear when he pulled her back inside.

~ ~ ~ ~

The lobby doors burst open with a bang as General Sun Li and his men burst into the hotel. The soldiers, outfitted in combat gear, carried their rifles across their chests. The general smacked his hand down on the welcome desk, causing both attendants to jump. They quickly gave him the room number of the Hunters, AKA the Butlers. Storming toward the elevators, several men entered each one; another two stood at the stairwell. The general also gave instructions to block the exits on the first floor.

Entering one of the elevators with two soldiers, he focused so hard at the panel showing numbers of the ascension, he wondered why holes didn't form as a result of his anger. When the doors opened, the soldiers stormed out and followed several halls until they stopped outside the room occupied by the Hunters. They waited for Sun Li to join them. He passed the key card to the bigger of the two soldiers. At the sound of the lock being released, the door was thrown open so that it banged against the wall. General Sun Li followed them in as they approached the two twin beds.

He tilted his head toward the beds. The soldiers pointed their guns at the stretched-out bodies beneath the covers and fired several rounds until General Sun Li held up his hand. Bending over the larger of the bodies, he jerked the covers away only to find pillows. He hurried to the other side with the same result.

"Search the room," he demanded.

There was nothing of any consequence. After all, they had left their luggage behind in Wuwei.

He marched to the tour guide's room with the same kick-down-the-door attitude.

John, startled, sat up in bed, and tried to swing his legs to the floor at the same time the two soldiers dragged him to his feet.

Sun Li approached him casually, enjoying the terrified expression in the man's wide eyes. Taking a moment to survey the room as he flipped on an overhead light, he saw nothing out of the ordinary. John squinted from the sudden burst of light and tried to shake the soldiers off without success.

"Where are the Butlers?"

"The Butlers? Do you mean the American adoptive parents?" He cleared his raspy throat. "In their room. What time is it?"

"After midnight. They are gone."

"Gone?"

"Stop responding to me with another question. Where are

they?"

"They left the restaurant after dinner. Said they were tired and the baby was fussy. They arrived late. We had a nice dinner, made plans for tomorrow, and they said good night. The others soon followed. What is this about?"

One of the soldiers jammed his rifle into John's gut, causing him to release a loud grunt of pain.

"This is about them leaving without my permission. The man tried to kill me in Wuwei, and I want to know why. I suspect he is an American agent of some kind who should not be taking one of our babies. No telling what they will do to her. They are dangerous."

John tried to straighten only to be shoved down on the bed, followed by the barrel of the rifle pushed against his chest. "They planned to go on the tour tomorrow. That is all I know. I thought everything was fine."

"Who brought them here?"

"I heard they arrived by a limo. It carried a Chinese diplomatic flag. I didn't get a chance to ask because several families had a problem at the American consulate with their papers. I had to fix that then take them to the medical clinic for the final exam so the babies could leave for America."

"Did they go to the consulate to get their final papers?"

"At dinner, the talk involved the process and how they were sworn in. The Butlers admitted they were sorry they missed it with the group, but it went well there for them with no problems."

General Sun Li believed the man, since his voice and body trembled. He would have been a fool to lie to him.

"Any idea where they might have gone?"

"No, sir." His eyes were bulging at the rifle pointed at his chest. "I warned everyone not to leave the hotel after dark unless in a group and, even then, I needed to be with them. Everyone is ready to go home because they are so tired from being new parents. They just want a good night's sleep. I have known new parents to stroll their baby around the hotel to get them to sleep." He gulped then licked his dry lips. "Maybe you will see them on security cameras."

"Strangely enough, they are offline due to a tropical storm that rolled through two weeks ago. They have not yet been repaired."

He moved toward the door. "Thank you. You may go back to sleep. For your sake, I hope you are telling the truth."

"I-I am telling you what I know, sir."

He said nothing more as he left with the soldiers following as if they were ready for battle.

CHAPTER 45

Tessa dismounted the motorcycle with the help of one of the men who had picked them up at the airport. Lotus snuggled against her chest inside the baby carrier. Buzz had dressed like a native and made sure she matched the style. No one would have guessed an American rode behind him. Besides, at this time of night, no one paid much attention.

She took Chase in quickly who dismounted his motorcycle easily, and also dressed like a local. Except for his height, he didn't appear so different from their protectors. His dark skin and almond-shaped eyes were cover enough. His ability to speak Chinese added a layer of confidence. She moved closer to him. Doing so gave her a sense of safety, even though this remained a dangerous situation.

"Are you sure those security cameras were down?" Chase asked when he surveyed the area.

"We were the repairmen. Just removed a few pieces that won't get repaired. They are on backorder because that storm took out a lot of security systems. The high-profile business and government offices used the only parts available. A hotel is not high priority." He grinned. "Too bad. So sad."

"Is that the Pearl River?" She took a few steps away from her protector who followed without being invasive. "How are we leaving?"

Chase joined her. "I'm guessing that is our ride."

Tessa squinted to try and navigate the darkness. "Is that one of those fishing boats we saw at dinner?"

"Yes." Her protector motioned for them to follow him down the wharf where a boat bobbed up and down in the water. "We paid this couple a lot of money to take you down the Pearl River to the South China Sea where you'll head north toward the Taiwan Strait. You'll then enter international waters."

"Oh my gosh," Tessa moaned. "The Chinese claim those aren't international waters." She turned to Chase. "There's got to be another way. That passage is closely monitored."

"It's monitored by us too," Chase responded calmly. "We can't stop at Hong Kong. They'll be waiting for us, maybe even on the river. This is our best chance to get out."

"Then what? We can't take that boat all the way to California?"

The young couple stood waiting on the deck. Tessa couldn't tell if they were nervous, but she was terrified. Her knees were knocking so loud that the authorities would soon be descending on them.

"Mrs. Hunter, you'll only go as far as Taiwan. There will be a ship waiting to pick you up then a plane will take you home. I know you're scared, but no one knows where you are." Buzz laid a hand on her arm.

The second protector, Jimmy, followed up. "Just so you know, we chose this couple because their baby died in childbirth two days ago. They are grieving. I know you're going to think we took advantage of them, but we had to make sure they would be anxious to ease their grief by helping you with this child. We explained why the baby was important. I know it's cruel, but we suggested this virus may have killed their baby."

"That was a lie."

The young mother unfolded her arms when she saw Lotus.

"I know. But the part about saving other children wasn't. Sometimes you have to be wrong to be right," he said firmly. "Be gentle with her, Mrs. Hunter. She can help you through the night so you can get some rest." Jimmy squeezed her arm in support.

Tessa knew his actions were for the greater good. Her heart

would be permanently crushed if something happened to one of her children. In spite of knowing she would soon have to relinquish Lotus, the child had become one of her children. Thinking about surrendering her weighed heavily on her heart.

The four were helped into the boat, and introductions quickly followed. Chase took control of the conversation, and she could tell by their nods and shy expressions, they were satisfied with their new passengers. The woman spoke to Tessa and pointed to her eyes.

"She says she has never seen blue eyes and that they are pretty." Chase slipped an arm around her for just a moment, which gave her confidence.

Tessa nodded and said thank you in Chinese. The young woman switched her attention to Lotus and spoke softly to Chase.

"She wants to know if she can hold her for a while." Tessa hesitated to give her permission, but Chase removed Lotus from her chest carrier. The sadness on the woman's face became bright and serene as Chase placed the baby in her arms. She felt compelled to touch the woman's arms rocking the baby. Instantly, they bonded.

The two CIA men helped the boat captain to slip away into the darkness. Until that moment, Tessa didn't realize they were moving. Somehow that made her feel a little better about their chances.

"You two get some rest. We got this," Jimmy promised. "If anyone comes snooping around, they'll believe we're just a couple of Chinese fishermen. We even have papers saying as much. Go below. I'll keep an eye on Lotus. Probably two or three hours until we reach international waters, if this boat can keep up the speed. I want to be out in open waters before daylight. Darkness is our friend."

A three-quarter-size bed crammed into a small space with a faded blanket and one pillow was the only place to rest. Exhausted, Tessa didn't worry if there were bedbugs or spiders. She climbed into the bed and waited for Chase who searched the cabin for what she knew would be some kind of weapon in case of trouble. When he joined her in the bed, he turned on his side to face outward. He reached back and pulled her forward into his back. Snuggled against his body, she dared let her eyelids close and let fear ebb away.

~ ~ ~ ~

A scream woke him up. Chase rolled to his feet, dragging Tessa out of her deep sleep. Something had gone wrong. The realization the putter of the boat had stopped and the shuffle of feet no longer existed, drove home they were in danger. Tessa laid her hand on his hip. Several minutes passed before they ventured to the ladder. As they did, a soldier jumped down, knocking both of them off-balance, then pointed a QSZ-11 compact pistol in Chase's face.

Tessa stumbled backward quickly as Chase knocked the gun out of his hand and landed a fist like a hammer, crushing the bridge of his nose. A spray of blood landed on Chase as he directed another blow to the man's jaw, which took him down, long enough for him to grab his weapon. The dazed attacker tried to wipe the blood from his eyes, giving them seconds to figure out what happened.

"Maybe you should come up, Captain Hunter."

Chase recognized General Sun Li's venomous voice and instantly knew they had been boarded. He hoped they were in international waters. How the general found them so quickly remained a mystery.

"Stay behind me," he ordered Tessa. Her arms went around his waist with a quick hug and maybe a light kiss against his shirt. The idea she expected this to be the end made him more determined to prove her wrong. The years of anger, war, and killing had led him to her gentle healing, and he refused to relinquish that miracle because of a brutal general. "Be alert. If you can escape somehow, do it." The chances of an escape grew slimmer by the second.

Coming on deck, Chase spotted his two CIA friends crumpled on the deck, blood oozing from cuts on their heads. Their hands had been bound and their bodies shoved face down. The boat owner stood nervously next to his wife who clutched the baby securely. Tears rolled down her cheeks as she patted Lotus to keep her quiet.

"I am beginning to think you are avoiding me, Captain Hunter, and that you prefer the likes of these peasants over me. It says a lot about your tastes." He smirked.

"It certainly does," Chase admitted, meeting his sinister gaze with one of his own. "How did you find us?"

"There are cameras everywhere in the city. It took some time, but through the process of elimination, we discovered your trail." He turned to evaluate the CIA men. "Besides being traitors, I'm not sure who they are. We managed to secure a yacht out of Hong Kong"—he threw his arms wide—"and here we are. We dropped anchor about a hundred yards from you. The small dinghy had a battery motor. Virtually silent against the racket of this pathetic excuse for a boat."

"You think four men plus you will be enough to handle things here?" he asked sarcastically as he eyed his options and their positions.

"Two are disabled. The boat owner has promised not to take action. I think it was because I promised his wife to my men." He released a deep breath. "Then there is Mrs. Hunter." He moved toward her only to have Chase cut him off.

"Get out of my way," General Sun Li growled then tilted his head toward one of his men who slammed a rifle butt in Chase's abdomen. As he bent over, the general reached around and pulled Tessa away from him. "There is no need to worry that I will hand you over to my men." He eyed her with pleasure. "I am keeping you for myself." The soldier hit Chase again as he lunged toward the general. "Actually, before I kill you, maybe you'd like to watch."

The sound of a baby whimpering took the attention off Tessa for a few seconds as the general pivoted away and grimaced at the Chinese woman. She caught her breath then turned and ran to a stack of baskets and lifted out a baby. Tessa couldn't help but join her.

"And you said your baby died and you couldn't bear to get rid of these infant supplies." He clicked his tongue. "Shame on you." He turned back to Tessa. "Is this your baby?" When she said nothing, he shouted, "Is this your baby?"

When she still didn't answer, he pointed his gun at the husband of the woman and fired his gun, hitting him in the shoulder. Both women screamed. Tessa grabbed Lotus as the fisherman's wife reached for her husband. "Throw him overboard," he ordered one of the soldiers.

"General, you don't have to do this. He is an innocent." Chase tried to step forward, but a soldier lowered his weapon toward him.

"If he were an innocent, he wouldn't have taken you on as a passenger."

"I paid him to do it."

"Where were you going? Surely you don't think he could have gotten far in this piece of junk."

"I hired another man who said his boat could get us to the Philippines. From there, we could get a flight home. We were to meet him at dawn."

The general twisted his mouth in impatience. "You are more gullible than I anticipated. That or you are just a liar." He spoke out of the corner of his mouth and tilted his head toward the wounded man. "Throw him overboard." His cold eyes returned to Chase. "He won't get far swimming with one arm. And he is bleeding. Did you know that the South China Sea is home to many species of sharks?"

Without warning, the wife picked up an iron pole and screeched as she ran toward the general. A soldier knocked the pole away. He picked her up like a bag of feathers and tossed her overboard too.

Baby Lotus cried at the top of her lungs. Nothing Tessa did would console her. The general's expression turned to stone as he watched her speak softly to the child. His eyelids slowly blinked like a snake.

Chase could feel a familiar fire of anger and revenge being stoked inside him. He needed to act quickly. It was now or never.

"Captain Hunter, has anyone ever told you that you are more trouble than you are worth?" General Sun Li's words sounded like scratching a chalkboard.

"Yes, but none of them lived to share that information. Probably why I'm still around."

When the man guarding him shifted his body to look at the general for a second, Chase charged him, grabbing the rifle and pulling the trigger. He fell as another man got off a shot toward him, clipping the top of his ear. When he lifted it to shoot again, Chase jumped on him, hitting him rapidly with his fists. The soldier fought back until yet another man intervened and managed to hit him with the iron pole that the fisherman's wife had tried to use. A shot rang out near Tessa, causing him to freeze.

When he spun around, he saw the general holding the baby in

one arm and a pistol under the chin of his wife. The general stood near the cabin and motioned for a soldier to come forward and tie her hands. He stepped closer to Tessa and said loud enough for Chase to hear.

"I won't be but a minute, then you can scream all you want."

He walked to the railing and dropped Lotus into the black waters of the Taiwan Strait.

Both Tessa and Chase lunged toward the railing, only to be pushed back. The desperate cry of pain escaped deep from inside his wife and caused Chase to fall to his knees.

The general dragged Tessa back and slammed her against the ladder that led to the upper deck. Chase felt strong hands yank him up as he witnessed the general run his free hand down Tessa's hair then her cheek. He could see something caught her eye as she focused past both the general and him toward the back of the boat. Although it was dark except for a little dappled light from the upper deck, he also saw something crawl over onto the deck. Then a second. A third.

One soldier went down with a twist of the neck and two others met with a knife. A grunt caught the general's attention as he pivoted to see his men falling. He quickly pulled his knife and held it to Tessa's throat as Chase snatched up a harpoon gun he saw lying on the deck.

"On the count of three, Tessa," Chase spoke calmly. "One. Two. Three."

Tessa stepped sideways and drove her fist into the general's crotch, the sudden jolt of pain catching him by surprise. When he released her, Chase aimed and fired the harpoon at the general, piercing his body so that it pinned him to the wall of the cabin. His eyes were wide with horror as blood gushed from what was left of his beating heart.

Chase moved closer and leaned in. "I guess you won't be telling anyone I'm a pain in the ass either."

A man in a wet suit came along side of Chase. "Captain Hunter?"

"Yes. Thanks. You guys know how to swoop in just in time."

"I'm Lieutenant Schaffer. We need to go."

Another SEAL helped Tessa who had become unsteady on her feet but made her way to the back of the boat. That's when they heard crying.

Tessa hurried to the railing and stared to the darkness below. A dark figure held up Lotus for her to see. "Ma'am. We caught your baby."

A wave of relief washed over Chase as she scampered down into the waiting boat. To his surprise, the boat captain and his wife were also in the delivery vehicle.

"Do you guys always go around like this, making us Delta Force guys look bad?" Chase asked as the vehicle sped toward darker waters.

"It isn't that hard, Captain Hunter," Lieutenant Schaffer offered good-naturedly. "And to top it off, we're better looking."

"Guess I'll let my wife be the judge of that."

Tessa gave the SEAL a thumbs-up.

"She's made her choice, Captain."

~ ~ ~ ~

After being delivered to one of the new Tuo Chiang class corvette ships, they were taken to Taiwan where they boarded a plane for home. The fisherman and his wife received medical treatment and decided to stay in Taiwan to make their home, since neither had family on the mainland.

Once in the air, they received a call from Director Benjamin Clark explaining all that had transpired while they were gone and how things went sideways with Robert. He assured her that the children were safe and never in any danger, thanks to Dr. Wu and Agent Dennis Martin. Dr. Wu had managed to save Robert's life, but needed to remain in the hospital with his injuries. He'd been transferred to Sacramento Medical, a part of the University of Science and Technology and Engineering.

The difficult part of the mission came later the next morning when they met the parents of Lotus. They waited at an undisclosed location at a safe house north of San Francisco. Tessa dressed the baby girl in a new outfit and managed to make a bow for her short hair.

"Tessa, they're here."

"Director, are you sure they are a good family?" She kissed the baby girl and enjoyed a giggle.

"Yes, Tessa. And you knew from the start this was going to be the outcome." The director didn't resist slipping an arm around her shoulders.

"Give her to me." Chase took the child from Tessa and cradled her as the parents came through the door with Agent Dennis Martin in the lead. "Great. The FBI is here to try and keep me in line."

Introductions were quickly made. It was not lost on Chase that both women sized each other up like opposing forces. Finally, Lotus's mother spoke.

"I am Mae Hie."

Chase handed the baby to her and stepped back to hold Tessa's hand.

The woman stepped closer to Tessa with tears in her eyes. "Thank you for being her mother. I will always remind her of the mother and father who saved her life."

Tessa choked on her tears and leaned in to kiss Lotus for the last time. "I will always love her as if she were my own."

"She is lucky to have two mothers."

Jun Hie, the father, extended his hand toward Chase. "I owe you a great debt."

Chase took his hand. "Just give her a better life and save the rest of the children who depend on her."

"I will."

In minutes, they left. Director Clark told them they would be returned back to a safe place while Dr. Jun Hie finished his work. A good portion of the formula had been completed.

"There aren't enough words to tell you how much you two have managed to accomplish here. The president has already contacted Beijing and voiced his displeasure at the attempt to pull a fast one. Although the evidence is clear concerning the adopted children, they have denied it. But it is enough to put them in their place for the time being." The director handed Tessa a box of tissues as she walked to the window to watch the family pull out of the driveway. "You two need some rest. Go home and be with your family."

"I'm going back." Chase expected a confrontation when she turned to face him. "Tessa?"

"You can't leave them over there. I understand that."

The director took a deep breath. "I suspected as much. We've put a plan together."

After stopping at the hospital to check on Robert. Tessa felt shock when Robert thought she'd take care of him while he recovered.

"That's not going to happen, Bobby," Chase informed him. "I know a nurse named Helga, and she'll take care of you."

He appeared interested. "That sounds Scandinavian. That could work."

When they left the hospital, Chase showed a picture of Helga to Tessa. "She's a nurse, but also a weight lifter, wrestler, and bouncer on the side. She is a man hater, well, except for me, because I got her out of jail a few times."

"You are so bad."

"To the bone actually."

Arriving home, the kids stormed them with attention and questions. They told them about their adventure and that their dad must be a hero because he stopped Phoebe from stealing American secrets.

"I'm really going to have to kill that guy, you know?" He gathered Tessa in his arms and kissed her.

"How soon will you leave again? I know your family is waiting for you."

"As soon as I can approve the plan."

"You won't go alone."

"I already have some people I plan to take with me."

EPILOGUE

Night closed in on the group of men who waited at a small airport outside San Francisco. The smell of distant forest fires from the interior burned Chase's eyes as he evaluated his travel companions approaching with their gear. Plans rested in the hands of those in China who could help complete the mission. Then he wanted to start the process of letting go of the life that had nearly destroyed him.

"Dr. Wu," Chase said, extending his hand in friendship. "I wasn't sure you would want to come after all the grief I've given you over the years."

"It is my duty to finish this. I have one final lesson to teach the woman who put Tessa's children in danger and betrayed our family. It will be my honor to see your mother once more. I am both comforted and in awe of her survival."

"And my sister— Is it true you were in love with her and wanted to marry her from a young age?"

"Yes. We reconnected when she went to college. I had left for Hong Kong to finish up some work for my master's degree. I hoped to secure a job when I returned. Then I planned to approach you to ask for her hand. I discovered what had happened when I returned a few weeks later."

"Is that why you never married?"

"Yes. I love her still. Tessa's goodness reminded me of her, and

I felt that if I was there for her—to heal and help her continue being a bright light, maybe you would forgive me for not being there for your parents and your sister."

"I now know the truth. I am sorry I didn't trust or believe you for so many years."

"Your words are enough."

He climbed the steps to enter the plane and disappeared as Lieutenant Ken Montgomery raised his chin in greeting. "Good to have you back, Captain."

"Thanks for protecting the kids and for going with me on this."

"Your buddy over there is waiting for you. I guess you trust him, but I sure don't."

Chase nodded and strolled over to where Roman Darya Petrov, known as the Tribesman, leaned against a forklift. He straightened and picked up his duffle bag.

The two men clasped arms and stared into each other's eyes before letting a grin toy with their mouths.

"Thank you for coming. There isn't anyone I'd rather have my back."

"I feel the same."

"Darya, if anything should happen to me…"

"I will take care of her. But it is not your time. Focus on what needs to be done and then we will come home."

Chase nodded and together, they walked to the plane to begin what felt like another impossible mission.

ABOUT THE AUTHOR

Besides serving as a Solar System Ambassador for NASA's Jet Propulsion Lab, and attending Space Camp for Educators, Tierney served as a Geo-teacher for National Geographic. Her love of travel and cultures took her on adventures throughout Africa, Asia and Europe. From the Great Wall of China to floating the Okavango Delta of Botswana, Tierney weaves her unique experiences into the adventures she loves to write. Living on a Native American reservation and in a mining town, helped fuel the characters in the Enigma, Dark Side and Lipstick & Danger series. With 23 books, and four audiobooks under her belt, Tierney now enjoys working with writers in their quest to become a published author. Her new love is speaking at conferences and writer groups to help others avoid the potholes of being a writer. She is also a public speaker for community groups and book clubs.

You can be a part of her journey by signing up for her newsletter at tierneyjames.com. Check out her social media choices for some daily fun and information.

FROM THE AUTHOR

Thank you for reading China Dolls #11 in the Enigma Series. I hope you'll consider writing a review on different outlets, including social media to get the word out. Want to discover the other adventures in this series? Here are a list of the books exploring how Tessa, an ordinary housewife, came to be an agent for good against the evil forces of the world while she wins over Enigma with one chocolate chip cookie at a time.

An Unlikely Hero #1
Winds of Deception #2
Rooftop Angels #3
Kifaru #4
Black Mamba #5
Knight Before Chaos #6
Invisible Goodbye #7
Martyrs Never Die #8
The Hemlock Switch #9
Knight and the Sugar Plum Fairy #10
China Dolls #11

Other books by Tierney James

Dark Side of Morning
Dark Side of Noon
The Rescued Heart
House of Miracles
Dance of the Devil's Trill
Turnback Creek
Lipstick & Danger: A collection of short stories
Secrets, Lies & Chocolate Chip Cookies: Recipes to Die For – An Enigma Cookbook
Marketing: How to Write a Book Someone Besides Your Mother Will Read

Children's Books

There's a Superhero in the Library
Zombie Meatloaf
Mission K9 Rescue

My Social Media Links:

Regular Facebook Page:
https://www.facebook.com/tierney.james.7/
Facebook: https://www.facebook.com/AuthorTierneyJames/
Facebook Reader Group:
https://www.facebook.com/groups/2430789897157949
The Write Place to Create:
https://www.facebook.com/groups/JustTheWritePlaceToCreate
Twitter: https://twitter.com/TierneyJames1
Website: http://www.tierneyjames.com
Pinterest: https://www.pinterest.com/ptierneyjames/
Instagram: www.tierneyjames7
Blog: www.tierneyjames.com/blog

WHAT TO KNOW ABOUT CHINA

Adoption:

China stopped allowing foreign adoptions of its children in August 2024. The population growth shifted over the years, going from a fear of overpopulations to concerns about a growing aging demographic. The one-child policy was in place from 1979 to 2015. Adoption was an important part of solving what to do with the many abandoned children. Now the government has embraced larger families and offers tax deductions, maternity leave, and other benefits. The number of adoptions mentioned in the book may be higher than have been reported during those years.

The places I visited in the book are real. China is an amazing country full of history, beauty and innovation. I did not go to an orphanage but tried to create how it was described to me from other parents who had visited. As with many orphanages around the world, some are better than others. Our baby was from Wuwei orphanage in the Gansu Province where there was one caretaker for every four children. They were well cared for and loved. In the book, I share how the babies were handed off to the new American parents. That was my experience and it really was heart breaking to see these caretakers burst into tears at losing the babies to complete strangers.

Dragons:

The year of the dragon was celebrated in 2024. Who doesn't like a good dragon story? I tried to use the symbolism of this mythical creature as a force for good in China Dolls. I liked him so much I may have to give him his own series. Why is the dragon important? Along with being a symbol of good luck and prosperity some people believe it brings much needed rain for successful agriculture. The dragon and its connection with water symbolizes great wealth. You'll notice emblems in Chinese businesses and trade use the dragon.

Geopolitical Conflict:

The scenario of China creating a diversion was not true. They love their children like any other country. Although in the past the one-child policy created an undesirable outcome for families, especially mothers, in China, that is no longer a problem since 2015 when it was acceptable to have more than one child. However, the part of the story that spoke of the Spratly Islands had a great deal of truth. I started following this movement about ten years ago in my geography studies.

Why China wants the Spratly Islands?

These countries claim this group of islands or at least part of them located in the South China Sea. They are claimed in their entirety by China, Taiwan, and Vietnam, while portions are claimed by Malaysia and the Philippines. The group of these 45 islands are occupied by small groups of military forces from China, Malaysia, the Philippines, Taiwan, and Vietnam.

Some of the reasons why these islands are important have to do with a submerged reef coveted for its bountiful fish stocks. China has been using some of these islands for the construction of missile arsenals, aircraft hangars, radar systems and other military facilities. China has also built artificial islands that negatively impact marine environments. But it is the military ramifications that concern the United States.

By China monopolizing these waters it can be pictured as a perfect place for surveillance, communications and logistics capabilities. With a strong Chinese presence where miliary vessels are housed in disputed waters, control over marine resources puts smaller countries at a disadvantage. In the case of a prolonged conflict with the U.S. and its allies, the strategic advantage of China is a real threat to the U.S. The possible blockade of goods to other countries could cripple the world economy if they were in control of the South China Sea.

There is also the possibility of the invasion of Taiwan who creates sixty percent of the semiconductors. These chips are used in computers, smartphones, microwaves, cars, and advanced weaponry.

Does the US have to protect Taiwan?

"The TRA (Taiwan Relations Act) requires the United States to provide Taiwan with defensive weapons to be able to resist forms of coercion that would jeopardize the security, social or economic system, of the people on Taiwan." This does not make China happy and are constantly having military maneuvers off their shores to demonstrate a show of force.

I tried to tie part of these concerns into the book but there is so much more that is involved. It has been going on for years but it seems that only now the news media have stumbled upon the threat and are talking about it.

Are missionaries allowed in China?

In this book we talk about Captain Hunter's parents who were medical missionaries. I have known some medical missionaries who have worked in clinics there. While in Beijing, I was happy to see a Catholic church next to my hotel. I also got to visit a number of Buddhists temples. Missionaries were sent back to their home country as a result of COVID. Although there are laws in China that make being a legal missionary difficult, it is not impossible. Public assembly requires a permit and is often denied. The Chinese Communist Party has a long history of restricting religious freedom. It continues to be hostile toward Islam, Tibetan Buddhism, and Christianity because the government believe the converts are under foreign influences.

www.ingramcontent.com/pod-product-compliance
Ingram Content Group UK Ltd.
Pitfield, Milton Keynes, MK11 3LW, UK
UKHW020328130125
453411UK00014B/106